# The
# THREE
# LIVES
## of
# ALIX
# ST. PIERRE

# OTHER BOOKS BY NATASHA LESTER

*The Paris Seamstress*
*The Paris Orphan*
*The Paris Secret*
*The Riviera House*

# *The* THREE LIVES *of* ALIX ST. PIERRE

NATASHA LESTER

FOREVER

NEW YORK  BOSTON

Forever
Hachette Book Group
1290 Avenue of the Americas, New York, NY 10104
read-forever.com
twitter.com/readforeverpub

Originally published as a trade paperback in Australia and New Zealand in 2022 by Hachette Australia (an imprint of Hachette Australia Pty Limited) Gadigal Country, Level 17, 207 Kent Street, Sydney, NSW 2000

www.hachette.com.au

First Forever Hardcover Edition: January 2023

Forever is an imprint of Grand Central Publishing. The Forever name and logo are trademarks of Hachette Book Group, Inc.

The publisher is not responsible for websites (or their content) that are not owned by the publisher.

The Hachette Speakers Bureau provides a wide range of authors for speaking events. To find out more, go to www.hachettespeakersbureau.com or call (866) 376-6591.

Quote on page 1 from Penelope Rowlands, *A Dash of Daring: Carmel Snow and Her Life in Fashion, Art, and Letters*, Atria Books, New York, 2005.

Quote on page 7 from Christian Dior as told to Elie Rabourdin and Alice Chavane, translated by Eugenia Sheppard, *Talking about Fashion*, Hutchinson, London, 1954.

Quote on page 85 from Elizabeth P. McIntosh, *Sisterhood of Spies: The Women of the OSS*, Naval Institute Press, Maryland, 1988, used with permission.

Quote on page 145 from Marie-France Pochna, *Christian Dior: The Biography*, Overlook Duckworth, London, 2008.

Quote on page 237 as quoted in Scott Miller, *Agent 110: An American Spymaster and the German Resistance in WWII*, Simon & Schuster, New York, 2017.

Quote on page 275 from Penelope Rowlands, *A Dash of Daring: Carmel Snow and Her Life in Fashion, Art, and Letters*, Atria Books, New York, 2005.

Excerpt on page 355 from *Crusade in Europe* by Dwight D. Eisenhower, copyright © 1948 by Penguin Random House LLC. Used by permission of Doubleday, an imprint of the Knopf Doubleday Publishing Group, a division of Penguin Random House LLC. All rights reserved.

Quote on page 369 from Christian Dior as told to Elie Rabourdin and Alice Chavane, translated by Eugenia Sheppard, *Talking about Fashion*, Hutchinson, London, 1954.

Library of Congress Cataloging-in-Publication Data
Names: Lester, Natasha, 1973- author.
Title: The three lives of Alix St. Pierre / Natasha Lester.
Identifiers: LCCN 2022037038 | ISBN 9781538706930 (hardcover) | ISBN 9781538706947 (ebook)
Subjects: LCGFT: Novels.
Classification: LCC PR9619.4.L48 T48 2023 | DDC 823/.92—dc23/eng/20220812
LC record available at https://lccn.loc.gov/2022037038

ISBNs: 978-1-5387-0693-0 (hardcover); 978-1-5387-4263-1 (trade paperback—Canada); 978-1-5387-0694-7 (ebook)

Printed in Canada

MRQ-T

10  9  8  7  6  5  4  3  2  1

*To Kevan Lyon*

*Thank you for welcoming me to the pride, for being the agent of my dreams, and for loving this book from the very first moment of its existence.*

# PROLOGUE
## PARIS, 1937

*I've always been attracted by what I can, by some kind
of Irish clairvoyance, foresee in an artist...*
—Carmel Snow, *Harper's Bazaar*

I'm not coming with you," Lillie said to Alix on the day they were
supposed to leave their Swiss finishing school and travel to Paris to
truly begin the adventure called life.

Alix laughed. "You mean you're too lazy to pack and want me to
do it for you?" She pulled Lillie's suitcase out from under the bed of
the room they shared at Le Manoir.

But Lillie shook her head. "I promised Mother before we left LA
that I'd come home after a year. She wrote to remind me."

"But you let me think—" Alix cut herself off and sank onto the bed.

Lillie was lying on her back staring at the ceiling. In her hand—
gripped so tightly it was starting to crumple—was a photograph of
Lillie, Alix, and their friend Bobby, taken at a county fair in LA the
week before the girls left for Switzerland. The mangling of that cherished image of the three of them told Alix that Lillie was hurting
more than Alix, right now.

Alix slid onto her knees on the floor so she could stroke her friend's
hair. "I'm sorry," she whispered.

Her words made Lillie start to cry—no, to sob. "I'm sorry too."

"It'll be all right," Alix said softly, swallowing all the other words—*You let me think for this whole year that you were coming to Paris when the entire time you knew you weren't.* Because she could see in Lillie's tears that the plans they'd made of renting a room in a *pension* and taking French lovers and walking home at dawn from a night out in Montmartre via the Eiffel Tower had been a wish Lillie had made herself believe in, as if an enchantress were going to divide her in two, sending one part back to her mother and Peter Brooks—the man Lillie's mother wanted her to marry—and the other half on to Paris with Alix.

For the first time, Alix was glad no one had ever expected anything of her, that the only path she had to follow was the one she made for herself. Affection, a mother's caress, a father's pride were her losses, but Lillie's losses—the ability to trust herself and to choose—were substantial and painful too.

"I'll miss you so much," was all she said. Which was true. She'd seen Lillie every day of her life since she was thirteen years old. But when Alix went on to Paris and Lillie home to LA, who knew when they'd see one another again?

"Take this." Lillie thrust the creased photo of three smiling, happy people into Alix's hand. "I have another one at home. And Bobby has one too. I always meant to give one to you because..." She stopped, and Alix knew Lillie didn't want to say it aloud: *Because you couldn't afford to buy one yourself.*

"The Three Musketeers," Alix said, trying to make Lillie smile.

"No." Lillie was adamant. "A band of people can change their mind about one another. The three of us never will. We're..." She thought for a moment. "The three points of a triangle. Without one, the triangle doesn't exist."

Which only made Alix pick herself up off the floor and throw herself onto the bed, where everything disintegrated into a teary, soggy embrace.

Then Lillie drew back and smiled at Alix, "You're like the side-kick in a movie," she said, which didn't sound especially complimentary. Until she added, "Everyone thinks the star is the one they should watch, the one they should love. But sometimes the sidekick steals the show. And everyone wonders why they hadn't noticed her before. That's you," she said very firmly to Alix, who did not believe this prophecy at all. "You're the one worth watching."

Only the truest friend would say such a thing while she tucked her own dreams away and watched the person she'd always called her sister pick up her suitcase and go off and live them instead.

"I love you," Alix said, her eyes leaking tears again.

"Until triangles don't exist," Lillie said with a grin that had them both sniffing in a very un-finishing-school-like manner.

* * *

Two days later, Alix St. Pierre stood in the very center of the Pont Alexandre III between two nymphs that were poised and ready to dive with utter abandon into the water. Above her head, orb-shaped Art Nouveau lamps shone like a strand of full moons bejeweling the dawn. Adorning the bridge to her left and right were cherubs and flying horses and lions and scallop-edged seashells—everything that was spirited and wild and impulsive and impossible. But it was all right there in front of her, so it *wasn't* impossible—not now.

A smile burst onto her face and she leaned forward like the nymphs, her upper body stretching out over the Seine as far as it could. She opened her arms wide, embracing Paris, her delight too much to keep inside her. And she began to laugh.

How would she ever stop laughing now that she was in Paris?

As daybreak became morning, she straightened, opened her purse, took out the list of names Lillie's parents had sent her from LA, and threw them into the nearest garbage bin. Alix might have only a high school education to go with the introductions Lillie's family had wished to grant her via that list, but she couldn't—and wouldn't—live off the van der Meers' largesse forever. Besides, the names on the list were high society types who did little but spent a lot, and Alix would always be an outsider in that crowd. Here in Paris—in the country of her parents' birth—she would find people she belonged to.

She strode determinedly north to Printemps and spent ten minutes gaping at the grand façade: the Four Seasons sculpted dramatically onto the wall above the heads of the shoppers who streamed in and out, arms accessorized with bracelets of shopping bags. How could they be so unaffected by art, everywhere? By beauty all around? By Paris!

Alix almost took hold of the elegant collar of the woman stepping around her and exclaimed, "Look!" Instead she took hold of herself and vowed never to be so hardened to beauty—or so old as to forget that awe existed.

Inside, she purchased the largest cocktail shaker she could find. At a grocery store, she bought gin, vermouth, and olives, retraced her steps south and took a seat on a bench in the Jardin des Champs-Élysées—if she walked this much every day, she'd soon be able to find her way around without needing her breathless copy of *So, You're Going to Paris!*

Into the cocktail shaker she poured the gin and vermouth, added six olives and checked her watch. Half past twelve. Enough time to reapply lipstick, check that her hair was behaving as hair should when in Paris—stylishly and flawlessly—straightened her neat little teal hat, which, she was pleased to see, was at the height of fashion here, unlike in the States where the dull and heavy fedora pretended to be *à la mode*. Finally, she adopted the posture that Lillie's mother had always insisted was the most important thing a girl should learn: to imagine that an extraordinarily long pencil was fastened to the back of her head and Alix wished to draw with it upon the ceiling. This pretense was supposed to pull up her chin, lift her chest—but without throwing it audaciously forward—and, somehow, shrink her waist. The only part of Lillie's mother's advice that she ignored was to keep her eyes cast shyly downward; Alix threw hers up to the sky.

Her martini shaker accompanied her to 18 Rue Jean Goujon and the Paris studio of *Harper's Bazaar* where she waited in the lobby, eyes fixed on the rackety iron-cage elevator. Soon after one o'clock, it emitted a blue-haired woman with blue glasses and the kind of figure acquired—like Lillie's mother's—by never eating, or else by a studied reliance on a liquid sort of lunch. It was Carmel Snow, editor of *Harper's Bazaar*, in Paris for the collections—and the doyenne of the liquid lunch, or so Alix had heard.

"*Bonjour*," Alix said, smiling wide—her smile was her best asset according to Lillie, who meant it kindly, and also according to Lillie's mother, who meant for Alix to wonder about the shortcomings of all her other features.

She held up the cocktail shaker. "I heard you like a three-martini lunch. So I've brought one right to you. I'm hoping that, in exchange for an afternoon's worth of martinis, you'll take a look at my portfolio."

Carmel laughed, a big and effervescent sound.

Alix took that for encouragement and extracted one very expensive martini glass from her shopping bag. "Shall I pour?"

"You'd better," Carmel said, vowels cradling her Irish accent and imbuing her words with warmth. "But in my office."

Once there, Carmel glanced at Alix's treasured illustrations then deposited them in the wastepaper basket. "Your destiny is PR," she said. "You draw as if dresses were meant to shackle a body, rather than move with it. Give up on illustrating for now."

Alix tried not to wince, but she hadn't the fortification of vermouth, had only eighteen years on the earth and a dream of working in fashion in Paris, and it was, therefore, impossible not to flinch.

Carmel didn't withdraw her gaze and allow Alix the opportunity to have her hurt undiscovered. She marked it, and then indicated the cocktail shaker. "You know how to get someone's attention and deliver what they want. Which means the Service de la Presse is your calling. The best way to learn public relations is to write—understand how the press works before you try to seduce it. You start tonight at Marie-Louise's Thursdays—where you'll meet *le tout-Paris*—and then tomorrow, more officially, here at *Harper's Bazaar* as junior fashion editor."

Alix couldn't help whooping like a cheerleader.

Carmel raised her glass. "I wish they bottled and served your brand of spirits at the Ritz. It'd be better for me than three martinis—and its effects might be more long-lasting."

And then Alix was laughing with Carmel Snow in her office in Paris, an astonishing situation that made her believe for the first time in her life that it didn't matter that she was an orphan who'd grifted her way through life since she was thirteen, a girl who'd relied on the guilt and charity of Lillie's parents for the last five years, and who'd spent every last dollar to get herself to Paris. It also made her believe that Paris was the place where she would finally be the Alix St. Pierre she was supposed to be, the one she'd had to subdue in Lillie's hushed and highly polished mansion. *That* Alix could, at last, be unshackled.

# PART ONE
## PARIS,
## DECEMBER 1946–JANUARY 1947

*This is my zero hour.*
*Ten minutes pass.*
*It is up to me to give the signal to open the doors.*
*The show is about to begin.*

—Christian Dior

# ONE

Only if ladders and tins of paint were now being worn by fashionable Parisians could Alix possibly be standing in the doorway of a couture house. She ducked to avoid a passing plank and wondered—for at least the one hundredth time since she'd broken her contract and boarded a ship in Manhattan on the basis of just one scant telegram from Suzanne Luling—if she'd done the right thing. The salon was in a state of total *déshabillé* with nary a gown or mannequin in sight, and Alix's first and overwhelming apprehension was that this new couture house would probably topple off its pumps at its very first showing.

She should turn and run. But a chandelier was forcing its way in behind her, blocking the exit. She was trapped.

"Alix!" Down the staircase came Suzanne Luling, who pointed an imperious finger at the men hefting the chandelier, directing it onward. Then she proceeded to the ground floor and placed a precise but affectionate kiss on each of Alix's cheeks. "It's been too long."

"It has," Alix said warmly, before adding, "When you were so busy convincing me to work for this new couture house, you forgot to mention that the house itself was still getting dressed."

"Monsieur Dior wanted everything to be new," Suzanne explained, sweeping an expressive arm around her, making Alix see the graceful curve of the staircase rather than its absence of carpeting. "Including the house itself. I think it's the best way to begin, don't you—to bring nothing of old with you."

*Bring nothing of old with you.* Alix occupied herself with removing her hat to stop the shiver that was most definitely from old, from the past she kept thinking she'd discarded only to find, at moments like this, that it was still there—a gown with a stuck zipper, one she would never be able to take off.

Judging by the uncharacteristically serious look on Suzanne's face, Alix was certain she too was thinking of the last time they'd seen one another, on an incoherent night in April 1945 at Suzanne's sumptuous apartment on the quai Malaquais. It had been a stop on Alix's journey home from Switzerland to New York, and Alix had said very little but she knew the uncontrollable tremor in her hands had said much.

"Show me around?" she asked now, wishing to focus only on the new and the present.

"*Bien sûr, chérie.*"

Suzanne linked her arm through Alix's and they ascended the stairs. The older woman wore her typical uniform of black skirt and jacket which, combined with her statuesque build, seemed to act like armor, repelling all planks and paintbrushes. Alix, whose patience for suits had expired with the ration years of the war, wore a pair of cream and green tweed high-waisted, wide-legged trousers and a red silk blouse. Her only warning that she was about to meet the couture house's namesake was Suzanne's murmur, "I'll make sure *le patron* forgives you for the trousers."

Then Suzanne had vanished and Alix found herself standing in front of a man seated on the top step, sheaves of paper spread around him.

*Le patron*—Monsieur Christian Dior, Alix's new employer. Her first impression was of an endearing roundness. His head was domed like the Invalides, his mouth a circle of concentration. He wore a white protective coat over ordinary trousers, shirt, and tie. Nothing marked him as someone who understood the hearts and minds of women so well that he would be able to transfix them with his dresses. But Dior had worked with Lucien Lelong, president of the Chambre Syndicale de la Haute Couture, and his prewar Café Anglais dress for Piguet had been one of the most talked about dresses that season. He had talent. And he obviously wasn't averse to getting the work done in whatever space was available, given where he sat now.

"You like the view from up here?" she asked, indicating the curve of wrought-iron balustrading that stretched down to the construction chaos on the ground floor.

Monsieur Dior cast dismayed eyes over her trousers. Alix didn't quail or apologize; she was too used to men's judgments by now and had learned to withstand them—or at least to appear to.

"I like the spaciousness," Dior said at last. "There isn't enough room for my thoughts in the studio. Which you'll see for yourself, soon enough."

"Will the staircase be my office too or is there a closet somewhere I can squeeze into?" she said, risking a joke because maybe a man who worked on a staircase would be different to every other boss she'd worked with—besides Carmel Snow.

*Le patron*'s reply was such a rush of words that Alix wondered, nonplussed at the idea, if he was actually a little bashful. "You will need that sense of humor in the coming weeks," he said. "Especially when you learn that a fortune-teller convinced me to establish Maison Christian Dior. *J'ai la frousse*—I was going to pull out." He paused. "I suppose now you know I rely on fortune-tellers, you'll return to New York."

She was working for a man who not only didn't need an office the same size as his ego, but who also consulted fortune-tellers. She grinned and sat down beside him. "The fortune-teller must have said something encouraging, otherwise we wouldn't be here. So I think I'll stay. Just to find out how accurate fortune-tellers are."

Dior's mouth lifted into a petite smile. "Despite your trousers, I like you, as Madame Luling said I would. But what will you say if I tell you I've scheduled the first showing of the House of Christian Dior for February twelve?"

Alix's reply was blunt. "The American fashion editors always leave Paris before then—you know the shows are scheduled to finish the week prior. And if you want to be anything more than a specialist dressmaker with a few faithful clients then you need the American press."

"If that's true," *le patron* said contemplatively, "then you will have to persuade the American fashion editors to stay on for my show."

Which would be a task more difficult than convincing the American fashion editors to never drink champagne again.

By now, each would have booked their passage to Paris for late January, a journey that would have them departing France prior to February 12. Alix would have to persuade them to ask their editors-in-chief to pay for several more days accommodation, as well as the cost of amending their transatlantic bookings—and all for the sake of an upstart who didn't care about the inconvenience he was causing by showing so late in the season.

Except that Dior was neither upstart nor careless, she thought. She studied him with the same degree of shrewdness he was applying to her own countenance.

"You chose to show late deliberately," she hypothesized. "Show when everyone else does and you risk being lost in the crowd or overlooked by exhausted editors. Show late and, on the one hand, you might be saying you're a sight worth staying for but, on the other, that you're an ignoramus or an egoist. It's my job to foster everyone's belief in the former. And if I can't—well, then I'll be the ignoramus and you'll be the designer whose Directrice of the Service de la Presse failed to allow his talents to be discovered. It's lucky I enjoy challenges."

"Suzanne said you did."

"Suzanne owes me a drink," Alix muttered.

But a challenge like this—cajoling every single American fashion editor to book an extra week in Paris to witness Dior's first show—would take up all her time and energy, leaving her no unfilled hours for reflection. Which was just how she liked it, and why she'd come to Paris—to start anew, just like Maison Christian Dior. It made them kindred spirits.

So she nodded—as if there had ever been any chance of her doing otherwise given her purse now held only a few francs and she'd used all her savings to buy her third-class steamship ticket to get herself here.

"Spend today settling in and meet me here tomorrow morning at ten and I will show you the studio," Dior said.

Perhaps it was because she'd never before had a boss who sat beside her on a step, but Alix couldn't resist a parting jest—the kind of thing she might have said almost ten years ago when she was an exuberant eighteen-year-old. "I'll be sure to wear my trousers again as I don't think skirts and top steps are a very elegant combination."

With her sixth sense for knowing everything, Suzanne reappeared to conduct Alix away, eyes twinkling in a manner that told Alix she'd eavesdropped on the entire conversation. They climbed more stairs and, once at the top, the sounds of busyness particular to a fashion house began to filter into Alix's ears: the whisper of silk unfurling onto a worktable, the slicing of scissors into calico, the tinkle of pins spilled onto a floor.

"The ateliers are in the attic," Suzanne said.

Alix took in the rolls of fabric crowding the landing, leaning toward the attic as if desperate to be permitted entry. The sounds she could hear emanated from there and in seconds she had bypassed the disappointed lengths of taffeta and found herself in a workroom so full of energy she could almost see ideas dancing in the air.

The *petites mains*—the seamstresses—sat lined up in rows on stools at school desks from beneath whose lids they extracted a thimble or a *découd-vite* or a pincushion. They worked elbow to elbow, heads bent over needles, fingers delicately manipulating fabric that entered their hands in a flat and lifeless state and exited having been transformed into a sleeve, a sash, a swirl awaiting a skirt.

"This room is for the *flou*," Suzanne said. "The evening gowns in silk and chiffon and fine wool. Whereas this one," she walked through a doorway, "is for *tailleur*—the heavier fabrics for suits and daywear."

Alix's head swiveled from the bravura red of a bolt of silk-satin lounging on a worktable to the undulating silhouette of a half-finished gown standing theatrically to one side as if awaiting its cue. A ghostly collection of toiles lingered expectantly, ready for life to be breathed into them; indeed, there was an *étincelle* of magic in every corner. Alix's disbelieving hand reached out to touch it all: the silk-satin, the sketches, the gowns—and her own awestruck smile.

* * *

By midnight, the tiny space off the entryway that Alix now inhabited—and that must once indeed have been a closet—resembled something more like an office. Suzanne's half was as elegantly tidy and attenuated as its owner, despite housing an assistant, a dozen card indexes containing the telephone numbers of Paris's style-makers, two telephones, an outfit to change into at day's end, a bottle of brandy and several crystal tumblers. In contrast, Alix's portion housed only one desk, two chairs, one bookshelf, and no decorative *objets* whatsoever. It had been a satisfying day's work clearing away a great deal of clutter.

Despite the late hour, there was still work to be done—but not at the *maison*. Alix and Suzanne walked along the sparkling Champs-Élysées, crossed through the too-quiet Place de la Concorde where the postwar automobile shortage was most apparent, then turned north toward the undiminished glamour of the Ritz, which had survived the war like a true diplomat, keeping all sides happy.

Along Temptation Walk, Alix ignored the glass display cases filled with expensive things she couldn't afford, and smiled when they reached the Little Bar, which was discreet, and either tranquil or exuberant, as one's mood required. Tonight, Alix wanted the exuberance: just one celebratory toast to herself for coming to Paris—her third chance to do everything right.

"I'm buying," Alix told Suzanne, even though it would further deplete her tiny reserve of francs. "To thank you for the job."

"Then I will find us a seat," Suzanne replied, gesturing to a small table crammed tight with the Parisian editors and journalists Alix would need to charm into writing about the House of Christian Dior. "It's always best to begin work proper at almost one in the morning and with a drink in hand."

Alix laughed. "Maybe it is."

Once Suzanne was safely out of earshot, she turned to Frank, the American barman.

He smiled at Alix. "*Bonsoir, mademoiselle.* It's been a long time."

"It has."

"The usual?"

"Yes, and a cognac for Suzanne."

She watched him take out gin, sugar syrup, and a lemon, flourish the cocktail shaker a few times, pour the concoction into a *coupe* and top it up with champagne. "*Voilà,*" he said to her. "*Un soixante-quinze.*"

"You have an excellent memory, Frank," she said with a smile.

"It works well enough for the things that need to be remembered, but not so well for the things that don't. Especially wartime things. And your drink's on the house. Always will be."

His reply was everything she needed to hear. Which meant she was ready to reacquaint herself with *le tout-Paris.*

She slid in beside Suzanne, whose talent had always been to know not just who everyone was but their individual stories as well. She gave Alix a useful and exact précis.

Many Alix knew already—Michel de Brunhoff from *Vogue*, fashion illustrator Christian Bérard—but there were some new faces amongst the British and Americans, two of whom were doing what they could to keep up international relations, if the man's arm slung around the woman's shoulder and the giggles of the woman were anything to go on.

"That's Becky Gordon," Suzanne said. "English. So brand new she squeaks. She's with *The Times*—the goddaughter of someone or other who owns the newspaper. And looking as if he's about to swallow Becky for his evening digestif is Anthony March, third and profligate son of Montgomery March—the American newspaper baron. Anthony, now that his two older brothers are buried somewhere in France, has had to curtail his amusements somewhat and actually work. He's the editor of the international edition of the *New York Journal* and very louche and luscious, as you can see."

Alix wrinkled her nose, watching Becky follow Anthony to the elevator. "He's too…" She searched for the right word to describe his handsome but deliberate air. "Contrived," she settled upon. "Like he thinks he's about to be photographed."

Across the room, Becky's hand reached up to touch her hair, then her fingers worried at the cuff of her jacket.

"She thinks she's going to disappoint him," Alix guessed.

"A man like that, she probably will."

Alix wanted to take Becky by the arm and whisper a warning in her ear because, once upon a time, Alix had been as shiny-new as Becky. But there was no chance Becky would listen to Alix, a total stranger. So she said goodbye to Suzanne, leaving behind both her unfinished drink and the memory of a shiny-new girl who had had a lot to learn.

Outside, she saw a man leaning against the wall and smoking a cigarette as if he'd needed both the slap of the December night air and the solace of a solitary Gauloise. It was Anthony March, who couldn't possibly have finished with Becky that quickly. Perhaps Becky had been wiser than she'd looked and had gone up to her own room instead.

That thought put the smile back on Alix's face and soon she was at her tiny *pension* on Rue du Cirque where she sank into bed. She'd begun again—had sailed through a day and a night back in Europe, had consumed only one mouthful of champagne, and would be asleep in time to have around four hours rest, which she'd learned was enough.

\* \* \*

Alix chose her clothes carefully for her meeting with Christian Dior the following day. No trousers, despite what she'd said. Instead, a Schiaparelli suit several years old that she'd bought from Carmel Snow, who used to sell her hardly worn couture to her "girls" at *Harper's Bazaar* for a price Alix could just afford. The suit was black, and had the requisite peplum and padded shoulders, but was accented with a red trompe l'oeil waistband. Schiaparelli had meant for it to be worn with red gloves and a red hat, but Alix knew that was *de trop*. She opted for black for both, and crossed her fingers girlishly behind her back.

*Le patron*'s forehead rumpled even more than it had yesterday when he saw her. "One of the *premières* will have to make you a suit so you don't have to rely on my competition." Then he gave her one of his compact smiles.

Alix grinned. It was what she'd been hoping for, and his smile told her he'd guessed. Which meant she wouldn't be able to use a trick like that again. But a girl on a minimum wage in a city like Paris—where inflation was higher than the Eiffel Tower—had to use every advantage at her disposal.

Dior led her through the rooms in the *maison* that she hadn't seen the day before: the *cabine* where the mannequins would dress, the six petite fitting rooms for *les femmes*, or the clients—which was Suzanne's domain as Directrice of Sales—and the studio, which was in direct competition with Alix's own office for the smallest space in the building.

"As you saw yesterday, the workrooms are small. The *maison* is small," Dior said as he ushered her inside. "Why? Because I want to practice the best traditions of couture, and to the highest standards. And to help me, I have the 'three mothers.'"

At his words, three women entered.

"This is Madame Raymonde," *le patron* said, indicating the severest of the group, a woman who had come with Dior from Lucien Lelong. She possessed the demeanor of a person who spoke little, but who was always pointedly accurate.

"I don't sew," Monsieur Dior explained. "But I need to sketch only what can, somehow, be made. Madame Raymonde," he smiled, "is Reason. She makes my imagination possible."

He moved on to the next woman, Madame Bricard, who seemed to exhale seduction rather than air. With her leopard-print turban and a scarf of the same pattern tied at her wrist rather than her neck, she was the reason the word *flamboyant* had been invented.

"Madame Bricard lives for elegance alone," Dior said. "She is my inspiration."

*The muse, then.* Men seemed unable to exist without them—why should Dior be any different?

The final woman was Madame Carré, the house's technical director. She passed *le patron* a sketch, which he placed in Alix's hands.

The first thing she noticed was the line of the shoulders, soft sloping and seamless, curving gently over the body. It made her see that all the jackets women had been wearing—many of which had been reconfigured from men's suits due to fabric rationing—had, over the past few years, made women look rectangular, sharp-cornered. But women weren't. The bodice of the dress in the sketch didn't change a woman's shape; it revealed it.

"I can almost feel it move," she said, running her hand over the glorious swell of the pencil-drawn skirt, shaped like the *coupe* she'd drunk from at the Ritz.

Madame Bricard, obviously not yet convinced of Alix's credentials, inquired coolly, "Where would you wear it?"

"Where wouldn't I wear it? To the Ritz for a drink, to work, to dinner at La Méditerranée, or even to stroll through the Jardin du Luxembourg. Not that I'm one for strolling," Alix amended.

"Everywhere one wishes to be elegant," Madame Bricard said succinctly. "Which is anywhere."

Madame Carré spoke now. "Do you see how the skirt falls, like a…"

"*Coupe.*" Alix spoke her earlier thought.

Madame Carré laughed. "Just like a *coupe*. When I first saw the sketch, I thought it couldn't be done. We've had to relearn old couture techniques that time has stolen from us. We've used the entire width of the roll of silk, from selvage to selvage, but running horizontally around the mannequin. The bowl of the *coupe* is shaped just so because, folded under at the waist, is all the pleating of a thirteen-and-a-half-yard seam allowance."

Alix's eyes widened as she understood that what she'd thought must be some sort of intricate system of petticoats to make the skirt achieve the wonderful fullness was nothing of the sort—it was from hidden padding that the dress blossomed into its extraordinary shape. Alix coveted this dress as she'd never before coveted anything in her life.

"Suzanne calls it her dress. I'm told the seamstresses do the same," *le patron* said. "I've decided to call it Chérie. I heard Suzanne call you *chérie* yesterday. That means it's your dress. But," he added, speaking sternly now, "not until after February twelve."

It was impossible not to smile the same way she had yesterday in the atelier. Dior gestured to her face. "That's why I do this," he said. "I hope to make women happy."

The quick rush of tears to her eyes was so unexpected. Alix hadn't known she could still cry, or that a couturier, of all people, would be the one to make her do it. But what man in the world wanted to make women happy? Men wanted so many things from women, Alix had learned in Switzerland during the war, and most of them aimed to steal away their happiness, not gift them joy. That was why she almost wept now, over a dress.

* * *

That night, Alix didn't go to the Ritz. She returned to her *pension*, took out notepaper and pen and began to write.

*To Lillie,*
*From Paris*

*I have so many thoughts flying around my head, like skirts in the wind. If I was back home, we'd go out for dinner and by the time we got to ice cream, everything would make sense. These letters will have to be a substitute.*

*I've only been at Dior for two days but I can already see how different it is to every other job I had in Manhattan after the war. There was the War Department, where I was supposed to make posters telling women to give up their jobs to the men returning from overseas—the women could just find husbands and be perfectly happy making roast dinners, they said. I never told you that was why I quit—you wanted to marry Peter so badly I worried you'd think*

*I was critiquing your choice. Actually, I didn't quit. I told my boss the only thing I planned to roast was him and he fired me. Carmel Snow offered me a job after that but I knew that daily proximity to martinis would be too tempting. I didn't tell you that either.*

*So I took the job at* Glamour, *where I found out that negotiating with men for two and a half years of war had made me seem pushy—*willful *and* obdurate *were the words they used. That was why I threw myself back into the world of men; I thought it was the only place I fitted. And I used my talent for obduracy every day at Goldman and Sachs, a world where women were meant to be either secretaries or wives—and I left it because my boss appeared in my office late at night with a bottle of brandy in hand and an unsubtle offer to make me a Between the Sheets. By then I was so tired of using all my wits to escape versions of that scene that I told him I had a gun in my purse and could shoot straighter than his pinstripes, and the only thing he'd be doing with his brandy would be pouring it over my contract and setting it on fire. Writing it down now, I can almost see the humor in it—but it wasn't funny at the time. Another thing I never told you.*

*Here at Dior, nothing like that would ever happen. I'm wanted, Lillie. You have no idea how good that feels. And at last I have a goal that goes beyond surviving and forgetting. Dior is a genius. I've never seen a designer like him, whose pencil captures the divine. Just wait till you see his gowns. Suzanne believes he'll blaze a trail. And I'm going to throw myself headlong into that fire.*

*Love and* bisous,
*Alix*

Writing it down conjured it up, that night almost two weeks ago when Alix had decided at three in the morning to run away to Paris. She could see herself escaping her boss and returning to her apartment to be greeted by a newspaper proclaiming that the Nuremberg Trials of Major War Criminals were finally over and the judgments would be handed down within a fortnight.

And she'd known that in just a couple of weeks, justice would be served and that she should feel the guilt unclench itself, maybe even slip away. But it laced tighter still, as if telling her that even justice wouldn't free her—which was something she hadn't considered until then. No, justice was supposed to end it all.

So she'd met Carmel Snow at the Colony Club and tried to match her drink for drink. But Carmel's sorrow must have been more resistant to martinis than Alix's and the night had ended with Carmel wrapping liquid fingers around Alix's wrist and introducing her to someone as "my protégé." And Alix had seen, through a spinning haze of gin, how easily she could become just like Carmel. Numb enough not to feel her heart ache. For one moment, she'd been so very tempted to let it happen.

Which was the worst thing of all.

She'd hurtled back to her apartment and re-read Suzanne's telegram and discovered she had just enough of her meager salary saved to afford a steamship ticket. She'd been at the dock the very next day.

But she couldn't tell Lillie any of that, didn't want to relive that tantalizing moment of wanting to succumb to insensibility—didn't want Lillie to be as ashamed of Alix as Alix had been of herself.

# TWO

Morning dawned and it was time for Alix to tackle the press. But first she had to defrost herself. Coal was still rationed and the little kerosene stove in her *pension* was as useless at generating heat within her as a naked nonagenarian in her bed. A brisk walk to the Ritz would warm up her body and perhaps inspire her to embroider a phrase or two for a press release that would convince the fashion editors not to miss the House of Christian Dior's show.

But the farther she walked, the more she felt her spirits sag like the fatigued coats worn by the Parisiennes around her. Rather than the parade of elegant sleeves and pert collars and flirtatious buttons that had decorated the boulevards in the late 1930s, all Alix saw were threadbare skirts and the eyes of women etiolated by war, their wounds not yet hardened to scar tissue.

Alix knew, better than most, that many of them had been valiant heroines during the German Occupation. Perhaps the woman hurrying past her now had kept a safe house for downed pilots, had sheltered a Jewish child, had couriered messages between Resistance fighters. What did that same woman have now the war was over? Chilblains on her fingers. A half-empty basket over her arm, unfilled by still-rationed food.

That woman, like many other Parisiennes, deserved so much more than to be trapped in this strange gloaming—a time when color and joy and confidence were mere memories, possessions of past selves and a different era. Dior could change all of that—but only if Alix did her job.

So she sat down at a table in the Ritz's winter garden and pretended not to notice when Estelle Charpentier, the fashion editor from *Le Monde*, arrived more than twenty minutes late for their meeting.

Luckily Alix had learned a thing or two about game-playing during the war. Pleasantries concluded, she slung out the dice. "I don't know how I'll swing it," she said to Estelle with faux consternation as she frowned at the seating chart for Dior's show. "There are so few seats left. All the Americans have taken them."

She gave a helpless shrug to accompany her lie. No, it was a strategy. Her aim was to start a swathe of rumors about the special interest the Americans were taking in the show, with the outcome hopefully being they would all believe the gossip about their competition and thus amend their transatlantic bookings.

Estelle summoned the waiter over and ordered coffee without waiting for Alix to offer it. "But the Americans always leave Paris by then. Besides, Pierre Balmain has opened a *maison*. Balenciaga is filling the void left by Chanel. Why do we need Maison Christian Dior?"

Alix refused to validate that with a response and pretended to consult the seating plan again, permitting Estelle a peek at the names who'd supposedly been designated a place on the staircase. Estelle's eyes rounded when it appeared from Alix's fabricated chart that even the luminaries of fashion journalism had not been granted a seat in the grand salon. Then Alix allowed her face to light up as she spied a place where an extra chair could be squeezed into the third row of the main room.

"But don't tell anyone," Alix said conspiratorially. "If they find out I gave you a seat there but relegated them to the staircase..."

Estelle just shrugged in that irritatingly French way before departing and Alix understood she had much work to do before Estelle, and most likely the other fashion editors as well, believed that Maison

Christian Dior would fit them just right. And even more work to do to if she was to make her seating plan into anything other than a fantasy.

Her thoughts were interrupted by a girlishly English voice saying, "I'm here!" Becky Gordon, the English journalist from *The Times*, was twenty minutes early. Alix's spirits lifted a little.

"I'm so happy to meet you," Becky continued eagerly. "I thought you mightn't have known who I was. I've not been long at *The Times*, you see."

She forgot to remove her coat and had to stand up again to shoulder it off, gazing awkwardly around the room for someone who might take her dripping Burberry trench before it created a lake on the floor. "I was worried I mightn't be given a ticket to the show at all," she added as a waiter placed the offensive coat on one disdainful finger and ushered it out.

Alix could tell that if she offered Becky a nook at the top of the stairs where she could hardly see a thing, Becky would almost cry from gratitude. So, "This is your seat," Alix said, pointing to one of the very best positions, and feeling a gentle squeeze in her heart.

"For me?" Becky gasped.

Alix smiled as her heart squeezed again. "Yes."

They began to chat about how long Becky had been in Paris—just a fortnight. "My godfather owns *The Times*." Becky paused and Alix could see her mind tumbling through different ways to explain this next thing. She settled on, "He's helping me out."

Becky must have a tug-at-the-heartstrings story too. War had unraveled everyone's fates, it seemed. "How so?" Alix asked.

"Well..." A self-conscious fidgeting with the coffee cup, a tucking of the hair behind the ear. "My family have found themselves with an aristocratic name, a run-down mansion, no staff, and rather a lot of bills. Like many in England really. We're not so very unusual these days," Becky hastened to add.

And thus, by saying little and simply listening, Alix had found Becky's weakness.

She felt her body give a physical jolt, which she covered by reaching for her cup. Was she never going to be able to have a normal exchange again? Would she never forget that she'd been trained during the war to lead people into telling her things she could exploit?

Yes. She *would*. Mundane questions and unexceptional answers— that was what passed for ordinary conversation. So she asked Becky, "Are you enjoying Paris?"

"So much," Becky enthused. "Although…" Her smile fell away. "People in Paris are different from people in England. More worldly wise, I suppose."

"Men?" Alix asked, hoping it wasn't what she'd witnessed between Becky and Anthony March at the Ritz the other night that had rent Becky's optimism.

Her silence told Alix everything she needed to know and she jumped right in because here was a chance to stop one person from falling unwittingly into a disastrous future. "Tell me if I should mind my own business," Alix said, "but it's fine to make a mistake about a person. Once. Don't turn it into a pattern. Learn from it, and be more worldly wise yourself the next time."

Becky stared at her and Alix could see both shock at Alix's frankness and also a spark of something that hadn't been there before. "That's good advice," Becky said, then added, as if she'd learned a thing or two already, "and now I owe you two times over. Once for the seat, and once for the advice. Let me talk to my editor about getting an interview with Monsieur Dior into the newspaper."

* * *

She had silk, Alix thought with a smile as she walked to work several days later wearing the new suit one of the seamstresses had made for her. And she'd had a success with Becky. It meant this week couldn't be anything other than *magnifique*.

But the mood in the still-unfinished grand *salle* was more maleficent than magnificent. Dior was interviewing for mannequins to show his gowns. Demurely dressed girls were arrayed around the builders' scaffolding, whispering and staring at a woman who knew how to dress to show off every curve of her body. Her eyes were decades older than her face, but it was her provocative stance that was causing the backbiting; her nearly camouflaged pain had escaped everyone's notice.

"*Une pute*," one of the girls said in a very loud whisper, before laughing with her friends.

Alix hadn't shaken her habit of studying the newspapers each morning, still waiting for news out of Nuremberg, and she'd read about a new law that had closed down some of the city's brothels. A few of the now unemployed ladies of the night must have seen Monsieur Dior's advertisement and were hoping for a job that let them keep their clothes on—there were several other provocatively dressed women hiding in the corners of the room.

"You can leave," Alix said to the spiteful, giggling girl. "*Au revoir*," she added firmly, when it appeared the girl thought she was joking. "And you can come with me," she said to the woman with pain in her eyes, after the first had slunk away. "Please?"

The woman scrutinized Alix, then followed her.

"You've not worked as a mannequin before, have you?" Alix asked when they reached her office.

The woman drew back her shoulders, a cobra about to spit. "I've paraded before more people in my life than those other girls have."

Alix grinned. Another woman who hadn't quite had the spirit flayed out of her. Which meant Alix was bound to help her. "To get the job, you'll need to walk less like you're about to disrobe in a boudoir and more like you never want to take off anything you're wearing. Like this."

Alix, who'd seen hundreds of fashion shows during her almost three years at *Harper's Bazaar*, demonstrated the serenely self-possessed stroll of a mannequin. "You sway too much," she explained. "You don't need to. You could stand absolutely still and everyone would look at you. I'm Alix, by the way."

The woman smiled for the first time. "Fortunée. And yes, it's my real name. One of the only girls on the street who didn't have to change from a dull Juliane to a more exotic *nom de chambre*."

Alix laughed. "Then I hope it's auspicious today."

All credit to Dior, he auditioned every woman gathered downstairs, choosing six mannequins—including Fortunée.

*To Lillie, From Paris,* Alix composed as she finished her day in the Little Bar, drinking just one French 75. *I helped someone today. Last week too. And it felt so very good.*

* * *

Alix moved her meetings with Paris's male editors to the Little Bar, knowing the alcohol would motivate them even if she and Dior didn't. Despite the law forbidding Parisian women from wearing trousers in public places, she wore her trousers; Frank would never throw her out and she needed the meetings to be memorable. She paired the trousers with her red blouse, not abiding by the maxim that redheads shouldn't wear red. Besides, her hair was more an indeterminate fairish hue with enough highlights of red, caramel, and gold that she'd been called everything from a redhead to a blonde to a brunette. That day, she wore it loosely waved and unfashionably long, falling to the middle of her back.

The first gentleman, Henri Paquet from *Jardins des Modes*, was hilariously good fun, and had, back in 1937, introduced Alix to the Hemingway Champagne in this same bar, which had resulted in her giving up both American literature and absinthe for quite some time.

He still dressed as if it were the 1920s, she was delighted to discover, but was somewhat less pleased when he noticed she had only one *coupe* to his entire bottle.

"Try not to sit beside Carmel when she arrives for the shows, *ma chérie*," he said to her as he stood up to leave. "Or it will become even more apparent that you are now exceedingly scrupulous about how much you drink. Some might think it's a weakness they can exploit."

She ordered a coffee and hadn't quite digested the advice when Anthony March arrived for his meeting, early.

"Alix St. Pierre," she said, holding out her hand. "What can I get you to drink?"

"Alix St. Pierre," he repeated. "You sound like you should *be* a drink."

He was flirting with her at a business meeting. No wonder Becky had had her heart frayed. "I'm too vinegary," she said coolly. "Coffee?"

"You're worried that alcohol might make me even more obnoxious?" His tone was less self-deprecating than baiting.

It was an effort of no small moment to keep her professional smile fixed to her face. "You can be as obnoxious as you like. You're the one who has to live with the consequences. But I don't offer more than three times. Tell me what you'd like, or we'll get started."

"I thought PR princesses were supposed to be deferential. Shouldn't you be buttering me up so I say nice things about..." He shrugged. "Whoever."

*Don't be obdurate*, she reminded herself, but heard her mouth say, "Princesses get guillotined too often in France. And butter is for bread. Now, do you know anything about fashion?"

Unexpectedly, he laughed at the joke, sat down, and she thought he'd dropped the rakish persona—indeed, he looked suddenly younger, as if he might be only a year or two older than her. She finally saw the handsomeness Suzanne had enthused over, rather than the exaggeratedly bored and wealthy womanizer. But then he said, "Well, I know how to throw on a suit and—"

Alix's eyeballs wanted desperately not just to roll, but to somersault. Before he could say *take it off*, she interrupted, "There's a lot more to fashion than the ability to spend a colossal inheritance on superbly tailored suits that would look fine on anyone. Why don't you just live off the money, wear the suits, and leave the work to those of us who enjoy it?"

"Because then I'd be a cliché."

"Yes," she said, standing up. "Only then would you be a cliché. Call me when you're ready to have a professional meeting without the sophomore banter."

"Do professional meetings take place in bars?" he shot back.

Touché. She *had* been playing to clichés by arranging the meetings with the men in the bar. Another habit she hadn't lost—but she wasn't in Switzerland and nor was she spying on Nazis. She actually had an office in which to transact legitimate business.

She was so disappointed in herself for yet another lapse into past tricks that she almost stalked out. But then her irritation gave way to the laugh bubbling up inside her at the two of them, both wanting to play their own game but not enjoying it when the other did the same.

The laugh spilled out and she saw a flash of surprise on his face.

"You're right," she said, still laughing. "Only PR princesses and spoiled third sons have meetings in bars. As we're neither of those things, we should start over with a meeting in my office."

"I'm away until the end of next week," he said slowly.

And the week after that was Christmas. "The Monday after the New Year, then. Ten o'clock?"

He nodded. But just as she was about to leave, he said, eyes trained right on her, "I knew your fiancé, Bobby."

The sudden collision of her past life into her present was a shock all the training in the world couldn't have prepared her for. Her flinch was apparent, but anybody would flinch when reminded so abruptly of their now-dead fiancé.

Bobby: her sweetheart from a time when her heart was apple pie.

"Well," she said in the even tone she'd learned to drape over her words throughout the war. "We can talk about him at our next meeting."

* * *

Every muscle in Alix's body was concentrated on maintaining an undemonstrative stroll and a neutral expression as she walked away from the bar. Somehow Anthony March, one of the most arrogant men she'd met—and someone she wouldn't be able to avoid because it was part of her job to be nice to him—knew Bobby. *Keep walking*, she told herself as her steps faltered. *And keep smiling.*

Perhaps Anthony knew Bobby from before the war. They both came from families with too much money. And Alix St. Pierre was a black opal name—rare and memorable. If Bobby had ever mentioned it, it made sense that Anthony might recall it.

But her gut—which she'd trained to be a sense stronger even than olfaction—contracted when she recalled the manner in which Anthony had mentioned Bobby, tossing his name into the conversation like a grenade, intent on the fallout. His acquaintance with her former fiancé was no mere chitchat.

At the same moment, her gut registered something even more appalling. A newspaper headline at the kiosk on the corner shouted: "SS GENERAL KNOWN AS THE WHITE RAVEN—WOLFF WALKS FREE." Her eyes had to be playing the most dastardly of all tricks on her. Wolff was the blackest of all the SS ravens.

She stepped closer but the words steadfastly refused to alter.

In that moment, nothing else mattered except buying a copy of the newspaper. Once it was in her hand, she had only enough presence of mind to turn into a quieter road where understanding almost felled her.

Karl Wolff, SS General and Obergruppenführer, military commander for the whole of Northern Italy during the war, the man at whose hands so many had died, had been set free at the conclusion of the Nuremberg Trials. It was inconceivable.

He was a murderer.

"*Non*," she whispered, head shaking frantically and uselessly back and forth in protest.

If the man who'd been in charge in Northern Italy had been allowed to walk free, then what had happened to those who'd worked for him? Had they not been caught and locked up, keys thrown away, either? Was every colossal wrong they'd committed unavenged still?

The newsprint confirmed her fears:

*It is difficult to imagine how the Italian partisans who lost their lives as a result of Karl Wolff's orders would feel, especially as it was also revealed in the last week of the trials that Wolff's anonymous aides disappeared immediately before the Italian surrender and have never been found. The Italian Nazi command, far from suffering as those they killed suffered, are living a life of freedom.*

*Wolff's anonymous aides.* It meant the man who'd wrecked Alix, a shadow she'd believed would be brought out into the light at the trials where he would at last be destroyed, was still lurking somewhere, unpunished.

The justice she'd been counting on since April 1945 had not been delivered.

And if he was free, then Alix, who was the only person who could identify him, was in just as much jeopardy now as she had been during the war.

# THREE

A lix fled to a post office, slipping in just before closing time, rummaging in her purse for her address book, finding the necessary form and writing out a telegram in a shaking hand to Mary Bancroft, who Alix had worked with in Switzerland: Did they catch him stop you know Dulles won't tell me stop.

Allen Dulles had been Alix's boss in Switzerland, Mary's too—although *boss* wasn't really the right word to describe Mary and Allen's relationship. Dulles would certainly never speak to Alix again, not after she'd all but run away from Bern, abandoning her job and perhaps her country in April 1945. But he might speak to Mary if Mary was able to use all her wiles—and she had plenty—to ask him that question in such a way that he had no idea it was Alix who wanted to know.

It was a shot so long it was like shooting at the moon—but didn't she deserve just one grain of moondust?

\* \* \*

Each day that passed with no response made it seem as if the answer to that question was a firm no. The best distraction was, as always, work. So on the day of the toiles, Alix sat in the studio beside the three mothers, Madame Bricard at Dior's right hand. *Le patron* held a baton as if he were ready to conduct: to blend a silk soprano with a taffeta contralto, music that would fade into the final gentle notes of chiffon.

"*Monsieur, une modele,*" a voice called from outside.

In walked a mannequin outfitted in creamy-white cretonne. No color. No variety of fabric. Just the simplest, plainest muslin so that nothing could distract from the cut. These toiles were the very first realizations of Dior's *petites gravures*—his sketches—and they floated like ghosts on the mannequins, strangely beautiful in their pure whiteness.

"*Parfait!*" was the judgment handed to the first and it was allowed to be reconfigured into organza. The second was fussed over by Madame Bricard, trimmed, its neckline altered, the sleeves lengthened by a frog's hair, and then it was permitted to return to the workroom, more angel now than ghost, calico fluttering its own applause.

The next—a day dress with a narrow skirt and the subtly curved shoulders Alix had come to expect from *le patron*—was declared by Madame Bricard to be a horror. Her terrifying finger banished it from the room.

And Alix saw that the toiles were true shadows, revealing only outlines and promises, a silhouette upon which the gown proper would be made, the toile then scissored away and forgotten. Only Alix watched it leave, wanting to reach out and save it from the firing squad.

She felt someone's eyes on her and realized Dior had seen the sadness that was Alix's own distinct shadow. "They're like gods," she tried to explain, "deciding the fate of a dress that might have been."

"You don't like gods?" Dior questioned.

"How could anyone, after the war, admire gods? They're as cruel as humans."

Alix's declaration hung in the air like day-after sludge dirtying a pure white snowfall. She recovered quickly. "Not all humans. But I believe in fortune-tellers more than gods now." She summoned up a smile to accompany her jest.

But *le patron* was studying Alix's eyes and wasn't distracted by her words. *It's why there are so many women around him*, she thought. What appeared to be shyness was perhaps a deep kind of compassion. Men usually wanted the quick parry—jest and response—but Dior spoke to souls. How could he tell that her soul had kept her awake all night, asking questions whose answers were too frightening to face alone in a room in the dark?

"Fortune-tellers are for those who want to move only forwards," he said at last. "Gods are for those who look backward to what they've done and believe in penance as a kind of absolution. I don't know who those trapped in the middle should turn to." He frowned at his hands as if disappointed, for her sake, in his unawareness. Then he said, as if struck by inspiration, "Perhaps that was the idea I wanted to express in the line for the collection. I saw too many people trapped in the middle and I thought of this."

He waved a hand at the toile in front of him.

Alix studied it, and the one beside it, and she began to see that the "line" Dior often talked about, a concept Alix hadn't fully comprehended, was neither shape nor form, neither contour nor curve, neither profile nor pattern nor theme. It was a unifying silhouette that was similar in every model and yet somehow transformed into a new gown, a new suit, a new spectacle. And it was the silhouette, unashamedly, of a woman. The curve of breast and hip. The inward sweep of a waist. Dresses that showed who a woman really was, everything she'd been hiding since war had required her to shroud her true self and her true shape: everything she'd forgotten to reveal since the war had ended.

But now Christian Dior was saying, through his gowns—*Live*.

\* \* \*

Alix left the room, determined. Virginia Pope, fashion editor of the *New York Times*, was still planning to return to Manhattan before

Dior's show, as were many others. It was Alix's job to make sure they didn't; that they understood Dior's message and told every one of their female readers about it as well.

She needed inspiration, and the *maison* was too full of brilliance to let in any more ideas. So she went outside and walked without direction until a movie theater—a dark space where she could sit with her thoughts—caught her attention. She entered, and found herself watching Cary Grant recruit Ingrid Bergman to spy on a party of Nazis who had absconded to Brazil to continue their dirty deeds postwar.

*Dammit.* She should have paid more attention to what movie was showing. There was no inspiration to be found in Bergman thinking she could help her country by using her feminine wiles to unbutton the Nazis' secrets. Alix lit a cigarette and reminded herself that it was just a story. Not real. Bergman talked too much for a start. A real spy would never be so indiscreet.

The instant she had the thought, Alix was struck by her own inspiration. She saw herself—not in Switzerland or Northern Italy—but in the winter garden at the Ritz, making promises and telling lies and talking far too much. What if she didn't? What if she applied the few honest skills she'd learned in Switzerland to PR, took something useful from that time rather than imagining it had all been a terrible waste?

On the screen in front of her, Ingrid Bergman was swept into Cary Grant's arms. All the women in the theater swooned.

And the frisson of a perfect and brilliant idea had Alix leaping from her seat and hurrying out.

\* \* \*

A quick chat with Suzanne confirmed that Rita Hayworth was coming to Paris for the premiere of her new film *Gilda*, in which she played a seductress, a siren, a woman every woman wanted to be. And the premiere of *Gilda* was not long before Dior's show.

"Rita Hayworth," Alix announced to Monsieur Dior the following day, accosting him on the top step.

"Is a very fine actress?" *le patron* replied, mystified.

"She's a dream made real," Alix continued. "In the arms of a man like Cary Grant, and wearing a beautiful gown."

"Wearing a beautiful gown," Dior repeated slowly, as if he were almost following her admittedly very tangled thread.

"You need to make her a gown. We'll deliver it to her and hope she wears it to her Paris premiere. And between now and then, I take no more meetings with journalists. I ask for no more promises of press coverage. All I'll do is send out the tickets to the show."

Dior eyed her in a way that made it hard to tell whether he was appalled by her suggestion that she do no work between now and February, or wanted her to continue.

"Between us, we know people who talk. Which means I don't need to," she hurried on, her words like a bolt of satin unspooling ever faster. "The Service de la Presse at every couture house is talking nonstop about their upcoming collections. If we do that too, we're just noise. Imagine if we were quiet." She stopped speaking then, for effect. And the sudden change resulted in a kind of lush velvet quiet that one wanted to reach both hands into.

After a long moment, Alix began to speak again. "If we say nothing, then our friends—Carmel Snow, and Michel from *Vogue,* and Christian Bérard—won't be able to help themselves. Once they realize they know more about Maison Christian Dior than all the other fashion editors, the chance to show off that knowledge will be irresistible. From now on, we do one spectacular thing—send a dress to Rita, which will make everyone talk all the more. I don't want to hear a whisper about this show. I want a deafening, thunderous roar, a roar we won't contribute one single sound to because we won't have to."

"You're setting your sights at the stars," Dior observed.

"Aren't you?"

"*Oui*. But it's my name on the door."

"You don't have to have your name on the door to want to do a good job."

It had come out too abruptly and she almost gave too much of herself away. Dior watched her silently for a time and she stood perfectly still, as she'd learned to do, and endured his gaze.

He leaned forward, face serious. "Thank you for setting your sights at the stars. Let's look through the sketches and choose one for Mademoiselle Hayworth."

When told of the plan, Madame Bricard declared, "She cannot wear anything other than Soirée for such a soirée."

*Le patron* nodded. And Alix did too.

For the Soirée gown had a straight-edged, low-cut bodice meant for Rita's shapely figure to cascade out of, and a two-tiered skirt in which her body would be a single stem adorned with two perfect rosettes of pleated navy blue silk. Rita in Soirée would be unforgettable.

If Alix could convince her to wear it.

Her secret weapon was Carmel Snow. She sent a telegram to Carmel, who'd recently published a very flattering interview and series of photographs of Rita. That meant Carmel knew how to get in touch with Rita, and that Rita was already favorably disposed to Carmel.

In the telegram, Alix asked Carmel to write a note to Rita saying that if Rita wore the gown to her movie premiere, she'd be certain to garner more publicity for herself and her movie than a thousand interviews ever could. And that Dior would dress her for every movie premiere thereafter. In return, Alix promised Carmel exclusive rights to publish an illustration of the gown in *Harper's Bazaar*, and that she'd take Carmel to the Ritz when she arrived in Paris and buy her the most expensive martini Frank could possibly make.

Carmel loved new things. So Alix was staking everything on the hope that she would love the idea of movie stars making alliances with fashion houses—especially if she were the intermediary to the first execution of the concept.

Just a few days later, Carmel's participation was secured in a typically ebullient cable. Alix celebrated both that and Christmas Eve with just one brandy in her office with Suzanne, and a lot of laughter and reminiscences of the prewar years when Suzanne had been in advertising and Alix at *Harper's Bazaar* and they'd often been the last to leave a nightclub at five in the morning.

\* \* \*

It wasn't until the new year that a telegram finally arrived at the post office for Alix.

HE ASKED ME IF IT WAS YOU WHO WANTED TO KNOW, Mary's reply read. THEN HE SAID, TELL ALIX TO GO TO HELL. I'M GUESSING YOU CAN FIGURE OUT THE SUBTEXT IN THAT.

Alix wished Dulles was there right now and she could tell *him* to go to hell. But she knew as well as Mary did that Allen Dulles had spent so much time dealing with the devil that he wasn't the least bit afraid of hell.

She almost didn't read the rest of Mary's message and perhaps she shouldn't have because it said: LEAVE IT ALL BEHIND, ALIX. WHAT'S DONE IS DONE. NO MATTER WHAT YOU DO NOW, EVERYONE WHO DIED OVER ALL THOSE YEARS OF WAR WILL STILL BE DEAD. YOU CAN'T SAVE ANYONE NOW.

*Except myself*, Alix thought almost prayerfully. That was the one person she'd wanted to save by coming to Paris. And now that self was imperiled again—perhaps worse than before. Because the subtext in Dulles's response was, *No. They didn't catch him.*

* * *

Back in her tiny *pension*, the newspaper article that had started it all shivered in Alix's hand.

*Tear it to pieces,* she urged herself.

But that would make her a coward.

She read it again—maybe in her agitation last month she'd misunderstood. But no. It was perfectly clear that Wolff and his accomplices were unpunished. Then, at the bottom of the article, she saw the journalist's name: *Anthony March*.

Anthony March had known Alix's fiancé, Bobby. Bobby had worked for a secret American wartime intelligence agency in Italy. Now Anthony was writing about wartime Italy in his newspaper.

God, she wanted a drink. Her fingers flexed for her purse. She was sure to find someone at the Ritz. Maybe Carmel was in Paris for the New Year. Carmel, who relied on gin and vermouth to get through the day, tonics that meant the world always felt like chiffon, even when it was heavier than lead and sharper than pins. Except those tonics didn't just alter the world; they altered oneself. Alix only had to recall herself in Manhattan a couple of months ago to know the hard and aching truth of that.

So she didn't leave the *pension* and seek benediction in a French 75. She picked up her pen instead.

*To Lillie,*
*From Paris*

*I thought forgetting meant not remembering. Like you, I don't want to remember. Remembering feels like the slow unraveling of my heart, as if it were a length of threadbare ribbon. But what if forgetting actually means finding a man I think nobody else has been able to?*

Her pen clattered onto the desk and Alix rested her forehead in her hand. What had happened to mundane questions? To *How are you?* and *Tell me what you've been doing?*

Those things had all died in April 1945 when a Nazi informant made Alix into a murderess.

Alix had been his handler. She'd never seen his face, but she'd spoken to him—she was the only person working for the Allies who had. And she'd relied on information he had given her to organize a clandestine mission into Italy that had resulted in the deaths of nine men, including eight of America's best intelligence agents. One of them had been Alix's fiancé, Bobby.

And that Nazi informant, about whom almost all she knew was the sound of his voice and that he had worked for Karl Wolff in some capacity, had most likely escaped justice. And if he had, he was probably living in Paris. He'd told her it was where he would go after the war and she'd thought to herself at the time, *No, you won't. Because you will* never *win.*

But Alix had been so very wrong.

A flash of blond hair. Bobby taking her out to dinner when she'd had to quit *Harper's Bazaar* and return to America from Paris in 1939 after the outbreak of war. "You don't know anyone in New York," Bobby had said to her. And he'd dined with her every night for a week so she'd know at least seven places in Manhattan that served good food. "Food I can't afford," she'd said to him wryly and he'd just shrugged and smiled—Bobby would never understand not having enough money to eat at the Rainbow Room each night.

But Bobby would never take her out to dinner again. She would never scan a room for his sunshine-blond hair, would never eat at those seven restaurants, would always blanch at the sight of steak au poivre because that's what Bobby liked to order. None of those things would happen because of one treacherous Nazi informant—and because of Alix. That mission would never have taken place but for Alix and her supposedly watertight information.

The result: the lives of nine young men had ended. Those men would visit her in her dreams tonight and they would condemn her because there had been no retribution.

But was finding someone—a Nazi with more deaths on his conscience than just those nine men—the answer to nightmares and always being chased by ghosts? She remembered the sound of the Nazi's voice and she shuddered. Almost two years on, it still made her feel true and absolute terror.

\* \* \*

Alix woke the next day hungover with self-loathing, wishing that alcohol afflicted her instead—then it would be over by midday. But the cure was the same: a careful application of rouge and lipstick, a cup of black coffee and fresh air. Except she felt the effects of the coffee drain quickly away when she arrived at the *maison* and saw from a pile of telegrams that at least half a dozen of the most important fashion editors from Manhattan were still undecided about whether to stay in Paris for Dior's show.

Suzanne took one look at Alix and exclaimed, "*Chérie! Mon Dieu.* Was your New Year too celebratory? Let me put this in your coffee." She held up the bottle of brandy she kept in her desk.

"No." The word was said unwaveringly and God it felt good to be stubborn about that. Brandy would only fuel the nightmares and she needed a clear head if she was going to figure out how to fulfill the stubborn wish for justice she'd held on to since April 1945 now that it was apparent the authorities had failed. Not to mention how she was going to make sure she didn't, in fact, end up as the Directrice of the Service de la Presse who'd failed to allow Dior's talents to be discovered.

Suzanne replaced the bottle in the drawer, observed Alix for several long seconds and asked, "How are your meetings with the editors going? Your meeting with Monsieur March, for instance—was it successful?"

The recollection of that was enough to set a little more of Alix's spirit flickering. "No. He's like a Hemingway novel—aggressively male and not worth the effort."

Suzanne chuckled, propped an elbow on her desk and draped a cigarette between her fingers. "That is more like the Alix St. Pierre I know. The *petite orpheline* I met and marveled over nearly ten years ago because how many young women who lose their parents when they're just thirteen years old have the courage to do everything they set their mind to, like you always have? As you've seen, *le patron* has the talent to be the most famous couturier of them all—someone to make people forget even Chanel and Schiaparelli. But he'll be nothing without you and me. That is why I asked you to come back to Paris."

*He'll be nothing without you and me.* Wasn't that true about so much, war or no war? That even a man who worked on staircases was buttressed by women in an enterprise only he would be known for. But didn't it also mean that Alix had a talent for working in the shadows, for getting things done without anyone knowing she was doing them?

The flicker of spirit leaped higher. She was more afraid of the Nazi who'd betrayed her than she was of anything—and that fear had stolen all of her courage and her reason last night. But what if she worked in the shadows again? What if she could somehow search undetected to give those nine dead men the redress that had been stolen from them? Her informant didn't know she was in Paris or that she was looking for him, which took just a little of the fear away.

Alix stared at Suzanne who was, right now, like her own fortune-teller, plucking possibilities out of the hopelessness. And Suzanne said, "I wonder if perhaps you need to be honest with yourself about why you came to Paris after telling me you would never return."

Beneath Suzanne's owlish gaze, all else besides honesty fled. Words pressed to the tip of Alix's tongue. "I thought I came to find myself. But maybe I came to find someone else. Except..." She faltered, dropped her eyes to the desk. "I'm scared."

"Never refuse something because you're scared," Suzanne said gently. "Only refuse something because it's wrong."

Understanding was a quiet and painful thing. It ached, the same way that guilt and shame did. The past wasn't a series of events that had once happened, it was the substance of Alix's bones. Finding the Nazi who had made her the murderess of nine men was the right thing to do—the only thing to do. Because—*Live*. That was the message she'd seen in Dior's gowns. How she wanted to truly live once more.

Alix lifted an imaginary glass, feeling something good stir inside her for the first time since she'd witnessed the victories unfurl in Italy and known she had a hand in that. "To us. The invisible women behind the man."

\* \* \*

That night, Alix sat down at her desk and contemplated how the hell a resource-less woman who'd spent all her savings on her steamship ticket to Paris would find a Nazi who'd evaded the Nazi hunters, the police, and the armies.

*Remember your training*, she told herself. Being a spy was like painstakingly tugging every fine thread in a garment until you found the one in a million that unraveled everything. It was an awfully big coincidence that Anthony March had mentioned Bobby to her on the same day he'd published a piece about men escaping justice for what they'd done in Italy. War had taught Alix not to believe in coincidences. Luckily Anthony March was coming to see her on Monday. It was time to give his threads a little tug.

# FOUR

Anthony March appeared at the door of Alix's office precisely on time saying, "I know you don't ask more than three times, which means I need to be rude and ask for coffee rather than wait to be offered it."

In spite of herself, she laughed. "I'll be back in a minute."

She collected two coffees from the cafeteria and returned only to have him say, "They don't give you someone to make your coffee?"

Just like that he was back to being a jerk. Maybe he thought it would unnerve her, or that arrogance was attractive and she'd rush to notch herself onto his already well-scored belt. What Anthony didn't understand was that she was an expert in dealing with antagonistic men. Which meant this might even be fun.

"If I had someone to make coffee for me, they wouldn't know to put salt in yours instead of sugar," she said sweetly. "Shall I tell you about Maison Christian Dior? I don't imagine you have any questions prepared."

"I do actually," he said, eyeing his coffee, as if torn between drinking it anyway just to foil her and doubting she'd actually done what she'd implied. "Let's start with whether this couture house is just a way for Boussac to sell more fabric. The rumor is he's sunk sixty million into Maison Christian Dior." The depth of scorn attached to the last three words made it sound as if the house were named after a vagrant. "Some people have put the figure as high as a billion, but I'm not that gullible when it comes to rumors spread by PR princesses."

He picked up his coffee and sipped, grimacing when he discovered she'd actually added a dozen sugars instead of salt. She'd not done it to be petty but so she had an excuse to leave the room and refresh his cup if she needed to—when you were trying to unpick someone's seams, it was always good to have an escape route.

She responded coolly, ignoring the grimace. "When you come to the show and see something that bewitches even you, you'll know this is a premier couture house, not a front for fabric sales."

He was right to ask, although everyone else had danced around the subject more lightly. Pierre Boussac was Dior's financial backer and he was also one of the biggest fabric manufacturers in the country. It was possible that Maison Christian Dior had begun as a way to show-case Boussac's fabrics. But what Alix had seen over the past month made her certain it was now nothing of the kind.

"Something that bewitches even me," he repeated. "You don't think I'm easily charmed?"

She sipped her coffee, hoping to swallow her next words but they slipped out anyway, silk-toned, to distract from her lack of *politesse*. "I have a feeling you're so used to everyone trying to charm you that you think yourself immune to it. I'm also sure you think women's fash-ion is a time-wasting frivolity in a city where the bullets of two years before are still lodged in buildings and the Allied Control Council can't even agree on what the time is at midnight."

He acknowledged the joke with a short laugh but then segued with dazzling alacrity, asking, "How long have you been in PR?"

"Since I left Paris in '39." She'd let him keep asking questions; what he wanted to know might tell her whether he was just a red herring— or a button she needed to fit into a buttonhole.

"And during the war?" He lit a cigarette then exhaled smoke, loudly, irritatingly, eyes heavy-lidded as if he'd just rolled out of bed and was planning to return to it or some other decadence as soon as the meeting was over.

Alix wondered for just a moment what she gave away about herself in the nuance of her own exhale and resolved not to smoke while Anthony was in the room. "I was with the government," she said blandly. "I ran the campaign to recruit women into the workforce."

That was part-truth. But while she was at the War Department, she and her language skills—her parents had emigrated to America from French Alsace, and had thus taught Alix both German and French before they died—had, through a mysterious whisper network, come to the attention of other government officials. After a labyrinthine set of strange interviews and even more peculiar training—why would she need to learn voice recognition in this new job, was just one of the many questions she'd asked—she'd been sent to Switzerland by the Office of Secret Services, an organization for spies and their masters, an organization nobody was supposed to know about. But Alix knew because she'd been a part of it from late 1942 to 1945, doing things she was forbidden to speak about.

It was clear by now that neither of them had any interest in discussing Dior.

"And you?" she asked. "What were you doing before you took up the newspaper business?"

"I served in Europe, like most men. That's how I knew Bobby Du Pont."

It was still possible that Anthony had been a regular soldier, in Italy perhaps, and had run into Bobby in a bar on furlough. Or—Anthony was OSS too, just like Bobby and Alix had been. *I served in Europe* was the kind of nonspecific response an ex-OSS agent would give. And thinking along those lines helped quell the urge to blink at this second cavalier mention of Bobby's name, like he was worth only a shrug of the shoulders and a quick *Oh well*, rather than as if he was worth a hell of a lot more than the man in front of her right now. But if she didn't blink, then the sudden shine in her eyes might fall onto her cheeks.

Her resolve broke. She reached for a cigarette, letting smoke haze her face.

It gave him an opening.

"What about, say, 1943 to 1945?" he pressed on, eyes fixed on her. "I spoke to some folks in Manhattan who knew of PR wunderkind Alix St. Pierre who'd saved Bergdorf Goodman's skin in 1940, and who rescued Goldman Sachs from an embarrassing faux pas after the war. But I couldn't find anyone who knew what you did during those two years. It made me wonder—maybe she doesn't want anyone to know?"

The only reason anyone would be so interested in what she'd done between 1943 and 1945 was if they already knew she'd worked for OSS and were trying to lift off her mask and see what she was hiding.

"Is it because you find me so very alluring that you wasted so much time on transatlantic cables about me?" Her voice was as sweet as Anthony's coffee. "Odd, given I'm not the subject of this meeting."

"No. You wanted to flatter me with front row tickets to a show that's one of the least newsworthy things in Europe so that I would, in turn, knock out an article saying women should drape themselves in Dior," was his retort.

It was a wonder he could stand up with the weight of that chip on his shoulder. Everyone carried them these days—or at least everyone who'd been in Europe between 1940 and 1945. Alix's was a splinter stuck deep in her heart. But even if Anthony had his own buried shrapnel, she would not stand back wearing a publicist's smile while he abused Dior and fashion and her entire sex. This was the all too familiar point when stifling her words felt too much like stifling her integrity and it all came out—and she ended up getting threatened or cursed or fired.

*Don't lose your job over Anthony March,* her rational mind pleaded. *Don't be just another woman who lets him get away with being a jerk,* the fighting part of her mind begged. It won.

"I wasn't going to flatter you," she said, standing, straight-backed and unrepentant. "And nor was I going to offer you a front row seat.

Perhaps I could find you a place outside on the doorstep where you can contemplate how it will look when the *New York Times* has a double-page feature on Maison Christian Dior and you have nothing. There'll be no bullets at Dior's show, I'll grant you. But people don't just turn to the newspaper to find out about the bad things that are happening. They're also looking for a glimmer of light to help them cope with the bad things—the sequin hidden in the hopsack. You're selling hope as much as I am, and you won't sell papers at all if your headlines are only about guns."

She crossed to the door. "I have another meeting."

She expected he would make fast his escape to tell Dior his new publicist needed her mouth scrubbed clean with soap. But he was irritatingly slow to stand, smoothing his necktie and then drawing himself upright, towering over her at more than six feet tall. He was dressed in a navy suit—not shabby and worn and having survived wartime rationing, but new and cut with a tailor's expert precision. His shirt was pristinely white, as was his pocket square, and his tie was patterned geometrically with pale gold and ocher diamonds, colors that contrasted superbly with the navy. He mightn't care about fashion—women's fashion—but he kept himself well supplied.

Which meant she couldn't resist adding, "What were you trying to forget when you bought your suit?"

Anger sparked in his eyes. "Just how much time-wasting there would be in Paris." He strode out.

Immediately Alix crossed to the tiny window which overlooked a small square of the street below. After a few moments, her eyes picked out a tall man with dark hair who, when he reached Rue François ler, turned and took out a cigarette, flicked a lighter and frowned as he looked back at the *maison,* eyes scanning over each window as if he knew how to memorize internal floor plans and extrapolate them to the exterior, to figure out which window Alix St. Pierre was watching him from.

She didn't step away. She didn't think he could see her but if he could, she wanted him to understand that she knew how to observe someone's exits, and had enough smarts to work out what Anthony March was keeping from her. He hadn't reported her rudeness to Dior. That was both a relief and a clue.

He wasn't a Nazi, or the man she was looking for—his voice wasn't the one she'd heard in Switzerland. But he was definitely one knot in a tangled ribbon that led back to everything that had happened during the war.

* * *

There was nothing she needed more after that encounter than fresh air. She picked up her purse but before she could leave the *maison*, her phone rang. A husky voice, familiar from the silver screen said, "I like the dress."

It was impossible that Rita Hayworth was on the phone right now but it was either Rita or her voice-double. So Alix bet on the former and said, "I thought you would. And you'll come to Monsieur Dior's show, won't you? I've arranged a front row seat so you can choose your gifts this time, rather than have us choose them for you."

Rita said, "I think I will." And Alix almost squealed.

Subduing her excitement for the remaining minute of conversation wasn't easy. Her feet danced against the floor but only when she put down the receiver did she let her mouth say a very heartfelt *"Mon Dieu,"* and then break into a smile as big as the one she'd worn on her first day in Paris in 1937.

It was working! Rita had said she'd wear Soirée to the premiere of her new movie. That would surely persuade the fashion editors to stay in Paris for the show. Should she tell Dior? What if Rita changed her mind on the night and wore something else? *Le patron* would be felled by the disappointment, especially so close to the show. No, it was better to keep it a secret for now, until the premiere was closer and Rita's plans absolutely fixed.

But neither could Alix stay in the *maison* because someone was bound to notice a grin so ridiculously large and think she was drunk. She made a quick exit and achieved her earlier desire for fresh air—it was so chilly outside she could probably give up earrings altogether as icicles were now adorning her earlobes. She shoved her hands in the pockets of the cast-off mink coat Mary had given her in Switzerland and marched onward, not letting the cold steal her smile.

Along the Champs-Élysées, the pavement was crowded with Americans carrying shopping bags marked with the Chanel logo. Coco was still giving perfume away to the Allied GIs in Paris keeping the peace, who sent it home to their sweethearts—one bottle of liquid gold in exchange for a faithfulness the men most likely didn't practice themselves. But perfume was a currency many were willing to trade for, just as U.S. Army ration tins had been almost legal tender during the war in Italy. There was always something one could barter with, or for—cigarettes. Bodies. Secrets.

Secrets. Alix halted. She was an expert at trafficking those. And right now she knew a secret too delicious to keep under her tiny—and very chic—hat. What if the American editors found out about Rita Hayworth and Soirée now? Surely that would convince them to come to Dior's show.

She started walking again, faster now, going to the Hotel Scribe, which had long been patronized by the American press. She stationed herself outside, lit a cigarette and wondered how many she'd have to work her way through.

Four, as it turned out. It wasn't too bad as far as stake-outs went.

Mrs. Perkins from *Women's Wear Daily*, who always came to Paris early and who Alix had never met—having dealt with consumer magazines rather than trade in the past—emerged from the hotel. The minute Alix saw her, she slipped the doorman a few francs to disappear for the next ten minutes while Mrs. Perkins tried to hail a taxi in a city where cabs were as scarce as coal.

"I discovered when I arrived last week," Alix said, playing up the overriding American tenor of her accent and obscuring the French lilt, "that a taxi is as hard to find as a good man. I've taken to walking down to the Ritz so often to catch one that the doorman there thinks I'm a guest, only he can't figure out why I'm always leaving and never arriving."

Mrs. Perkins laughed. "Are you on your way there now?"

"I am," Alix said.

As they walked, Mrs. Perkins asked Alix how she came to be in Paris. Alix chattered on as if she were as green as new grass about how she'd just started as a publicity assistant at a new couture house and wasn't it exciting but she'd answered the phone that morning and Rita Hayworth herself had been on the line! And Rita was wearing a Christian Dior gown to the premiere of her new movie, truly she was, but—oh dear. That was still a secret and she shouldn't have said anything.

Alix arranged her face to look like an innocent creature who couldn't have identified a fashion editor even had she been in the offices of *Vogue*. Of course, Mrs. Perkins would discover in February exactly who Alix was but hopefully by then the magic of Dior would have been wrought upon the world.

"I wouldn't dream of mentioning it to anyone," Mrs. Perkins replied with a smile that gave away the fact she wasn't to be trusted, which was exactly what Alix was counting on. Surely it meant that Mrs. Perkins would reveal, in the biggest fashion industry journal in America, the news that Rita Hayworth was wearing new couturier Christian Dior to her next movie premiere.

\* \* \*

It was only when Alix returned to her *pension* at almost midnight that the joy faded and she found herself dressed in something more like contemplation—or perhaps it was trepidation. The witching hours were the only moments that were hers alone and could thus be expended on her quest. But how did you find a Nazi who'd evaded everyone?

No one knew the names of the shadows working behind men like Karl Wolff, just as nobody had known who Karl Wolff was back when he'd been a shadow working behind Himmler. There were always men who specialized in back doors and lurking, and all the cloak-and-dagger business of a war. La Voce—the code name she'd given her informant—was one of those unnamed and faceless men. She needed to know his name and his movements now, the places he lived or worked—a location she could give to the authorities where they could trap him at last and lock him away.

She had exactly five leads. One: La Voce had once told Alix that Brasserie Lipp was his favorite place in Paris. Two: he'd made his initial contact with the Allies via Frank at the Ritz. Three: Esmée Archambault had been the courier who'd passed the message on from Frank to Alix. Four: Chiara Romano, one of Alix's couriers in Italy, might know the names of Karl Wolff's aides. That was unlikely, as was the chance of Chiara replying to any letter Alix sent. Five: Anthony March had more than likely worked for OSS and he wanted something from Alix too.

She'd start with the first. Go to Brasserie Lipp and see whether it was the kind of place she could linger to listen for the sound of the voice she knew too horrifyingly well, or if it was too exposed for a stakeout. She'd also pay a visit to Frank—on a Sunday morning perhaps, when the bar was quieter. Anthony March had a suite at the Ritz, which meant she could ask Frank about him too. And she'd write to Chiara, and pay Esmée a visit—but she also had a job she needed to keep at a fashion house that was hurtling toward its very first showing, meaning Alix was busier than ever and would have to fit all of these things into the edges of her already too-full days.

\* \* \*

Brasserie Lipp proved to be less than ideal for waiting in obscurity and listening for voices. The walls were mirrored, reflecting the patrons to every corner of the room, and the tables outside were clearly in view of all passers-by along the busy Boulevard Saint-Germain. And it was Frank's weekend off, she discovered when she went to the Ritz, and Esmée Archambault was out of town.

But even as she found herself thwarted in her personal mission, her professional one was—she hesitated to say it for fear of cursing it too—edging close to a triumph. On her desk sat the latest issue of *Women's Wear Daily* with an article about Rita Hayworth's plans to wear a Christian Dior gown to her movie premiere.

*Yes!* There at last was the evidence that perhaps Alix wasn't going to be the *directrice* who failed to show *le patron*'s brilliance to the world. *Le patron* might even manage a full and complete smile when she told him, which was an idea that made every pore of her skin feel like a tiny sequin of joy.

With a smile on her own face, she continued to read her mail. Out of one envelope fell a sheet of plain white paper scored with red pen.

*Leave Paris.*

Her heart recoiled as if La Voce had just spoken those words aloud. It could only be from him.

When had it been delivered? There was no postmark on the envelope. No logo or letterhead or insignia on the notepaper. Just two words written in red.

He wanted to scare her. He wanted her to run.

*He knew who she was.*

Despite all her training, her limbs froze. Her breath too. Even her blood.

The only way La Voce could send a note to her place of work was if he knew her name.

The punch of shock had her bending double, bile and terror pressing into her throat.

A Nazi who'd taken not just nine lives, but perhaps nine hundred or nine thousand, was giving Alix one chance to leave Paris.

\* \* \*

She needed to stand up. To take a taxi—not walk—to her *pension*. Once there, a smart woman would pack her valise, then board a train or a ship and run far away.

That would mean leaving Dior and the chance for someone to be proud of her. It would mean not seeing the show she'd worked so hard to make a success. She'd be right back in the well-worn suit of the Alix dodging brandy bottles and temptation.

Her eyes flickered back to the *Women's Wear Daily* article. She thrust herself out of her seat.

She crossed over to the wall where she'd pinned a copy of her seating chart. Instead of ripping it down and throwing it away and running again, she picked up a pen and began to write in the names of every editor she hoped would come to the show after reading the article about Rita Hayworth and Dior.

This moment was like standing on the edge of a cavern and knowing it was dangerous and stupid and so goddamn painful to jump—but that you had to do it anyway. And so she leaped—into the life she'd started making for herself in Paris. Into the life she deserved to make for herself.

*Damn La Voce to hell.* She wasn't leaving Paris. In fact, he'd just spurred her on to work harder and faster than ever to find him—before he found her.

# FIVE

After the door of the *maison* closed behind her and she was safely inside, Alix shook off the alertness and fear that had accompanied her on her walk along only the busiest of sidewalks to the Avenue Montaigne. *Think of Rita Hayworth's movie premiere*, she told herself. Not the fact that she might be in tremendous danger every time she went outside and that she hadn't gone anywhere without her gun for the last few days.

But something was wrong at the couture house too. Three weeks before the show and the salon should have been filled with workmen dressing the room with gray and white wallpaper. Apprentices should have been jostling for space amongst the parasols, hats, and gloves. But the lack of noise was so absolute that Alix would have been able to hear the proverbial pin drop—except the atmosphere was such that no one would dare drop a pin right now.

As she ascended the stairs, everyone averted their eyes.

Suzanne waited at the very top. "You must go straight to see *le patron*."

"Why?"

Suzanne's reply was an expression of such extreme disappointment that Alix felt about as sick and winded as when she'd read La Voce's note. How had she ruined this too?

One foot proceeded the other to the studio.

Monsieur Dior pushed a copy of *The Times* across the desk.

Alix recognized the image on the fashion pages at once. Soirée. The gown she'd sent to Rita Hayworth. The sketch she'd promised to Carmel Snow. It had somehow been published already in *The Times*. And it wasn't a sketch from a copyist's hand, or the studio illustrator's hand. This sketch was the most secret and coveted of all—*le patron's* own.

It couldn't possibly be in the newspaper. Nobody was meant to see it until Rita wore it. Monsieur Dior wouldn't care about priceless publicity in *Women's Wear Daily* when his trade secrets had just been exposed.

And Alix knew she would take the fall for this. Would lose her job over it, even though, this time, she'd not done a single thing wrong.

Tears threatened. But it was funny how muscle memory worked. When one had trained one's body not to react in front of another person to anything—a gun, the cognac-scented breath of a Nazi at one's neck—the body recalled what to do. Not to remain still, as that in itself said much. But not to pale or flush either, not to quake nor bluster, not to allow even the slightest tremble into one's voice. Certainly never to let those tears well up, or fall.

No, Alix had learned to be like thread, able to be warped and wefted into whatever pattern suited that particular moment. Right now she was defiant red taffeta.

"I didn't give that sketch to anyone," she said furiously.

"I telephoned the journalist, Mademoiselle Gordon. She told me the sketch arrived with a note from you. She didn't know it was both stolen and embargoed," Monsieur Dior replied quietly. "She believed she was permitted to publish it."

Suzanne and Mesdames Carré, Bricard, and Raymonde—the people hand-selected by Dior—were beyond suspicion. Whereas Alix had had access to both the sketches and the press and while it seemed like the stupidest of all things to do—ingratiating herself with an English journalist in so public a manner that losing her job was the only possible outcome—everyone probably believed she'd been paid sufficiently well that she cared nothing for her job. That she'd run back to Manhattan with her payoff, put her feet up and laugh.

"I didn't send it to her," Alix insisted.

Dior, to his credit, didn't look away or protest that his hand had been forced. "Until some other explanation is discovered, you cannot work here."

Alix was so damn tired of being like thread. "I'm not jumping on a ship to Manhattan," she said. "I'm going to find out who did this and the minute I do, you're going to give me my job back—with a pay raise."

\* \* \*

Alix raced back to her *pension*, driven by so many things—fury, disbelief, single-mindedness. And maybe a little bit of pride.

It wasn't the first time since she'd come to Paris that she'd felt a stirring of the self-worth she used to possess. It was a fragile thing and she didn't want to look at it for too long in case it fled but she also wanted to let it spur her on. Had she been fired from this job two months ago, she might have thought it easier to quit than to fight.

Not now.

She got to work, changing into an old slate-gray suit from wartime. She tucked her hair up into a simple chignon and tamed her face by removing all of her makeup. Not that she thought she was a startling beauty, but Switzerland had taught her that when made-up and appropriately attired, her eyes—wide-set and as green as a cat's at night— and her full lips and high brow were arresting to some. She jammed a detestable fedora on her head, tilting it to one side and pulling it low to sit just above one eye, not wishing to be recognized by anyone.

She had an entire day at her disposal and two puzzles to progress: who was the man she'd only ever known as La Voce, a man who wanted to run her out of Paris before she ran him out; and who the hell had framed her with that sketch? She'd learned at OSS that when you had a thousand problems to solve, you started with whatever you had a next step for and sometimes that would untie a knot in a different thread.

The Ritz was a next step she could take right now. Frank was there. Anthony March had a suite there. And Becky Gordon, the recipient of the sketch, lived there too. Alix would tackle Frank and La Voce while she waited for Becky—and perhaps Anthony—to finish work for the day.

* * *

Alix took a seat at the far end of the bar, lifted her hat a little and caught Frank's eye. He polished a glass, flicked a towel across his shoulder and strolled over to ask, as if he'd never met her before, "What can I get you?"

"Something Italian," she said. "I'd like to meander down memory lane."

"Bellini?"

"Why not?"

She flipped open a newspaper, keeping the fedora tilted toward the main room, hoping it was too early for anyone she knew to be there. As she pretended to read, she was aware of Frank adding peach puree and raspberry juice to prosecco—God, she hated Bellinis—and recommending to the handful of customers seated at the bar that they'd be more comfortable over in the chairs, advice they seemed happy to take. Once the counter was clear of people, Frank carried the drink over to her and began to polish more glasses, whistling to himself.

Alix sipped the drink, did her best not to grimace, and said in a low whisper, "Tell me about Anthony March."

Frank laughed, which made Alix say exasperatedly, "I'm not asking on behalf of my heart or my loins."

That made Frank laugh even harder. "You know a bartender doesn't discuss his favorite customers."

Her first response was an incredulous, "Anthony March is one of your favorite customers?" But her second—Frank sounded a lot like he'd already had a very similar conversation—was the more astute, "He asked you about me."

"Maybe you two should just talk to one another," Frank said sagely.

"Why—"

He cut her off. "You get to know a man who prefers a table on his own at three in the morning to the charms of disappointed admirers. And I told him that you get to know a woman who jumps behind a bar at midnight when she can see it's too busy and that the bartenders can't keep up and then makes consummately timed Bloody Marys, which are the hardest damn drinks to make."

She smiled. She had done that a few times back in 1937 and '38, using all the skills she'd learned from a year spent as a part-time waitress while at her Swiss finishing school. "Okay. You won't tell me anything about Monsieur March but can you tell me…" She checked to be sure no one was within hearing distance. "Who made contact with you about Italy?"

Frank whistled a rousing chorus, then shook his head. "I don't know. The message was passed on via a German military intelligence officer who used to come here, one of the ones arrested and killed after Operation Valkyrie."

Alix knew the Little Bar had curlicues of secrets decorating her wallpaper, that it had been the watering hole for a group of disaffected Nazis during the war. Based on what Frank had just said, some of those Nazis were involved in the unsuccessful plot to kill Hitler. Which meant she could rule out the man who'd passed the message to Frank—if he'd been killed in 1944 for his part in Valkyrie, he wasn't Alix's informant in 1945. He was just a conduit.

More whistling from Frank, and Alix pretended to read an article in the newspaper about more punitive bread rations. Then Frank added, "He'd passed on genuine information before so I sent it to Esmée. I didn't hear anything after that, so I assumed it had found a handler."

"It did. Me. And I'm trying to find out who I was handling."

Alix's eyes fell back onto the newspaper as two customers approached and Frank asked them in a cheery voice what he could get them. They were not, unfortunately, inclined to sit in the chairs— no, they were tourists who liked to chat to the bartender.

She'd have to wait for Frank to get back to her after he'd had a chance to roam his memory for any link that might be useful. In the meantime, just as she'd already surmised, Esmée Archambault might be able to help. And yet another step was perhaps walking into the bar right now in the form of an impeccably dressed—as usual—Anthony March. With any luck, Becky wouldn't be far behind.

Alix tipped her fedora to the other side of her head, exposing her profile. Despite her understated appearance, Anthony recognized her. He frowned and drummed his fingers on the bar, glanced at Frank, then walked over to her.

"I heard you got fired," he said, folding his arms across his chest. "Why did someone want to set you up and cost you your job?"

Maybe it made her a fool—or maybe it just meant she was human enough to recall what it was like to sit alone in bars at three in the morning, thinking about all the things that had driven one to do just that. Instead of retaliating, she gave him the truth, "This time, I don't know."

She waited for him to heap scorn over that moment of truth but his frown deepened and he said, "Don't look at your enemies. Look at your friends. People you've done a favor for. People who've had to rely on favors often find them grating after a while."

*People you've done a favor for.*

Dior's sketch had been sent to Becky. Nobody had suspected Becky of having any part in the mischief because it seemed too obvious— you didn't expose your crime by publishing it in the newspaper you

worked for. Becky had been the most unlikely of suspects, an innocent caught up in a game. But wasn't the thing hiding in plain sight so
often the answer?

Alix had given Becky advice, and a front row seat.

But Alix had also given Fortunée advice, and lessons in deportment.

"Thank you," she said, actually smiling at Anthony and then hurrying out of the bar.

In three cigarettes' time, Fortunée left the House of Christian
Dior. Alix, waiting across the street, began to follow her, retracing her
footsteps—as it turned out—to the Ritz. Fortunée entered the main
bar and sat down as if she were waiting for someone. And Alix had a
very good idea that the someone in question would be Becky Gordon.
Indeed, when Alix went back outside, she saw Becky approaching
from across the Place Vendôme. Which meant she had about three
minutes to get Fortunée out of the bar before Becky saw her, and to
come up with a plan—and she couldn't afford to be too fussy about
how elegant it was, nor about who she relied on to help her pull it off.

The first person she asked was Frank. When she told him she
needed management to detain Fortunée in an office for half an hour,
he simply nodded.

The second person, she was sure, wouldn't simply nod.

But she'd had to ask for larger favors from worse people in the
past and she'd survived the trade-off with only her principles slightly
wrinkled. She'd iron them smooth tomorrow at the *maison* when
she got her job back.

She approached the front desk with a smile, a glance at the man's
name badge, and a "*Bonjour*, Monsieur Charles," because she'd learned
that bothering to find out people's names was never a waste of time.
She requested writing paper, scribbled a note, and asked Charles if it
could be delivered immediately to Anthony March's room, praying
that Becky wouldn't leave until Anthony replied, and praying he'd
gone up to his suite, as he hadn't still been in the Little Bar just now.

After only five minutes, the concierge tapped Alix on the shoulder and said in a low voice, "Monsieur March asked that you be shown up to his suite."

"*Merci*, Jean-Luc," she said.

\* \* \*

In the elevator, she remembered her lack of makeup; she'd never done something like this without a mask. She pulled off her hat, tugged her hair loose from the chignon and tried to finger-comb it into some sort of style, but the elevator ride wasn't long enough for miracles.

All too soon she was in front of a door that opened to reveal Anthony March, looking more informal than usual. His tie was off, top button undone and shirtsleeves rolled up so she could see that he had tanned arms, muscular arms, as if he spent time outside, or perhaps indulged in more exercise than simply lifting a highball from bar counter to mouth.

"Twice in one day," he said, leaning against the wall. He held a glass in the tips of his fingers, a glass filled higher than it should be with what smelled like vermouth. "To what do I owe the pleasure?"

It would be best to tackle this like a bone-dry martini—brazenly and without fear. "Despite what you said earlier about people who rely on favors finding them grating, I need a favor. We already find one another grating so it won't make too much difference in the scheme of things."

Anthony actually laughed.

"I wasn't expecting to find a sense of humor lurking up here on the sixth floor," she said, eyebrows raised.

Anthony shook his head as if he'd surprised himself too, then waited, humorless again, for her to elaborate.

"I need to see if Becky Gordon has a large quantity of money in her purse. The only way to do that without her suspecting and taking the evidence out before I see it is to get her up to somewhere like this, where she expects one thing, but—" She stopped and shook her head, hearing how it sounded.

There had to be a better way. But what? If Anthony had worked for OSS too then he knew how to persuade someone into a room better than anyone else of her current and proximate acquaintance.

"You want me to seduce Becky," Anthony said, and the corners of his mouth lifted into a smile as if he were rather enjoying her discomfort—which she probably deserved after the coffee stunt.

She exhaled. "What you two do once I'm finished is really up to her. I just need you to get her up here. I can beg, if that makes you feel better. And if you want to name a price for your services, go ahead. But I'd prefer to discuss that in your room rather than out here in the hallway."

She fixed her eyes on his face and he met them briefly before he pushed away from the wall, moved aside to let her in, raised his glass, tilted back his head, and swallowed more liquor. "How old *are* you?" he asked. "Bobby was a baby. But if you were his fiancée…"

"Then you thought I'd be a baby too," she finished. "If it's any consolation, right now I feel like one. So will you help me or not?"

He walked across to the window, staring out. "Despite an appalling lack of manners…"

Alix winced as she recalled how she'd just asked him for a very large favor. He spun around at the same moment and caught her, but she thought she saw him smile, as if perhaps he wasn't really annoyed.

"I will," he said. "And my services tonight are free."

"Thank you," she said. "See, I have manners."

She inched into the room, hovering near the incongruously delicate Louis Seize sofa. Anthony placed his now-empty glass on the coffee table, rolled down his sleeves, did up his top button, and picked up a tie that lay stretched out on a chair. She turned away; watching him put on a tie felt somehow too intimate for their strained and fleeting acquaintance.

"I'm dressing, not undressing," he said wryly.

She knew she was flushing—it was a singular drawback of pale skin—and she made herself turn back to face him, made herself remember what it was like in Switzerland and Italy in 1945. Back then, watching a man put on a tie was something she would gladly have done compared to all the other things she'd had to do.

"You didn't answer my question," he said, eyes on her in the mirror as he knotted his tie, frowned, unknotted it and tied it again.

"I'm twenty-seven. The same age Bobby would have been."

"You look like you're about twenty-one."

As he spoke, she caught a glimpse of herself in the mirror and she could see that yes, she did look especially young today: her lack of makeup and unfussy hair made it seem as if she still held on to a soupçon of innocence.

"The first time I met you at the Ritz, you seemed like you came from another world to Bobby. But today—" Anthony cut himself off, frowned again, then slipped on his jacket and walked toward the door. "I'll try to be back soon."

She recovered herself and said, with a mischievous grin, "I have no doubt this is one mission you'll be able to complete in record time."

She heard him laugh as he left the room.

*  *  *

Alix surveyed the suite. It reflected the Ritz's understated opulence: curvaceous oriental porcelain vases filled with hothouse blooms, a delicate chaise longue near the fireplace in dusky blue and several antique chairs in shades of pewter, cinnamon, and flint. They looked unused, the ornamental pillows still arranged at just the right angle by housekeeping.

To her right stood a large desk. The chair behind it was brown leather, soft with wear. The desk's surface was bare of anything except a pen and a lamp and a drop or two of water—condensation left from a glass.

Alix pulled herself up short before her outstretched finger could move toward those drops. This was how she'd scrutinized every room since late 1942 when she'd been taught how to tell something of the person who owned a space by the traces they left behind. But there was little of Anthony here. All she could discern was that, whatever time he spent there, he did so at his desk, which perhaps meant he did more work than she would have credited.

She should be safe for at least ten minutes, despite what she'd said to him about his likely speed in accomplishing his mission. She pushed open the door to the bedroom. But it was just as bereft of the personal. In the bathroom, the only items on view were Ritz soap, a toothbrush, a shaving brush, and a razor.

She washed her hands so that if Anthony came back sooner than she'd expected, she could pretend to have been using the facilities. And that was when she saw it. Behind the shaving mirror was a pocketknife she recognized—because she'd given it to Bobby for his twenty-first birthday. She stared at it for a long time before picking it up and running her hand over the engraving. *To B. Love A.*

She slipped it into her purse.

Anthony would know who had taken it. The price of getting it back would be to explain why he had it.

*Leave Paris*, the note had said. She closed her eyes against it, heard the words again in La Voce's voice as she braced her hands against the vanity. La Voce wanted her to leave but she hadn't, was foolishly thinking she could keep skipping through the city streets and somehow evade a Nazi killer. Becky appeared to be up to something that involved making sure Alix lost her job. And Anthony March had some sort of business with Alix too.

But was it for good or evil?

If it was the latter, that meant she'd walked straight into the lion's den. Luckily she wasn't a sheep.

She pressed her hand against the outline of the Beretta service pistol in her purse. *Deal with Anthony and Becky first*, she told herself. La Voce couldn't get to her in a private suite at the Ritz.

She returned to the sitting room and barely had time to arrange herself in a chair before the door opened. Anthony really must be an excellent flirt.

Becky turned to Anthony, expecting passion, but he spun her around to face Alix and said, "I'll leave you to it."

"If you could stay," Alix said, voice hard like it had needed to be with Allen Dulles in Switzerland, "a witness would be useful."

Becky's head swiveled from Alix to Anthony, and Alix saw the precise moment when awareness slapped her on the cheek.

"Was it your idea or Fortunée's?" Alix asked, wanting to know who had been the instigator and who had been the fool.

"I don't know what you mean," Becky said, eyes wide, a countenance Alix imagined might work with her daddy but would never work with Alix.

"Then you won't mind if I look in your purse."

"My purse?" Becky squeaked.

"The black rectangular object in your hand," Alix said, knowing that soon it would all be over if she just kept her cool and didn't let herself jump up and implore, *Why? Why did you do it?*

Behind Becky, Anthony leaned against the door, bearing witness as Alix had asked him to, but also frowning at Alix as if she were a surrealist play he was trying to understand.

"The money I have in there is for—"

"A Dior gown?" Alix interrupted.

Becky's voice trailed away and there it was. The moment your prey gave in. They mightn't let on, might thrash a few more times, but it was over and Alix felt suddenly very tired.

Becky turned to Anthony as if she expected him to save her and Alix almost said, *Always save yourself, never rely on a man*—but she knew it would be as soundly ignored as the last piece of advice she'd

given Becky. Anthony inclined his head in Alix's direction and
Becky's face transfigured into that of a petulant child. She opened her
purse, pulled out an envelope stuffed full of the cash she'd obviously
planned to give Fortunée in payment for stealing the sketch. "There.
You've seen it."

But Alix had seen something else. She pushed herself out of the
chair, crossed the room in a second and took the envelope from
Becky's hand.

On the front were some handwritten words. Alix had seen that
handwriting before.

Her eyes locked with Becky's and all pretense of wide-eyed innocence and capitulation was gone. Becky's eyes were diamond-hard
with hatred.

Becky had written the note that said *Leave Paris*. Not La Voce.

Then Becky leaned forward and spoke in the lowest and coldest of
whispers so only Alix could hear. "You should take my advice."

"Wh—" Alix cut herself off before she could look or sound even
more like a stupid, shocked fool than she already did.

Triumph flashed in Becky's cruel and quick smile. Alix had just
given away both the fact that Becky was the victor in this round, and
also that Alix had no idea what the game even was.

Becky rearranged her face and by the time she turned back to
Anthony, the faux-naif had returned. She waved an arm at the door
and said crossly to Anthony, "May I?"

"You may," Alix answered, pulling herself together at last, mind
finally operating as it had in wartime. If she pushed Becky now, Alix
would be the certain loser because Becky appeared to know a hell
of a lot more about Alix than Alix knew about her. All Alix could
surmise was that Becky's loathing of her was deeply personal, and
also that Becky didn't want Anthony to know there was anything
more to her than the part she had played—Alix had to admit—very,
very well. If Alix acted vanquished right now, it might make Becky

overconfident—and overconfident people always made mistakes. In the meantime, Alix would be tailing her very closely and doing her damnedest to find out enough about the not-at-all-innocent Becky Gordon so that at their next meeting, Becky would be the one conquered, not Alix.

"Tell Fortunée to spend the money wisely," Alix said, trying to regain just a little of the wise-cracking, impenetrable Alix she ordinarily was.

Becky's parting shot at Anthony before she left was to say, "I wasn't that interested in you anyway."

The utterly convincing pettiness in Becky's tone made Alix laugh, quite helplessly. Which was a damn good thing—it made certain her own façade was intact before tackling the next person who had a secret agenda.

She kept the smile on her face as she said to Anthony, "You might regret having helped me when you realize that now I'll be back at Maison Christian Dior and you'll have to keep sparring with me about dresses."

"I definitely wouldn't have missed being called a cynic and having my suits critiqued." He conjured up a fleeting smile.

"Thank you for your help tonight." He was so tall she had to tip her head back to meet his eyes, which made her feel spectacularly young once more. What would he do now? Ask her about Bobby again? Tell her who he really was and what he wanted?

He opened the door. "Like I said, I don't want anything for my part in this. Knowing that someone who deserved it got their comeuppance is payment enough."

But she didn't take the chance to leave because his words were sinking like stones inside her: *Knowing that someone who deserved it got their comeuppance.*

She said to him, testing, "Rather than getting her comeuppance, you know Becky will continue on as before. It's always the ones with money who win, even when they lose."

"Which makes them more dangerous. And ever more due for their just reward."

He knew. He *knew* there was someone out there who'd not met their deserved fate. Did he know it was La Voce, or that a La Voce even existed? Or did he think that person was her? Because, in a way, it was her. What just reward had she received for sending nine men into the mountains to be murdered? A silk Dior gown. A job in Paris. A life still lived.

It was plain that she and Anthony March were due for a showdown. But not here in his suite at the Ritz where he was in charge.

"Come and see me when you're ready to talk," she said, noting the start of surprise he wasn't able to hide. "Number five, Rue du Cirque."

# SIX

Anthony frowned as he stepped onto his terrace, which overlooked the Place Vendôme. He couldn't see her. She must have taken the Rue Cambon exit. He was almost certain she wouldn't look quite so nonchalantly unhurried once out of his sight—but he also wasn't entirely sure. From a redhead in trousers with a champagne-house name in the bar at the Ritz—he was positive women weren't allowed to wear trousers in bars and restaurants in Paris, so how did she get away with it?—to a silk-clad tigress in a couture house accusing him of using tailor-made suits to cloak his sorrows, to a...what? What had she been tonight? Shrewd, and maybe even wily.

Back inside, he fixed his frown on the chair where she'd made Becky Gordon quail. God he'd wanted to laugh at the end, just like she had. Or clap. But he'd also wanted to...He crossed over to the bedroom and into the bathroom. The pocketknife wasn't where he'd put it when he'd received her note. She *had* gone snooping.

The sound of the telephone roused him. The front desk advised that a woman named Anjelica was asking to see him.

"Send her up."

He lit a cigarette and poured another vermouth, knowing he should fix Anjelica a drink too, but intensely disliking the idea of company right now. Besides, he and Anjelica had worked together for long enough that she'd know he wanted to be left alone.

He opened the door a second before she knocked and she breezed in the way she usually did, occupying all the space in the room with her presence. Anjelica wasn't just larger than life, she was larger than the goddamn universe.

"I think I'll be fired from Dior tomorrow," she said.

Anthony rubbed a hand over his brow and said, probably too brusquely, "Is he firing everyone?"

Anjelica pouted.

None of this was her fault, he reminded himself, and she *was* helping him. "It doesn't matter," he said by way of appeasement. "It was a long shot you getting a job there anyway, which you pulled off admirably"— he found a brief smile, knowing he should never have doubted her talents—"and I'm hoping that by tomorrow I'll know enough about Alix St. Pierre that I won't need you following her anymore."

He took his wallet out of the desk and gave her a decent handful of francs. When she opened her purse, he could see she already had a handy sum tucked inside. "Paris is just as profitable as Naples?" he asked.

"So far, so good. But don't you want to know why I'm being fired?"

He laughed. "I'm guessing you said something you shouldn't have. Although Dior seems to have a few outspoken and impetuous women working for him."

"Is she impetuous?" Anjelica said astutely, which was why he liked working with her—she'd seen almost every character and could read them all fluently.

He shrugged.

"You might think what I did was impetuous though." Anjelica placed her hand on her hip, allowing a dramatic pause before continuing. "Becky Gordon is up to something that involves your Alix St. Pierre. I'm the one who helped her steal the sketch, hence my purse-full of francs. She's a lead you missed. I'll let you pay me to keep chasing her. And I'll leave Mademoiselle St. Pierre to you."

So Becky and Alix's little showdown earlier wasn't about mere industrial espionage. But how the hell was Becky involved in everything? He pulled more money out of the drawer and passed it to Anjelica. "Let me know what you find."

She blew him a kiss, made for the door but stopped when she reached it and said, "I don't think Alix is the guilty one."

She put a hand on the doorknob as if she was going to leave. Which was what he'd wanted earlier, but right now he wanted her to stay and explain. But of course she knew that because, just before the door closed and when he couldn't pretend anymore not to be too damned curious to let it slide, he said, "Why?" at the same time as she said, "Because," and then they both laughed.

"You're forgetting I've seen you pretend to be a million things in Italy," Anjelica said. "So I can tell when you're playing at disinterested."

"I was trying to forget Italy," he agreed, his meaning a little different.

And maybe she sensed that, because she gave it to him painfully straight. "When a woman's seen every dark side of mankind, it layers a shadow in her eyes. I'm not one for poetry and souls having windows, but I'm not blind either. Alix St. Pierre has a whole moonless night in her eyes."

And then Anjelica had gone and he was pouring another vermouth—which would mean the staff replacing the bottle for the second time that week. He sat down at his desk, remembering the strange emerald green—not moonless black—of Alix's eyes when she'd seen whatever was inside Becky's purse.

Tomorrow night, he decided. Alix would return to Dior with her explanation of who was behind the sketch Becky had published. Which meant that by evening, she'd be jubilant and relaxed. So he'd go to 5 Rue du Cirque then and have her explain her involvement in what had happened on the mountain in Italy that night in April 1945 and whether it was her fault—or someone else's.

As for Becky Gordon, thank Christ he'd never slept with her. But he should have noticed that her interest in him had been too avid, rather than just accepting her attention like a narcissist.

He swallowed a mouthful of vermouth. It didn't really matter. He'd have his answer from Alix tomorrow night regardless. And perhaps expecting people to be genuine these days was like expecting repentance from a Nazi. But Jesus, wouldn't it be nice if the world wasn't a place where everything was for sale, ready to be bought and bartered and sold; if the world wasn't a place where trust was a notion more outdated than justice.

\* \* \*

At the *maison* the following day, Ferdinand the doorman let Alix in, exclaiming, "*Je vous ai manqué!*"

"I missed you too," Alix replied, returning the smile. She'd sent Monsieur Dior an explanation that morning, advising he could telephone Anthony March for corroboration, and she'd been asked to report back to duty that afternoon.

"*Chérie!*" Suzanne called, before bestowing a dozen kisses on each of Alix's cheeks and dressing her from head to toe in apologies.

"Stop," Alix said, laughing. "I won't be able to walk up the stairs carrying the weight of all this contrition. Buy me a drink and we'll call it quits."

They were interrupted by Dior himself. "Mademoiselle St. Pierre," he said gravely, before his round button of a mouth transfigured into the closest thing to a beam Alix had ever glimpsed on his face. It was the best thing she'd seen all week.

\* \* \*

Alix's first task was to telephone Carmel Snow, who'd just arrived in Paris for the early shows, to apologize for *The Times* having already published the Rita Hayworth sketch Alix had promised to *Harper's Bazaar*.

"Take me to lunch and we'll call it even," Carmel said affection-ately. "I know it wasn't your fault."

So Alix found herself at the Ritz that afternoon, where Carmel wrapped her in a heartfelt embrace. Carmel's hair was bluer than ever, obviously having just been refreshed by her dear Parisian hair-dresser. Her glasses were a matching shade of blue, and her pillbox hat was perched in its usual place, as was her Jean Schlumberger brooch and emerald engagement ring. She summoned the waiter over and ordered a martini. Alix requested mineral water.

Alix had barely finished promising Carmel a mannequin and the actual Soirée dress for an exclusive shoot before the first of the marti-nis was gone. She wondered uneasily if the customary three-martini lunch had long since been abandoned in favor of a vermouth flood. It made her fix her eyes on Carmel, brilliant Carmel, and pose a ques-tion Alix had never, not in ten years of friendship, asked.

"How's Palen?" she said, referring to Carmel's husband, a man who lived a life of hunting and horses completely separate from his wife.

Carmel paused, glass not yet to mouth. "How's Palen," she repeated, olive bobbing drunkenly in her gin. "I cannot recall the last time any-one in Paris asked me that."

"Have you seen him lately?" Alix prompted, not sure if she was helping or hurting, but avoiding and drinking didn't seem to be assuaging anything either.

"I spent the weekend before I came here out at the house with the children. Palen was there."

Palen was there. It didn't automatically follow that Carmel had seen him.

"Do you know," Carmel said after a very large—even for her—mouthful of martini, "what it's like to have two lives? One that is intoxicating and energetic and full of people like you"—she smiled brilliantly at Alix—"and another that's the life I am supposed to have and want and treasure, a life that exacts far harsher judgments behind hands at parties when I'm not quite out of earshot?"

Two lives. Yes, Alix knew what that was like. A secret agent and a secretary for the American mission in Bern. Bobby's fiancée and the woman who knew she would never marry him. The director of the Service de la Presse—and the woman she was expected to become when she did what custom and convention dictated and gave it all up and peeled shells from lobsters for dinner-party bisque rather than metaphors from her imagination for eloquent press releases.

She only said to Carmel, "I'm glad you have Paris," understanding Carmel would not speak any more of the man she'd married twenty years ago and who, when set beside Carmel, was like drab homespun stitched alongside cloth of gold. Nor would she speak of the three daughters raised by housekeepers and absence—because she didn't want Alix to judge her for any of it either. Which Alix never would. Life was a relentless sacrifice; giving up something you hoped was of lesser importance in exchange for something finer, but you never knew until the end if you'd chosen the right thing—or given up what you should have valued.

\* \* \*

She didn't leave the *maison* until almost midnight; the *Women's Wear Daily* article had started a flurry to rival a hoop skirt and she had more than a day's worth of cables and telephone calls to return. As she stepped onto the pavement, she turned her face up and stood for a moment, bathing in starshine and lamplight, not minding the chill of a late-January evening, wondering if the frost on the air might twirl a snowflake or two through the sky. She lingered a moment, reveling in how good it felt to not search every corner and opening, every intersection and shadow for a Nazi. She hadn't realized how much strain had coiled into her temples over the last few days and she let it all unwind, like hair unbound from a too-tight chignon.

Farther along the pavement, she found herself stopping in front of a tailor's shop, her eye caught by a handpainted silk jacquard necktie with a bright red swirl down the middle, three tropical leaves in teal, ivory and red sitting in a perfect posy in the middle. It was the kind of tie she would once have bought Bobby—she hadn't been allowed to write to him when she was in Switzerland so instead she'd sent him a tie occasionally. She liked to imagine him unwrapping them and laughing, both of them knowing he would never choose what she selected—his preferred palette was more subdued—but both of them also knowing that he would wear it the next time he saw her, whenever that might be.

She smiled at the memory, rather than searching for a way to lose it forever. Then she walked on, trying to stay with the promise of snowflakes and remembrances that were more sweet than bitter but, as always, her mind turned to La Voce, the man around whose neck she wished to knot all of Bobby's ties until he pleaded for her to stop.

Would she stop? The thought arrested her, made her look into one of the deepest pockets of her soul and consider: was she merciless enough to wrap La Voce's neck in silk in the first place? And which of those selves could she live with afterward? The one who stopped, or the one who didn't?

She hated most of all that there was someone out there who would make her ask those questions.

And now there was Becky to consider. Alix could take up a full-time job as a secret agent again and she still wouldn't have enough time to fit together all the pieces of a puzzle that was growing too big for one woman to even fit in her head, let alone solve. Still, there was a good chance Esmée Archambault might be able to help with Becky, which meant paying her a visit was moving to the top of Alix's list. It was too late to tail Becky tonight. Alix would have to tackle that on her weekends too.

The chill on the air turned, settling into an unpleasant frost. She picked up her pace and almost didn't see the man waiting on the steps of her *pension*, his elbow propped on bent knee while he smoked a cigarette.

"Anthony?" she said incredulously, then remembered: she'd been the one to throw down the gauntlet. Time to re-armor herself—if not with steel gloves, then with wit.

He stood and passed her a bottle of champagne. "Peace offering," he said. "To celebrate you getting your job back. And to thank you for sending me a ticket for a seat inside the salon rather than out on the doorstep."

"Your ticket," she said, unable to suppress a smile, "is not just inside the salon. It's in the front row, beside Becky. If her godfather owns the newspaper then there's nothing I can do to make her atone for her dirty tricks. But I can rub her nose in my success in uncovering those tricks. I thought you'd enjoy the joke—and I know Becky will hate it."

And provoking Becky might just tempt her out into the open where Alix could more easily discover her real motive.

She tucked the champagne bottle safely under her arm and climbed the stairs, Anthony following behind. She pushed open the door, found a water glass and a teacup, opened the champagne and poured as he gazed around at her one tiny room.

"Why do you stay here?" he asked, clearly a little appalled.

It was tempting to get mad. But she passed him the glass, sat down in the one comfortable sofa, curled her legs up beneath her, and said, "This is clearly something of a surprise to you, but as you once told me that the serious matters of the world interest you more than the frivolous, I'll explain. A woman gets paid, at best, half of what a man does.

When I took over the publicity reins at Goldman Sachs, my salary was forty percent of my predecessor's—a man, of course. Besides," she said, wishing to return the conversation to less personal ground, "it's a waste to spend money on lavish rooms when I'm almost never here. And impermanence is something I became used to long ago. Take a seat." She gestured to the lumpy chair that had survived the war like so much in Paris—only just, and with bruises showing.

He sat down reluctantly, sipped his drink, and they regarded one another over their mismatched cups.

"You were OSS too," she said.

"Too?"

"Yes, too."

They had both confessed. But behind that confession lay so much more. An organization that didn't exist: the Office of Strategic Services, a top-secret agency devoted to wartime espionage that recruited some women into its ranks to decode messages and man cable desks and re-create the topography of foreign countries in plaster— and where a very few were deployed to gather information about the Nazis.

"You weren't based in Italy," he said, finishing the champagne in his admittedly small cup and refreshing it and hers too, which had similarly vanished.

"Switzerland," she said, propping her head on her hand. "But you already know that."

"Okay," he admitted grudgingly. "But I know you didn't just come to Paris to..."

She braced for him to say something derisory like *to hype dresses*. But instead he said, "To run Dior's PR for him."

So she replied, "I came for Bobby," which was part-truth and part-lie.

"You loved him?"

"He was my fiancé."

"Love is rarely the reason people marry."

She was surprised into a short laugh. "True. But I did love Bobby." She almost stopped but if they were going to get anywhere tonight, it meant plunging on into the darkness and hoping not to stumble too badly.

So she gave Anthony some very small pieces of herself to see what he would do. "Bobby was a precious part of my life for years. I first met him when I was thirteen and living in LA with my friend Lillie and her parents—for a time," she added, as if that arrangement had been a temporary rather than a necessary thing. "He took me to my high school prom when I didn't have a date; he let me cry on his shoulder at that same prom when..."

She paused. Could she say this to the man in front of her now? Every single word was a risk because the big question was: would he use it against her in some way? Or would it help? God, she needed help, although she hated to admit it.

"When?" he prompted, sipping more champagne.

"When Lillie's mother told me the dress I was wearing—it was bright red—was shocking and not meant for a debutante." A part-truth again. What she held back was that the dress had been her mother's and she'd cried because she had no mother to tell her she looked beautiful on prom night.

She kept going, past the deepest of all hurts and onto a different hurt—or perhaps it was yet another guilty secret. "Bobby was wholly and perfectly nice and I loved him for that, even though I knew marriage would never have worked with him. He thought I had too much ambition." She shrugged. "Women's ambitions are meant to be limited to having children, planning dinner menus and looking decorative on their husbands' arms. It's very easy to look decorative with all this Dior," she indicated her dress, "so it doesn't really keep one's mind engaged."

"I think that, remove the Dior and you'd still be beautiful."

She smiled a little. "I'm not removing my Dior."

"It was worth a try." He grinned, and she couldn't help laughing.

The slight relaxing of the tension in the room, made her tell one absolute truth. Her voice was low when she spoke and Anthony had to lean forward to hear her.

"Everyone—Lillie's parents, maybe Lillie too—thinks that if Bobby had lived, I wouldn't have come to Paris and taken this job. But I would have. And Bobby would have come to visit me here after six months and he would have known it was over: that he wanted a wholly and perfectly nice girl who spent her days thinking of him, not her work. In him dying, I get to be the grieving fiancée people pity instead of the woman who broke off her engagement for Dior."

Anthony moved over to the sofa, sitting on the opposite end. "You can't beat yourself up over what might have happened. Hitler might have won the war, for Christ's sake. Bobby's dead. You didn't have to break off your engagement. Those are facts that hurt, sure, but they aren't life sentences."

He flinched, as if he expected she might throw her teacup at him after that frank summation of facts. Instead, she said, "You're right."

The ensuing silence was transparent, a length of chiffon she could see right through and into the next moment when he would speak. When he did, he asked the question she'd been expecting, the one that confirmed he did indeed know that someone needed to pay, and very dearly.

"Did you arrange the mission into the mountains that night?" he said.

"I did." She drained her teacup. "But why do you care about that?"

He looked over at her, eyes a strange silvery-black. "We've run out of champagne."

"Then we'll have to see what it's like to speak about the past without the prop of alcohol."

More silence. This split second would be the defining moment of their entire conversation. She'd offered him some information about herself and her past, and she'd answered his question about her role in Switzerland. In return, Anthony had given away very little about himself. Right now, he needed to tell her what he was chasing because there were only two reasons for him to be in her *pension*—to find the man she wanted to find, or to find her. The former meant that maybe he was on her side. The latter meant he most definitely was not.

He rubbed one hand over his face and, for just a moment, Anthony wasn't the impeccably suited, too-wealthy, rakish man he excelled at being. He was someone who hurt like she did and who tried to cover it with a champagne smile. Then he reached his hand around and pressed his fingertips into his shoulder, grimacing as if there was something there that ached.

In that action, she knew exactly who Anthony March was.

At the same moment, he asked, "Why do *you* care?"

A question, not an offering.

She almost laughed, but the malignant sound of her disappointment would give her away, and she needed a moment. Last night at the Ritz, he'd been studying her and planning this. That was why he'd agreed to help her with Becky. And in studying her, he'd decided that a handsome man with a bottle of champagne who alternated between a flirtatious joke, a studied flinch, and the giving of life advice was all it would take for her to break.

She put down her teacup. "You want a great deal from me, Anthony. And you thought planting my fiancé's knife in your bathroom and appearing on my doorstep with champagne would be enough to get it. It's not. Don't forget that if I was OSS too, then I must be at least as intelligent as you, although after this poorly executed attempt to reel me in, I'd have to say my intelligence is superior to yours."

This time, she was sure his flinch was real.

"I'm not interested in someone taking what I know and leaving the room and embarking on a solo crusade to hunt down a Nazi without me. I won't be interrogated and used and cast aside. *If* that's why you're here."

She stood and walked to the door as she spoke. "Or perhaps you had some other more brutal reckoning in mind, which you might as well get over and done with now. We've both been trained in how to kill people, but I'm smaller than you, and alone. You have the upper hand physically. So if you want revenge for Operation Lycaon, then do your best—or worst."

His muttered curse was filthy. He stood up too and their eyes clashed, hers accusing, and his…chagrined? Impossible.

"I'm not in the business of attacking women," he said, voice rough.

And she thought, for only as long as it took to inhale, that he might relent. That he might say that yes, he too wanted to find the man she was searching for and that, with two minds sharpened on the whetstone of wartime intelligence, they might somehow flush out the Nazi who had caused her to have a hand in the slaughter of nine men.

But he brushed past her and she knew he never would. He was the lone gun, the kind of man who would never trust a mere woman in a Dior gown.

She shut the door a little too loudly and stood motionless beside it. Then she let all of the memories pour in, didn't shut them out or run from them. She let them haunt her—no, she let them drive her.

A white silk dress. A room at the Bellevue Palace Hotel. A border strung with barbed wire. Smoke, and so much fire. Sitting on the floor of a mountain hut and waiting with a savage, pagan desperation for Matteo to come.

She felt it all, pain by pain, as another of the too-few stitches still holding her heart together snapped. And she knew that while the definition of justice might be to find La Voce and leave him to the authorities who would charge him and lock him away, that wasn't enough for Alix. Bobby and the others would continue to haunt an Alix St. Pierre who did only the lawful thing—because that was the cowardly thing.

Retribution for those who'd died meant standing in front of

La Voce and saying something that would skewer the deepest and most cherished part of his soul. The only way to unknot the ties of guilt and shame that bound her in a too-tight skin was to make him a ruin too.

Since April 1945 she'd been an Alix St. Pierre who was unforgiven, afraid, less than she'd ever wanted to be. Only by asking La Voce why he'd chosen to make her the gun with which he'd killed those men would she ever be able to be anything more.

She strode across the room, took out sheaves of paper and started to write it all down: what she already knew—that Becky was a loose thread she needed to sew into place; that Fortunée was too; that Anthony March had certainly been on the mountain with Matteo and Bobby that night.

She stuck the papers on the wall. She drew lines connecting the few pieces that had certain links. In the middle of it all she wrote: *What I know about La Voce—the sound of his voice.* And: *What La Voce knows about me—what I look like.*

She worked until morning because it didn't matter that she was alone in her quest; it didn't matter that she was afraid. This was *her* moment of reckoning.

She was no longer searching: she was hunting down.

And Anthony March could go to hell.

# PART TWO
## WASHINGTON, DC, AND BERN, SWITZERLAND, 1942–1943

*From this office were issued orders that sent OSS men and women to secret training camps where they learned to forge documents, dissemble, kill.*
—Elizabeth P. McIntosh, *Sisterhood of Spies: The Women of the OSS*

# SEVEN

Y ou were at school in Switzerland?" the man with no name asks Alix before he clips the end off a cigar, puts it in his mouth for the raw draw then lights a match to toast the foot, singeing the edges evenly and expertly. He rotates the cigar through the routine of the preliminary puff then turns the end to face him, the corner of his mouth twitching upward at the pleasure of no darkened patches: a ceremony well executed.

A man who takes so much time and trouble over the lighting of a cigar is a rich man of influence, Alix has learned. Why she's been asked to travel from Manhattan to DC, to take a cab to the end of Constitution Avenue and enter the building behind the flagpole where armed guards lurk at each corridor intersection is a mystery, but she suspects it isn't to teach her the art of cigar smoking.

He waits.

She waits.

At last he says, "You didn't answer my question."

"You didn't ask me a question. You told me I was at school in Switzerland."

A spark of something like interest flashes in his eyes and is then hidden by the cloud of smoke he lets drift from his mouth. He's the kind of smoker who sips cigars. And he's the kind of man who, like Lillie's father, thinks that if you offer a woman a silent room, she'll rush to decorate it with words. Once upon a time, Alix would have.

Indeed, the first time Mr. van der Meer called her into his office at his home in Beverly Hills, she'd convicted herself in that courtroom of silence.

Mr. van der Meer had simply said, "You were enjoying yourself at the party," and Alix had assumed his subsequent wordlessness meant he knew she'd slipped into a closet with a boy—looking for any kind of human touch to make up for the fact that her parents would never hug her again, but finding only sadness. The second time, she was missing her mother so much she couldn't open her mouth to speak and was thus dismissed without having disclosed anything.

"All right," the man says now. "You attended Le Manoir in Switzerland for your final year of schooling with your friend Lillie Marie van der Meer. You were the only scholarship student."

Alix nods.

He writes something on a piece of paper and, despite herself, Alix leans forward, trying to see what it says. She corrects her posture almost immediately; she's sat in so many job interviews with company bosses that she knows it's best to be cool. Interest shown and money paid in salary are inversely related.

"You'd like to know what I wrote down," the man says, resting the cigar in the ashtray.

Alix would kill for a cigarette. "I'd like a clue about why I'm here," she replies. This entire scenario is ridiculous. Maybe he's Mafia and he wants to use her PR skills to win the public's approval for drug running. That would explain the cloak-and-dagger setting, and the cigars. A smile tugs at her mouth.

"That amuses you," is his deadpan response.

"It does." She agrees to move things on. Otherwise they'll still be here at midnight.

But hurrying isn't his style. "You must have worked hard to win that scholarship."

"When you're poor and parentless, you have to work hard." A

thousand times harder than everyone else, she doesn't add because this man knows nothing of what it's like to be someone's ward, to know you're costing them money, to be so grateful you have a home—but to also want to escape from the oppression of charity the minute you can.

"How did you acquire the French, German, and Italian languages?" is his next question. "They don't teach languages explicitly at Le Manoir."

*Boy, he's done his homework.*

"If one wants to know what the girls are whispering about in their beds after lights out, then one learns a language very quickly," she replies, wondering if she should just curse at him in French, Italian, and German to demonstrate her proficiency, but he's ready with another question.

"The school moved from Lake Geneva to Gstaad, near Bern, each winter. So you know Bern well?" he asks now.

"Yes."

He picks up his cigar, sips smoke again. "You speak less than I would have thought for a person who peddles persuasion for a living."

"Listening and observing are critical skills when persuading. Which I think you know." She succumbs at last, opening her purse and extracting a cigarette, inhaling smoke like it's the best thing she's tasted all year.

"What have you observed?" He folds his arms.

If she hadn't been told the interview was about something critical to the war and virtually ordered to attend by her current boss at the War Department—where she organizes domestic propaganda—she would leave.

She exhales a little too forcefully. "That you'd like to intimidate me. That you have a lot of money and a great deal of experience with cigars. That how I've lived my life is somehow important. And that you're intrigued enough to have let this interview go on for longer than you'd imagined."

He almost smiles but halts the action with another question. "You moved to Paris after Le Manoir. The van der Meers paid for your relocation?"

Pride clenches her hand, squashing the cigarette enough that she's forced to stub it out in the ashtray. "I paid," she says crisply.

"How?" He feigns surprise but he must know the answer. All he wants to hear is how she'll describe it.

"I worked as a waitress at a hotel near the school. Tourists tip well."

"You must have been a good waitress."

She gives him the raw, unadorned truth. "I had to be. I couldn't get to Paris without money."

There's a mortifying quiver on the last word as that horrible pressure she'd felt from the time she was an orphaned and penniless thirteen-year-old until she was finally a free and salaried eighteen-year-old squeezes her throat. The desperation not to be a burden on the van der Meers, not to have them throw her out to become one of those haunted girls who strolled the Strip in Los Angeles, the fear of knowing that permission to be friends with the van der Meers' daughter was one transgression away from being revoked.

He senses weakness and moves in for the kill. "How did you meet Bobby Du Pont, your fiancé of…what?" He consults his notes. "Three months?"

"The Du Ponts are friends of the van der Meers," she says a little too coolly.

She pictures Lillie and Bobby at the lawn party at the home of some Hollywood mogul almost ten years before, where they chatted over Shirley Temples in the area designated for children while the adults preened by the swimming pool.

"This is my sister, Alix," Lillie had announced to Bobby. Lillie had always believed that if she said something aloud enough times, it would come true. And Mr. van der Meer liked to grant wishes—they were easier to give than affection. So after Alix's French immigrant parents, who'd worked as costumiers in Hollywood, had both died tragically and romantically—Alix had convinced herself at age thirteen—in a scenery collapse on set, Alix had been semi-adopted by Lillie's parents. Lillie had begged and cajoled, and she'd also reminded her father that Alix's parents had been working for him when they died, thus the whole situation was partly his fault.

"You've leapfrogged your origins in a spectacular fashion. You could almost make a movie out of it." He leans back in his chair and scrolls his hand through the air as he sums up what he thinks has been her life. "Girl grows up in two-room apartment on the wrong side of town, befriends the daughter of a Hollywood mogul, and spends the rest of her life in a Beverly Hills mansion."

"Hardly the rest of my life," she says, knowing he's trying to anger her with the implication that she manipulated her way into a life she didn't earn. It's true, in a way. If she and Lillie hadn't both broken their arms at their separate schools when they were ten, they would never have both been at the van der Meers' Hollywood studio, Alix hiding in piles of organza while her parents made costumes, Lillie having run away from her father's secretary to explore. They'd bonded over having plaster casts on the same arm, and the bond had cemented into something unbreakable by the time Alix had shown Lillie her secret castle of tulle and chiffon. "I haven't lived with the van der Meers since I went to finishing school."

He grants her this concession to his rose-colored motion picture with the words, "You know how to live in all worlds though. The poor and the moneyed. Although Bobby's one of a lesser branch of the Du Ponts, really. Lesser in terms of money, I mean."

"Only someone with a hell of a lot of money would consider Bobby's wealth to be lesser."

"So you're marrying him for his money?"

"I've earned my own money since I went to Le Manoir. I'm marrying Bobby because he asked me to."

*Oh God.* That is a much crueler explanation than what she'd meant. He lets her wallow in the aftermath for a very long minute.

But how does any girl say no to a man who's down on one knee at a party organized by Lillie, supposedly for Alix's birthday, but really to celebrate an engagement everyone presumes will happen? How does anyone say no when newly engaged Lillie is grinning at her, arm around her fiancé Peter's waist, and calling out—before Alix has a chance to say anything—"Yes! Of course she says yes!"

How do you refuse a man who's been her sweetheart since she returned from Paris in late 1939 to find he'd moved to Manhattan, where she'd also based herself? The man who wooed her with dinners where they'd chatted about those long-ago Hollywood parties populated by rich Hollywood kids, safe in their cocoon of privilege. She'd been the only one who couldn't wait to emerge from the chrysalis. But now she's trapped herself in it because—how do you refuse a friend when he asks you something with tears in his eyes? A friend who thought he was being shipped out to the high seas of Europe to attack U-boats—or else to be attacked by them.

The only thing to do had been to say yes and hold him until he could blink away the shine in his eyes and smile too.

But Alix will not say any of that to the man in front of her now.

Luckily he stands. "If you could report back here tomorrow."

"What if I want to stay in Manhattan?" she asks incredulously.

"By tomorrow, the War Department will have given your job to someone else."

\* \* \*

The women call it the Oh So Secret. The men call it the Oh So Social because so many of the Office of Strategic Services' recruits are old money, from an exclusive network that Lillie's mother pretends has accepted her new-money Hollywood family but knows never will until Lillie marries into it via Peter Brooks. Alix calls it the Oh So Spontaneous: everything is made up as they go along and it seems that if you speak French, own a few tuxedos and treat hundred-dollar bills like cigarettes, you can get yourself a job in this new and so-called intelligence agency.

For six weeks she goes to Maryland's Congressional Country Club and is taught to shoot a gun, which is easy; to steam letters open—a skill Lillie's mother would love to learn; to send coded messages; to tail people on foot and in a car—she has to learn to drive for this one; to recognize the intonations and patterns of voices; to navigate on foot by the stars.

And to drink.

On the first night, when she sees the quantity of liquor that's been provided for a small number of OSS recruits, she knows it's a test so she doesn't accept any offers of private rendezvous with young men in various closets. Nor does she say anything much about herself. She doesn't have to—these moneyed men and women are so full of their own important words that it doesn't take more than a drink or two before they all come spilling out, messily and hard to clean up later.

The following evening, some of the faces from the night before are gone, some new ones appear, but the quantity of liquor stays the same. Alix learns to run each morning uphill and through an obstacle course with a pounding head and a nauseous stomach, the only sign of her hangover a paleness to her cheeks.

Then two months of cooling her heels on the cable desk at Q building where she had her initial interview. It's on the cable desk, where messages come in from all over Europe and Africa, that she begins to understand the whole point of OSS: to learn whatever can be learned about the Axis powers. The Americans know little to nothing, not even the precise physical location of geographical features like lakes and mountain ranges in the various Axis countries. They don't know what exactly the German secret police do, what uniforms they wear, who in the Vichy French government can be trusted, how many troops the Germans actually have and in which countries they're located. Their ignorance is staggering.

At this rate, the Allies will never win the war.

She's thinking this as she walks back to the apartment she's been housed in and almost doesn't see the beautiful blonde with red eyes and tear-stained cheeks waiting on the top step.

"Lillie!" Alix exclaims, embracing her friend. "What are you doing here?"

Lillie grips her so tightly that Alix knows it's bad news. "Daddy lost it all," she says in a low and bitter voice.

Dread curls in Alix's stomach. Lillie's last letter mentioned financial difficulties but Alix thought the van der Meers had so much money that "financial difficulties" meant taking only two vacations abroad next year instead of four. She steps back and examines Lillie: immaculate Lillie, pampered Lillie, loyal Lillie—but now a very sad Lillie, a version Alix has never seen.

"Let's get dinner," she says and they walk over to the Trianon, where the food is true-French, rather than a redacted version absent of duck fat and Toulouse sausage.

Once seated and with drinks in hand, Lillie explains, a sob trapped in each word. "The house has been repossessed and the studio's been bought out by the Warners. That gave us enough money to get to Manhattan—Mother won't stay in Hollywood where everyone knows what she's lost—and rent an apartment on Park Avenue."

*So you're not absolutely destitute*, Alix thinks wryly. "Are you all right?" she asks.

Lillie dissolves into weeping.

The man at the next table sends over a drink. Lillie accepts it with a watery smile and fresh tears.

Alix holds her friend while she cries. Even before this, she would never have wanted to be Lillie. Lillie's mother has pursued Peter Brooks relentlessly, never allowing Lillie to wonder if she was in love, but telling her any girl would love a man like Peter, who's from the kind of old establishment American blood that either owns or runs half the country. Lillie's life has been placed before her like a path leading to one destination—to be just like her mother, but richer.

Alix pulls a handkerchief out of Lillie's purse and passes it to her. "You need a job. Go see Bobby tomorrow. Money is your immediate concern. But right now you need to go back home to your mom."

Lillie shakes her head. "She won't even take time out from planning who we should meet in Manhattan to cry. She keeps telling me that my eyes are so red I'll frighten Peter away."

"That's how she loves you. And when you're sad, you need someone with you. She needs you."

"But I need *you*."

"You need someone to pet you," Alix says with a smile, "just like that day we went picnicking in the Hollywood Hills and you got sunstroke. Remember how Bobby drove us home at walking pace so you wouldn't be sick again and I told you bad jokes the whole way to cheer you up? Bobby and I will always pet you, but sometimes you need to pet someone else in return."

Lillie, who's always admitted her shortcomings once they've been pointed out, makes a face and sighs. Then she passes the drink the man had sent over to Alix. "You never need petting," she says and her eyes well up again. "I can't lose you too. I know you have an important job and you don't really need me but..." She scrubs her face with the handkerchief and in her next words, Alix can hear the sound of love—an exquisite hoarseness, because love is sometimes too much for prosaic human words. "You'll always be my sister."

"Lillie," Alix says, and now she's crying as well. Then she laughs at the two of them in a nice restaurant with free drinks and happy-sad tears. "You petted me when I needed it most," she says, her voice raspy too. "In September 1933, you sat down on my bed and brushed my hair and it was the only thing that made me get up and go to school."

Lillie smiles a little. "I did," she says. "And I'm glad I did."

"Me too," Alix says and they hug, perhaps too hard on Alix's side because she isn't sure when she'll see her best friend again. The one person in the world who, in the days after Alix's parents had died, had sensed that the gentle stroke of a brush through hair, the soothing, calming quality of such a mundane thing, would let the small steps of daily life back into Alix's future, which had seemed back then not to exist at all.

So Alix sends Lillie back to Manhattan and her mother. Maybe Alix hadn't liked Mrs. van der Meer's methods—the same day Lillie got sunstroke, Lillie's mother told Bobby he had her permission to date sixteen-year-old Alix. She knows now that it was out of fear: fear of this other young woman suddenly living in her house and whose future it had fallen to Mrs. van der Meer to fix—a young woman competing with Lillie for husbands. Lillie's mother had thought Bobby was perfect: rich enough for Alix but a far cry from what she wanted for Lillie. And with the benefit of distance, Alix can be grateful for that maneuvering because Mrs. van der Meer could have put Alix in a maid's uniform and forbidden her to date anyone at all. In the end, she'd taught Alix a lot about what was really best. To always be able to take care of herself. To follow instinct and adventure. To never fall into the trap of thinking marriage was love and it conquered all: it only ever conquered the women, not the men.

\* \* \*

The next day, Alix is up at dawn writing a letter to Bobby, whose call up for duty three months before had not landed him on the high seas chasing U-boats, but doing some essential war work in New York. She tries not to believe the Du Pont name has kept him out of a military training camp and barracks living. She hasn't seen him since she arrived in Washington, isn't allowed to tell him what she's doing, realizes she's only written one letter—and that he hasn't replied.

She wonders if war and absence will let them drift gently apart and return to being friends. She loves Bobby the same way she loves Lillie—a twenty-four carat gold kind of love that's solid and genuine and ritualistic. She and Bobby can't plan a picnic without double-checking that everyone has a hat to ward off sunstroke; they sometimes drink Shirley Temples when they go out to dinner for the sake of nostalgia. So many people live with a hell of a lot less love than that, so maybe they could make a marriage work out just fine. But just fine is so much less than she wants. And it's less than she wants for Bobby, too.

*Dear Bobby*, she writes.
*From Washington, DC*

*This will arrive after Lillie but in case she isn't persuasive enough, let me just say, please—please help her find a job. I know you think the idea of women working is barely tolerable but you also know that America needs women to work now. And Lillie needs a job. I don't trust Peter. The wedding isn't until next year and I worry that three bankrupt van der Meers might cool his ardor.*

*Thank you, Bobby. I hope you're well. And I hope the tie makes you smile.*

*Love and* bisous,
*Alix*

She encloses a silk tie the same color as her prom dress, then goes to work.

When she arrives at Q building, a man is waiting for her, telling her she isn't required on the cable desk. He takes her to the office where she had her first interview. Mr. Cigar is waiting. He prepares his cigar and cuts to the chase.

"You've seen, over the past three months, that while OSS is called an intelligence organization, intelligence is something we lack," he says a little grimly. "We need to know everything about every Axis-occupied country in Europe, from the location of aircraft factories and railway infrastructure, to where there are any pockets of resistance fighters willing to work with the Allies, to order-of-battle intelligence, to who in Germany might be swayed to work against the Führer. Sweden and Switzerland, both being neutral and well patronized by Germans, Italians, Bulgarians, Hungarians—everyone—are the ideal places to set up stations to run agents who'll collect intelligence. That intelligence will be fed back to Washington and then dispatched to military command. I want you in Switzerland gathering information from whoever you can. You speak all the languages, you know Bern, you're whip smart. You won't be able to tell anyone what you're doing and will need to inform your fiancé and the van der Meers that you'll be out of the country on confidential business and that letters will be few and far between. You may find your engagement doesn't survive such cavalier treatment but perhaps that's a stroke of luck. You're to go with Allen Dulles, ostensibly as his assistant. His cover is that he's working as a special attaché at the American Legation in Bern."

"Ostensibly as his assistant? Or actually his assistant?" is all she asks while her mind works furiously to process everything he's said. "And are you asking me if I want to go to Switzerland or telling me?"

"Do you think Roosevelt had the luxury of choosing whether to declare war against Japan and Germany?" An exhalation of cigar smoke underscores his impatience at her questions, the answers to which are apparently obvious.

The door opens and another man enters. His blue-eyed stare from behind rimless glasses is hostile and he's chewing aggressively on his pipe.

"This is Allen Dulles," her friend with the cigar says. "He'll be heading up OSS's Swiss operations. Mr. Dulles does not want you to go with him."

Alix can't help it; she laughs. She has a feeling Mr. Cigar actually likes her and is looking forward to seeing what will happen next.

"Dulles is Agent 110. Code name Mr. Burns," Mr. Cigar continues. "I thought you'd like to choose your own code name."

The urge to irritate Dulles is one she can't suppress. "Bisous," she says. "A little French kiss in Switzerland."

"Jesus Christ," is Dulles's response.

# EIGHT

Bern is two things: beautiful and flawed, like a Hollywood goddess who always has one drink too many. The twelfth-century old town's narrow cobblestone streets wind past charming medieval sandstone buildings. But the people inside those buildings and on those streets are, Alix discovers, the run in Bern's silk stockings.

There are spies like her and Dulles—some loyal to their country, others acting as double or triple agents, able to be trusted with nothing. There are also the camp followers—those with information to sell, often of dubious quality, but she's been taught to peer beneath every muddied hem because you never knew when you might find an antique lace trim. There are many, many women offering up their bodies to gain favors, protection, money, or some other patronage.

Even in neutral Bern, war means blackouts and food-rationing but ski holidays are still de rigueur, as is fine dining and drinking. Bern has the nonchalant ease of a place around which war is happening, a place where it's safe to mock Nazis without being shot, and hardly anyone appears to realize that to do the same thing just one hundred kilometers away would mean death.

These are the observations Alix makes in her first week in Bern.

At the end of that time, Dulles establishes himself at 23 Herrengasse. Arched windows, planter boxes, and a fountain out front give no indication that ungentlemanly business happens within. From the back, the same impression of gentility is preserved; the turquoise ribbon of the Aare River winds past and the Jungfrau, the Eiger, and the Mönch rise majestically beyond in a rampart of white.

In Dulles's office, Alix sets up the radio telephone, the scrambler telephone, and the telegraph beside a small table Dulles has filled with every alcoholic beverage he could get his hands on. Next to that is a mantelpiece topped with a photograph of his wife, Clover, and a roaring fire beneath. He intends the warmth, the red drapes, and the liquor to do his work for him. And perhaps it will, Alix thinks as she sends her first message to Victor, otherwise known as HQ in Washington.

FROM BURNS AND BISOUS TO VICTOR. ARRIVED. 23 HERRENGASSE.

Dulles, having spent the day at the tailor effecting a makeover from Wall Street lawyer to casual Swiss diplomat, returns in flannel slacks and blazer, a fedora slung low on his head as if trying to be jaunty or incognito—neither of which he achieves. "Off you go, kid," he says to her. "Find me something useful or find your way back home."

It's a useless threat. With the borders completely sealed now that the Allies have invaded North Africa, there's no way she can get back to America even if she proves to be as inept as the Scarlet Pimpernel's nemesis.

Still, a long-ingrained instinct for proving herself pushes to the fore. "Do you think OSS would have sent me here if I were completely incompetent?"

"I can't answer for OSS," he says, "but I will answer for myself in a few days' time. Being a schoolgirl in Switzerland isn't quite the same as gathering intelligence the entire Western world is depending on."

There's nothing she can say to that. It's true, even if exaggerated.

She leaves the apartment and wanders through the arches of the endless Lauben, not seeing the antique shops, the bookstores, and bakeries she used to linger over as a schoolgirl. She descends into the vaulted stone cellars that hide theaters and bars, orders a drink and ponders how exactly a former Swiss schoolgirl will find out anything that might change the course of a war that has recolored most of Europe in Nazi brown.

Dulles will be sure to share cigars with every important man in Bern—the industrialists, politicians, exiles, foreign nationals. Which leaves Alix with the other half of the population: women—the unimportant, like Alix herself. And if there's one thing she's learned from life so far it's that men are at their most unguarded when eating and drinking, and, she's heard—she has almost no experience in the area herself—when they're in bed. That means talking to chambermaids at hotels. Waitresses at ski lodges. Dancers at nightclubs. And prostitutes, she supposes. While Alix can't claim any expertise in the other occupations, she's been a waitress before. So she'll start at the Bellevue Palace Hotel.

* * *

At the end of the horseshoe of river that cups the Altstadt, the Bellevue Palace Hotel sits like a maiden aunt, dated but imposing, and with perfect posture. Alix heads directly for the restaurant overlooking the river, arriving in the dead time between lunch service and dinner when waitresses are sitting down with a cup of coffee, dreaming of not waiting on anyone. She sits at a table, spreads out one or two old copies of *Harper's Bazaar* and some typed papers and pretends she's making alterations on the manuscript before her.

She shakes her head at the first waitress who approaches; it's no one she knows. Surely Chiara Romano is still here? No sooner has she had the thought than a dark-haired young woman with olive skin and a mischievous set to her countenance emerges from the kitchen and Alix grins.

The woman starts, opens her arms, and exclaims, "Bella! *Ammazza!*"

so loudly that the few people seated in the restaurant all look up to see her fling herself on Alix in a tempest of laughter and tears.

Alix emerges from the flurry, smiling. *"Ti sono mancato,* Chiara?"

Chiara subsides into a chair and wipes her eyes. *"Nobody,"* the emphasis on the word is dramatic, "has been as much fun to work with since you left. Especially now." With those words, the drama and ebullience are gone and a more subdued woman takes the place of the Chiara Alix had once worked alongside.

"How's your family?" Alix asks. "Are they still in Italy?"

"They are. They pray each night for Mussolini to die but so far neither he nor Our Lady Madonna is listening. But tell me why you're back in Bern? I thought the Americans were staying as far away from Europe as possible."

Alix ignores the dig at her country's late entry into the war and gestures to the magazines in front of her, knowing that until she's reacquainted herself with her old friend, she needs a cover story. "I'm working at the American Legation. And—do you remember I worked for *Harper's Bazaar* in Paris a while back?"

Chiara nods; they used to exchange letters, back when mail was delivered rather than drowned at the bottom of the sea by a U-boat.

"I told Carmel Snow I'd write a few pieces for her on what women are wearing in Europe so I need to find parties and glamour."

Chiara's eyes romp the way they had six years ago when she and Alix put away their aprons at the end of the night, slid into dresses and slipped into whatever party happened to be kicking up its heels at the hotel, despite the fact that Alix was seventeen and the school would have thrown her out had they ever discovered her escapades.

Chiara turns the pages of the magazine, sighing over impossibly beautiful dresses worn by models arranged with carefree glamour beneath a chandelier in a sparkling room. Then she opens Alix's purse and extracts a cigarette as if they were both still seventeen and shared everything. "There's a very big party here on Saturday. For all the fancy people—some are coming from Zurich and Paris. Esmée will be there."

"Esmée? As in your sworn enemy Esmée Archambault?" Alix says incredulously.

Chiara grins. "We're friends now."

"That's like . . . I don't know," Alix searches the bowels of her mind for a suitable comparison and comes up with, "Hitler and Churchill exchanging love notes."

Chiara laughs hysterically and it's just like one of those hilarious nights at the end of a party when they'd walked back to the school—where Chiara worked as a maid during the day—laughing over a man who'd invited her to Saint Moritz to ski. Chiara had refused, devoted to a life free of men, because, "In Italy, I can't vote like you can in America," she'd once told Alix on a gloomier night. "To go to university, I have to pay double what it costs for a man. I'm supposed to marry and have lots of babies for the Fascist Patria. They're scared of women in Italy," she'd added darkly, exhaling cigarette smoke into the night.

"Chiara!" A voice calls from the kitchen now. "Break's over."

Alix squeezes her hand. "It's good to see you."

"You too. I'll get you tickets to the party—you'll want one for your boss, too, I know." Chiara grins, then hurries away.

Dulles had given her a few days but, it turns out, Alix only needed one.

\* \* \*

When she re-enters Dulles's office it's with a smile and a hell of a lot of self-control, which helps her not to blurt out, *I told you so.* Instead, she says, "We're going to the Swiss consul's party at the Bellevue Palace Hotel on Saturday night."

He almost double-takes but he's as good at self-control as she is. "I'd have been able to get to that party myself."

"Maybe," she says, "but not without making it look like you *want* to go. This way, people know straight away you have the influence and connections to get into the party of the week after only being in town for a few days. It makes you look good, Dulles. Accept it with a smile and don't be quarrelsome. And you can forget about sending me back to Manhattan; I'm not going anywhere."

\* \* \*

The next day, she eavesdrops on conversations at the Bellevue Palace Hotel while pretending to write an article for *Harper's Bazaar*. It isn't long before she overhears that Allen Dulles is an American spy. She jolts. Only half an hour later, the same words are spoken by two Italians at the table beside hers. After they've gone, Alix snatches up their newspaper and sees an article announcing that Allen Dulles has arrived in Switzerland as Roosevelt's "special envoy." Even an idiot can interpret that subtext.

She's about to hurry back to Herrengasse but Chiara approaches and says, "I have a ten-minute break."

Alix is marched out of the hotel and into a side street. "You know the Swiss government has ears everywhere," Chiara says hurriedly. "Every conversation in that hotel is listened to. And I don't want the Swiss government to know that I asked you if you're really here as a secretary or if you're a 'special envoy' too."

Alix extracts two cigarettes, hands one to Chiara and strikes a match. "You know me," Alix says cheerily, as if she's just taking a walk with a friend and chatting about frivolities. "I've always been special."

"Then you need to know this." Chiara's eyes are intent beneath her light-as-air-smile. "There'll be an Abwehr agent at the party. Hans Gisevius. His job as the Vice-Consul of the German mission in Zurich is just a cover."

An Abwehr agent. The Abwehr is the Wehrmacht's military

intelligence service. Just as it's illegal for Allen Dulles and Alix St. Pierre to be practicing spycraft in Bern, it's illegal for the Nazis to have an agent working in neutral Switzerland.

"How can you know?" Alix whispers.

"The things I hear as a waitress are worth pockets full of francs."

Which means Alix was right to have begun with Chiara, who will now be her first informant. "I can pay you," she says.

Chiara's response is vehement. "Money isn't enough. The Blackshirts arrested my father twelve months ago. We don't know if he's dead or alive. We need the Allies to do something. I need you to *do* something."

"I will," Alix promises, rashly, hopefully, and most likely foolishly.

As she walks through the Kornhausplatz to Herengasse, she sees none of Bern's beauty, only the Kindlifresserbrunnen, the Child Eater Fountain. The ogre sits contentedly on a pedestal high above his domain of water, stuffing a child into his mouth, more children cradled in his arms and wriggling in his sack, ready to be main course and dessert, like Hitler and Mussolini devouring countries and their citizens and their freedom.

Alix had come to Switzerland because of an unquenchable need for adventure—and also because she was virtually ordered to. But as she stares at the ogre's white teeth clasped around an infant's head, she realizes she ought to have come for Chiara and for Chiara's father and for all the other people she doesn't know but who face dangers she's never dreamed of. What will an Abwehr agent do to Chiara if he finds out she knows his true vocation? How many Abwehr agents are on the streets of Bern right now? And how many more fathers will go missing in the night before all of this is over?

\* \* \*

Mary Bancroft, dark-haired, red-lipsticked, and carrying herself as if she believes everyone is looking at her, is nothing but noticeable and, at the party at the Bellevue, Alix sees Dulles do a hell of a lot of noticing. Alix has already heard of Mary—daughter of the owner of the *Wall Street Journal*—and it isn't long before Mary and Allen are huddled together, her hand touching his arm, him angling his body toward hers. Mary's husband, Jean, on the other side of the room, doesn't notice, or doesn't care.

Alix wishes she was surprised. Who Dulles chooses to sleep with while his wife waits in Manhattan isn't a concern of hers, but it's a reminder never to be the wife of a wealthy man, feigning ignorance at a husband's indiscretions, and never to be like Mary, so conspicuously unhappy in matrimony that her reputation precedes her into rooms like a flag-bearer.

Suddenly, Alix wishes she could write to Bobby. But how can she tell him she's already foreseeing a future when he'll cheat on her? He'll deny it, but his father is just like Dulles, his older brother too. It's in the genes.

But it's not the time to be thinking of Bobby. So she circulates and discovers that gathering information from the gentlemen in the room isn't difficult as long as she's happy not to defend her cleavage from roving eyes or her buttocks from presumptuous hands. Twenty minutes in uncomfortable proximity to one man has her learning that the Hungarians are trying to withdraw their troops from Russia, and a hand on her ass leads to the discovery that the Rumanians are rioting. Washington will want to know all of it, just as Alix wants to know now if the reason Mr. Cigar chose her was for her ability to cut a fine figure in a dress, rather than her ability with languages.

On the other side of the room, she sees a man who is exceptionally tall and handsome in that cool, Germanic way that matches Chiara's description of the Abwehr agent. Dulles approaches him and Alix is crossing the room to join them when Dulles gives her a subtle but firm shake of the head and beckons Mary over.

Dulles has teamed up with Mary, not Alix, to charm the Abwehr agent. Which means that, somehow, Alix needs to find a lead even bigger than a German military intelligence officer if she wants to be more than Dulles's secretary.

She swears and whirls around to deflect another attack from a hand on her back but finds Esmée Archambault, fellow schoolgirl—and never a friend—from Le Manoir.

"Alix St. Pierre," Esmée says, grinning. "If we chat here, everyone will stare because we're the most attractive women in the room. I suggest we withdraw somewhere quieter."

Despite the fact she's hardly spoken to Esmée in her life and definitely recalls playing a practical joke or two on the undisputed queen of Le Manoir, Alix hears herself say, "The service elevator," as her curiosity overpowers her. "Get Chiara to show you where it is."

Esmée nods and Alix exits the bar, slipping through the corridors of the hotel. The service elevator arrives only a moment after Esmée and the women step inside and Alix presses the emergency stop button.

"So," Alix says, smiling a little, "the queen finds herself mingling with the peasants."

Esmée laughs. "I might have been the queen, but you were definitely the empress of mystery. Too busy with Lillie van der Meer to talk to anyone else and when you weren't with Lillie, you were smoking in the stables with the grooms or sneaking into your room after curfew. I could never tell whether you were a snob or a libertine."

It's Alix's turn to laugh uproariously. "I guarantee I was neither."

"And I was no queen," Esmée replies, smiling too. "My friend Anthony says that when I was born, I probably told the midwife exactly how I wished to be birthed—which is ridiculous because he's just as bossy as I am. It's just that some personalities are larger than the bodies they've been given to contain them. Mine is constantly popping the buttons and splitting the seams."

This explanation doesn't lessen Alix's laughter, not least because it's entirely accurate. But she can't hold the elevator up all night. "Chiara tells me I can trust you," she says, swallowing her giggles. "I need information."

"It turns out you and I have a mutual friend—Frank at the Ritz. The hotel is occupied by Germans who do a lot of talking in the bar. Frank hears it all." Esmée is speaking quickly and Alix is impressed that this woman she'd disregarded at school as rich and vacuous is probably more experienced at these kinds of meetings than Alix, and must be involved with the Resistance in France in some way.

"I don't know how much longer I'll be able to keep coming into Switzerland," Esmée continues. "My family has business interests here and so far I've been able to get an *Ausweis*—a travel permit— from the Germans. But we might need to resort to letters if things go awry. Which means we need to be able to write things down in such a way that only we can understand them."

"Reminiscences of school," Alix jumps in. "If we visualize the school like it's a map, that would make the dining room into France, the stables into England, the front gardens into Italy—"

"That'll work. We'll assign the names of the girls to some of the people I might write to you about."

"And it's always every fourth sentence or fourth word in a list that's the important one," Alix finishes, remembering how she was taught to hide information amongst trivialities.

It's only as she releases the emergency stop button that Alix looks properly at Esmée and sees a subtle tiredness in her eyes, a thinning of her face into sharper angles than the soft and pretty seventeen-year-old heiress used to possess. "Are you careful? Doing this must be—"

"Believe me, someone who lives next door to an Oberführer knows this is dangerous," Esmée says in the regal manner Alix remembers from school. "But I would prefer not to live next door to an Oberführer. So…"

The elevator doors open and Esmée departs.

# NINE

Dulles is ebullient the next day when he tells Alix, "Mary's joining us."

Alix can't stop her mouth from falling open. "The most well-known gossip in Switzerland?"

"Exactly," he says, smiling the way men do when they've just had a night that's kept them up in a satisfactory manner. "She's going to charm Hans Gisevius into telling her whether he's a double agent or not. He says he wants Hitler's downfall. That makes him valuable—if he isn't lying."

The plum job has well and truly been whisked away from Alix before she's even taken a bite. And Dulles has proven himself the kind of man who's happy to have women do some of the work—but only if they sleep with him too.

That night, while she waits for Esmée to write to her, she flirts so determinedly with everyone at the Bellevue Palace Hotel bar that she's at risk of having to deliver more of herself to the men around her than she wants to. But Chiara's father is in prison and Esmée lives next door to an Oberführer so, really, Alix's problems are trivial.

Someone takes the seat beside her and Alix braces for another round of coquetry. But it's Mary.

"You're keeping busy," Mary says derisively, eyeing the Italian Alix has had to use all her ingenuity to send away without the cocktail he thought he deserved.

"Doesn't Dulles want us to be busy?" Alix doesn't quite manage to wrap the same mocking lilt around her vowels and sounds chagrined instead.

Mary nods. "I just want to make sure you understand. It's easier all round if you know upfront that you're being used rather than discovering it later."

Anger flares. It's too hot in the bar. The fire is blazing and the odor of melting raclette, caviar, and sausage render the air pungent, salty, and male. The blackout means the world outside the bar doesn't exist and Alix misses the vista of snow softened by lamplight.

Mary summons the bartender over and orders a drink. "Let's be honest. You see me as a rich woman who Dulles wants for his own reasons and who you think is going to be a hindrance? Is that about right?"

Alix lets out a surprised laugh. She's always considered herself forthright but Mary is brutal. "Yes," she says, finding it a relief to be truthful after all the dissimulation she's been practicing over the last couple of hours. "Although," she adds, her own forthrightness making her judge herself by the same standards she's applying to Mary, "I'm doing nothing especially useful besides sending cables for Dulles."

Mary's, "Ah," in response is either patronizing or amused. "Washington would get nothing if Dulles didn't have you to send his cables for him," she says. "So you are being useful. It's just that your usefulness isn't acknowledged by anyone. That's what's really galling you."

Mary is baiting her, looking to discover if Alix will choose to be offended or if she'll thicken her skin and accept the facts. Alix realizes she could probably learn something from Mary about the intelligence business—a woman who's been conducting clandestine affairs for years must know a thing or two about both men and discretion.

So she chooses to unlock some truth from its bolts. "What galls me," Alix says, downing her drink, "is that if Dulles were a woman, nobody would come into his office and tell him anything. It'd be his ass being groped, not mine."

"You know that," Mary says obliquely as she taps ash off her cigarette, "power is the opposite to love."

"Power is the opposite to love," Alix repeats, trying to understand what Mary means. Is Alix's love for Bobby some kind of strange oppositional force to her ever having control over anything? "I always thought women were the opposite to power, not love," she says soberly.

Mary laughs heartily. "I guess that's true as well. But what I mean is…" She sighs, squashes her cigarette, and motions to the waiter for another drink. "What I mean," she repeats, "is that I don't want you to ever find out what I mean. Goodnight. I think it's time your ass had a break from molestation."

And thus Alix is dismissed.

\* \* \*

The next few months offer up more of the same. Sometimes the information Alix cables to Washington comes from her own sources: Esmée provides excellent updates about the state of the French Resistance; Frank sends over the gossip of Nazis from the Ritz bar, where disaffected military intelligence officers congregate; and one of the former kitchen hands from Le Manoir now runs a gentleman's club in Bern and provides a constant stream of news.

By 1943, Washington wants information about Italy, which Chiara gathers from her brother Matteo, who send letters written in Piedmontese so they mostly escape the censors' understanding. The letters detail troop strengths and garrisons, locations of manufacturing plants, geography, and everything the Allies need to know for a purpose Alix hopes, for Chiara's sake, is an invasion.

By summer, nothing like an invasion has happened. Chiara's brother's letters tell her that the Italians are starving and they want action from the Allies besides a landing in far-off Sicily, which has made the

Nazis position themselves to take over the entire north of the country where Chiara's family lives.

"I'm sorry," Alix says despondently to Chiara as they sit by the river with ice cream in hand.

"Don't be," is Chiara's grim response. "At least I know you *want* to do something. Whereas I have no idea if the Americans or the British really do. Matteo's last letter said he's had to hide in the mountains because everyone knows he hates the Fascists. If the Nazis take over the north, they'll kill him."

What begins as fury ends in tears and, for the first time since Alix has known her, Chiara cries. The only thing Alix can do is hold her. Just like she held Lillie in Washington. Then, she'd been sure she could help her friend. Now, she has no such conviction.

* * *

Every day, more cables arrive from Algiers, where the Allied Forces Headquarters has been established, but none arrests Alix as much as this: ALIX, I KNOW IT'S YOU. I RECOGNIZED THE BISOUS.

The only people who would recognize the *bisous* are Lillie and Bobby. But the only person who would send such a thoughtless cable is Lillie.

Alix sits down in a chair. For Lillie to see the *bisous*, she has to be working at the cable registry at AFHQ in Algiers. She shouldn't be surprised. Alix gave the OSS Lillie's name because Lillie has the pedigree and language skills OSS needs.

But now Lillie has used Alix's name in a transmission. If anyone sees this, they'll be fired. OSS depends on as few people as possible knowing the names and locations of its agents, so if one is caught, they won't blow the whole organization apart. Alix crumples the paper in her fist and composes her own message. BISOUS, AND ONLY BISOUS, SENDS YOU GROS BISOUS.

The reply, when it comes, is typically Lillie. GROS BISOUS RECEIVED WITH PLEASURE. I'LL TRY TO COVER SWITZERLAND AND LEAVE FRANCE TO THE OTHER GIRLS. PLEASE SEND MORE BISOUS.

Alix grins. She needs a friend. No, she needs Lillie.

Not long after, another cable arrives: OPERATION AVALANCHE. This cable is more important than all the others, with its briefing at last on the forthcoming invasion of mainland Italy by the Allied armies.

It's almost impossible to wait until it actually happens on September 9 but as soon as it does, Alix rushes into the Bellevue, grabs Chiara's arm, hustles her outside and says, "They've landed in Salerno."

Chiara's shriek is surely the loudest sound ever heard in Bern. *"Ammazzo!"* she says again and again, thanking Madonna and hundreds of saints.

"Tell your brothers," Alix says, beaming, "that I need everything they can send."

"They will tell you the color of Mussolini's underpants," Chiara replies and they both start to laugh.

That moment is worth all the months of drudgery. As is the thought that, given Alix is the one with the contacts in Italy, she'll finally be able to do something more worthwhile than sending Dulles's cables for him.

\* \* \*

It's October when Alix, returning to her apartment, hears footsteps hurrying after her. Chiara is behind her and she looks both scared and proud and Alix knows that whatever she's about to say, she can't say it there.

Perhaps she has a letter from her brother, which Alix is desperate for. Italy is in chaos. The Germans have rescued Mussolini from prison and set him up in the north of the country as the head of a new Fascist State. Chiara's family are trapped within its violent boundaries.

The Allies, after advancing toward Naples and gaining control of the southernmost regions of the country, are now stuck on the wrong side of the Volturno Line—a long way from Rome and so far from Piedmont they might as well be on the moon. The mood in Washington and at AFHQ in Algiers is somber, and the clamor for information, especially about what the hell is going on in Italy's inaccessible and Fascist-controlled north, is deafening.

Alix thinks quickly. She needs to take Chiara somewhere private and settles on Mary Bancroft's room at the Hotel Schweizerhof, which Mary never uses, preferring to stay with Dulles.

"How silly of me," Alix says for the benefit of any listening ears. "I forgot we were supposed to meet at the Schweizerhof for a drink."

"I'm bringing a friend," Chiara says. "I'll meet you there."

At the hotel, Alix crisscrosses the floor impatiently. Ten minutes tick by and then another ten. Finally, footsteps and a tap on the door.

There, Alix finds Chiara and a man perhaps a year or two older. His exhale, once he's on the right side of the closed door, is one of stupendous relief. He looks tired, dirt mars his olive skin, and his hair hasn't seen a comb for several days. His lips, when he smiles at Alix, are delicious.

"This is Matteo," Chiara says, a quiver of love in her voice. "My brother. He smuggled himself through the border last night because he has a proposition for you."

"He smuggled himself through the border? But…" Alix's words are lost to her astonishment. How did a young man from Italy, doubtless without travel papers, escape Fascist patrols and Swiss border guards and get himself to Bern?

In the gaping silence, apprehension sweeps over Matteo's face, and Chiara's too.

"Well," Alix quips, trying to ease the rising tension, "I've always been partial to propositions from handsome young men."

\* \* \*

Even though Matteo must be exhausted from walking or skiing clandestinely from Italy into Switzerland, he won't sit down. He paces as he talks about everything that's happened in the last month since German troops occupied most of Italy, and the Allied advance stalled near Naples.

"It's not just me hiding in the mountains," he says, animation making his brown eyes spark gold. "The Italian army, in the mess right before the German Occupation, abandoned their weapons. So we've been collecting cannons and guns and ammunition—"

Alix interrupts. "Matteo, who is 'we'?"

He stills, eyes not gold now but carrying the shadows of someone who's endured a Fascist government for most of his life—a government he's openly rebelled against—a man who's put himself in grave danger to come here. "Men like me," he says, passion gone, anger settling in and underscoring the point: men in their early twenties with their whole lives ahead of them should not have to scour the countryside for guns. "About ten thousand of us, spread over the Val Pellice, the Germanasca, the Val di Susa. And we're hiding about two thousand British prisoners of war."

"Ten thousand partisans and two thousand Allied prisoners of war?" She repeats the words because she has to be sure she's heard him right—the numbers are staggering. Such a body of men with guns and ammunition in the seemingly impenetrable Italian north is a force she must be able to do something with. And Allied POWs too. At the very least, the Allies will want their soldiers back.

"Please sit down," she begs him. He looks exhausted, as if he might fall asleep while standing. "I'll get wine and food sent up."

"*Grazie*," he says with a grin, perching on the edge of the bed, then shuffling back, leaning against the wall, and closing his eyes for a moment.

It doesn't take long for Turin vermouth, saucisson, and onion tart to be delivered. Alix passes Matteo a drink, which he downs in one swallow. Then he falls upon the tart, devouring it in only a few bites.

As Matteo eats, Alix's mind works furiously. Italy is an unknown quantity. Mussolini's rule has gone on for years, cutting the country off from the world. The north is widely believed to be a hotbed of communism but Matteo's letters have always expressed support for the Partito d'Azione. America might support the Action Party, especially if they're affiliated with partisans in the mountains who are willing to fight the Nazis and the Fascists. But...What will Dulles say? He'll want proof of their loyalty.

"Matteo," she asks, sitting on the end of the bed where she can watch his face, "you want freedom from the Fascists and the Nazis, but what else do you want?"

Matteo stands and shifts restlessly over to the window, staring out at Bern in the fall, the city's most beautiful season. The leaves of the trees are a vibrant red-brown, matching the roofs of the houses so that the entire canopy of the city seems to hang suspended, waiting to flutter downward.

But what Matteo says next is bereft of any charm. "In a town not far from where my family live in the Val di Susa," he begins and Alix can see from the way Chiara stiffens at the mention of their family that he hasn't told her whatever he's about to say, "the Nazis started burning down houses. Two of my cousins had some ancient guns from the Great War. They fired on the Germans to protect their homes, but what can an old pistol do against a machine gun?"

He turns to focus on Alix and she feels sick at the idea that she's making him give evidence of grave violence before she helps him.

"The Nazis killed twenty-three people I know that night, including my cousins. They destroyed five hundred houses. They threw petrol on the parish priest and burned him alive. What I want," Matteo says quietly after another swallow of vermouth, "is for that not to happen again."

"*Madonna mia,*" Chiara gasps, scrambling over to embrace her brother.

Matteo holds his sister, his gaze on the wrenching beauty of the free and unburned city that lies beyond the glass. His jaw is clenched but his head is held high despite fatigue and despair. He has not only witnessed horror, but he has brought it here and placed it before Alix because he believes she has the power to help. It's a power she hopes to God she possesses.

\* \* \*

"The French Resistance's sabotage campaign has been a huge irritation to the Germans," Alix tells Matteo a little later, drawing on everything she's learned from helping Esmée over the past few months. "The Nazis are using the factories around Turin to make weapons. So you need to destroy the bridges and railways they use for transport. I should be able to get you explosives and weapons. But," she joins Matteo at the window, "they might retaliate by burning more houses. And…"

"By killing more people," he finishes the sentence she hadn't been able to. "I'm not scared." His eyes flash a furious brown.

This is what courage looks like, Alix tells herself so she can remember it later when she asks Dulles for the equipment Matteo needs. The urge to promise him everything is overwhelming but not within her control. Still, she gives him a vision to look forward to, one she believes she should be able to arrange.

"I can get the Allies to send in radios, ammunition, and men trained in resistance tactics," she tells him. "That's how you and your friends become an army who can protect the villages, harass the Nazis, and be ready to fight with the Allies when they reach Northern Italy."

Matteo smiles as if he can taste the dream of future freedom she's promising him. But there are practicalities—again, Alix has learned this from Esmée.

"Until we can get radios in, you need some way of communicating with me and with the partisans in the other valleys," she says. "The French have couriers to run messages around the country. But you're holed up in the mountains, so how will you do that?" This part is crucial. She knows Washington's price for guns and radios and leadership will be information.

"We have *staffette*," he says. "Our sisters, mothers, girlfriends. They pass messages to us and bring us food. The Nazis think they're out shopping—they don't think women are a threat."

As he speaks, an idea forms in Alix's mind. It's perfect—and also selfish.

"Chiara," she says to her friend, "we've run out of vermouth and they don't do room service after midnight. But you know the bartender—can you ask him for more? I have a feeling we're going to be here for a while."

Chiara nods and leaves.

Matteo grins cheekily at Alix. He has one dimple in his right cheek and his smile is at once magnetic and charmingly old-fashioned. "You could have just told her you wanted to be alone with me," he says.

Alix laughs. "I sent Chiara away because I have an idea. But I want to make sure you won't bite my head off. I prefer my head on my shoulders."

"I like your head on your shoulders too. It's a very beautiful head." His smile now is gentle and perhaps a little sad, as if he understands that for as long as it takes to get the Nazis out of Italy, all he'll have with women are brief flirtations. It's impossible for him to have anything more when he's living a life of hiding in mountain huts and shepherds' granges, a life where blowing up bridges is about to become normal and moonlit strolls and romantic dinners will become the stuff of nightmares because who knows when they might happen again?

Soon, maybe. If Alix does this right. Bracing herself for Matteo's outrage—Chiara's told her that all the men in her family have traditional values—Alix says, "Chiara would be the perfect *staffetta* to liaise between you and your partisans and me. Just until I can get a radio to you." It will put Chiara in danger—she'll have to cross the border many times—and moving back to Italy will mean Chiara loses the Swiss visa she obtained in the interwar years, but Chiara might be happy to make the sacrifice.

Matteo frowns.

Alix adds, gently, "It's Chiara's choice. But I want you on her side. She'll have to travel back to Piedmont with you and I don't want you to lose her at the border crossing so she has no choice but to return to Bern."

Matteo's laugh is a resonant sound, burgundy plush that wraps itself around Alix's heart, giving it a little squeeze. Then the door opens and Chiara appears with wine in hand.

Matteo reaches for the bottle and opens it. "Alix thinks you should come back to Italy with me. Liaise between her and the partisans." He lifts his glass, waiting for his sister's response.

Chiara's beam is broad and determined. *"Alla nostra."* She doesn't just clink her glass against her brother's, she kisses his cheek.

Alix wonders whether she will regret this—and suspects she most likely will.

\* \* \*

"You've got to be fucking kidding me." Dulles is predictably incredulous when she tells him she wants to fund and equip a band of Italian partisans.

"I'm not," she fires back. "The Allied Control Commission is in Brindisi, on the opposite side of Italy. The partisans can't get intelligence information down to Brindisi. But they can get all that and more to Switzerland."

"One charming Italian comes through the border and you think you can run a Resistance circuit? Did he kiss you? Or more? He must have been good at it."

The temptation to throw one of the crystal decanters at Dulles is strong. Because now he's made her doubt herself, just a little. Matteo *had* flirted with her. And he *was* good at it. But he's also seen twenty-three people die.

"That charming Italian has been feeding us intelligence via his letters all year, intelligence you've thought highly enough of to let me pass on to Washington," Alix snaps, hoping her instincts are right. "He's the one who first told us about the CLN," she adds, referring to the Comitato di Liberazione Nazionale, formed by Italy's main opposition political groups to fight fascism and resist the Nazis. "Through the charming Italian, we now have direct contact with the CLN. And direct contact with the partisans who are independent, uncoordinated, and leaderless. You want to have a hand in who ends up in power in Italy once the Germans are pushed out? This is your foot in the door."

"*My* foot in the door. I didn't hear you say anything about me being involved." Dulles pours himself a whiskey.

Alix lights a cigarette and strolls over to the drinks cabinet. "How would you get me back to Washington if I suddenly became incompetent at coding your cables?" she asks innocently.

His laugh is a bark. "There's no going back to Washington. We're surrounded by enemy territory. You'll just have to do the work."

She picks up a decanter of something and fills a glass. Dulles's mouth twitches in annoyance. He's the one who proffers the drinks, not her.

"So I'm stuck here for the duration," she says after taking a sip. "We can either make that duration productive and I continue to do all your coding, cabling, and organizing, in return for which you let me do this—or I won't do anything except be decorative." She smiles her most decorative smile and drapes herself in a chair.

"By God, I could fire you right now," he storms, chewing on his pipe the way he'd like to chew on her.

"You could," she agrees, "but you know you won't find anyone to replace me who's even half as good as I am. So, you decide. It's in your hands."

Another barking laugh. "It's not in my hands and you know it. Fine, make a start on Italy. If you screw it up, I know nothing and you were doing it without my approval."

She raises her glass. "And if I succeed, I was doing it under your orders?"

"Damn right."

# TEN

In Alix's tiny apartment, which sits above a spaghetti restaurant in the old town on Kornhausplatz and looks out over the Child Eater Fountain—a macabre backdrop—Alix takes Matteo and Chiara through an intensive training session. She can't bring Matteo into the office as he has no papers and the Swiss officials who visit Dulles occasionally will detain a paper-less Italian partisan.

They start by discussing the courier line they'll need to set up to pass on messages and supplies until parachute drops and a radio can be organized by Alix's OSS counterparts at Brindisi. Alix has never had to arrange airdrops of supplies before; Esmée deals with the British agents servicing France for all that, but Alix doesn't think it will be difficult to coordinate. Obviously partisans need radios and weapons to be effective.

"You'll have to come back through the border at least once more so I can brief you after I've put the border-to-Bern half of the line in place," she says to Chiara. "And so you can brief me on your half too."

It's Matteo's turn to sigh. "*Porca miseria*. If our mother ever finds out I've let my sister become a *staffetta*, she'll kill me in a manner more gruesome than any German ever will."

"You see what I mean?" Chiara says to Alix. "Overprotective."

"I see that your brother loves you." Alix's heart twists a little with what can only be envy. How nice to have someone care for you like that.

She reaches for the vermouth bottle but it's empty. Matteo takes the glass from his sister and passes it to Alix. She walks over to the window with it, hips leaning against the sill, the fountain behind her obscured by blackness, returning from sentiment to practicality. "There's enough money in that envelope," she points to a package on the table that Dulles had reluctantly handed to her earlier, "to pay everyone you recruit."

"Thanks, Alix. Cigarettes and whiskey will encourage people more than cash, though. I promise not to drink or smoke it all myself." Matteo grins and the dimple on his cheek reappears.

She laughs. "I won't tell Dulles you even joked about that."

His grin doesn't fade. "We need warm coats too—especially for crossing the border in winter."

"Fur or wool?" she asks, smiling too, before she checks off the next item. "I have some grenades and small explosives for you. I'll send more via the courier line once it's set up and then a whole lot more by parachute."

"You know," Matteo says, stretching out on the sofa and leaning his head back on the armrest, "you don't look like a person who can shift from jokes about fur coats to plans to supply grenades. But," he shrugs, "who does look like that?"

His grin is gone and his face wears an expression that makes him look younger and more uncertain than he has at any time over the last three days. He's become, suddenly, a vulnerable man in his twenties. It's Alix's job to make him forget that, even though his vulnerability makes him human rather than a cog in the war machine paid for and controlled by the Americans and the Nazis.

"Matteo..." She needs to warn him, but what dangers can she, living in Switzerland, possibly speak of to a man whose home is a freezing grange in the mountains of an occupied country?

"You both need code names," she says instead, after swallowing the last mouthful of vermouth. "I can't use your real names in cables and memos. You choose."

"What's yours?" Matteo asks.

She blushes. "Bisous."

"Then I'll be Bacio," he says. "Italian kisses are far superior." His eyes on her are both teasing and intent.

Chiara groans. "She's engaged," she tells her brother. "To a rich American."

"I hope your rich American knows how lucky he is," Matteo says gently.

Alix turns around and sees that outside, unseasonably early snow-flakes are falling in a soft bridal white, sparkling in the air like falling stars before they melt into nothing. Matteo has known her for three days and flirtation is a reflex for him the same way breathing is, but still his words rattle her.

*She's* the lucky one. That's what Mrs. van der Meer always said, and Lillie too. Just last year, Alix had believed them. Nobody had ever thought Bobby was equally blessed—no, he was lowering himself to Alix.

"What name will you choose?" she asks Chiara as another snow-flake disappears.

"*Sorella*," Chiara says, eyes on her brother. "Sister."

\* \* \*

Chiara falls asleep not long after and Matteo joins Alix at the window. "It's good-luck snow," he says, indicating the world beyond covered in white. "Enough to cover my tracks but not enough to slow me down."

"I'm glad the snow is blessing you." She can't help smiling at his irrepressible dimple.

"What about you, Alix St. Pierre? Are you blessing me too?" His dimple deepens.

"Yes." Her smile becomes a laugh. Matteo is all uncontained energy at the prospect of a border crossing back to Italy that would make most people quail. Then her smile fades and seriousness takes hold. "Last night I dreamed about a priest on fire. I know that's ridiculous because I wasn't there, but..." Her voice is vehement now. "This has to work, Matteo. This can't be the world we live in."

He touches a hand quickly to her cheek, his eyes espresso-dark. "When Chiara told me there was someone in Bern who might help us, I almost threw the letter away. The Allies are so busy blaming the Italians for creating our own mess that they don't really want to help. When they do, it's a grudging kind of help for a nation they think are fools. We aren't fools, Alix. I never supported Mussolini. Nor did anyone I know."

The dimple is gone, replaced by the steel of a man who has seen death and who wants to protect his family and who has no certainties other than war. He presses his palm flat against the glass. "There are thousands of men in the mountains who want to fight our way out of this mess. All we need is someone who trusts us. And you have. So no, I don't think this will be the world we live in. Whatever strengths the Germans have, they don't have trust. And isn't that worth more than fire and violence and death?"

He withdraws his hand from the glass and Alix fixes her gaze to the faint haze left by the heat of his skin, wanting to know more about this man who in three days has become a significant part of her life. "Tell me what you did before all of this."

She shouldn't ask; it's best to keep a distance from your informants. But she learned that back in Washington, when an informant was an idea rather than a man willing to organize disparate bands of young men in Northern Italy into a fighting force, despite the personal danger.

"I was training to be a doctor. We'll need doctors in the months ahead." He takes up position beside her, their backs to the snow, their shoulders touching. "I also dreamed of dark-haired Madonnas worshipping me but I can see," he indicates her hair, "that I was narrow-minded."

She can't help but smile again. "Then tonight my dream will be that, in the not too distant future, you won't have to dream of dark-haired Madonnas because you'll have one of your own, and a band of children too, and a medical practice, and everyone will speak of the handsome doctor who fought bravely in the war and who's now devoted his life to healing."

The shine in his eyes is visible, as it probably is in hers. "I like your dream," he says softly. "And I might borrow it from time to time. But don't think too badly of me if sometimes the Madonna has red-gold hair and a beautiful smile."

* * *

Once the Romano siblings have disappeared over the border, Alix gets to work. She changes into a dress that flatters her figure, packs money into her bag, and heads to the border station near Lugano, where the landscape allows for an easier crossing into Italy and where the barbed wire Chiara will have to crawl back through is within sight of the guards' posts.

"*Bonjour* and *ciao*," she says to the guards, smiling brightly, passing around flasks and figuring out which guards are amenable, in return for money, to turning a blind eye to anyone lifting the barbed wire.

Then she takes the train to Zermatt, which is both near the border and home to some people she knows from school—people who might help her establish the courier line—a series of people and places who will pass messages along either from Alix to the partisans, or from the partisans to her. The Keller brothers who worked at Le Manoir—one as a ski instructor and the other as a stablehand—came from a ski lodge here. She finds their sister in charge of the ski lodge now, which is in an almost perfect location overlooking the Italian border. Alix's heart races with the hope that the Keller sister is as nice as the Keller brothers were.

She is. "I remember you!" the woman exclaims and Alix recalls a younger version of her—Nina was her name—visiting her brothers at school. Alix had given her a list of the best nightclubs to visit in Geneva, an experience Nina had returned from with a glowing smile.

Nina makes coffee and tells Alix about her brothers. "Rafael drives the intercity trains into France and Italy," is the one thing she says that makes Alix the one with a glowing smile.

She knows she looks too thrilled by such prosaic news—and that Nina has noticed.

"We have a range of visitors at the lodge," Nina continues, producing cake and a slug of brandy for their coffee. "German businessmen. Italians. And Rafael sees a lots of different people on the trains. I've always said the American Legation would be fascinated by some of the things we overhear."

It's Alix's opening and she takes it. A train driver going into Italy is the perfect start for her courier line. She thanks God, who she's never thanked for anything before, that her various friendships with all kinds of people from stablehands to maids have reaped such rewards.

Because once you find one person willing to help, you suddenly have dozens. Nina has a cousin who delivers food to the markets and who is happy to transport messages. He has a son with a business in Lugano who can collect anything that comes through the border there. Each of these cousins and sons and friends become Alix's means of getting her courier line up and running.

\* \* \*

Even Dulles is impressed by the report she delivers detailing everything Matteo told her: the location of Nazi garrisons in Piedmont and Milan; a precise overview of the political situation in Italy's north; the names of influential Italians who don't support the Nazis. He reads to the end, whiskey glass by his side hardly touched, pipe unsmoked.

Then he takes off his glasses and says, "You need money. Supplies. But the Brits, who think they run the show when it comes to parachuting equipment into Resistance cells, will be hard to convince. They think Italy's north is a communist hotbed and that helping the partisans will turn Italy from Fascist to Communist quicker than you can say *ciao*. But they're getting Parri up here for talks soon. You should come along."

Alix wants to whoop. Ferruccio Parri is the underground leader of the Action Party in Italy, and president of the CLN. With a man of Parri's stature meeting with the Allies, and men like Matteo working at the grassroots level beside women like Chiara, and intelligence reports like the one Alix has just written, the British will be easily persuaded.

\* \* \*

At the meeting, Parri welcomes Alix with a smile that's impossible not to return. He's in his fifties, with a neat mustache and glasses behind which his eyes are bright. He has spirit, and the air of someone driven by principle and purpose.

"Our friend Matteo asked me to tell you he received your message," Parri says to her. "Cris Cross is working."

Alix's grin widens. Cris Cross is the code name for the courier line. She sent her first messages along it last week and they've already reached Matteo!

But her smile soon fades. Parri pleads for equipment to supply a partisan army, but John McCaffery, the Dulles equivalent on the British side, chokes on his coffee and says, "All I want from the Italians is a spot of guerrilla work in the areas we can't get to. No partisan army. For that, you have only yourselves to blame."

*The areas we can't get to.* As if that's just a small patch of dirt. As if the Allies are in control of most of Italy, which is a lie fatter than a blimp.

The Allies are stuck well south of Rome. It's the Nazis who occupy the country. But the British aren't prepared to negotiate with a man who could help them control the north with a partisan army. Alix has no manpower in Switzerland so she can't just find a pilot and load a plane with supplies. Her OSS counterparts in southern Italy have the manpower but they are, right now, subordinate: as Dulles warned her, the British have the lead role in dealing with partisan groups.

It's a political quagmire—but priests are burning. And she promised Chiara and Matteo parachute drops of radios, explosives, guns, and more. She *promised*.

"A group of partisans," she interrupts, "blew up the Arnodera Bridge last week. To do that, they stole three thousand kilograms of explosives from the Nobel factory and used mules to take them to the base of the bridge. When the track ran out, the men traipsed over ice, each carrying forty kilos of explosives on his back. The bridge was once the main route into and out of Turin. Now the Nazis can't transport the supplies they need to hold the Allies back. Even the Germans said the sabotage was a work of art. Imagine how many more masterpieces of resistance could be created if the partisans were properly armed with equipment from parachute drops?"

"Who is she?" McCaffery spits at Dulles. "Keep your secretaries quiet."

"She," Dulles taps his pipe on the desk in a kind of quiet anger that could be directed at either Alix or McCaffery, "is the woman who wrote the highly praised report on Italy that made its way onto Roosevelt's desk a fortnight ago."

"I don't care if Roosevelt wallpapered the White House with her report," McCaffery says, glowering at Alix. "I'm not supplying a partisan army that might well turn into the next Russia and attack us in the end."

So Matteo's partisans are to be left virtually defenseless against the Germans who, in reprisal for the bridge sabotage, will surely find their mountain hideouts and clear the weaponless partisans out with just one tank. And Matteo will think Alix is a liar who can't deliver anything she's promised him.

\* \* \*

To douse her fury, Alix drags Mary to the bar at the Bellevue, which is perhaps a poor choice—asking Dulles's lover to commiserate with her over something Dulles didn't fight hard enough for—but there is no Lillie or Bobby to drink with, and Esmée hasn't been able to get an *Ausweis* for months. Perhaps a woman with Mary's experience of the world is what Alix needs.

Mary folds herself languidly in a chair. "Is it a hard liquor conversation?"

Alix nods.

"Two Scotch whiskeys please," Mary says to the waiter.

What would Mary do in Alix's position? Alix has no idea because, compared to Mary, Alix is an ingenue. Alix has never been married, or had children, or affairs—has only ever slept with one man, one time. "Does everything come back to power or seduction?" she asks Mary now. "Is that what you were trying to tell me the first time we came here? Even if I could stomach it, I don't think sleeping with McCaffery is going to help me or the Italians."

"Last month, Hans wanted me to go away with him for a weekend," Mary says, referring to the Abwehr agent whose confidences she's still collecting. "I said I couldn't; I thought it would be disloyal to Allen."

She doesn't mention her husband, who she perhaps has no loyalty to, just a broken vow barely binding them together. "When I told Allen about it, he got angry—not at Hans for wanting to whisk me away for the weekend, but at me for letting an opportunity to gather information pass me by." She reaches for her Scotch. Her tone is matter-of-fact and perhaps that's worse than her meaning—that Allen is happy to share Mary if the outcome is intelligence.

What would he be happy to do with Alix for the same outcome? Definitely not sleep with her. But use her? She studies Mary, this woman who isn't her friend, nor her conscience, nor her future—she hopes. What is Mary then? Alix's warning? "I..." She can't finish her sentence. What advice could an ingenue possibly give to Mary?

"You know," Mary says, smiling faintly. "You're one of the most private—or perhaps careful—people I know. Allen once told me that if you share one personal thing with someone, then if the person is on your side, they'll share something too. It's how you can tell if you have a true ally or not."

Alix thinks back over all their conversations. She's told Mary she grew up in LA and that she's engaged, but little else. Whereas Mary has told her that Dulles is happy to hurt her—but that she sleeps with him still. "I'm scared I'll fail the partisans," she says, staring at her hands. "That I'll be their downfall rather than their salvation. They've given me their trust and I..."

She's floundering for words and Mary is eyeing her with—what? Impatience? Alix wishes she hadn't said anything at all.

"Isn't it ironic," Mary says, "that our jobs rely on gaining people's trust. Yet the people we work for..."

*Aren't to be trusted.* Perhaps that's the truth Mary's been trying to impart. It's a view that presupposes life will always hurt.

Alix takes a too-large swallow of Scotch. Her throat burns and her eyes water. Does that mean she's wrong to have given Matteo and Chiara her trust? Who will they fight for, in the end? And who will she? One thing is certain, she won't fight for a life like Mary's, a life Mary probably doesn't deserve.

"It's hard to believe, when you're in your twenties, that your life will turn out like this," Mary segues, her voice softer than Alix has ever heard it, wistful too, her gaze fixed to Alix's eyes—which aren't only

damp from the whiskey fire now. "Then suddenly, you're in your for-
ties and it has and it's too late to do anything about it."

Mary finishes her Scotch and leaves Alix to her thoughts.

\* \* \*

Alix returns to the office soon after. She's been waiting for the partisans to be supplied with radios and better weapons before they try
to ferry the Allied POWs through the border from Italy. But those
POWs are perhaps the bargaining chip she needs. Mary's advice—to
be more like Dulles and less like herself—is painful but probably true.

There are two parts to her plan and the POWs are the second. The
first part is a cable she writes out. When she's finished, she taps on the
door to Dulles's private rooms where Mary is now curled in a chair
and Dulles is laughing. Alix raises her eyebrows in Mary's direction
and Mary takes herself to the powder room.

Then she shows Dulles the cable she's written for the OSS station
at Brindisi: FURTHER TO McCAFFERY AGREEING TO THE PARTISANS'
ROLE AS SABOTEURS, WE NEED AN AGENT, SUPPLIES, AND RADIO OPERATOR
IN PIEDMONT ASAP. BISOUS.

Everything she's said in the cable is true. McCaffery *did* agree to
the partisans' role as saboteurs. She may have conjoined facts to imply
McCaffery's approval of the parachute drops, but that's in the inter-
pretation, not the words she's written. By the time everyone works
out that she's lied, she'll hopefully have some rescued Allied POWs to
offer as proof of the partisans' value.

Dulles studies her, pipe in one hand, glass in the other, cheeks
pinkish with warmth and food and wine and Mary. "Why make it so
hard?" he asks. "Why not just do all the other work—there's plenty
of it." Then he shrugs and says, as if he knows her, "I guess you and I
both like the road that runs along the cliff's edge."

It's partly true. Dulles sends long cables about psychological warfare and policy, and things that are most likely outside his remit and that ruffle some feathers in Washington. But while his road as a man born into the same circle as those running the country might occasionally veer close to the edge because he likes to offer unasked-for opinions, Alix's road is still being built on the valley floor.

"I'll take that as permission," is all she says.

Then she waits nervously for the cable to do its work and the air-drops to be arranged and McCaffery to find out and call Dulles, raging about his lying secretary—who he'll want fired, at the very least.

# ELEVEN

While she waits, Alix puts in place the second part of her plan, the part that will save her—if it works. She sends a flurry of packages via Cris Cross to Chiara with false identification papers for the Allied POWs, instructions about how to select someone to accompany the POWs so they don't have to speak to any German patrols, and information about where they should cross the border. She makes sure her Swiss couriers can transport not just messages, but humans, to Bern.

Soon, a cable comes through from OSS Brindisi advising that they've arranged an airdrop of sabotage supplies, ammunition, a wireless operator and a radio for the following month. She feels her gut twist, wondering if they'll get airborne and the mission complete before McCaffery discovers what she's done.

March 1944 is almost over when she receives the message she's been waiting for from Cris Cross. She's about to show it to Dulles when the door of 23 Herrengasse flies open and McCaffery appears, red-faced and vicious. He advances on her, continuing to walk forward even when he's right in front of her so she has no choice but to step back into a wall.

"You bloody liar," he shouts, face inches from hers. "I did not authorize any airdrops. I'd court-martial you if you were real military."

He spits the next sentence at Dulles. "Do you know what she's done?"

And Alix remembers what Dulles told her: *If you screw it up, I know nothing and you were doing it without my approval.*

He won't save her. She'll have to save herself, if she can.

Dulles lights his pipe. He takes his time and McCaffery can't bear it. "Dammit, do you need me to fire her for you?"

Alix hears it then—the sound of the back door opening, the door that's screened from eyes on the street. The door that allows secrets to enter.

She steps forward, even though it means her body coming up against McCaffery's, and he lifts his hand as if he's going to push her back against the wall.

"It's that special delivery I told you about," Alix says to Dulles, ridiculously glad that McCaffery's physical and verbal aggression have made her hate him, and that hatred has allowed her voice not to waver beneath his menace.

*Play along, Dulles*, she thinks desperately. She just needs five more minutes. And if she lets Dulles share in what she hopes is the arrival of a victory, there's a small chance he might not fire her.

It's a hope as ridiculous as a child wishing Santa was real.

Indeed Dulles doesn't tell McCaffery to step away. He continues to light his pipe, to suck in smoke, to pump it out like a dragon and say, "Well." He looks at McCaffery, not at Alix.

Then the door to the office opens and Alix sees them. One, two, three, more. Maybe twenty. Even thirty.

"Who the bloody hell are they?" McCaffery demands.

"British prisoners of war," Alix says, trying to be calm but triumph rings possibly too smugly in every vowel. "Smuggled from Northern Italy by the Italian partisans you refused to—"

*Refused to help*, is what she means to say.

Dulles cuts her off, which is probably for the best.

"Do you want these thirty soldiers and all the rest waiting to come through from Italy?" he asks McCaffery coolly. "I don't have time to do everything. It seems she can be useful." He indicates Alix.

As far as compliments go, it's the most tepid one she's ever received. But she's so happy not to be fired, to have this proof that Matteo and Chiara can get things done even with minimal help, that she doesn't care.

"Americans prefer a little more personal space than the British obviously do," Alix says grimly to McCaffery and he finally steps away. She feels her shoulders plunge downward, her teeth unclench.

"If she sends any more cables giving orders I haven't authorized—" he starts.

"Then I'll fire her," Dulles finishes.

She's sent out of the room to arrange safe houses for the POWs. The Swiss will want to place them in internment camps to wait out the war if they discover them, but McCaffery wants them smuggled back to Britain. She gives Dulles a look before she leaves that she hopes conveys the price he needs to ask for their help—airdrops for the partisans.

\* \* \*

She gets her airdrops. Well, she gets them scheduled. She stupidly thinks that's enough and she buys Mary not just drinks but a meal to celebrate. She doesn't thank Dulles, who lit a pipe rather than ask a man not to fence her in against a wall. He expects thanks and when he doesn't receive it, he growls for days.

But her excitement about the promise of airdrops is premature. Her OSS counterparts in Brindisi have to rely on British planes. The pilots are either incompetent, unlucky, or have been told by McCaffery not to try too hard. The first drop is canceled because of bad weather. The second drop overshoots its zone by miles and returns to base. The third time there is engine trouble. Then they have to wait until the following month as the moon is waning and the pilots won't be able to see the drop zone. Without a damned wireless transmitter on the ground, Alix can only keep sending messages via the courier line and it's much slower than her impatience can tolerate.

The next month, June 1944, her impatience increases when incredible news comes through. The Gustav line is breached and the Allies have liberated Rome. But Rome is more than four hundred miles from Matteo and Chiara—too far to have any immediate impact on their own fight for survival in the north. And the Germans will be outraged by the Allied victory—and still more outraged, she frets when, two days later, the Allies invade France too. What will enraged Nazis do to partisans who are becoming a blade, rather than a thorn in their side?

She takes matters into her own hands again, starting with cabling AFHQ, now based in Caserta in the south of Italy, and doing something she's never done before: she specifically addresses her cable to Shirley Temple, hoping that if Lillie isn't the one who receives it, whoever does will holler for Shirley Temple, and Lillie will realize Alix needs help. She asks Lillie to find out who's in charge at OSS Brindisi so she can cable them directly rather than cabling anonymous people who clearly don't have the authority she needs.

She waits for a day and hears nothing. Still another day of waiting passes so she cables again.

SHIRLEY TEMPLE, I NEED THAT INFO URGENTLY. BISOUS.

A reply comes back almost immediately.

SORRY. MEANT TO REPLY YESTERDAY BUT DISTRACTED BY BIG NEWS! THE THIRD POINT OF THE TRIANGLE IS IN ITALY! HE PASSED THROUGH CASERTA ON HIS WAY TO HIS POSTING. HE'S OH SO SOCIAL TOO. YOUR BRINDISI CONTACT IS LEONE.

The third point of the triangle. Bobby.

Alix's fingers fly. She can't believe Lillie has once again been so indiscreet. And there are no excuses for forgetting to respond.

No more secret info, she writes. And don't forget to cable again. Lives depend on it. Bisous.

Alix takes her annoyance with Lillie out on Leone, grimacing. What kind of man names himself after the king of the jungle?

She writes the cable the way a man would, with profanity adorning every sentence, demanding Leone get his shit together and send in a wireless transmitter, a wireless operator, and some goddamn supplies. She appends to the cable a report with the latest intelligence from Matteo and Chiara about Nazi troop movements in the north.

Leone responds almost immediately saying that the best he can do is get a British agent sent in but if Bisous can send more detailed info, Bisous might get what he wants. Leone thinks she's a man, of course. His cable ends with, I want more men in Northern Italy too. So get me what I want and I'll make it happen. And who the fuck calls themselves Bisous?

*More detailed info.* How to get that without a wireless operator on the ground? While she ponders that, Leone is as good as his word and she hears a couple of weeks later via Cris Cross that an agent has arrived. It's a start—a tiny victory. But, as with every tiny victory, it's followed by a colossal defeat. The following month, one lone Allied POW arrives at Herrengasse, brought up from the border by the man she's paid to keep a watch. His face is gray.

"The Nazis tracked us down," the POW tells her. "They shot the guide. I got away, just. But no one can use that route through the border now. It's blown."

He passes her a coded note. It's Chiara's writing. *Major crackdown on partisans announced by Wolff.*

Alix's curse is explicit.

"The Nazis we ran into were gloating," the POW finishes. "They said they've captured the entire partisan military command."

*No.* After successfully getting almost two hundred POWs through the border, their route is blown. Their guide shot. Karl Wolff,

Obergruppenführer and SS general, military commander for the whole of Northern Italy, is hunting down the partisans. And he's already caught their entire military command. She'll never get more detailed info now.

Alix takes a train to Zermatt. Her backup plan with Chiara and Matteo has always been that if the route via Lugano is ever blown, the route to Nina's ski lodge is the fallback. And she knows that if the partisan military command has been arrested, Chiara will be on her way through the border.

What will she say to Alix? *We trusted you. You failed.*

\* \* \*

Alix says a hurried hello to Nina and then, binoculars in hand, takes up residence in the shed that has a view over the border. On the second night, a shape appears behind the barbed wire. Alix is out the door and running toward it immediately.

When she's close enough, she sees that it's Matteo, not Chiara. She halts. The partisans must be furious if they've sent Matteo.

But he swoops her into a hug. "Can I kiss you?" he murmurs and she wants to say yes because his hands on her back are gripping her as if he values her. Bobby's hands had only ever touched her in a casual way, not as if she were a necessity.

She manages her first smile in two days and shakes her head. "I can't."

"But you want to?"

She nods, still smiling.

"That's enough for me," he says.

She ushers him into the shed and leads him over to the blanket on the floor where there is a liquor flask, a coffee flask, and a plate of bread, salami, and cheese. The kerosene lamp is turned down low but even in the semi-dark, she can see that Matteo's dimple is gone, lost to a hard-set jawline and drawn cheeks. He's leaner too, but also more filled out, as if he spends all his time working his body hard, running from Nazis.

She wishes she had let him kiss her.

"Eat," she tells him. "And definitely drink—whichever is better for you right now: vermouth or coffee."

He sits on the blanket beside her, tilts his head and rests it against the top of hers. "I try to keep thinking of the victories, Alix—the invasion of France, the liberation of Rome," he says tiredly. "But yesterday morning the Nazis murdered the entire Piedmont military command. So many of our best men gone. Doctors can't heal the dead." He props an elbow on his knee and rubs his face with his hand.

She takes his other hand in hers and squeezes it. It's all she has to offer and it's so little.

He reaches for the vermouth flask. When he next speaks, his voice is low, anger still flaring in it. "The Allies have taken almost a year to get to Rome. At this rate, it'll be 1950 before they reach the north. Meanwhile, they drop bombs all over Italy; Milan is a ruin, Alix. The supply drop finally happened two days ago but there was no wireless transmitter and the agent they sent last month to teach us how to fight is *un cazzone*—nobody understands his so-called Italian."

Her fingers tighten on Matteo's. She wants to storm down to AFHQ in Caserta and shout: *This is how you lose a band of men. Just one worthwhile supply drop to give them hope is all they need.*

"What can you give me?" he asks. "I'm part of the new military command and I need supplies for my men."

She indicates a pathetic bag by the door. "All I have are more grenades, money, cigarettes, identity papers. But give me a week and I'll have everything. *Everything.*" She repeats the word like a prayer she needs the gods at Caserta to hear. "I'll light a fire under HQ that won't stop blazing until you have what you need."

"*Grazie,*" he says, but she hears the doubt in his voice.

He squeezes her hand and stands up, hoisting the heavy rucksack onto his shoulders, preparing to face the danger of the journey back to Occupied Italy with nothing more than her empty promise. She watches him walk resignedly toward the coils of barbed wire.

And she knows what she needs to do.

The only way to gather the information she needs to send to Leone is to go and get it herself.

"Wait!" she calls. "I'm coming with you." She throws the food into her pack. "If I see exactly what I'm fighting for, then I can fight all the better."

"No…" But Matteo catches her expression and his mouth breaks into its first smile.

It's about sixty kilometers to the Val d'Aosta, a difficult hike that will take all night and most of the next day. For the next several hours as they walk, they hardly speak. There's a haunting kind of silence in the no-man's-land they cross through. Alix is used to being in the mountains when they're covered with snow and she's flying along on skis and everything is vigor and breathlessness and magical white. In midsummer, the mountains are perhaps more beautiful, brooding over her and putting up a protective wall of rock within which the only sounds she can hear are her footsteps and Matteo's, their exhalations, the rustle of their eyelashes when they blink.

The fir trees, undressed without their covering of snow, lay themselves bare to her. And in a way, Matteo does too, catching hold of her hand when the path allows it, threading his fingers through hers and sometimes running his thumb over her skin—not flirtatiously, but as if making sure she's really there. The mountain pastures are dotted with flowers nodding their colorful heads and their every step is tracked by the mountain rabbits and eagles. The air is scented with truffle and earth. Every time she meets Matteo's eyes he smiles and her heart feels like one of the alpine gentians they pass by, saturated not with color or love or romance but with the deepest and richest kind of affinity. And she knows he's glad she's coming, that he needs her to see what she's fighting for too.

It's stupid and foolish and dangerous—but also, she knows as her gaze meets Matteo's again, necessary. If she somehow makes it back to Switzerland safe and sound, Dulles will kill her. But that's a sacrifice she's prepared to make for all the people in Italy's north who sacrifice so much more each and every day of their lives.

She just hopes she's prepared for whatever she'll find when she reaches Italy.

# PART THREE
## PARIS, 1947

*This was woman incarnate—unashamedly flirtatious in her nonchalant disregard of the stir she was causing, sensual, sensational, crazily chic and, above all, supremely sure of herself. This was the long-awaited image of Paris reborn, an explosive cocktail, a breathtaking fantasy.*
    —Marie-France Pochna, *Christian Dior: The Biography*

# TWELVE

In the overfull studio at Maison Christian Dior on February 11—the day before the show—a mannequin stood in a toile, rather than a completed dress. Monsieur Dior frowned at her side. Madame Carré kept darting away, raven-like, and returning with a treasury of pins and chalk and thread. Madame Raymonde tunneled through fabric rolls, finding the one she somehow knew was buried in the middle. Jeannine—or Boutonnette, as everyone called her—lingered by the wall with trays of buttons, waiting to be summoned forth with flat, shank, or toggles, in mother-of-pearl, cut-glass, or gold.

Alix tried desperately not to pace, tried to expend her nervous energy on smoking and eating the peppermints and nougat that sat on plates around the room. It was impossible that everything would be ready. She hadn't even been able to get the programs printed yet because dresses like this one were hardly started, let alone finished.

Thirty or more different rolls of black wool were draped one by one over Margaux Jourdan, the mannequin who, despite her undeniable beauty, had scars in her eyes and Alix knew her war had been a bad one too. Right now she was statue-still, gaze fixed above the hubbub, at the center of a process Alix had witnessed two hundred times over the past two weeks: the scrunching and stretching of fabrics, each identical on the roll but when unfurled and pulled this way and that, their subtle differences became apparent. One was more supple, another luxuriously weighty, the last was the deepest possible matte black—a night without stars.

She hadn't realized she'd spoken aloud until Dior pointed his baton at her.

"*Répétez, s'il vous plaît*," he said.

"A night without stars," she repeated cautiously, as Madame Bricard, who was somehow late for everything but exactly on time the instant she was needed, entered the studio.

She nodded at Alix and said, "*Exactement*. We will call it that in the program."

That was precisely what Alix needed to hear. Some finality. They were running out of time and Alix knew there was no chance any of them would be going home that night.

"And this one?" Madame Bricard's heavily braceleted arm indicated a roll of palest pink that had been selected for the previous dress.

Alix sighed, because it was all innocence and childhood. "Sigh pink."

Dior's almost-smile began to hover near his mouth. "*Continuez*," he said, tapping the wall of fabric with his baton.

Everyone in the room focused on her—even the previously mentally absent mannequin—and Alix knew that if she was to fully redeem herself from her firing in the eyes of each *petite main* and *arpette*, each tailor and *première*, and most especially in the eyes of the three mothers, she needed to do what she'd once done with Carmel Snow—*Get everyone's attention, and give them what they want*.

She looked at silk-satin and saw the Paris sky she'd embraced when she was only eighteen. "Rose Boréal," she said. Another pink, in duchesse-satin shot with silver. She christened it Rose Rêveur because it was both a dawn moon and a moonstruck young lover.

"Daybreak Gray," she continued, indicating a wistful length of chiffon. "And Morning Coffee," she finished, smiling at a richly brown bolt of wool.

*Le patron* actually laughed, as did Madame Bricard, whose throaty ebullience drowned out Dior's more muted but no less extraordinary enthusiasm. And Alix felt the wariness in the room disappear as she was pleated back into the fabric of Maison Christian Dior.

Then Madame Bricard turned to Margaux Jourdan, still draped in black silk velvet. "Dreadful," she exclaimed.

The offending roll was whisked away.

"Try it in red," Madame Bricard said.

Madame Carré unraveled a cascade of red wool-jersey over Margaux. The three mothers, Dior, and Alix all smiled and said, "Success!"

Success was a well-cut dress in bravura red that made a roomful of women smile.

* * *

The staff, who'd been able to go home for an hour or two of rest, returned to 30 Avenue Montaigne before dawn. Workmen were still tacking down the carpet in the grand salon. Elsewhere, hammers pounded as the house rushed to complete construction before its seams were tested by the pressure of hundreds of guests. It was below freezing outside and the newspapers had just announced that bread rations were reducing from three hundred and fifty grams to just two hundred per day, and that coal was rarer than gold. Alix ignored it all, studying the miracles that had been wrought inside the *maison* the night before while she'd been flying around the city having programs and press releases printed.

The shoebox that she had doubted could ever be transformed into a boutique was now the most charming miniature shop with *toile de Jouy* covering the walls in tendrils of blue-gray and white. Hatboxes inscribed with *Maison Christian Dior* were stacked artfully on top of cupboards and in otherwise dead corners, making the eye jump from one delight to the next. Vases of blue delphiniums and white lily-of-the-valley, their petals folded and crimped like the pleats and godets of fabric soon to billow through the salon, had been arranged by Christian's sister Catherine—just enough and not too many to compete with the gowns.

In the *cabine*, the mannequins dressed in white coats and under-wear looked variously frightened almost to death, hungry, bored, or exhausted as they were painted and primped. Several sipped from miniature bottles of brandy in this room made for twelve, and that now accommodated thirty people as well as parasols, hats, shoes, and a plenitude of nerves.

Two assistants trailed Alix through the grand salon as she placed a numbered card on each chair. She gave one final adjustment to the *Vogue* sofa, and did the same to Carmel's.

With half an hour to go, she found Monsieur Dior in the studio with his eyes closed and his hands over his ears, trying to block out the hubbub.

"Your heart and soul are about to be presented to the world," she said to him.

"And the world will judge me for it," he replied.

"Luckily your heart and soul are the finest I've known."

He kissed her cheeks, then clasped her in his arms for a long and entirely sentimental moment. He'd done the same thing a fortnight ago when Rita Hayworth had worn Soirée to her movie premiere and the fashion press had been unable, for days, to speak the name of any couturier besides Dior.

Alix had refused all requests for interviews with Dior, had not issued a single press release about Rita's dress, had simply mentioned in a note to Carmel Snow that Christian loved to use black for his evening gowns—an unusual choice in these post-Chanel times—and that Soirée was the most libertine example of Christian's new line, the other dresses being more like Soirée's sultry younger sisters. The following day when Alix had walked past the Little Bar, she'd seen Estelle Charpentier from *Le Monde* trying to wheedle Carmel into telling her exactly what was happening at Maison Christian Dior while the American fashion editors eagerly eavesdropped. With no information being given out by the House of Christian Dior, gossip filled the silence, reaching its grand crescendo last week. Now, the show was full, quite literally, to bursting.

Only two hundred and forty people could be accommodated in the main and petite salons. But so many journalists had requested tickets that Alix had needed to create thirty standing-room places around the edges of each room, and have a minor staircase removed to enlarge the landing to fit forty more spectators. Not to mention the forty she'd squeezed onto the main staircase, herself included.

Maison Christian Dior was poised on the cusp of legend. Succeed or fail, everyone would know about it.

It was a thought that made Alix sink down beside Dior. This— witnessing the fervor build, taking her first steps toward the stars, having done her job well and honestly and having got all that she'd wished for—was everything.

Dior raised her hand to his lips and kissed it. "Do not forget that today you're watching your own brilliance sail through the room too."

"Goddammit," she said, scrabbling in her purse for a hanky she didn't have. "How is it that you always make me cry?"

He laughed and passed her his own hanky. "I didn't make you cry. You made yourself cry—that is what happens when one is rightly proud of oneself."

Which only made her cry all the more. Dior was the first man in her life since her father who'd ever told her to be proud of herself. "Thank you," she whispered. "For more than what you just said."

*Le patron* pointed to the words on the front page of the program. Under the heading *Coloris dominants* were listed: *A Night Without Stars, Rose Rêveur,* and *Rouge Scream.* "And thank you for more than what you did here. Most people would have refused to return to a workplace they'd been asked to leave, would have let wounded feelings trump everything. Madame Raymonde is reason, Madame Bricard elegance, Madame Carré technique, and Suzanne a black book filled with names. You are courage, and it makes me feel a little braver to have you by my side."

At that, Alix dissolved completely into sobs.

When she'd mopped herself up, she drew back to study *le patron*'s face. "Will you watch the show?"

"I cannot."

"Then come and sit in the *cabine*. You'll be able to tell how it's going from the faces of the mannequins. And you won't need to plug your ears—you'll hear nothing whatsoever over their shrieks."

He found a rare smile, then gestured to a gown hanging from a rail. It was Chérie, the dress she'd admired weeks ago, shimmering sapphire. "Put it on, if you wish," he said.

It was Alix shrieking now. "The roof falling in wouldn't stop me from putting it on."

Monsieur Dior clapped a horrified hand over his mouth, touched one of the multitude of lucky charms in his pockets, and shooed her out of the room lest she say anything else inauspicious.

In her office, she removed her trousers and stepped into her dress, which was romance and tenderness and everything she found hard to express caught in navy blue taffeta. She unpinned her hair and let it fall down her back, touched red onto her lips and mascara onto her eyes and saw in the mirror the woman she might have become had the war not happened. She saw the awe and the wonder and the innocence she was hoping to wrest back from La Voce, when she found him.

"Alix, come and see!"

The call of her name roused her from that one lacerating moment. She left her office and gaped at the crowd gathered outside, swaddled in mink and staring pleadingly at poor Ferdinand. "Twenty more minutes," she heard him say and the chorus of disappointment was operatic.

Twenty minutes later, in they all came. Carmel headed straight to the most prominent sofa before the fireplace. Bettina Ballard from *Vogue* was seated at her right hand. Then Mrs. Perkins from *Women's Wear Daily*, Lucie Noel from the *New York Herald Tribune*. And the women invited for their influence and social reach: Lady Cooper from the British Embassy and Susan Mary Patten from the American; Liliane de Rothschild; Rita Hayworth; Daisy Fellowes.

They all kissed Alix's cheeks and asked some variation of *What are we going to see today?* to which Alix replied, "The making of history."

Becky Gordon arrived near to last. She ignored her numbered seat and strode over to an empty chair right up front, which was the photographer's. She yawned theatrically and said to the editor at her side, "We'll see very soon why Dior had to leave Lelong. Take it from me, Dior's an apprentice who'll never live up to his master."

*Oh, Becky*, Alix thought as she marched across the room. *Attack me all you like but never attack my friends.* "You need spectacles, Becky," she said. "Your seat is over there."

"I prefer this one," Becky said with an overconfident smile.

Alix smiled too. "Perhaps you think being fired means my position here is precarious. But I guarantee the only person Monsieur Dior will be throwing out of here today is you. If you'd like to test that theory, or my ability to forcibly shift you into your proper seat, then let's get started."

Suzanne, tall and large-boned, materialized at Alix's side. "You are in the wrong seat." Her voice carried across the room and heads began to turn.

Becky scowled, then collected herself and gave a little laugh. "It doesn't matter where I sit. The best couturiers have already shown. I have everything I need for *The Times*."

"I think *The Times* might find itself a little behind the times tomorrow," Alix said, sweet as sugar and trying not to be overconfident too.

If Becky took her personal vendetta against Alix out on the House of Christian Dior in her newspaper, that would quickly become a problem. *The Times* was a powerful newspaper in England and Dior would like English clients to patronize the house. Victory against Becky in this skirmish meant very little. Especially as tailing her had resulted in nothing. Becky went to the office, to the bar at the Ritz, and to her suite. Nowhere else.

But the show was about to begin. Becky had taken her proper seat. Anthony March slipped in while Alix was occupied with a paint-splattered Christian Bérard and his dog, Jacinthe, who apparently couldn't miss the show. Alix took her place on the staircase, tucking her sapphire-blue silk-taffeta around her.

Somehow, the room quieted itself seconds before the *aboyeuse* called, "*Numéro Un*. Number One."

Tania, the first mannequin, stepped out. She wore Soirée, already famous, and its placement as the show opener was, of course, meant to ensure that everyone was paying attention.

Every face in the room looked suddenly bewitched. It was no longer possible to suggest that the dress was only beautiful because it had been worn by Rita Hayworth. Here in the salon, back-dropped by white woodwork, gray curtains, and mirrors to double and redouble the effect, Soirée bloomed, the most rare and precious midnight-blue rose.

The eruption of applause was spontaneous, and profuse.

Corolle came next, reinforcing the line and the expression of Soirée, but in understated black wool and with a high neckline rather than low. But Corolle needed no low-cut neckline to make her magnificent—the lavishly full skirt, that had required an immoderate fourteen meters of fabric to bring to life, made every set of female calves in the room long to feel that glorious excess sweep against them.

A sudden change to the En Huit line and the black wool and velvet Maxim's dinner dress drew all eyes to the seductive spill of cleavage hiding behind an oversized bow. Rita Hayworth devoured it with her eyes and Alix made a note to send it to her that afternoon.

Dress after dress glided through the salon, each a living thing with passion and heart and so much joy. Every woman in the room—except Alix, the three mothers, Suzanne, and the mannequins—unconsciously tugged at her now too-short and too-slim skirt, or grazed her fingers in despair over her square padded shoulders, understanding every article of clothing she owned had just been made *démodé* and could never be worn again.

And Alix believed that everyone in the room was seeing the gowns the same way she did and that, over two hours on February 12, 1947, fashion had changed forever.

# THIRTEEN

*B*usy wasn't an adequate word to describe the next few hours of Alix's life. Her office inhaled and exhaled fashion editors and *coupes* of champagne. A smile ran unchecked over *le patron*'s face, which was also adorned with red lipstick. Carmel's maxim—"Dior saved Paris"—and Bettina Ballard's words—"There has never been an easier or more complete conquest than that of Christian Dior"— echoed through the *maison*.

Becky had scuttled out—vanquished for now. There was no doubt Dior was the true master and Becky was going to have to rewrite her report for tomorrow. But that only meant a short reprieve—Becky would find another way to attack Alix soon enough.

Amidst the bustle, a card arrived that Alix almost didn't open for lack of time but the letterhead caught her eye: the *New York Journal*. She unfolded it warily.

*Alix*, it read. *When it comes to fashion, Dior is the only name anyone will remember this year—and maybe for years to come. Congratulations. Anthony March.*

She reread the note a dozen times. If she wasn't mistaken, that was an apology. Or perhaps just another tactic.

The phone shrilled, demanding she return to the work of scheduling in more meetings for *le patron* than he would agree to accept, of placating less-fortunate editors with Bérard's or her illustrators' sketches, of booking the promised shoot for Carmel Snow. She neither ate nor drank a single thing until night fell when she found Dior in the studio with the three mothers, each trying to placate him.

"What is it?" she asked in alarm.

"With only two ateliers, we cannot possibly make everything that has been ordered," he lamented. "We need a new building."

"But this building was only finished this morning," Alix said, unable to imagine how everyone would survive months more of construction with the added pressure of orders to fill, if indeed a new house *was* to be constructed.

Then she laughed. For it was ridiculous that they were saying this beautiful *maison* was inadequate, ridiculous that they were lamenting the success they'd all hoped for.

Madame Bricard was the first to join Alix, throwing back her head and allowing her throaty chuckles to spill into the room, followed by the quieter mirth of Mesdames Raymonde and Carré. And then Dior added his rolling baritone to the cacophony. Everyone rushed to the studio to find out what was going on and stood bemused, watching the five of them wipe tears from their cheeks.

Once *le patron* had calmed himself, he held out an arm to Alix and said, "Marie-Louise Bousquet"—Carmel's Paris editor—"has invited us for dinner, *non?*"

"She has," Alix agreed and they swept down the staircase, replaying the show in minute detail. "Did you see Tania trip?"

"*Oui*, I thought she would never go back out there, she was so upset."

"Lucky went out with one black shoe and one beige!"

Dinner was a rambunctious affair. The quietest amongst them was Monsieur Dior, which was usual. There was just one moment of formality—Bérard's toast.

"My dear Christian. Savor this moment of happiness well, for it is unique in your career. Never again will success come to you so easily: for tomorrow begins the anguish of living up to, and if possible, surpassing yourself."

\* \* \*

*To Lillie,*
*From Paris*

*I realized tonight that I spend most of my time thinking about all the days and nights when I did not surpass myself. For example, "Nobody marries for love," you said to me a week after I accepted Bobby's proposal and we'd found out he was to stay in New York rather than be shipped overseas, and I told you I was going to break off the engagement. We were in a diner eating ice cream and you went on to say, "You marry for everything Bobby can give you. That's what women are supposed to do. Bobby knows that."*

*It was the first time I ever thought you sounded like your mother, and I remember thinking maybe they weren't your mother's words. Maybe they were every woman's words.*

*"What does Bobby get?" I asked you.*

*"Well," you said around a mouthful of chocolate sauce, "Bobby gets you."*

*I nearly cried then because you didn't sound like your mother anymore. You sounded like Lillie, the closest thing I've ever had to a sister. So I said, "We've always been a package deal. So Bobby gets you too. He's one hell of a lucky guy."*

*And we both laughed till we cried.*

*I went home thinking it was okay. That I didn't need to surpass myself in marriage. That I was lucky to be marrying a friend rather than a stranger.*

*But the night before I left for Switzerland—I couldn't tell either of you where I was going, just that I wouldn't be in touch for a while—we all went out for dinner. You and Bobby had a row, and between you and Bobby giving each other the cold shoulder, and Peter goading Bobby about giving me a fond farewell, and me wondering what I would find in Switzerland, Bobby and I ended up under a yellow chenille quilt at a cheap hotel, him finished in a couple of minutes and me staring up at the ceiling.*

*I did not surpass myself that night.*

*I think I did in Switzerland though, and look how that ended.*

*I think I am here in Paris too—but I want the ending to be different this time.*

*I know you want the ending to be different too. And we both know that's impossible.*

*Love and* bisous,
*Alix*

She shoved the letter away. She'd been so happy until Bérard's toast. But everywhere there were triggers—tiny words, insignificant gestures, meaningless sounds—that were so replete with memory that the happiness fled and there was only the echo of her cry in La Voce's room the night she had presented herself in her white dress for what she'd thought was the terrible settlement of a debt—and was really the beginning of the horror.

\* \* \*

Alix was at the Ritz early, before work, where Frank gave her a list of the people he recalled being in the bar around the time he received the inquiry that had put her in contact with La Voce.

"I don't know if your man was ever here though," he reminded her. "He used third parties to get his message to me, so maybe he was never in France."

"I know," Alix said. "But I have so little to go on that I have to chase down anything. And," she paused, wondering if it was foolish hope pretending to be intuition, "he's the kind of man who liked to observe. He won't have delivered the message, but I bet he witnessed its delivery."

Frank's list was around fifty names. It took a lot of willpower not to ask him to make her a French 75 for her to cry into. When would she have time to investigate fifty people to rule them in or out? And the more she probed, the more she risked drawing attention to herself. Only while still anonymous in both her name and in her quest could she pursue her strategy of identifying La Voce without him identifying her. A chase turned perilous when the hunter became the hunted.

\* \* \*

It was well into March before Alix was able to pay a visit to Esmée Archambault, who'd been escaping the winter at the Riviera. Despite the always-clamoring piles of work, Alix left the office at eight o'clock and walked north and west toward Parc Monceau, shivering in the minus sixteen-degree cold, wishing coal would miraculously appear in her *pension* in a large enough quantity to warm her permanently frozen hands.

At Esmée's apartment, which was splendidly located overlooking the park, Alix knocked on the door, cursing as she heard the unmistakable sounds of conversation, music, and mirth. Before she could hurry away, the door opened and a maid asked for her name.

"Could you tell Esmée that Alix St. Pierre needs five minutes of her time?"

"I'll take you in to dinner," the maid said.

"No." Alix was vehement. She was wearing her green tweed trousers, not dinner-party attire. And she wasn't sure how Esmée would respond, given they hadn't seen one another for years. "I'll wait in the hall."

The maid set off, returning a moment later with the words, "A place is being set for you."

Alix almost swore aloud. She hadn't given herself a glance when she left the office and had no doubt her nose was bright red with cold and that to the guests from Esmée's high-born circle, she'd look like a cross between Rudolph the reindeer and a bohemian nonconformist. She wasn't just wearing trousers; she'd paired them with a leopard-print blouse made from an offcut of fabric for her by Dior's chief tailor, Pierre Cardin. Everyone else would be wearing gowns it would take Alix a year to afford, and then only if she ate nothing and lived on the streets.

The doors of the dining room opened and a welcome gust of heat wrapped around her.

"Alix St. Pierre!" a woman declared in a stagey voice. "It's been too long."

Esmée Archambault, who'd been imprisoned and interrogated and narrowly avoided deportation to a concentration camp in late July 1944, descended upon Alix in a flurry of kisses. In a low whisper, she said, "It's very good to see you."

Alix's eyes prickled as she hugged her tightly, this woman most knew as wealthy and indolent but who was actually a flame-bearer for the good that could come out of war. And she knew that her silence postwar was forgiven and that, between two women who'd worked so hard to save others, no absence would ever diminish affection.

"We've only just served main course so you'll be able to catch up," Esmée said, reverting back to her role as hostess and ushering Alix over to a chair beside, of all people, Anthony March.

This time Alix did swear.

*My friend Anthony says that when I was born . . .* Alix remembered Esmée telling her in the elevator. How could that Anthony possibly be Anthony March?

Esmée grinned. "I thought putting the two of you together would be fun." She squeezed Anthony's shoulder in a way that suggested intimacy before she returned to her seat on his other side.

* * *

Anthony almost swore too. This was *not* on the agenda for the evening. How the hell did Alix St. Pierre know Esmée?

Conversation resumed and knives and forks clattered once more as he watched Alix reach a little too eagerly for her champagne glass and schooled himself not to do the same. Because there was something hidden a long way beneath the shallow carapace he dressed himself in that made him hear her voice saying: *I'm smaller than you, and alone. You have the upper hand physically. So if you want revenge for Operation Lycaon, then do your best—or worst.*

She'd sounded angry—furious, in fact—rather than scared. And in that moment he'd felt more repugnant than all the monsters he'd met during the war. Because months ago, when he'd found out that a woman named Alix St. Pierre had sent him the piece of intelligence that had made him send his team out on a fatal reconnaissance expedition into the Alps, he *had* wanted to tear her head off her shoulders with his bare hands. But standing in her cheap and tiny room as she invited him to do just that, he knew he never could—and that perhaps it made him human after all.

"I'm sorry," he said.

A look of complete surprise swept over her face. Then her lips quirked almost mischievously and she opened her green eyes very wide. "For what?" she asked and he knew she wanted him to grovel a little.

Which he probably deserved. He reached for his glass. "For trying to use you. And," he hesitated, swallowed champagne, and added, "for being a jerk."

"As you've confessed to some of your main faults, I suppose I'll have to forgive you." She held up her glass then seemed to think the better of it, peering inside. "Salt? Sugar? Shrapnel? What did you decide to poison me with in retaliation?"

He laughed before he realized what he was doing. At the same moment, Esmée reclaimed herself from the man on her other side and turned back to them. "Apologies are so old-fashioned," she said in her faux-hostess voice. "I prefer more novel ways of making amends. Such as, for example, if someone were to put a toad in your bed, you might then serve that someone a toad disguised as *poule* when next you dine with them."

He had no idea what that meant but Alix obviously did because she looked as if she wanted to spit her mouthful of chicken across the table—which was exactly how he'd felt about the coffee she'd made him. She swallowed with a shudder and said, "You wouldn't."

Esmée's glee was extravagant.

"Maybe I'll change seats with Esmée and then this conversation needn't happen over my head," Anthony said.

Esmée laid a placating hand on his arm. "Darling, no. Alix and I were at school together in Switzerland. She was there because—"

"Because of the fine company," Alix interrupted, shooting what seemed like a warning glance at Esmée, who shrugged and went on.

"There was an incident one evening with an amphibian in my blankets," Esmée explained. "Put there by one of the maids I was foolish enough to offend, but caught from the lake by Mademoiselle St. Pierre here."

"Your face," Alix chortled.

"I'm sure it was priceless," Esmée said, laughing too.

"But now you're the kind of friends who visit one another unannounced and while—" Anthony began.

Alix cut him off. "And while completely underdressed. Yes— and before you offer up any unsavory quips, I said *under*dressed, not undressed."

He laughed again and caught her trying not to smile too, strangely pleased when she was unsuccessful. Her smile was an action her whole face threw itself into so even her hair glowed redder, brighter. Which was a very unexpected thought.

Then Esmée added something still more unexpected. "Did you know, *mon cher*, that the identity papers for the pilots you had me hide in Monte Carlo came from Alix? She befriended a train driver who'd once been the school's stablehand and convinced him to make a secret compartment on the train that ran from Switzerland to Lyon, just big enough to hold identity papers. She even had him make a lever so that if the train were searched, he could trip the lever and the documents would be dumped in the boiler. She saved more than a few lives."

"Yes, I managed not to kill quite everyone." Alix's reply was more than a little sad. No, not sad—it was self-accusatory, as if she carried guilt like a lead ball in her chest too.

When Esmée next spoke, her voice was very low. "You know I love you," she said to him, slipping her fingers into his and squeezing tightly. "But I also love Alix. And I only love good people. I don't know what you were apologizing to Alix for, but I'm almost certain it was to do with you being too high-handed. And you," she turned to Alix, "being too stubbornly self-reliant. And also you both hurting too much."

The look on Alix's face was quite possibly an exact replica of the expression on his—disbelief that somehow Esmée, who he trusted beyond anything, also trusted this other person so much that she was basically cutting each of them open and saying, *Here, look inside.*

His eye caught Alix's. She reared back like a frightened colt as if she wanted nothing less than for him to see inside her. And he suddenly wished his apology had been more earnest. If he didn't already hate himself for making her think he might harm her that night in her *pension*, now he loathed himself because he understood that beneath the wise-cracking façade, she was more than a little wary of him.

*I would never do that*, he almost said. But Esmée was saying, "I think Alix wants to talk to me. We'll be back before dessert. You can entertain everyone."

Never in his life had he wanted so badly to gatecrash a tête-à-tête he wasn't invited to. Before tonight—before seeing Esmée and Alix together—he would have sat back with his champagne glass and been content to do the entertaining, confident Esmée would tell him later what she'd discussed. But the way Esmée was with Alix—not just close but intimate, like two people bound by a crypt of sorrow—made him doubt whether Esmée would tell him anything at all.

*  *  *

"Anthony can either be hard to love or much too easy to adore," Esmée said cryptically as Alix followed her into another room. She gratefully accepted the offer of brandy, even though it would put her one drink over her supposedly strict limit.

"He was on the mountain the night everyone died," Alix said, remembering the way he'd pressed his fingers into his shoulderblade at her *pension*, remembering the cable she'd received the morning after that terrible tragedy: Nine dead, including guide. One agent survived with gunshot wound to the right upper back. "Does he have what must be a nasty looking scar on his right shoulder blade?"

She realized what she was asking Esmée—*Have you seen Anthony March unclothed?*—and she downed a large mouthful of brandy. "Don't answer that—"

"He does," Esmée cut in crisply. "And I saw it on a beach and not in a bedroom. I didn't know..." She sat down opposite Alix and shook her head. "I didn't know he was caught up in all that too. We have an agreement, you see."

Alix held up a hand, not wanting to know about the kind of agreements Anthony made with women, but Esmée said, "An agreement not to talk about the war. I knew he was in Italy, but that's all." She sighed, then smiled a little. "It's very good to see you."

"You too. And I'm sorry about the toad," Alix said softly, as if that was somehow the cause of everything.

"I'm sorry about a lot more than the toad."

It was Alix's opening and she took it. "Do you still have contacts in England from the war? I need to find out whatever I can about Becky Gordon, *The Times* fashion editor. And maybe her godfather too. I know your Resistance circuit was sponsored by the British so I'm hoping—"

Esmée sank to her knees beside Alix. "It wasn't your fault. Just like I have to believe it wasn't my fault for arranging the meeting between you and that man in the first place. It was *his* fault, whoever he was."

"And that's just it," Alix said desolately. "Who is he? And how the hell do I find him? I have to find him, Esmée. Otherwise…" She swallowed the brandy. "I feel like I'll hate myself forever." She heard the break, like torn silk, in her voice.

Esmée circled gentle fingers around her arm. "*Chérie*, there are too many blameless women who cannot forgive themselves for the things war did to them. Let me make some inquiries from whoever is left of my network. It's the least I can do to make amends for introducing you to someone who only wanted to betray you. And Alix…"

Esmée's voice was the one splintering now. "Be careful. He killed at least nine people. Most likely more. I don't want…" Another crack. "I don't want to lose you to him too."

Alix threw her arms around her friend and their embrace was both unendurable and necessary, reminding Alix of how beautiful life could be and also how agonizing it was. Because if your most cherished friends could make you weep, then what wretchedness could your enemies wreak upon you?

# FOURTEEN

I predict trouble in your future," Frank said to Anthony at two in the morning in the bar at the Ritz.

Anthony swiveled his head in the direction of Frank's gaze and saw Esmée charging toward him. "I think that means it's goodnight," he said to Frank, hearing how gritty his voice sounded, as if he'd swallowed cigarettes rather than just smoked too many of them.

"Can you send about a dozen bottles of mineral water up to Monsieur March's suite," Esmée said to Frank. To Anthony she said, "I've seen a lot over the years but I've never seen a vermouth strong enough or a woman intoxicating enough to drown anyone's sorrows."

"Ain't that the truth," Frank said as Anthony followed Esmée to the elevator.

Once the doors closed, he said to her, "I've had exactly three vermouths and zero women. Tonight, I've done nothing that would chase my reputation deeper into the gutter than it already is. I couldn't sleep, that's all."

"Have you even tried? Or do you ordinarily climb out of bed at this hour wearing trousers, tie, and jacket?" Then she smiled. "Actually, you're always so impeccably dressed, it wouldn't surprise me if you did."

He laughed, glad she'd relaxed and hating to think he was the cause of her irritation. In his suite he glanced at the vermouth bottle but refrained, watching her pace for a moment before she said, "Becky Gordon is using her mother's maiden name."

He sat down in the chair behind his desk and couldn't stop the lift of his hand to his shoulder blade, or the accompanying grimace.

Esmée sent him one of her imperious glares. "I told you to go and see my doctor about that. It certainly won't be helping the insomnia."

"No," he agreed. "Nightmares, and having my shoulder blasted open by a machine gun, are proving to be pains more tyrannical even than you."

The imperiousness shifted from her eyes to her voice. "As I'm the only person who ever tries to order you around, I have to do it twice as forcefully. And I don't think my news is going to help your shoulder or your sleep. Becky's name is actually Rebecca Fitzgibbons. Her brother Francis Fitzgibbons died in Italy on April tenth, 1945."

His head shot up. "That's the same day—" He cut himself off. They didn't talk about the war. It was their solemn pledge.

"The same day Alix's operation went wrong and a whole lot of people were slaughtered?" she asked quietly.

He stood up and came around to the front of his desk where he could see her face better. If she was breaking her oath and bringing up the war, there must be a damn good reason. Here by the lamp, her eyes were so dark they reminded him of what Anjelica had said about Alix's eyes—moonless—and he wanted to reach back into 1944 and take Esmée out of Paris so she would never be captured and tortured by goddamn Nazis.

He shrugged out of his jacket and tossed it onto the desk. "Come here," he said and she really must have been feeling the past stalking into the present because she let him embrace her, seemed to need it in fact, holding on as if she might fall out of now and back too far in time if she didn't.

"You know," he said after a moment, "you might just be the only woman intoxicating enough to chase away all troubles. In fact,

I remember I once made you promise to marry me if we were both still single at thirty. Which is not that far away for me."

He heard her laugh, which was his intent, and she pulled back a little, smiling and wiping her eyes. "You know I love you too much to ever want to marry you."

He smiled and kissed her forehead. "Same."

She drew away, said a quick, "Thanks," and nodded as if yes, she was steady enough now to resume the conversation.

So he told her what he thought. "The Brits sent one SOE agent up the mountain with my team that day. I only knew him by his code name but I'm betting his real name was Francis Fitzgibbons."

"And that Becky wants revenge."

"Jesus, *she* should have been the SOE agent," Anthony said, shaking his head. "She's the best damn actress I've come across in a long time. I'm guessing she thinks Alix St. Pierre is to blame for her brother's death. But how did she find out that Alix was involved?"

Esmée was blunt. "I don't know how you found out but I'd say you used similar techniques. My British contact told me that her godfather, who's equally furious and bent on revenge, bullied enough people into telling him the operation his godson died in was conceived in Switzerland. Most people with business in Europe during the war had an inkling Allen Dulles wasn't in Bern to ski. You find out that Switzerland is the link, then you find Dulles. And from him, so long as you know the right people, it's just a short hop to his so-called—"

"Secretary," Anthony finished. "Alix St. Pierre." He expelled a breath. "Half of Paris is chasing her."

"And you should be the one to tell her that."

"I don't think she'll want to hear that news from someone she despises."

Esmée's tone was implacable. "Alix is..." She hesitated and Anthony waited, curious to know how that sentence would end. Alix was what? Damn smart. And damn beautiful. But what else?

Then Esmée shook her head. "I told you I wouldn't talk about her with you, and I'm not going to."

He turned around and leaned his palms on the desk, needing to think. Since Alix had thrown him out of her *pension*, he'd spent all his time trying very hard to convince himself that what had happened in Italy was unfixable—and that he most likely was too. But he'd also thought about Alix from time to time, especially in the last month since Esmée's dinner party when he'd seen many different facets of her: the woman who played improbable practical jokes on Queen Esmée, of all people; the woman who'd done a hell of a lot of things during the war that he'd relied on and benefitted from.

His shoulder fired another round of pain into his bones. He swore, reached up and undid his tie, scrunched it into a ball and tossed it onto a chair. It made absolutely nothing feel better.

Alix St. Pierre, he was now certain, had not been the one who screwed up Operation Lycaon so disastrously. She hadn't lazily sent on half-assed and unverified information from an unscreened inform-ant, like he'd first thought. No—right now he'd bet it was the per-son she'd received that information from who'd played them all. And if Anthony had been able to ride roughshod over enough people to find out the name of Dulles's secretary, and Becky's godfather had as well, then wasn't it only a matter of time before that person hunted Alix down too?

Leaving it to Esmée to tell Alix about Becky's brother was pigeon-hearted. "I'll go see her tomorrow," he said.

Esmée beamed and kissed his cheeks, and told him to go to bed and imagine he was lying on the beach at her house on the Riviera. And God he was tired. Maybe tonight it would be that simple. Even the throb in his shoulder had eased a little, because maybe he and Alix St. Pierre were chasing the same thing. And maybe it'd be a damn sight easier if they chased it together.

\* \* \*

Alix frowned as she read Becky's latest piece in *The Times* decrying Dior's extravagant fashions that would send everyone straight to the devil. She was certain Becky didn't just think women should be perfectly happy in much-mended skirts that kept them in their place—dowdy and dreamless—but that Becky still wanted to ruin Alix. Unfortunately, there were others who agreed with Becky's views about Dior's offensive profligacy with silk, and Becky was expertly inflaming their outrage. Alix would need to act soon—but goddammit, she needed to know more about Becky first.

She'd stopped tailing her as it had proven to be a waste of time. Frank was eavesdropping on Becky's conversations at the bar, but he'd heard nothing that gave any hint as to what her business with Alix was. Alix had also spent weekends searching through old newspapers at the Bibliothèque nationale for information about Becky's family and her godfather, as well as the names from Frank's list, but that was proving to be a tactic that would take far too long.

Somehow it was summer and she'd achieved nothing in her search for La Voce or for clues about Becky's motivation, whereas the work at Dior had increased a thousandfold. She needed a new strategy for the first two assignments, but right now she had back-to-back photo shoots to attend and then had to rush the dresses to the Ritz because Daisy Fellowes had summoned Suzanne and the same gowns to her suite that afternoon. And nobody refused Daisy Fellowes.

She jotted a note to Becky, thanking her for the publicity, and hoping to goad her into something. Then she had the mannequins and dresses loaded into a van, spent a couple of hours at the Seine with photographer Willy Maywald and Carmel Snow, before heading to Montmartre, where Corolle's stupendous skirt would rival even the cupola of the Sacré-Coeur.

The dressing room for this shoot was a bar on Rue Lepic near the historic Moulin. There was an unnatural degree of noise and activity rebounding off the cobblestones, but they *were* in Montmartre. Alix couldn't expect the cancan queen of Paris to be subdued, even for Dior.

Soon Tania had Corolle swinging like a jazz club as she paraded along the street, past posters for Vivien Leigh's new film, the dress outshining even Leigh's doe eyes. A shout echoed from behind, then from nowhere, a woman launched herself at Tania, screaming, "*Putain!*"

Another woman hurtled over and grabbed Corolle, a stream of invective spewing forth denouncing Dior, his profligacy, and his extreme offensiveness in this postwar time. They tore and they tugged and they attacked Tania's dress like lions mauling prey.

"Stop it," Alix shouted, throwing herself into the fray, trying to cover Tania's semi-nakedness and earning an elbow to the head and the decapitation of her hat. But fury kept her fighting. Because newspaper photographers had arrived and they weren't helping Tania, but taking pictures of her clothes being ripped off as two women blamed one girl for everything that wasn't her fault.

One of the women wrenched Tania's skirt so hard it came clean away. She knocked into Alix, throwing her so entirely off-balance that she fell to the ground, hitting her head on the edge of the pavement. She swore as pain rattled her teeth and spasmed into her stomach.

She looked up once to make sure Tania was being escorted into the bar, that someone else was dragging away the two incensed ladies, and then she let herself close her eyes and exhale so she wouldn't be sick.

*Merde.* She'd have a headache for at least a couple of days, and she hadn't even the satisfaction of too many French 75s in the earning of it.

"Are you all right?" A male voice spoke in her ear and she felt someone push a hanky into her hand.

She opened her eyes and realized she must have cracked her head worse than she'd thought. She was hallucinating Anthony March.

* * *

The woman on the pavement was an Alix St. Pierre with blanched cheeks, bereft of snappy rejoinders. "Are you real?" she asked him.

"Probably more real than you'd like," he conceded. He crouched beside her. "Lean against the wall."

For once in her life, she didn't argue. Her head really must hurt like hell.

"What *was* that?" she asked weakly. "And why are you here?"

"That was a protest by the few women in Paris who prefer their dresses to look more like dead blooms than fresh roses. There was a tip-off that something was happening in Montmartre. I'm guessing that's why those fellows are here too." He pointed to the newspaper photographers. "Can I get you an over-sugared coffee to help rouse you back into fighting spirits, or will a glass of water do?"

She smiled, then winced. "Ouch. No smiling. Maybe not even any talking."

"I don't know how you'll survive," he said drily and was rewarded with another smile, followed by the same wince.

"Stop trying to cheer me up," she said, voice a touch stronger now. "You've managed extreme seriousness in every other encounter we've had so surely you can manage it now. Give me a hand to stand up."

There was an obstinacy to her words that had him, despite his misgivings, pulling her up.

The minute she was on her feet, she looked like she was about to be sick. He was surprised she hadn't been ill already after that blow. Alix St. Pierre was a tiny woman in silk but she was obviously a lot tougher than she looked. He took the hanky from her and dabbed her temple. "You've got blood in your hair."

He saw her brace and close her eyes again and wasn't ready for her to blink them open. She caught him in the act of studying her face. Five strange and silent seconds passed by, one of his hands under her chin, his fingers against her skin able to sense the movement of her blood in a way that was deeply intimate.

He stepped away. "It's not so bad. You could almost pretend you slipped with your lipstick."

"That makes me sound like I'm in my *coupes*," she quipped, more like herself. She ran a hand over her rumpled dress. "I need to check on Tania and then I have to get to the Ritz. Daisy Fellowes is waiting."

"With a head injury?"

"It's an overzealous application of *maquillage*, remember?"

He laughed. How did she do that every time? Find the humor in a situation and make it sparkle. A thought pressed in—some of his men in Italy wouldn't have treated a battered head with quite so much éclat.

"Thank you for your help," she said, turning to make her careful way inside.

There was nothing for it but to follow her into the bar where the mannequin was weeping, people wielding unidentifiable cosmetic items were wailing, and Alix was pressing a hand to her brow against the noise. He stepped back onto the street, hailed a cab, and ushered the mannequin outside in the hopes of reducing the commotion by a few decibels.

He returned to the bar shaking his head in bemusement. If anyone had told him he'd be cleaning up blood and mannequins today, he'd have thought *they* were in their *coupes*. He leaned against the doorframe, watching blood trickle down Alix's face, and said, "You need to sit down for at least five minutes with a handkerchief and preferably ice on your head."

She looked up as if she'd forgotten he was there, swiped her fingers over her brow and they came away smeared with red. She hastily dropped the torn dress she was holding—which couldn't possibly be any more ruined even if it was covered in Alix's blood—opened her purse and rummaged around, finding nothing to clean herself up with.

Anthony crossed the room, took her by the shoulders and, not forcefully but insistently, pushed her into a chair. "Tell me what you need done and I'll do it so the rumor doesn't go around that I hurt your head and then abandoned you, bleeding and senseless, in Montmartre with hundreds—thousands?—of dollars worth of couture at your feet, just waiting to be robbed."

She didn't argue. She accepted his hanky once more, pressed it to her brow, and started to explain how to cajole one of the suits into a crate.

"I don't even know what a peplum is," he said with a wry smile, but doing his best to avoid catching the jacket's flare in the lid.

She managed a small laugh, then unexpectedly bent down to retrieve the crate at the same time as he was lifting it. She received a thump on the other side of her head and she swore, very loudly and very profanely, in Italian.

"You didn't learn that at Maison Christian Dior," Anthony said, trying to hide his smile at this woman who breezed through head injuries and swore more colorfully than any man he'd worked with during the war. "Now you have a dent on the other side too."

At which point she collapsed with laughter. "This is not how my day was supposed to turn out," she spluttered.

"Come on," he said, deciding he might as well just enjoy the ride he seemed to have stepped onto. "I'll get you and your peplums to Daisy Fellowes's suite—it's on the same floor as mine—without any further injury, I promise."

And because Alix was exactly the person he'd come looking for that day, he added, "After that, let's go to Brasserie Lipp for dinner."

And she said, "Okay."

# FIFTEEN

*La soupe à l'oignon, le cassoulet, et puis la tarte au chocolat, s'il vous plaît."* Alix handed the menu back to the waiter with a snap.

Anthony stared at her as if she'd just ordered worms. "That's a lot of food."

"I'll pay for it," she said testily. Although, she thought now as reason overtook hunger, all that food in a place like this was going to cost her two weeks wages.

Before she could summon the waiter back and rein in her order, Anthony shook his head exasperatedly. "I don't give a damn how much your dinner costs. I just didn't pick you as someone who ate," he said, eyeing her figure, which was, she had to admit, shown off to its best advantage in another of *le patron*'s day dresses—a deep green this time, a color so similar to her eyes that Dior had smiled over the bolt of fabric and said, *Everyone will think I'm a churl if I don't make you a dress with this.* Thus Alix's sparse wardrobe had filled out a little more.

"I tend toward excess," she said, lighting a cigarette. "But only one indulgence at a time. French 75s one night, cassoulet the next, silk on another—although tonight I seem to have a decent quantity of that too. And knocks to the head," she quipped, sipping water, which she planned to stick to.

Anthony smiled and his face relaxed; even his eyes allowed the merest shimmer of lamplight to break in, enough that she could see they were an uncommon color, so dark it was easy to think they were brown. But they were actually the deepest possible blue before it tipped into black, the same hue as her Chérie dress.

"Does it still hurt?" she asked, indicating Anthony's shoulder, trying out his tactic of deft conversational segues.

He started and she saw him lift a hand as if he were going to press his fingers into his back, just as he'd done in her *pension*. He caught himself and shifted his wineglass back and forth instead before saying, "You were Bisous."

She nodded.

"Given your already rock-bottom opinion of me, it won't surprise you to know I thought Bisous was a man. A young blowhard with a bad sense of humor."

"And I thought Leone, who I assume you were, was a young blowhard with an inflated sense of ego." She grinned and he laughed and Alix decided she quite liked the sound. It was a bit like Dior's smile— rare, but strangely satisfying when witnessed.

"After some of our encounters here in Paris, you're probably convinced that you were about right," he said.

Now she was the one laughing. "I'm willing to change my mind." Esmée and Frank had both vouched for him. He could have left her bleeding on the sidewalk today. And in Italy, as Leone, he'd helped her.

Which was perhaps what made him ask, "Cassoulet or confessions first?"

Alix's head still ached and she was starving. "Cassoulet. Otherwise I might eat your confession."

Another laugh. "I can see why they had you in OSS. You can be quite disarming when you try."

"I'm not even trying yet," she said with a smile.

He gave his head a wry shake. "Maybe you do have concussion. After our encounter in your *pension*, I didn't think I'd be laughing with you over dinner just a few months later."

Alix stubbed out her cigarette. "After the cassoulet, remember? But what will we find to talk about until then? Not dresses, obviously." And just saying the word *dresses* made her realize something she should have thought of earlier, but for her headache.

"If there were photographers there," she said, "then there are photos of poor Tania having her dress torn off, photos that will be published somewhere tomorrow. Damn," she said at the same moment the waiter placed two bowls of soup on the table. She looked regretfully at it. "I have to tell *le patron* what happened."

"Eat the soup," Anthony said. "I'll use the telephone here to see if I can find out who the photographers were. Then you can call Dior with all the information, not half of it. And you can still have your cassoulet—and we can still talk."

"Yet another favor on the already overfull pile."

"Maybe you will have to pay for your dinner after all."

The surprise of laughing yet again. Maybe this dinner would be more fun than she'd thought. "Touché. I won't mention favors anymore. But..." She hesitated, pensive now. "The women this morning. What they did to Tania. It reminded me of..."

She looked up from her soup. Anthony was waiting for her to continue.

"It reminded me of *les femmes tondues*—the women accused of being mattresses for the Germans." She swirled soup around with her spoon, intending to stop, but more words escaped. "The ones stripped and shaved and paraded for all to see," she went on. "The women who'd needed food, or who had children to protect, or who, even if they had said no, wouldn't have been listened to. The newspapers will print Tania's picture the same way they printed pictures of women being spat on right alongside photographs of heroic GIs standing next to their shining tanks. Nobody ever printed a picture of Pig Alley— did you know that was what the women called Rue Pigalle?"

She didn't wait for him to reply. "Just like nobody ever published a photograph of the ten thousand American soldiers a day the French prostitutes had to service. Why shouldn't Tania wear a dress that flatters her figure? She's being vilified for the kind of behavior that doesn't even come close to what a man can not only get away with, but be praised for. Women are blamed for everything—and that's something that never changes."

Her voice died out as she realized how vehemently she was talking about things nobody was supposed to speak about—and certainly not with someone she hardly knew.

"I..." Anthony began, looking uncertain for the first time ever, as if he'd never contemplated any of this—and why would he?

Thankfully the waiter interrupted again, clearing away the soup bowls and placing the cassoulet in front of them, which Alix turned to in order to escape the awkwardness. "Cassoulet's here," she said crisply. "So let's start with how you knew I was Bobby's fiancée."

Anthony leaned his elbows on the table and rested his chin on the backs of his hands. "At the Ritz one night in early December, I heard a couple of editors talking about an Alix St. Pierre who was coming to Paris. The name made me pause but I told myself there must be another lady out there with an extravagant name who'd be older or plainer or somehow not the same one Bobby had spoken about. Then you walked into the Ritz that night in trousers and a red blouse and I knew it was you. Bobby liked to say that you were beautiful, but not in the way you're meant to be beautiful. He said you were like the sun: too dazzling—and dangerous up close. I said to him, 'Isn't that going to make married life difficult?' and he told me what you'd said: the two of you would never get married."

Anthony reached for a cigarette.

She read the stalling implied by the gesture. "What? Tell me."

He sighed. "You want to know what I think about Bobby? Maybe he thought you weren't going to get married because he carried a picture with him of someone who definitely wasn't you."

It took a moment for that to sink in. "Jesus," she said, because it hurt a little—that they'd both kept secrets. That they hadn't had the chance to just be honest.

She picked up her fork, seeking solace in the cassoulet. "Go on," she said flatly.

"Bobby thought you were on the cable desk in London," Anthony continued.

"But he didn't know I was OSS."

"He did."

The jolt this time was such that she managed to spill water on her dress. Perhaps the fact that she couldn't tell Bobby what she was doing had made him suspicious. It couldn't have been Lillie who'd told him because then he would have known not just that Alix was in Switzerland, but her address and bra size, given how profligate Lillie was with information.

"*Merde*," she swore as she swiped her napkin over the water. "I can't believe that after calling *you* a disappointment, here I am finding out that I may have been cheated on, that my ex-fiancé is a liar, and that I have the filthiest mouth in Paris. And where the hell is my chocolate tart when I need it?"

Anthony laughed, more than she'd ever seen him, and the sound was a rich and resonant *marron*, the same color as the tart she was hoping for.

"Let's take it with us," he said, standing. "I hate sitting still for so long."

Alix indicated the brasserie. "This isn't a street vendor with chestnut cones at the ready."

"I'll buy the plate and fork then. And if you put any money on the table," he added when she opened her purse, "I'm going to knock you on the back of the head to match the two bumps at the front. I invited you. I'm paying. You can keep the plate. Judging by the lack of crockery at your *pension*, you need it."

She was still laughing when she went to find the bathroom.

* * *

True to his word, Anthony was waiting out front with a plate of chocolate tart. "Heaven," she said, her mouth watering.

His lips quirked into a smile. "If you ever look at a man the way you're looking at this tart, you're going to be in trouble."

"I've never met anyone as delicious as this looks," she said. "Hand it over."

They walked in silence, Anthony with hands in pockets, all of Alix's senses alert to voices and footsteps and the shadows in side streets. She'd heard nothing at Brasserie Lipp to give her cause for alarm but that didn't mean it was time to relax.

"No one's following us," Anthony said. "I'm certain. I can't remember what it's like to walk down a street without all my faculties operating at one thousand percent. I kind of miss just strolling. Wish I'd done it more."

She glanced up at him and startled herself with the thought—perhaps Anthony was as handsome as everyone said. His perennially bored and arrogant expression had fallen away and he was, in that instant, a man with the kind of jawline that issued invitations to hands and lips.

*Mon Dieu.* She must have injured her head more than she'd realized.

She turned abruptly into Rue Dauphine. "Let's go up here." Walking meant there was nothing but the two of them and their words. She needed backdrop and noise and—the thought was like a whoosh of Alix rushing into the body she'd left behind—a little bit of fun.

He followed her to a building with the word *Tabou* above the portal. The faintest sound of jazz leaked from under the door.

"We're going in there?" Anthony said doubtfully, which was reasonable given the unprepossessing façade.

"You might have to lose the jacket and tie. There's a cloakroom upstairs."

"And by lose, you mean literally? It looks like thieves' paradise."

She laughed. "Oh, come on. You have to leave the Ritz occasionally. And we'd never have been able to go to a place like this during the war. There are no exits whatsoever and thus no means of escape."

"You're making it sound so appealing. And I'm a newspaper editor, remember? Some of the places I end up in make this look like a palace."

"Well, this is a troglodyte club, and I guess that's about all you need to know."

She heard him laugh as she pushed open the door and they were confronted with both a descending staircase that gave new meaning to the word *precarious* and the jubilant blast of a saxophone. "Ready?"

"It's not going to matter if I say no, is it?" But he smiled and she was glad it was dark because she had a feeling that if she could see him a little better, it might be the kind of smile that started wildfires burning.

They made it down the stairs alive and then they were in a cellar where the air was white with smoke, the music hypnotic, and dancers' limbs swayed perilously close to whiskey glasses on tables as well as to the patrons sitting at those tables. But somehow everyone had impeccable timing, lifting the glass to their mouth at the exact moment a hand got too close, turning their head to laugh whenever a body dipped too proximately in an extravagant swoop.

"Over there," Alix said, spotting a tiny table for two that had just been vacated at the opposite end to the band.

It was necessary to slide her hand into Anthony's to lead the way through the occasional gaps in the crush of people. She felt his fingers wrap over hers, her palm half the size of his but somehow a perfect fit—like the sliver of gin essential for the tonic. And with the same delicious kick.

She let go of his hand the instant they reached the table.

"It survived," she said, turning her attention to the chocolate tart—which was also delicious and, on balance, much less likely to be damaging to her health.

With a mouthful of bitter chocolate on her tongue, and a cascade of notes slipping like satin from the trumpet, she relaxed. Here, where everything around them was shameless and carefree, she could perhaps whisper her own cares and shame into the darkness where they would sound no echo.

Anthony unknotted his tie, slipped off his jacket, rolled his sleeves, and ducked to avoid a dancer's arm, just managing to avoid being beheaded, which was quite a feat given how tall he was. "How did you find this place?" he asked as a couple nearby took their dance off the floor and up the curved wall of the cellar.

"Suzanne told me about it. Her nighttime activities have always been more outrageous than mine." She grinned. "That statement could be interpreted in so many incorrect ways."

He laughed more than she'd ever seen him. "I'll try not to decode it then. But if we're having the kind of conversation that requires this much of a mise-en-scène, I might get a vermouth. Come and look for me if I'm not back in half an hour. Water?"

She nodded.

When he returned he lit a cigarette, then very unexpectedly passed it across to her. It reminded her painfully of how she and Chiara used to share cigarettes, and made her frown at the lit tip of a gesture she'd always equated with close friendship.

"I'm not going to ask you a question. I've asked too many before and said too little," he told her. "You need to know it was my team, men I was in charge of, who died in Operation Lycaon. I stupidly let Bobby take the lead because he'd been asking for weeks and I'd promised he could take charge of the next one. But with Lycaon..." Anthony reached out a hand for the cigarette and she passed it back to him.

"I said no," he continued. "I don't know whether your gut works like mine—it knows more than logic says it should. When I told Bobby I was going to lead Lycaon, he thought I was doubting him. And I was about to be transferred to France and I needed to get my team ready to work without me. So... I let him. But I was the one who gave the order to go ahead. Which makes me as responsible as anyone for those deaths. It was very convenient for me to try to shift the blame onto you, firstly because it took it off me and secondly because..."

He picked up his lighter and drummed it on the table, exhaled smoke and said, "Back when I found out a woman had sent us that intelligence, I was furious. I grew up being taught that women had no smarts at all. Then I met you and, as a very smart woman once said, you're at least as intelligent as I am."

A surprised bubble of a laugh escaped her. And she remembered what it had been like with Matteo—they'd shared both the most awful and beautiful things: spectacular orbs of light within the darkness. It was why some journeys were better not taken alone; sometimes you needed another person to help you find the single star hidden in the storm.

The drummer was making a determined effort to be heard on the other side of the Atlantic so Alix shifted her chair a little closer to Anthony's—although if she moved any closer, she'd be sitting in his lap. *Merde.* She touched a finger to her temple. What was the cure for concussion? Talking.

"A Nazi in the Italian command gave me the information we used to plan Operation Lycaon," she said. "He must have worked with Karl Wolff, given everything he knew. I never saw his face, and I don't know his name. But he was *my* informant. Which makes me responsible. If I'd never..."

She shook her head. The *If I'd nevers* were endless. Never met with La Voce. Never asked him for anything. Never got too close to Matteo and Chiara. Never needed to save them. She swallowed some water, wishing it was Anthony's vermouth.

"The only person I blame and want to find now is your informant," Anthony told her. "You have the advantage of knowing him. And as a newspaper editor, I have the advantage of access to documents and people and resources. I asked you to dinner because as partners, we might find him a hell of a lot quicker. What do you say?"

\* \* \*

Alix took the Gauloise from him, and her gaze as well, training it fiercely on the cigarette. But he could still see that her eyes were very wide and very green and it was like looking into a mirror. Reflected there was all the guilt and disbelief that he'd somehow been made into a person he'd never wanted to be.

He almost put out a hand to touch her wrist. But he remembered Esmée—how, after the war and being imprisoned by Nazis, touch was something she didn't like to receive uninvited, and then only from a select few. And he saw in Alix that same tendency to rear away, recognized a person whose trust had been broken so violently that all she had left were tiny, glittering shards, too precious to give away to someone like him just because he'd asked to be her partner.

So he said, "Let me tell you what happened on the mountain that night."

"All right," she said, very quietly.

How to explain the strange exhilaration that took hold before a mission—of knowing you were about to do something that could kill you, of fear mixing with adrenaline and expressing itself in some kind of tic. Bobby had always jogged his knee up and down on the plane in an irritating, rhythmic shudder; one of the other men had talked unstoppably about horses. Anthony had always smoked and gone over the plan in his head again and again.

"The edginess that night was like...I don't know—a snowstorm coming in," he said at last. "It's why every mission needs a good leader—someone who knows how to keep everyone on such high alert that the pores on their goddamn toes can sense danger, but not so keyed up that it becomes a hazard. That night I was thinking I was going to have to step in and take charge—somehow without undermining Bobby. Then we found the guide—Bacio, but I guess you already know that—and he had everyone steadied within just a few minutes."

He saw Alix blink for a second too long. Something about that had rattled her. She stared out into the club, eyes emptying of green and blending into the smoke-filled air around them. He tried to ease his voice into the same tone that had let a little slack into the tight-strung nerves of his men on missions past. "Bobby and Bacio took the lead together."

That made her close her eyes completely. Then they flew open as if she'd remembered she was with a man she was trying to trust but wasn't yet able to.

He took out the last cigarette, lit it and said, "Here."

She inhaled gratefully. "Thanks."

That *thanks* made him hope she was considering giving him one of those little shards of her trust. So he kept talking, here in this crazy cellar club with jazz music slipping into all the tiny gaps between bodies, the two of them sitting so close he could feel the warmth of her leg a quarter inch from his, the gentleness of her exhale drifting over his cheek.

"I was in the back," he said, reprising the story. "Where Bobby put me. And I let him because you don't want your boss breathing down your neck when you're leading your first mission. It had started to snow; it was beautiful actually. You know how sometimes when you're doing something ugly, you see glimpses of the most sublime damn things?"

She nodded, the green easing back into her eyes, lips curving around the cigarette before she passed it back to him.

"That was the last moment of beauty, though," he said, drawing on the cigarette, then cutting away and asking, "Did you go to Italy? I'm guessing you didn't, that OSS didn't let women take any active assignments."

"I did. Twice. Each time worse than before," was all she said and it gave him the nerve to go on. If she'd faced Italy, then so too could he face it in the retelling.

"Nobody heard anything," he said, hand tightening on the cigarette that was all but smoked out. "Then I felt something in the air, like a different scent maybe. At the same time, Bacio turned around and I felt my feet push me forward, needing to get to the front to knock Bobby out of the goddamn way of whatever it was, but the whole world exploded. Because I'd already started to move, I had momentum enough to throw myself into a snowdrift at the same time as something ripped through my shoulder. I don't know if I can describe that kind of pain. It's like setting fire to your goddamn heart."

It was his turn to glare ferociously at the table, then pick up the cigarette packet, forgetting they'd run out. He tapped it on the table and said brusquely, "God, I need a cigarette."

"I think we've smoked at least a week's worth tonight," she said gently. "You can stop if you want to. I've never been more convinced that you're nothing like a young blowhard with an inflated sense of ego."

He lifted his eyes up to meet hers. He'd never told anyone this, never wanted to even remember it, but telling her was like cutting away a little of the evil that had attached itself to him that night.

"The Nazis were laughing, Alix," he said grimly. "Laughing over the dead bodies of my teammates. I've never wanted to kill anyone but I wanted to murder all of them that night. Except I had maybe ten seconds of consciousness before everything went black. Being unconscious saved my life—they thought I was dead. But those few seconds awake just about killed me because what kind of people laugh while they murder?"

"I'm sorry," she whispered, touching a very quick and gentle finger onto the back of his hand.

That tiny moment of empathy hurt worst of all and he spoke to get away from it. "When I woke up," he said flatly, "there was only silence. That was worse than the laughter because it meant everyone was dead. I crawled down that damn mountain and passed out maybe a dozen times, but I made it back to the rendezvous point four days later with my shoulder torn to shreds because nobody should die to the sound of a Nazi's taunts. For all the hours it took me to get to the bottom of the mountain, I had integrity. But I lost it over these last two years. Now I want it back. Which means I need to look him in the eye because... Wouldn't it be nice to take all that blame off our own shoulders and throw it at his feet instead?"

"Yes," she said, voice as vehement as his. "It would."

They were both very still, and he could almost feel her eyes reading in his all the things he hadn't said. The rank nausea of knowing you'd been shot but not how badly, and that maybe with every step you took you were killing yourself. The sight of those bodies—men he'd trained and calmed and cajoled, men who'd told him in frightened moments about the hidden things caught deep in their souls. How much blood there was, the snow a furious ocean of red.

"We can be partners," she said then. "Let's find him together. But that means we're equals. I'm not weak or stupid. If you treat me like I am, I won't just put too much sugar in your coffee or a toad in your bed." She smiled a little, as if she knew they both needed levity right now. "I don't know what I'll do, but based on what I've been told over the last couple of years, I'm an expert at irritating men."

He laughed, not just at her words but at how incongruous they were as the saxophone let loose another husky line of notes that had everyone in the club focusing their gyrations ever more intently on their partners. "Anyone looking at us right now would think I was about to kiss you and instead you're threatening me."

It was clearly the wrong thing to say. She folded her arms and glared at him. "We are definitely not partners of the kissing kind. I'm not your type."

His glare matched hers. "Equals means you not treating me like I am my reputation and that my only interests are women and spending my inheritance on parties and new suits."

"I suppose that's fair. I promise I will never again mention how incomparably *à la mode* your suits are." Then she grinned, brilliantly and beguilingly, and the sultry air in the club blazed through him, as did the tantalizing scent of her perfume, leaving behind an urgent need for more.

He pushed his chair away. No wonder she treated him like he was only interested in women.

"Becky Gordon's brother was one of the men killed that night," he told her, effectively dousing every unbidden sensation in his body.

"So I have both a Nazi and an avenging sister to deal with," she said, voice low. Then she added, her smile gentle and very beautiful now, "You could have just told me that at the outset, rather than sharing everything else. It's the kind of information that would have made me agree to be your partner anyway."

"I know. But I wanted you to trust me, not just agree because you thought I was useful."

# SIXTEEN

A sharp rapping woke Anthony after only—he opened one eye and tried to read the clock—ten minutes sleep. *Jesus.* His eye closed but the knocking continued.

He swore again, rubbed his hand over his face, located his pajama pants, pulled them on, yelled, "I'm coming!" and decided he would kill whoever was on the other side of the door. He wrenched it open and someone scented very appealingly breezed in, strode over to the drapes and flung them open, letting in too much light.

"What the hell are you doing here?" Anthony asked, staring in disbelief at Alix St. Goddamn Pierre.

"This is going to have to be HQ," she said, waving her arm to indicate the living room of his suite. "There's nowhere else private enough or large enough. We need to put down everything we know—I've been up since five making sure my notes are legible so you can look over them before you go to Germany."

Last night they'd thrown ideas back and forth about their next steps and had decided, given he could get access to the transcripts from the Nuremberg Trials, that he should go to Germany and bring back a mimeograph of the transcripts relating to Wolff and Italy. "Someone must have known his name, and maybe they mentioned it at the trial," he'd reasoned. And Alix said maybe they'd find a name in those transcripts that matched a list Frank had given her.

But right now she was hefting a painting of an eighteenth century maiden off the wall and setting it on the floor. "She won't mind resting her smile while I use the wall space," he heard her say.

"I need coffee." His voice sounded bleary, as if he'd been up drinking—or worse—all night.

"It's on its way up."

"It's on its way up?" Incredulity sounded in each word. "Feel free to make yourself at home. Hopefully you won't mind waiting until I've drunk my coffee before I can make either civil or intelligent conversation."

As soon as he said it, he wanted to take it back because he was being a jerk again. But he'd had no sleep, and now that Alix was standing in his suite wearing an incredibly sexy leopard-print dress, he thought maybe he'd been dreaming about her—but why the hell was he dreaming about Alix?

"You can't be that tired. It's half past seven. We left Tabou at two." She turned to face him and he recalled he was wearing only a pair of pajama pants, a fact she seemed to notice for the first time too.

Her eyes flickered from him to the closed bedroom door. "Oh," she said. "Is someone in there?" A flush blazed over her cheeks and she looked as if she was about to run for the door.

She was *still* treating him like a womanizer. He mightn't have had any sleep but it wasn't for the reasons she thought, and besides, he *never* fell asleep beside anyone. "No," he said testily. "Not some*one*. There are three women in there. One is too boring for me."

"Three?" She clapped a hand over her mouth as if she actually thought three half-dressed, naked, or angry women were about to come storming out.

She really did believe he was nothing but a libertine. But he remembered how he'd turned up at her *pension* with a bottle of champagne and smooth words about her being beautiful, the way he'd let a stream of nameless women at different parties tempt him into darkened rooms, and he knew he had only himself to blame. So he made a concerted effort to regain his sangfroid.

He expelled a breath and saw the flush on her cheeks retreat.

"You almost got away with that," she said, one hand on her hip and a flash of a smile on her face, laughing at herself now.

He managed to locate his own smile, rubbed a hand over his jaw, felt the stubble scratch his palm and realized he needed a shave as well as clothes. "While you transform my living quarters into HQ, I'm going to get dressed. If my reputation is as bad as you say it is, then I should probably have a little more on when I'm meeting a woman in my suite at seven in the morning."

He'd meant it as a joke but now she was staring at him and he could have sworn her eyes were tracing a path over his torso. Christ, he must still be dreaming. Except her cheeks were flushed again.

Thankfully the doorbell rang. "Who else do I need to entertain?"

"It's room service. I'm hungry."

He finally laughed and it suddenly felt more like it had the night before. "How you can be hungry after all that cassoulet I have no idea, but in return for letting you rearrange my living room, can you at least pour me a coffee?"

"Yes," she said. "Get dressed. I'll have coffee waiting when you return."

He shut the bedroom door, exhaled, and willed himself to wake up. If there was one thing he'd learned about Alix, it was that he needed to keep his wits about him.

He shaved and showered as quickly as he could, threw on a pair of trousers and a shirt in crisp, palest blue and reappeared in the living room only fifteen minutes later. The walls were papered with lists. Alix was working with a croissant in one hand and tape in the other and she'd left a plate of pastries and a coffee on the table for him.

"Thanks," he said, taking a sip and stepping in closer so he could read her notes.

In the middle was a piece of paper that read: *Bern*. Around that were various names—*Sorella, Esmée, Bacio, Mary, Allen*—brief accounts of the intelligence operations she'd worked on, and a list of questions ranging from the most important—*Who was the informant?*—down to the smallest and possibly irrelevant—*Why did Bobby want to lead that particular mission?*

"Sometimes the things that don't seem to be related actually are, so I wrote everything down," she explained.

Anthony took another sip of coffee, and asked, feeling like a jerk but it needed to be said, "In that case, do you need to add another question about Bobby?"

"You mean who's the woman in the photo he had?" Alix's voice was quiet.

"Yes."

She took out a pen and wrote so slowly he couldn't help saying, "If it's any consolation, Bobby could be an idiot sometimes."

"I'm not mad at him. I just…" She shrugged. "I miss him. He was a really good friend." She placed a quick hand on her heart as if all her dead people lived there, just like they did in his own heart, and then she tore it away as if she didn't want him to know that.

But then she added, voice so raw he could almost hear it bleed, "I want to be able to look at the faces of those nine boys when they visit me every night in my dreams. I want to say to them, *Here is justice.*"

He inhaled sharply because hearing the same words that he thought every minute of every day made him want to press a hand to his heart too. While everything on the wall in front of him told him she was the best kind of partner because she was thorough and thoughtful and smart, everything she'd just said told him she was the worst kind of partner because she made him feel—and that was the first rule of OSS training: *Don't feel anything.*

But he heard himself say, "Sorry for everything I said earlier. I really do need coffee in the morning."

"Next time I break into your room this early, I'll remember to send coffee up first." She glanced sideways at him, and now he was laughing and she was the one who'd made *him* feel better.

She picked up her purse "I have to get to work. Let me know when you'll be back from Germany."

\* \* \*

Yesterday's contretemps on the streets of Montmartre had resulted in the women of Paris snaking in a line of mink, crocodile, and desperation up and down the staircase of the *maison*, onto the street, and around the block, ignoring Suzanne's reservation system. Every newspaper carried pictures of Tania having her dress torn off. Some commentators—like Becky—raged that the House of Christian Dior was wanton, while others overflowed with gratitude at having been freed from utility suits. Still more (the men, needless to say) mourned the shrouding of female legs, but seemed to be in favor of the more conspicuous bosom. Yet another article put forward the view that Dior was the great savior of marriages as husbands were happy to spend money on feminine Dior gowns in place of the mannish suits of the years before.

Somehow Alix was simultaneously the enslaver of women to their husbands and tradition, a demon of immoral profligacy, and a liberator of female confidence and desire. Her insolently ringing telephone saved her from having to contemplate how all of that was possible.

It was Bettina Ballard, who said, "I want to photograph Cocotte for *Vogue*."

"We're only allowing the dresses out if you can provide assurances of security for our mannequins," Alix replied.

"Next you'll tell me your dresses want green rooms of their own," was Bettina's sardonic reply.

"Now that you mention it—" Alix grinned and Bettina rang off, lest she be required to commit to any further extravagances.

Alix left her office only once more that day to arrange the shredded Corolle on a dress form near the entrance to the salon, accompanied by a sign that read, *Everybody wants to get their hands on Dior.*

*Take that, Becky*, she thought with satisfaction. She'd invited the photographer from the *Daily Telegraph*, Becky's main competitor, to photograph the display and they were only too eager to run the first pictures of the battle-scarred dress in an article that would, in return, be effusive about Dior. Thus she'd turned Becky's machinations against her into a victory. For now.

All the press attention was sure to lead Becky to plan new ways to garrotte Alix. But Alix knew what was motivating her now. And Anthony would be back from Germany soon with documents that might help them find a name for the man they sought. Until then, she was going to focus on her work.

"Poor Corolle," she said, stepping back to admire the display.

"Indeed," came *le patron*'s voice from behind.

Alix welcomed him with a smile. "Every photo shoot from now on will be a production worthy of the silver screen. The mannequins will wear white sheets over their outfits until the final moment so nobody will know what profligacies are hiding beneath, and I'm limiting outdoor shoots to one per month. Not to drive the press mad, but to make sure Suzanne will still speak to me."

"But also to drive the press mad," Dior said with his understated smile. "Now, can I tear you away from unlucky Corolle or do I need to employ a guard just to speak with you?"

"For you," she said cheekily, "I'll make an exception."

She followed him to their favorite place at the top of the staircase and almost toppled down when he said, "I've been invited to America to accept the Neiman Marcus fashion Oscar."

"Bravo!" Alix exclaimed.

Dior settled his kindly and slightly mischievous eyes on her. "Who should go with a couturier to a foreign country when he's accepting an award?"

"You need public relations support. I know some people in Manhattan," Alix said, thinking through and discarding names as not being sufficiently exceptional for *le patron*.

"Of course I will need the Service de la Presse. And *you* are the Service de la Presse."

"You want me to go to America with you? Gosh." Her mind raced over what that would mean for her mission with Anthony. "When? And for how long?"

"We'll leave in one month's time and be gone for around two months."

\* \* \*

That left her with one month to find a man who didn't want to be found, Alix reflected as she returned to her desk to clip and save all the press about Dior. She was on to the international edition of the *New York Journal* when she saw something that arrested her. An article with Anthony March's byline titled, WOMEN ARE BLAMED FOR EVERYTHING AND THAT'S SOMETHING THAT NEVER CHANGES. Her own words from the night before.

The article referenced Corolle's fate yesterday and *les tondues* and the notoriety of the ex-GIs now in Paris on the government's money. It mentioned everything unmentionable: the Parisiennes who'd traded their bodies for bread rather than starve, and the ones in Naples who did the same; and referred—obliquely enough not to get anyone from government too hot under the collar—to women who'd helped just as much as men in the war effort but who'd been told to return to domestic duties since then and were now treated as not even smart enough to decide for themselves what to wear.

At the bottom was the line: *Thanks to Alix St. Pierre for many of the ideas contained in this article.*

The ideas might have been hers but the words were Anthony's—and what words they were. Anthony was a lot smarter than he pretended to be and could give F. Scott Fitzgerald stiff competition for writing a damn beautiful sentence.

Suzanne burst into her office like a champagne cork, followed by Madame Bricard. Suzanne stabbed a finger at the newspaper. "There you are!" she cried, pointing.

"There I am," Alix repeated, her mind processing what this meant: Anthony had not had any sleep and nor had he been indulging in nefarious pursuits. He must have gone back to his office to write this and submit it to the typesetters, returning to his suite in time for ten minutes rest, which she'd interrupted.

"He is so charming," Suzanne gushed to Madame Bricard. "You remember him from the show. The very tall American. Those dark eyes."

"*Oui*," Madame Bricard nodded. "*Très charmant.* We spoke about Biarritz."

"He looked after her when she hit her head," Suzanne continued.

Alix absentmindedly touched the healing gash and, really, she must still have concussion because now she was remembering how she hadn't been able to, for one long minute, drag her eyes away from Anthony that morning. His torso was muscled as if he'd kept up the physical training from OSS, and it was also tanned as if he spent time outside—swimming perhaps, her OSS-trained mind reflected. His cheeks had been covered in dark stubble and while that, combined with his unkempt hair, should have muted his handsomeness, it somehow didn't. And in his suite, she'd thought to herself: if Anthony looked that good when he'd just woken up, then it was a wonder he had to settle for only three women in his bed.

Which had been a joke, she reminded herself. And why was she thinking about Anthony in his bed anyway?

"I have work to do," she told them firmly before shooing them out and making herself think only of Dior gowns for the rest of the day.

* * *

Three days later, Anthony was due back and Alix—doubtless out of the need to prove herself that had entrenched itself in her from the moment she became a parentless thirteen-year-old—was hiding behind a stand of potted palms in the lobby of the Ritz. Anthony had spent three days on their quest and she'd done nothing. Equals as partners meant equal work, thus her plan for that evening.

She'd left work at seven, and had asked Frank to send word out to her when Becky appeared in the bar. It was now nine o'clock and the man who'd let her borrow notepaper a few months back was hurrying over. "Frank advises you should go now." He slipped her a key.

"*Merci*, Monsieur Charles," she whispered, taking the elevator to Becky Gordon's—or Becky Fitzgibbons's—suite.

Once inside, she ran her eyes around the room. Dresses on chairbacks. Powder spilled over the dressing table. Cigarette butts on the floor. This would take hours, and she didn't know how long she had. Frank was going to do his best to send someone up to warn her the minute Becky stirred from the bar, but that might be in two minutes or two hours.

She started with the dressing table. The overfull ashtray told her that Becky spent much time there, preening perhaps. Scattered around it were a couple of red lipsticks, lids off. Blue pills. Francis Fitzgibbons's dog tags.

Alix slid into a chair. *Dammit, dammit, dammit.* She shouldn't have come. The blue pills told her that Becky couldn't sleep without help, and the dog tags told her why. All of which added to Becky's potential for volatility. But it also made Alix pity her, and no spy worth a damn should ever pity their quarry. *Get up*, she told herself. *Keep going.*

She opened the drawers and sifted through the contents. Handkerchiefs. More pills. A book of Shakespeare's love sonnets. A photograph of Becky with her arm around a man, beside another couple holding hands. She turned it over and read, *Me with Viscount John Shervington, and Francis with Miss Louisa Bagshawe.* Had Viscount John Shervington melted away when the money had gone, just like Peter had with Lillie? All the more reason for Becky to be bitter.

But something about that photo made Alix sit down once more. Becky had light hair like Lillie's. And Miss Louisa had darker hair. It could be a photo of Alix and Bobby, Lillie and Peter. Lillie's dressing table had always looked like this: a strew of Kleenex and cosmetics and expensive baubles. And, later, blue pills too.

A sound. She froze, ears reaching out into the corridor. Just a set of footsteps passing by. She remembered to breathe. She needed to hurry, not wander around in the goddamn past.

She lifted the lid off a jewelry case whose contents were blindingly impressive. Pearls. Little drawers of earrings. Even a tiara. Under the top tray, a card. An invitation to Comte Étienne de Beaumont's Venetian Ball.

When she froze this time, it wasn't because of a sound. It was because beneath the delicately italicized text detailing the time and place—the Piscine Deligny, a swimming pool on the Seine—someone had written in ink: *Piscine. Minuit et quart.*

*Mon Dieu.* The hard kick of adrenaline against her heart. Her breath like a frayed ribbon. She'd seen that handwriting before. In a note slipped into a hymnbook in a church: *You want Matteo Romano's sister.*

How much could a hand tremble? More than an ocean in a tempest.

La Voce was summoning Becky to a meeting. They had either joined forces or were about to. And he would be at this ball.

"Mademoiselle?"

She half-gasped, half-screamed. Someone was right beside her and she hadn't heard anything. Had been so lost in the long and hideous reach of La Voce's menace that she could have been attacked, given herself away to Becky—anything. My God, she was no better than an amateur.

Thankfully it was Jean-Luc, the concierge. "She is coming," he said insistently. "Hurry."

Alix shoved the invitation back in the box, shut the lid and fled into the bedroom. Where would she hide? And how the hell would she get out if Becky was on her way up?

Jean-Luc gestured to a panel in the wall that had been opened. A secret door. Relief urged her into its shelter. The concierge sped out of the bedroom and into the main room at the same time as the suite door opened. Becky snapped, "What are you doing?"

"Delivering a message for you," Alix heard the concierge reply with perfect calm.

Under cover of their conversation, Alix closed the secret door behind her as quietly as she could, then hastened along a dimly lit passage and down two staircases before reaching another door. She opened it slowly, finding herself in the mercifully empty ballroom. From there, even though it was only half past nine and Anthony had said he mightn't be back until ten, she took the elevator straight up to his suite.

# SEVENTEEN

Anthony was taping notes to the wall when a knock sounded. He frowned; he was in his shirtsleeves again and he'd meant to at least put his tie back on before Alix arrived. Although, he supposed as he opened the door, having a shirt on was a distinct improvement on what he'd been wearing the last time he saw her.

Alix's face was almost as white as when she'd hit her head. She stepped past him with her back very straight and he recognized her "tell"—her posture improved the more fragile she was feeling.

"You should fire me as your partner," she said, before telling him she'd been in Becky's suite and had almost been caught.

*Goddammit.* "I won't fire you for being shell-shocked at finding out that Becky's teaming up with your informant. But I might fire you for going to Becky's suite without telling me." He was trying not to be gruff but, really, he was pissed.

"I know," she said. "But you were getting trial transcripts. I was doing nothing. I've learned my lesson. And I'd say we're now even on proving to one another that, at times, our intelligence is anything other than superior." A wan smile accompanied the jest. "All I need to do now is get one of my printers to make a copy of the invitation so I can get into the ball. Then, next week, I'll see who La Voce really is."

Her final words were muted rather than triumphant.

She was clearly terrified of her informant. Which meant there was no way he could let her go to that ball by herself. He'd been gathering trial transcripts, yes; but without her, he'd wouldn't have known what he was searching for.

He walked over to his desk and pulled out a card. "I have an invitation and it says Monsieur March and partner."

"We can't go together," she said exasperatedly.

"Why not?"

"Because everyone will think I'm sleeping with you."

She said it as if the Eiffel Tower was more likely to fall down than she and Anthony ever become anything more than business partners. And also as if she still thought his reputation was execrable. He felt his jaw tighten at the second and, deep inside, was aware of a punch of disappointment at the first.

The next instant she was standing next to him, saying, "I'm sorry. I promised to stop treating you as if you deserved your reputation. We're partners. We'll go together. Who cares what people say?"

"It's fine. You don't have to."

"I'm almost afraid to say this because it's a little like breaking my promise again, but is this the first time in your life you've had to persuade someone to go to a ball with you?" She finally found one of her trademark grins.

Even though she *was* breaking her promise, he laughed. "How about I order up some French 75s, we agree we're going to the ball, I show you where we're working tonight in an attempt to demonstrate that even the Ritz has some secret corners that can take your breath away, and we forget for a moment that next week we might see someone you're scared to even talk about."

"That," she said, "is an excellent idea."

"Then come with me."

He drew back the sheer white drapes over the windows, opened the door hidden beneath and showed her out onto a terrace.

"Oh," he heard her say and now he was the one grinning.

"It's not Tabou but…" He gestured to the verdigris column of the

Place Vendôme, the top few feet visible against the kind of sky that couldn't have looked more spectacular had he ordered perfection. The golden glow of the City of Lights stretched on forever, sending the darkness into permanent exile.

"We're on the roof. I had no idea any of the rooms had terraces," she said as she turned her entire body from side to side. "Now I understand why your suite has those curved ceilings. You are quite literally in heaven."

"Nope. Somewhere better. No disapproving gods here."

She smiled. "That *is* an improvement. But as you said the other night—if what we're about to do requires this much of a mis-en-scène, then I'm very much looking forward to my French 75."

On cue, the drinks arrived and Anthony gestured to a pile of boxes. "That," he said, "is why we need the backdrop."

She lifted her eyebrows. "A little light reading? We'd best get started."

He watched her open a box, take out a mimeographed report, sink into a chair, kick off her shoes and curl her legs up underneath her as if she was about to read a novel, not a report on war criminals. While she read, he took the chance to examine her—this woman who'd settled onto his terrace as if she belonged there.

He never invited women back to his suite, besides Esmée and Anjelica and one was a friend and one was business. He'd never sat with anyone out on this terrace. He lit a cigarette and she looked up at the strike of the lighter so he carried it over to her and she smiled at him—just a little—but with a hint of the beautiful exuberance he'd noticed before. She took the cigarette and smoked so contentedly that he did it twice more, rewarded each time with the same smile. He liked the fact that it was after midnight and he was exhausted but couldn't go to sleep and dream nightmares because she was there and they had work to do.

And the more he scrutinized the trial reports, the more he was glad she wasn't alone. He'd read through the notes she'd stuck to his wall so he knew exactly what kind of intelligence this La Voce had given her, and therefore which names mentioned in the trial reports might be relevant.

There was one in particular, mentioned only a few times, and not by name—*Wolff's valet* were the words used. *Wolff's valet paid nine thousand lira for every Jewish man or woman turned in to him*, read one witness statement. *He approved the use of the torture chambers in Milan*, read another, *including Pietro Koch's.*

He had to close his eyes then. Pietro Koch's savagery went far beyond the frontiers of a nightmare and into the realms of utmost horror. Only a monster would sanction what had happened there. As if to confirm the thought, he next read, *Wolff's valet sent the Jews he paid for to Auschwitz. He kept a tally on the wall of how many died. It numbered almost two thousand the last time I saw it.*

Anthony stood up, crossing to the edge of the terrace where he could see the former *hôtels particuliers* lining the square. Cream façades, stacked rectangular windows, each with the same precise distance between them. So much light that the square seemed paved with gold.

He felt Alix step in beside him, saw her eyes trace over the vision below as if needing to reassure herself too that the world they were reading about no longer existed. How had it ever?

"It's Wolff's valet, isn't it?" he said.

"It must be."

She'd sat down not a foot away from this man and spoken to him. And now she wanted to tail him at a ball.

Her hand rested beside his on the balustrade and he had such a fierce urge to hold it inside his, just as they'd done for only a few seconds at the club the other night, that he shifted abruptly away to the safety of the Gauloises pack.

"We need to know his name," she said, braver than him right now.

"How do you find the name of a man who hid it from everyone?" she asked the night.

"We don't need his name," he said, drawing on both Gauloises smoke and inspiration. "It's clear in these reports that he took what he knew about the surrender of Italy and made sure he escaped to safety a few days beforehand. I bet he didn't take his identity with him. He shed it on one of the ratlines and got himself a new one. And I'm also willing to bet that he doesn't use the same name now."

Alix turned to him, a frown on her face. "That makes sense," she said slowly. "Which means we need to use the ball to find out what name he's adopted."

Anthony nodded, then he asked the question that was burrowing into his mind like a goddamn tick. "How does he know Becky's got a grudge too?"

"I don't know. Did Esmée asking questions about Becky tip someone off?"

She shifted her attention up to the stars and he watched her neck elongate, back straighten. All of his muscles contracted, knowing she was about to say something that scared her.

In a carefully unconcerned voice, she told him. "He knows what I look like. So I'm hoping it's a masquerade ball."

Anthony exhaled very loudly, understanding now how truly rattled she'd been when she arrived at his suite earlier with her mask peeled back a little and fear plain on her face. It was as if she worried about showing him any weakness, as if the world had taught her too much about all the ways weakness could be exploited. And an appalling question asked itself: what had La Voce made her do in return for the information he'd provided?

He stared at her profile: creamy-white skin, dazzling green eyes, mouth maybe a little too large—but it suited her. There was an energy that thrummed from her, and a smaller mouth would have been lost amidst the red of her hair, the glitter of her eyes and the spark of her presence. How much of that had La Voce seen—and how much of it had he wanted?

If he asked her that, she would stalk out, he knew.

So he waited in diabolical silence for her to speak about a plan to find a Nazi who Anthony now thought he might easily be tempted to murder.

\* \* \*

"It is a masquerade ball," she heard Anthony say as he passed her a cigarette, the action she'd come to understand was his way of trying to make her feel better.

Instead of saying thanks, the words that came out of her mouth were, "Have you ever killed anyone?"

"Yes." The twist of Anthony's mouth offered a reply more expansive. "Have you?"

"No." She hesitated, wondering what eloquence her own face possessed. And the explanation worked its way free. "I've seen murdered people though. Horribly, savagely murdered people."

Anthony flexed his fingers toward his glass and spun it slowly around. "Well, I've killed the ones who did the horrible, savage murdering. Does that make me a murderer too?" He shrugged, lifted the glass and drank deeply. "The semantics don't matter much. It still takes away part of what makes you human. And you never get it back." Another swallow.

"I think..." Alix began, but the sudden shuttering of every emotion on his face made it clear he did not want her sympathy, or her compassion. She said it anyway. "A person who still thinks about Nazis laughing over his dead friends has more than just the embers of a soul left."

His jaw tightened and she braced for a retort but instead he leaned his back against the wall where the lamps didn't quite reach, his eyes blacker than the sky. "When we find him, will we just hand him over?"

It was a deeply personal question, asking her why was she talking about killing people. And it struck her, as she rested her back against the edge of the terrace, that in some ways he knew more about her than anyone else. He didn't know about her parents or her years with Carmel, had never met her best friend, but he knew the gloaming inside her, the way it tried to blacken everything.

"I plan to," she said quietly. "But I also know it might depend on what he says. Justice might look different when we're in a room with him and he tells us why he sometimes gave me information that let other men go free, but not those men, that night. Most especially, I want him to know that it's me who caught him—that he didn't destroy me after all, which I know is what he wanted to do."

A long silence followed. A clock sounded twice, telling her it was two in the morning. She rubbed her eyes. "All we can do is go to the ball and eavesdrop on Becky and La Voce's conversation—we'll have to work out exactly how to do that once we're there and can assess the crowds and the noise levels. Hopefully we can tail him afterward and find out where he lives."

"And I might have another source who can pal up to Becky, find out what name he's using now."

They made their way back inside and when she saw the pieces of paper he'd added to the wall, she walked over to them. "We should run through the names we have here. Maybe there's some link or connection." She scanned the pages, saw Esmée's name and said, curious now, "You never did tell me how you know Esmée."

"Her family and my family have been friends for decades. I met Esmée when I was two and she was six months old. Apparently I tried to push her into a lake, which I'm sure that"—a grin, not malicious but mischievous, quirked his lips upward—"even as a baby, she deserved. She's the closest thing I have to a sister."

"So not all the women you grew up with were uselessly ornamental and stupid."

"I guess not," he said, "but if you know Esmée, you know that's what she pretends to be. It's why she has me stand in as her partner at dinner parties. So she won't take her role-playing too far and marry herself off to someone who thinks they're getting an ornament for a wife."

"Won't being cast in the role of her partner at dinner parties make it hard for you to find your own ornament of a wife?" It was possibly a too-personal question, but Alix was even more curious now. Men like Anthony always ended up with wives.

His answer was unperturbed. "I'm only in Paris until the end of the year. So wives, ornamental or otherwise, aren't on my agenda right now. I'll worry about that when I'm back in New York."

Alix only just curtailed her eye roll. While Esmée was lucky to have enough money that any eccentricity when it came to preferring to remain uncoupled would be overlooked for now, Alix—at twenty-seven and with a distinct preference for working over wife-ing—was rapidly approaching either scandalous willfulness or spinsterhood. Anthony's casual certainty that marriage would be there waiting for him when he was ready for it was yet another reminder of the vast gulf that lay between her and the wealthy, people who could mold life into a shape that suited them.

To mask her irritation, she stared at the other names she'd written down: *Allen, Mary, Sorella, Bacio*. But not Lillie. She should add her to the list. But what if it made Anthony ask about her?

At the same moment, Anthony indicated her list, "This is everyone?"

She didn't even hesitate before saying, "Yes."

"Okay, tell me about Bacio," he said, perhaps with the same unerring instinct that had made him a good agent. "Strange coincidence of code names. Bisous and Bacio. Kisses in two different languages."

The whole room spun nauseatingly off-balance.

"It wasn't a coincidence." She didn't want to say any more, didn't want to think about that carefree day when Matteo had sat in her apartment in Bern, turned his dimples on her and told her that Italian kisses were far superior. But her mouth said, "You have the eight souls of your OSS agents on your conscience. But nine men died that night. On my conscience are all nine."

\* \* \*

The next day, the *maison* was full of women being fitted for gowns to wear to the ball at Piscine Deligny.

"That ball will be the highlight of the season," Suzanne said triumphantly to Alix near evening. "So many women all wearing Dior. Schiap must be gnashing her teeth."

How had she not thought of it before? Alix didn't own a ballgown. "It's going to be completely extravagant, isn't it?" she asked, more than a little fretfully.

"I hope so," Suzanne said. "Why is that a problem?"

Alix blurted, at the exact moment that Dior and Madame Bricard entered the room, "Because I'm going to it with Anthony March."

Suzanne's smile was knowing and Madame Bricard's eyebrows raised suggestively.

Monsieur Dior spoke. "You need a dress."

"A dress like no other," Madame Bricard added.

"It should be a surprise," was Suzanne's contribution.

They hustled out, whispering.

"You don't have to do that!" Alix called after them, but they ignored her.

And to tell the truth, she was glad. The anticipation of a glorious Dior gown was about the only thing that would help her not to think about the clawing terror of coming face to face with La Voce in just a few days' time.

* * *

It was decreed that Alix should get ready for the ball at Maison Christian Dior and use the services of the makeup artists and hairdressers who ordinarily worked on the finer canvases of mannequins.

"Your hair is an unusual color," the hairdresser declared when presented with Alix's locks.

"Pffft," Madame Bricard responded haughtily. "It's better than being one amongst a thousand blondes."

Next it was the turn of the makeup artist. "You have a wide mouth."

Alix smiled her very widest in response.

Above, on the platform over the *cabine* where the most full-skirted and splendid dresses were usually lowered down from the workrooms, Alix could hear the rustlings and whisperings of the *petites mains*, who'd all stayed behind to see Mademoiselle l'Américaine in her custom-made Dior creation.

"It is the most beautiful dress of all," she heard one sigh.

"I sewed a lock of my hair into the hem," another whispered, which was the tradition with bridal dresses.

"I sewed my heart into it," a third commented wistfully.

"Excuse me," Alix said to the makeup artist.

She reached for a water glass to ease the gentle ache in her throat. That the women thought so much of Alix's dress that they had sewn hopes and dreams and charms into it was touching beyond anything, and for a single, exquisite second she felt the ghostly toile tiptoe into the room, take a seat beside her and say, *You can have hopes and dreams too.* Hopes like finding a way to track La Voce tonight. But maybe, as someone who'd never been to a Paris society ball, she also dreamed of an evening that combined the audacity of Tabou, the magnificence of Anthony's terrace, and the wonder of a Dior ballgown. Surely that wasn't too much to wish for?

Suzanne bent down to say, "Let's see the dress, *chérie.*"

Down from above it descended.

Alix had been expecting dramatic black. But what appeared was a silvery blue, a prismatic hue she'd seen perhaps once before in the deep crevasse of a glacier—the blue of spells and enchantment and most definitely of magic.

The seamstresses clapped their hands delightedly as it dropped over Alix's head and Suzanne turned her attention to the fastenings.

"I should probably do it myself," Alix said, "otherwise I won't know how to get it off at the end of the night."

Madame Bricard snorted. "This dress will be torn off you at evening's end."

It was Alix's turn to snort at the weight of expectation on the shoulders of Anthony March, who had no intention of removing even a loose thread from Alix's body. Then Suzanne spun her around to face the mirror—and everyone quieted.

She almost put a hand out to touch the looking glass because the woman standing there could not possibly be Alix.

Her neck rose creamy-white out of a strapless bodice. The luster of the fabric reflected like moonlight in her eyes and through her hair— one more deeply green than ever, the other more brilliantly red. The bodice was astonishingly shaped—wet-draping, Madame Carré was explaining—in ruched folds rippling over her breasts and around her waist.

It looked as if she'd been wrapped in seawater and, with one gentle tug, the dress would drop in a silvery-blue puddle at her feet. But the internal architecture held everything together in secret so what appeared from the outside to be stilled water, bound temporarily in place while the spell lasted, would never actually fall at midnight.

Alix's fingertips brushed over the stunning velvety flowers that were somehow part of the fabric.

"*Velours au sabre*," Monsieur Dior explained. "The jewel of all couture."

"It's indescribably beautiful," Alix breathed. "But the flowers aren't printed. They almost look like they're blossoming out of the...satin?" she guessed.

Dior nodded approvingly. "When we say *velours au sabre*," he explained, "we refer to a technique that creates the rarest of all fabrics. The very best of the *petites mains* uses a *sabre* to cut, with extreme delicacy, the topmost layer of double-warp duchesse-satin to create a pattern—in this case, blue roses. Once the threads are cut, she caresses them with a brush of wild boar hair, revealing the velvet beneath. *Et voilà*, the image—your roses—appears on the gown in relief. One can only finish a few centimeters each day, and it must all be done by hand. There is no machine that can perform work so *incroyable*."

"It's too much," she said, almost too frightened to move or do anything that might spoil this most extraordinary—and expensive—of gowns.

She was drowned out by a chorus of protest from the *petites mains*. Monsieur Dior inclined his head at them. "It would be a tragedy for this dress never to be worn. And no one else can wear it as it's been made precisely to your measurements. Its name is Compiègne— a touch of royalty for my Queen of Courage."

There was nothing else for it but to throw herself on *le patron*, envelop him in a hug and kiss his cheeks.

"*Merci*," she whispered. "It's the most wonderful thing anyone has ever given me."

"He's here!" One of the seamstresses rushed in. "We were watching below."

Alix shook her head. "This is really not an event worth so much attention."

"Wearing a dress like that, it is," Madame Bricard said decisively. "*On y va*." She motioned everyone toward the door.

Off the procession went, Dior and Madame Bricard in the lead, followed by Mesdames Carré and Raymonde. Then the horde of seamstresses. Alix went last, her hand held in Suzanne's, the dress sweeping grandly through a salon that had hosted so many incomparable gowns but Alix still thought she heard the carpet sigh with satisfaction beneath her feet.

At the door, everyone stepped aside to let her pass through. There, parked by the curb, was a flamboyantly art-deco-looking car. Leaning against the car, smoking a cigarette, and wearing a black tuxedo, was Anthony March.

# EIGHTEEN

Alix shivered, but not from the cold. The night air felt like silk gliding over the pores of her skin. The smile that flew to her face was impossible to stop.

But Anthony's expression didn't alter. He even looked away, tilting his head up to exhale smoke.

Her smile fell away. Her steps across the sidewalk slowed.

When she reached him, he said, "I think that dress will be just extravagant enough." Then his mouth lifted upward at last. "I know you said we're not partners of the kissing kind but we're going to disappoint our audience if I don't at least kiss your cheek."

He gestured behind her with his cigarette and Alix turned to find that everyone from the *maison* was clustered in the doorway. Those positioned behind the lucky few in front were craning their necks to see. Now her cheeks were on fire, which Anthony would find very entertaining.

She tried to modulate her voice into carefree lightness. "As they put so much work into my dress, I don't want to disappoint them."

She raised herself onto her tiptoes as he leaned down toward her. Their cheeks touched as they moved right, then left, then right. While their bodies were just inches apart and she could smell the citrus of his cologne, spiced with woody amber and musk, Anthony whispered in her ear, his breath warm against her skin, "I can't compliment you on how you look because there isn't a word I can think of that's enough."

Her entire body flushed. She couldn't look at anything other than the ground, and was thankful when Suzanne interrupted, calling, "You forgot your mask."

A line of seamstresses passed it down the steps—a thing of beauty too, also made of *velours au sabre*, with dark blue roses climbing up one side.

Anthony held up a matching mask, but without the feminine frill of roses. "It arrived at the Ritz for me this evening so I thought I'd better wear it."

Alix glanced over her shoulder to see Suzanne beaming and Monsieur Dior smiling and she couldn't help laughing. "Obviously I'm such a non-Cinderella that the idea of someone taking me to a ball is so beyond the scope of normal human activity that it creates more fuss than it ought to. Shall we go?"

"Won't it spoil their fun?" Anthony said, grinning.

"No," she said firmly, stepping past him to the car.

* * *

He didn't think he would ever forget, for the rest of his life, the sight of Alix St. Pierre in the doorway of the *maison*. And it wasn't just the dress; it was that smile. It was like snowflakes catching the moonlight against a black sky, diamonds suspended for an instant before they vanished. He'd felt his eyes smart, and then he couldn't look at her at all.

When he'd tilted his head back down, he could tell his apparent indifference had hurt her. He'd tried to resurrect the moment—but it was ruined.

They were silent as his driver crossed the Pont Royal and drove along Quai Anatole to the Piscine Deligny. From the outside it resembled a floating wooden barge but once inside, it revealed itself to be a swimming pool with a theatrical flair, edged with balconies and late nineteenth-century adornments.

"*Mon Dieu*," Alix said, gazing around.

"I swim here every morning," he said.

"Aha!" she said triumphantly. "I was right."

He raised a quizzical eyebrow.

"I can't drop the habit of creating a mental dossier about people," she explained. "You're tan, so I thought perhaps you swam."

"I'd forgotten you'd seen me in a state of *déshabillé*," he said wryly. To move on from that recollection, he said, "How about I get champagne and you circulate? You say you'd know his voice, so we'll listen to as many people as possible and try to work out which one is him. But keep your mask on," he added.

She nodded but looked uncertain, as if she wasn't quite as comfortable in a large and outlandish party as she was on the terrace of his suite—which was an absurd thought—then made her way over to watch the black gondolas ferrying guests up and down the pool.

On his way to the bar, he passed by cascades of fairy lights, their glister only just outdoing the guests' jewelry. At one end, a façade had been erected to mimic St. Mark's Basilica, and a flock of faux-pigeons gathered in a well-mannered group beside. Nearby, the Bridge of Sighs arched tragically from one balcony to another.

Through it all passed Aly Khan, the Coopers and their *compagnon de chambre* Louise de Vilmorin. Cocteau, Élie de Rothschild, the Vicomtesse de Noailles. Diamonds and bared cleavages and lascivious intentions strolled in on a line of wealthy and worldly people who had long ago acquired the kind of urbanity that was only satisfied by excess, an excess that would flaunt itself lavishly by one in the morning when the ball would become what it was always intended to be— a club that would make even the Moulin Rouge blush. He couldn't wait to get away from the bar, from the people kissing his cheeks, and return to Alix.

It took forever to reach her, by the poolside still, her eyes huge. He passed her a *coupe*. "It's the optimistic version of Venice, isn't it?" he said, casting his eyes over the faux-Lido. "One for those with stars in their eyes. Which we're all supposed to have tonight. Except you. Your eyes are so green right now they're like...bottled absinthe. Did you know that green eyes are an optical illusion? You have no green pigment at all in your eyes and yet..."

He broke off. He'd had one sip of champagne and was talking like a soak.

Thankfully Alix was always ready with a one-liner. "So my eyes are liars too," she quipped. "Perfect for a spy."

"What I was trying to explain, poorly," he said, "is that, if your informant is here and you looked anything at all like you do now when he last saw you, then I don't think a mask is going to camouflage you."

"Believe me," Alix said, gesturing to the dress, "I have never looked like this." But her shoulders were bare so he could see them turn inward, as if her fear of La Voce had pushed hard against her chest.

Which made it suddenly push hard against his own chest too—but for her.

He said without thinking, "Maybe you should...I don't know, go home. I can look for him. You shouldn't be here if he knows what you look like." And why the hell hadn't he thought of that before?

She looked up at him, fire in her eyes, fire directed—somehow—at him. "Would you say that if I was one of the men you worked with in Italy?"

"That's not fair."

She scowled at him and he scowled at her, and he remembered promising he wouldn't treat her as if she were weak. But he only had to look at the size of her shoulders, like fine wishbones able to be snapped by someone's pinky finger, to know that he should never have made that promise.

"I suggest we circulate," she said coolly, "rather than stand here arguing. I don't know a single soul so you'll need to do the introductions."

She started to walk away so he guided her over to a group he knew. One of the women slipped an arm through his. Another woman he'd once left a ball with, and who didn't seem to care that tonight he was here with someone else, accosted him too. Which, on any other night, would have been unremarkable—the person one took to a ball wasn't necessarily the same person one retired with. But tonight he didn't want his arm taken hostage, nor his departure plans anticipated.

On the other side of the circle he saw Alix standing austerely between two men who fixed their eyes to her décolletage. After she'd introduced herself, one man exclaimed, "Good God, you're the woman who costs me a fortune every week. You and that Dior."

Alix looked as if she might hit him and, God, Anthony wanted her to.

He never did things like that, did he? Maybe he slept with more women than was good for him but he didn't speak to their chests instead of their faces and he didn't mock them. Except he *had* mocked Alix and her work at Dior when he'd first met her.

His mind was racing—she always did this to him. Made him think. Like that article he'd written after their dinner at Brasserie Lipp. He prided himself on knowing everything about the news of the world, but he'd never considered that a mannequin having her dress torn off wasn't just a spat about skirt lengths but something that went much deeper, something he barely understood.

And now he'd been lost in a mess of thoughts for too long and Alix had vanished. "Excuse me," he said to the women on either side of him, reclaiming his arm and maneuvering through the thick crowd as fast as he could. A goddamn Nazi killer was here and Alix was missing.

A flash of red hair. There she was, waiting to order a drink at the bar. Nearby, he caught a glimpse through bodies of a woman with no mask and an exaggerated walk. Anjelica.

And he recalled that Anjelica had been involved in the stolen sketch fiasco and he'd forgotten to mention to Alix that he'd paid a sometimes-prostitute to tail her a few months ago—and that the same woman had helped Becky get Alix fired.

*Shit.* He indicated with his head that Anjelica should meet him out front, away from the crowds and away from Alix, who'd be safe at the bar for now.

It took him another ten minutes to reach the doors where he said apologetically to Anjelica, "I know this sounds like I think I have a right to tell you what to do. But you'll make my life a hell of a lot easier if you leave."

She gave him her best pout. "You're one of the only people in the world whose life I like to make easier. But you know they hired me for later—to be the Catherine wheel when the fireworks start, so to speak."

He shook his head, hating suddenly that he lived in a world where he went to balls that supplied their guests with a side serve of *demimondaines* to go with their champagne. And hating too that he wanted to say to Anjelica that if she left, he'd pay her everything she would otherwise have earned by staying, but was afraid that made him just as bad as the men hiring her for all the rest.

She must have seen the conflict written on his face because she laughed. "How about I ease your life and lighten your conscience. I have information for you about Becky. I'll go get myself some dinner and come to your suite later, where you can pay me handsomely for that information."

Before he could thank her for saving his skin, she'd gone.

He hurried back inside. He hadn't seen Becky, was no closer to finding La Voce, had a hell of a secret to break to Alix, and would give anything to be back in the claustrophobic exuberance of Tabou, where there was only music and dancing and laughter and none of the shit.

Alix wasn't at the bar. She wasn't dancing. His movements through the crowd were hampered by all the damn people he knew who wanted to spill flirtatious banter into his ears and champagne on his shoes, like the one whose fingers closed around his arm as she said, "I see you've taken a shine to redheads. Working-class redheads, no less. Someone told me she's a seamstress."

"She isn't—" he began, more than a little impatiently.

"Isn't planning to stitch you up?" the woman tittered. "Let us know when you tire of the talents of the proletariat."

He turned his back and stepped on more than a few trains as he continued to search for Alix, who'd maybe been right when she'd said she shouldn't go to the ball with him. Somehow she'd been cast in the role of coquette and demoted to seamstress. Usually when he came to these things with a woman, people just shrugged. But... when had he ever gone to a ball or a party with a woman who worked like Alix did—not just dabbling at being a hostess at society luncheons or patronizing a gallery by bringing along her moneyed friends, but throwing herself into it so wholeheartedly that a blow to the head was all in a day's work?

He found her at last, out by the pool all alone, and he stopped for a minute to observe her. She was staring at the water, one arm crossed over her torso, elbow resting on her palm, a bored—no, a lonely expression on her face. She crossed to a sun lounger at the far end of the pool and dropped onto it with a sigh. And he realized that while he knew almost everyone here because their parents knew his parents, or he'd been to school with their friends, Alix didn't appear to know a single soul—and nobody appeared to know her. She'd said as much to him at the start of the evening and he hadn't understood what it meant—that Alix St. Pierre's background was nothing like his.

\* \* \*

Alix sat down, thankful it wasn't long until midnight. Then she could go home.

She hadn't heard any voices that sounded familiar, hadn't seen Becky at all, had seen Anthony with about a million different women draping their arms around his shoulders, transforming him into the well-to-do rake for whom dark corners and married women were mere appetizers—warm-ups for a scandalous main course. Which he had every right to, but it was hard to imagine he was the same man she'd been sharing confidences with. She felt like she was back at finishing school, or the van der Meers' house, or at the Rainbow Room for dinner with Bobby—an outsider lost in a world she didn't belong to.

She opened her purse only to discover she'd left her cigarettes in the *cabine*.

"Here." A lit cigarette appeared in front of her, held out by Anthony. She accepted it, breathed in and watched the exhalation glitter like glass in the night.

Anthony sat on the side of the lounger opposite her, studying her face. She tried to empty it of expression, only her hand with the cigarette moving, her sangfroid attenuating like the smoke.

"I know OSS recruited mainly from the elite," he said at last. "And you know Esmée and you knew Bobby, so I assumed you knew everybody here. But somehow you don't, and I think I've made a hell of a lot of assumptions about you that are all wrong."

"I think we're both guilty of making assumptions," she said quietly. Then she smiled. "I mean, I actually believed for about ten seconds that you were serious about your *ménage à trois* or *quatre* or whatever number you said. And you assumed I belonged in these social circles just because everyone you know does."

He didn't smile, wasn't going to let her get away with a flippant aside. So she tapped ash off the cigarette and explained as matter-of-factly as she could, "My parents were French immigrant tailors. They died when I was thirteen and I was taken in by people who moved in the same social circles as Bobby's family. As Esmée almost blurted at dinner, I was the only scholarship student at Le Manoir, hence my being friends with the maids. I came back to Paris last year with exactly three suits, one blouse, one pair of trousers, and no ball-gowns," she finished, tossing the cigarette on the ground, hands itching for another. "I work because I have to—and sometimes I love it. Here in Paris I do, anyway."

She shrugged. "It's fine if you want to find yourself another partner now that you know I'm just one of the mob."

"I've worked with everyone from prostitutes to—" He cut himself off. "That didn't come out right."

Her mouth turned up just a little. "But you made me smile. Although it was one hell of a faux pas."

"Seems like that's my specialty tonight. It's just…" He paused, as if he was searching for a phrase that wouldn't offend. "Your manner, or the way you walk or something…I thought you'd been born into this." He gestured to the extravagance around them.

She raised an eyebrow. "Then how could you possibly explain my room at the *pension*?"

"I thought you were rebelling against your family's wealth."

Laughter spilled from her now. "Only the truly wealthy can afford to rebel against money, Anthony."

"Touché." He grimaced. "Which makes me a jerk again."

It wasn't his fault he assumed everyone was just like him. That you could move to Paris for a year, live at the Ritz, and return to New York to pick up your old life when it suited you, adding on the necessary adornments of wife and children when it was time to leave the role of idle gallant behind. Only she, always an outsider, could see the locked doors of the palace he lived in, the walls built of dollar bills too high to climb over.

"Maybe you'll seem less of a jerk if you tell me your history," she said very sneakily, deciding to take full advantage of his contrition. "Suzanne told me you had two brothers."

He walked over to sit beside her, the folds of her gown like quicksilver spilled around them. He took out another cigarette, lit it and passed it to her, waiting for her to inhale and exhale before he held out his hand to take it from her, this strangely intimate act they'd fallen into several times now.

"I did have two older brothers," he said flatly, as if he either didn't care at all or as if he really cared too much. "One died at Omaha Beach on D-day. The other died the day after from a gunshot wound he received as his boat pulled into the shore. They were both dead within twenty-four hours of getting to France."

A burst of hilarity from a group farther down the pool made him flinch. She touched a quick hand to his knee, a little stricken at having made him resurrect something so obviously painful. "I was being nosy. You don't have to tell me any more."

He shrugged, rested one elbow on his knee and smoked determinedly for a minute. "There I was in Italy, doing work that was meant to be the most dangerous thing of all, but I was alive and my brothers weren't. I was embedded in a resistance group at the time so I couldn't leave and see my old man, see how he was taking the news that his spare child—the one who hadn't done the law degrees necessary to take over a newspaper empire—was the one who would."

A mirthless smile. "So that's why I'm in Paris until the end of the year. I'm 'learning the business' is the official explanation—my father's probably more accurate private description is that I'm getting rid of all of my irresponsibilities. Given how many of those I possess, we've allowed eighteen months. Then I'll be ready to become Mr. March Junior, the responsible man in charge of the *New York Journal* and its associated mastheads."

"You like writing," she guessed, having sensed as much from the article he'd written about what had happened to Tania in Montmartre, "but you don't like—"

"Responsibility," he cut in as if he thought he was preempting her censure.

"Yet you still feel responsible for your OSS team. You're going to have to try a lot harder if you want me to believe you're an irresponsible rogue."

He smiled properly at last. "That's almost an offer I can't refuse. A chance to prove myself an irresponsible rogue at a party like this."

On cue, the sound of moaning issued forth from somewhere beneath the balconies. Their heads swiveled in unison. The sound came again and they turned back to one another and exploded into laughter.

"All this ball is proving is that you're better off not being the kind of person who's invited to these things," he said wryly and she followed his gaze around the pool deck and saw that, yes, inhibitions near midnight were *démodé* and half the party were misbehaving in plain sight. Even the Bridge of Sighs sagged drunkenly and the pigeons had been used in a boisterous game that had de-feathered them.

A firework exploded overhead, raining down gold light. The breeze rustled in, bringing with it the scent of citrus, amber, and spice with a bass note of vermouth and Gauloises—the scent of Anthony. As they passed the cigarette back and forth, the pocket of summer night air between them became suddenly quiet, and also full of peculiar things—the warmth of Anthony's shoulder touching hers, the brush of his fingers when she took the cigarette from him, the inexplicable urge to let her hand curl into his, to let the slight quiver of something turn into whatever it foreshadowed.

But a working woman's reputation was as easy to lose as a one-franc coin—and harder to earn back than diamonds. Which meant ignoring all quivers and moving on to the reason they'd come. "How long do we have?" she asked.

Anthony checked his watch. "Half an hour. What's our plan? I've been around the room inside. It's crowded and it makes sense he'd want the privacy of being lost in the crowd while he speaks to Becky. Why don't we go up onto the balcony where we can see everything?"

The balcony afforded them an excellent view over both the interior and exterior spaces. But ten minutes passed and Becky was still nowhere to be seen.

"Dammit," Alix swore, tapping her fingernails agitatedly on the railings.

"You know him," Anthony said, turning to her. "Where would he go?"

"Somewhere confined?" she speculated. "I never met him out in the open."

"The change rooms."

But they were empty of anyone except lustful revelers. And five more minutes had flown by.

"Where the hell are they?" Anthony said through clenched teeth.

Alix closed her eyes, wishing it was quieter. It was impossible to conjure up La Voce in all the noise.

"What does your gut say?" Anthony asked her.

So she made herself feel, let his voice echo through time.

*Piscine Deligny*, her gut reminded her. That was it! The location of the ball was already on the invitation so he hadn't needed to write it down, unless... "They're meeting by the poolside," she said. "Come on."

Instantly, his hand was in hers and they were running to the swimming pool, ducking and dodging groups of roisterers exercising their appetites.

Once there, their eyes met, the same question reflected—where to hide?

"In plain sight," they both said at the same time. It was the first lesson of OSS training.

Alix climbed the five steps to the diving platform, dragging

Anthony behind her, him already tugging off his tie as if he knew exactly what she was thinking. In the pool, they'd look like just another amorous couple for whom beds were passé.

"Three minutes," he said.

"I'm hurrying," she replied, sensing his impatience but also glad he knew better than to suggest he help her undo all the damn hooks on her dress.

He was the first to strip down to his underwear and he dived in a few seconds before she was free of her gown, glad that her pink corselette was no more revealing than a swimsuit. Then it was her turn. She swam underwater until her breath ran out and surfaced, gasping, to find Anthony coming up alongside her.

"I'm guessing we have about a minute," he said.

She brushed hair away from her face and leaned back against the edge of the pool, getting herself into a position where she could see everything and not be seen. Thankfully Anthony was so tall she'd be completely hidden from view behind his torso. And now it was time to play at being in the *piscine* for a different reason entirely to a stake-out. Smiles and casual conversation were required.

"How tall are you?" she asked, fixing a breezy smile onto her face.

"Six foot four. About a foot taller than you, I'd say. Although you look even shorter without all that Dior, which I didn't even have to talk you out of." He grinned and moved closer, the bulwark of distance created by her skirt gone. Then he asked, smile gone now, replaced by an expression more grave, "You ready? If we're right, you'll hear his voice in about thirty seconds."

Maybe it was just part of the role he needed to play. But she still felt a gentle thrum in her heart at the understanding that, despite being seconds away from a breakthrough, Anthony was concerned about how hearing La Voce might make her feel.

It was as if, out there in the dark, she'd found the shadow Anthony concealed and it was velvet soft, the tenderness hidden like the roses in her *velours au sabre* dress until the outer surface was slowly cut away, thread by fine thread.

For five long seconds there was nothing at all in Paris except Anthony March and Alix St. Pierre standing in the Piscine Deligny, staring at one another.

# NINETEEN

The rustle of silk-satin. Alix tore her eyes away from Anthony. "It's Becky," she whispered, because Anthony had his back to the other end of the pool and she needed to be his eyes.

"You're late." Out of the shadows, a man appeared. A man with a voice she'd hoped never to hear again.

Her entire body tensed, adrenaline rushing even into the ends of her eyelashes.

"That's him?" Anthony asked, voice low, stepping in even closer, shielding her. "All we have to do is listen. And make damn sure he doesn't notice you. We're just two partygoers in the pool." He tucked a strand of hair behind her ear, keeping up the charade. "I could make a terrible joke about being happy to be stuck in a pool with a woman in her underwear but I'm worried you might hit me."

The attempt at humor made her relax just a little, allowing her to refocus on the man talking to Becky.

"Tell me what you can see," Anthony prompted.

"Not much. He's wearing a tuxedo. His back is to me and he has brown hair like almost every other man in the world. He's keeping his hands in front of him and I can't see his face."

"He's good at keeping himself hidden."

Becky spoke, voice faltering a little, not so brave now. Or was she acting still? "I didn't know exactly where you'd be."

"What now?" La Voce asked Becky as Alix used everything she'd learned about voice recognition to study the timbre and cadence of his words. She heard not just a question but a touch of amusement—was he playing Becky too, just like he'd once played Alix? She also heard the briefest trill of victory.

He still thought he'd won. Fury surged. It must have shown on her face because Anthony laid a hand over hers as if he thought she was about to fly out of the pool and hurl herself at La Voce. It was very tempting.

"Well," Becky said in her shrill little voice, "you chose a very public place for our first meeting." Her eyes darted over the groups clustered beneath the balconies. "You wanted me to prove tonight that I could follow instructions and come alone. I've done that. I think we should go somewhere more private for our next meeting so we can actually talk about our shared interests. I suggest the Parc des Buttes-Chaumont at midday tomorrow. On the *passerelle suspendue*."

La Voce nodded and then he was walking away. Alix scrutinized his gait with desperate eyes but it was unremarkable—no limp, no peculiarity. He was of average height and weight. Utterly ordinary. Her hands tensed on the side of the pool, ready to lift herself out— ready to throw herself at him now.

"Let him go," Anthony said urgently. "We know where he's going to be tomorrow. You always take the future certain win rather than the immediate but far riskier chance. You cannot run after him now—believe me, Alix St. Pierre out there in her corselette is going to attract far too much notice."

Another joke to bolster her jangling nerves. And Anthony was right. If she charged over the pool deck in her drowned state, he'd know exactly who she was and she'd lose whatever tiny advantage she had. She let her hands fall to her sides and heard herself exhale.

Becky, frowning, walked back inside looking more than a

little frightened by whatever she'd conjured up. *Serves you right*, Alix wished she could think, but even Becky didn't deserve to be used and discarded by La Voce.

"Are you okay?" Anthony asked, hitching his right shoulder as if it was hurting him again.

"Sorry," she said. "You watched people die while La Voce's men laughed. All I did was—" She cut herself off; she could never talk about what La Voce had made her do. "I'm supposed to banish fear otherwise it drives our decisions. I'll do better tomorrow. I promise."

"Alix," Anthony broke in, "I'd be worried if you *weren't* scared. It doesn't make you less brave. Think about where we are now compared to where we were three months ago. Both of us hating ourselves for what had happened but too damn messed up to do much about it. In the last few days we've found out that he might have been known as Wolff's valet, but he was a hell of a lot more. We know he's making an alliance with Becky. We know what her motivation is. And we know where they're both going to be tomorrow. All we need is the name he's using now and then we can probably find out where he lives. We're so damn close. He'll be a hell of a lot easier to tail out of a park tomorrow where there are less people around. If you can do all that while you're scared, then being scared isn't holding you back."

His eyes on her were intent, his bearing too. He had a wrecked shoulder, and the vicious Nazi responsible for that had been within hearing distance just minutes ago but Anthony was still trying to make her feel better.

"Thanks," she said. "You must have been a damn good captain."

"You mean you doubted it before?" he said with a smile and she actually managed a laugh.

"God, I need a cigarette," she said, tipping her head back to look at the sky, stretching her arms along the edge of the pool and exhaling one long breath.

"How about a swim instead?"

She laughed again. "Be serious. We have a rendezvous to plan for tomorrow."

"It's hard to be serious when you're wearing a pink corselette."

What had started out as another joke didn't sound so much like one by the end of the sentence.

Night music played on behind them—a provocative laugh, a piano ballad, the pop of a cork. The breeze dropped.

Alix tipped her head back down and met Anthony's eyes. And all at once it was like that split second before Becky had appeared and Anthony was all she could see.

A different kind of adrenaline now. Her fingers curled around the edge of the pool.

"You're staring," Anthony murmured, his eyes suddenly very blue, like the heart of the hottest flame.

"So are you," she whispered, some heedless part of her trying not to blink, to never interrupt this moment.

"There's not a chance I could look away right now."

Her rational mind asserted itself at last, reminding her that his words meant nothing. *She* meant nothing. Not to him.

She folded her arms over her torso and dragged her eyes away from his. "I know I'm at the zero end of the scale of women you want to talk out of their clothes but I still think I'll get dressed." She started to turn away but he reached out a hand to stop her.

"Alix," he said slowly, carefully, "there is nothing about you that is on any kind of scale I've ever experienced."

What the hell did that mean?

She felt her head turn back toward him. Her eyes fell from his face to his torso, the tan and toned torso of someone who swam each day and took very good care of himself. A drop or two of water clung to his skin, one breaking its surface tension and trailing like a fingertip toward his stomach.

In that moment, there was only closeness and heat and silence and fire. Her eyes held by his, his falling just once to her lips.

Then he blinked and gave his head the tiniest shake.

She knew it meant he wouldn't step any closer. That every joke she'd made about his reputation meant he wouldn't reach for her unless she was the first to move. It was so very tempting. Because surely in kissing, in touching, there would be forgetting.

But there never was.

God, was this what life was still?

She braced both hands on the wall and lifted herself out of the water. "I'm going home," she said.

* * *

She needed air, and there was no air to be found in a cab. She'd promised Anthony she'd take one, couldn't endure a ride home in his car, but she walked instead, only to find there wasn't much air in Paris that night, or at least her mind wasn't refreshed by the quietude of the small hours. She'd left the ball in such a hurry that she hadn't made plans with Anthony about the park tomorrow—she had to go to work, not stake out a park. And there was something worrying her about the conversation they'd overheard, like a blister from a badly fitting shoe.

What?

Becky's faux or real hesitancy. La Voce's amusement.

And then she understood. It had been too easy. The conversation had taken place exactly where she could best hear it, and with most of the details spelled out. Intelligence was never that simple, otherwise everyone would be a spy.

It was a trap, not a breakthrough.

Her pace slowed. At the same time, the footsteps that had been tapping behind her stopped.

She reached for the rail of the Pont de la Concorde and her eyes and ears searched the night. There was the Eiffel Tower to her left, the Jardin des Tuileries to her right. There was the black water below, the current of darkness rushing onward. A couple embracing as they gazed at the city. A man staring at nothing. The drip of her wet hair onto the ground.

Alix ran a hand over the jacket Anthony had insisted she take, and which she was glad of now because her dress was a beacon. She might as well be standing on top of the obelisk at the other end of the bridge, shouting, *Here I am! Here's Alix St. Pierre.* One only ever wished to tease an opponent out into the open if one was prepared for that opponent—if one knew their strengths and their weaknesses. And she did not. She should have taken a cab.

Perhaps she was overreacting.

Or perhaps she was right. If she was, it meant that La Voce knew who she was and he intended to meet her face to face tomorrow. And someone he paid to do his dirty work was perhaps following her right now.

She hurried to the end of the bridge, then on to her tiny room where nobody would ever think to look for her, warning bells clanging. If her identity—and possibly Anthony's—was known, it meant La Voce knew things about her. Such as where she lived.

She continued on past her *pension*, listening. Nothing. Regardless, she walked around the block to the service entrance and waited in the maintenance room, hackles up. Her eyes roamed the darkness and stopped at a pile of flour sacks the landlord had stored there. One of them would have to do. It was heavy enough to be a decent weapon, but not barbaric enough to do irreparable damage.

She kicked off her shoes, wrung out her hair again, took a sack in her hands—God, it was heavy—and climbed the stairs. Outside her door, she waited and listened.

There was definitely someone in there.

She could somehow hear them breathe, sense the slightest of all movements—lungs inflating, chest expanding, a finger making the faintest crack.

Sack in both hands, elbow on doorknob, one push, the door was open, and she was bringing the sack down on a body. A groan, and a man fell to the floor.

*　*　*

She shut the door quickly, feeling the fast throb of her heart and the adrenaline kick that made her mind think, rather than panic. Panic should always be saved for later, when the mess was cleaned up.

She snapped on a lamp and studied the man on her floor. No one she knew.

She couldn't move him by herself. It meant taking out her sturdiest scarves, tying his wrists and ankles in case he woke, gagging him too, locking the door, hurrying back down the stairs, finding the nearest telephone booth, dropping in coins and asking the operator to connect her to the Ritz.

"Yes?" Anthony's voice came onto the line, quick, impatient.

"In the interests of sharing everything with my partner," she said, aiming for breezy, trying to still her heart and slow her breathing, "there is now a man on the floor of my *pension* who is either dead, maimed, or just knocked unconscious."

A woman's laugh sounded in the background. *Goddammit, Anthony.* Alix hung up the phone.

Then she hurtled back to her *pension*, sank into a chair and stared at the mess. *Think.* Discard emotions, go back to the training.

If your safe house was found, you packed up and got the hell out.

Alix took down her suitcase. From the wardrobe, she pulled out Chérie, the leopard-print, the green dress, and the two suits Dior had made for her. In the bathroom, she threw her toiletries and cosmetics into their case. Hats in hat boxes, all the while keeping her eye on the man. He didn't move.

A sound outside the door. She slipped her hand into her suitcase and drew out her Beretta service pistol. She pointed it at the door.

It flew open to reveal Anthony March.

Behind him was Fortunée.

Alix's shocked gasp was very loud. Anthony's face twisted with guilt.

Becky's brother had gone into the mountains with Anthony. Then Becky had teamed up with Fortunée to try to run Alix out of Paris. And now Anthony was here with Fortunée.

There were a lot of names she wanted to call him right then, but fear sliced through her like scissors into chiffon and she found she couldn't speak at all.

Anthony's eyes darted around the room, not meeting hers, taking in the scene—the man on the floor, the bag of flour, the papers on her desk that had been rifled through, stopping at one she'd kept since 1944 and that was now sitting on top of the others. He picked it up.

*To Alix,*

*Bisous and Bacio.*

*All my love,*
*Matteo*

"Who the hell is Matteo?" Anthony snapped.

She was so stunned by the utter incongruousness of the question—and hadn't she told him already?—that she answered. "Matteo was Bacio."

"In those last weeks in Italy," Anthony said grimly, "Bobby was looking for a Matteo."

# PART FOUR
## SWITZERLAND AND ITALY, 1943–1945

*An intelligence officer should be free to talk to the devil himself if he could gain any useful knowledge…*
—Allen Dulles

# TWENTY

Matteo and Alix arrive the following afternoon from their cross-border expedition at the partisan command center, an old talc plant in the mountains. The lookouts, two men with hero-worship for Matteo in their eyes and deep suspicion of Alix, let them pass through. Alix is exhausted but she refuses to show it. She has never walked so far and for so long with so little rest. She's drunk so much coffee her eyes feel like they might never close.

It's sunny, and the partisans are sitting outside on ledges and rocks like mountain goats enjoying the sunshine. At the sound of approaching feet, their hands fly to their guns and fall away when they see Matteo. Several bound over to greet him—one whose face is still smooth and unacquainted with a razor, another whose shoes are too big for him, like a little brother with ill-fitting hand-me-downs. It feels like a strange kind of summer camp until another group of men stroll over. They are closer to Matteo's age and have lines etched into their brows or around their eyes and she wonders, despairingly, how long it will be before the boy with too-big shoes looks like this too.

Everyone stares at Alix. When Matteo says she's American, they curse.

"Don't speak to her like that." At Matteo's words, they look sheepish.

"Spit on me in a month's time if I don't deliver what I promise," she says. "For now, show me everything. I can't fix what I don't know about."

They stare at her in surprise, having not expected the dialect—fluent Piedmontese, which she learned from Chiara.

"See this." Matteo leads her past a wall of silos and into the steel-gray of the talc plant, a grim backdrop, and she knows why the men prefer being outside. Matteo points to a man wearing, inexplicably, a British uniform.

"This is Colonel Stephenson, the *cazzone* I told you about," Matteo says.

The younger men who've followed them inside smile, whereas the uniformed man doesn't flinch, has no idea he's just been abused. And Alix realizes with a jolt that this must be the agent her OSS counterparts sent in to help the partisans—or the agent the British forced them to send in.

"He thinks," Matteo says, his voice dangerously congenial, "that he's here to lead and organize the partisans. But his Italian is incomprehensible, he won't take that damn uniform off and he has no idea how to even find Turin."

The agent takes a step away from Matteo's scorn and addresses Alix. "Who are you?" His manner is magisterial, just like Mrs. van der Meer.

Alix wants to swear worse than she's ever sworn in her life. Months of begging has produced this. What a goddamn waste.

She erupts. "Do you want me to order these men to take you up into the Alps and leave you there to fend for yourself? Take your uniform off. The partisans shouldn't have to shield you as well as themselves."

"How dare you." He steps toward her.

Matteo steps forward too but Alix puts out a hand to stop him. This is her fight. "I will not ask for another piece of equipment to be dropped in to help you unless you follow the partisans' orders," she tells the agent, voice hard. "I can action your requests for more guns to protect you—or not."

It's the agent's turn to swear now, at her, before he stalks away.

The partisans jeer as he departs, then turn to look at her with something more like admiration than disgust. She catches Matteo's eye and all of a sudden sees the ridiculous side of what just happened—a man in an occupied country wearing an enemy uniform, unable to understand even the most basic curse words. Her mouth smiles a little and Matteo grins in reply.

"I've been bad-tempered since last night," he says to her. His eyes trace over her face before he touches a finger quickly to hollows beneath her lids. "And you've walked for hours only to be sworn at by everyone here. I'm sorry."

The boys around them wolf-whistle but they're interrupted by the sound of running feet. A young man skids to a halt before Matteo. "Another *rastrellamento*," the youth says. "The Nazis are on their way to Susa."

Matteo's first instinct is to turn to her. "Don't worry about me," she says. "Tell me where I can find Chiara. I'll stick with her."

Then they make their way down lower into the valley.

\* \* \*

It's easy to hear the word *rastrellamento*—roundup—and assume it means the herding of something—animals perhaps—into a confined space. But roundup means nothing of the sort when orchestrated by Nazis.

At a shepherd's hut farther down the mountain, Alix finds Chiara. The young man who escorted her darts away to join his friends. Alix and Chiara have time only for a quick embrace before they nod. They're not staying in the grange, despite what they've been told.

They keep safely behind the partisans, who are armed with stolen weapons and borrowed weapons and outdated weapons and the weapons Alix supplied—but also with determination.

The Val di Susa, like the Val d'Aosta she and Matteo walked

through earlier, must ordinarily be breathtaking. It's a vast cradle of green scooped out between the Alps, the peaks of which intersect dramatically with the sky in a pattern of proud gray on hopeful blue. But now there's smoke where sky should be, holes where houses should be and the view is of fire, not majesty.

They're too late. The Germans have already wreaked their revenge on the partisans' families and friends.

Charred pieces of floral drapes flutter to the ground where rhododendrons once grew; a melted silver photo frame sits in a smashed window; a child's brass rattle clatters on the road where it will never be played with again.

She and Chiara catch up to Matteo in the town square. His eyes burn like the flames that tear at the walls of the few houses still standing as a woman tells him, "We tried to hide in the church but they dragged us out and made us watch while they marched the men into the square and..." She sobs as she points to a pile of what Alix now realizes are human bones, scorched of flesh.

Her stomach leaps into her mouth and she has to hold on to a wall to stop from retching. She reminds herself that this is what she needs—evidence gathered with her own eyes. "Do you know anyone from here?" she manages to ask Chiara.

Her friend's eyes are damp and her mouth, which Alix has always known to be laughing or spilling over with words, is a tight line holding back tears. "My older sister lives here with her husband. I haven't found her yet."

Which is why a grim-faced Matteo, Alix realizes, is methodically searching every street.

Alix swallows. "I'll help you look," she tells Chiara.

It is Alix who finds them.

There are five of them, swinging from trees like a medieval performance of grotesqueries. Alix steps closer, unsure of what she's seeing.

"*No.*" The sound is meant to be a scream but it is barely a whisper.

Her eyes close and her stomach disgorges. *You're just a witness*, she tries uselessly to tell herself. This isn't a horror she's forced to live. But even with her eyes closed she sees it.

Five women tied to trees. Three with stakes riven through them. Then there are two whose bodies flutter like tragic butterflies. Their stomachs have been torn open but even then it is still possible to see that they had been pregnant.

Chiara drops to her knees. Profanities and sobs stream from her mouth like prayers. Above her, the sky is alight with the remains of the fire, an angry red-orange hue as if the sky is bleeding too.

The partisans move toward the five women, some crying, some howling, some silent. Alix watches Matteo reach out for the hand of one of the women. He kisses it. And she knows that this is Matteo and Chiara's sister. Not just dead but destroyed, her unborn child too.

\* \* \*

They can't go back to the talc plant. In clipped tones, Matteo tells everyone he thinks Susa was torched because it's quite a distance from partisan headquarters, which means the Nazis knew the partisans would arrive too late. And that means the Nazis know where the partisans' base is located.

"Do you think they know who you are?" Alix hears Chiara ask her brother. "Who I am? That they chose Susa because—"

He cuts her off. "This is the Nazis' fault. Not ours."

But the despair in his eyes says that his thoughts are at odds with his words.

The partisans disperse into small and silent groups. Alix, Chiara, and Matteo pass the night in a deserted shepherd's hut in the mountains where they talk, not about war and death, but about the past— that lovely, safe place where the outcomes are known and the hurts already suffered.

"Chiara was my first patient," Matteo says quietly, swallowing a too-large mouthful of grappa. "I almost cut off her finger with a saw."

Chiara takes a medicinal gulp too and holds up her hand to show Alix the scar. "He was sawing firewood and I jumped in to help, except I put my hand under the blade. He wrapped my finger up in his shirt and carried me to the doctor—and he's wanted to be a doctor ever since."

"I thought being able to heal was the most powerful thing in the world," Matteo says. "But the *fottuti Nazisti* knew all along that the most powerful thing in the world isn't to heal, but to kill."

His mug clatters on the ground as he stands and disappears outside, the fierce set of his face stating plainly that he wants no company besides his grief.

Alix looks across at Chiara, whose face is streaked with ash and tears. "Do you wish you'd stayed in Bern?" Alix asks quietly, feeling somehow responsible for what had happened that day, which is both narcissistic and partly true.

Chiara, who used to make beds for spoiled schoolgirls and who now runs messages across Northern Italy past murderous Germans, shakes her head. "Do I wish not to know how my sister died? No. Because knowing what others are capable of—*that* is the most powerful thing in the world, if you let it drive you."

Chiara's strength gives out at last and she begins to cry in Alix's arms. When her hiccups quiet into sleep, Alix steals out of the grange, following the scent of cigarettes on the air.

It's impossible to imagine that Matteo has been doing anything other than crying too when she finds him. Her heart squeezes with what this man, all of twenty-five years, has had to endure.

"Tell me about your sister," she says, taking a seat on a rock a little way from him so he can have both company and privacy.

He draws on his cigarette and exhales smoke in a wistful stream.

"She was always going to marry and have babies and be completely happy. It was only Chiara and me who wanted more. She'd bake birthday cakes for us every year and last winter she came up into the mountains with a cake she'd made from flour she'd saved all year. She told me to be careful. I should have told her the same."

And Alix knows that, despite what he told Chiara, Matteo is blaming himself for his sister's death.

"Come here," she says softly, standing up.

He walks over to her and pulls her in so closely, holding her body against his as if he won't survive without something tender, one second of beauty amongst the ruins. She reaches up to touch his cheek and he presses his forehead against hers, his breath warm on her face, molded together in a closeness that would be more physical if either of them let it, but she knows she can't allow herself to fall in love with Matteo. His eyes, resting on hers, say the same—that falling in love would make him powerless. He has to give everything he has to the cause of Italy, especially after tonight.

They return to the grange hand in hand and she lies down with her head on his shoulder, tucked into his side, his arm wrapped around her. For a moment she almost wants to cry again—that the most intimate thing she's ever done with a man is right here and right now, fully clothed, not even kissing, just letting the slow stroking of her thumb on his chest and his finger on her arm speak of what it might be like if the world was a different place.

"If this were another time," he murmurs.

She presses one very light and very soft kiss on his cheek. "Yes," she says.

* * *

The following morning before she leaves, Matteo tucks a piece of paper into her hand. It reads:

*To Alix,*

*Bisous and Bacio.*

*All my love,*
*Matteo*

"Sometimes I feel like I'm not me anymore," he says to her, very quietly. "Like I'm turning into Bacio and he isn't—" He cuts himself off, tries again. "I'm trying to hold back a part of myself from all of this, Alix. I have to not give everything to Bacio because he has to deal with Nazis who are no better than savages. Hardly anyone calls me Matteo anymore. So I'm giving Matteo to you to save for me for a time when all of this is over."

Alix blinks once, then again, and a third time too but the tears slide down her cheeks anyway—useless tears because there is no physical human response that can possibly express the pain she feels at him asking her to be the custodian of his soul.

"Matteo," she says in the unsteadiest of voices and he smiles, just a little, at the sound of his name. "I promise."

# TWENTY-ONE

Back in Bern, Dulles flays her with vitriol for vanishing without warning until she tells him about the so-called secret agent wearing a British uniform and then he flays the British with vitriol instead. Alix's plan is to start stirring OSS Brindisi into action, but waiting for her is a note from Esmée:

> *I was drinking a French 75 with a friend from school the other night. We were talking about gardens we like to visit—and then we got onto churches. We made a list of our favorites: the Sainte-Chapelle, the Mont-Saint-Michel, the Duomo di Milano, the Paroisse Française, and the Basilica of Saint Francis of Assisi. It made me remember to go to confession this month to say some prayers. Salut ô Reine is a favorite; I remember yours was Mère de Miséricorde. I'm too busy to go on Sunday and I sleep late on Wednesdays. Fridays could work as Saturdays are for late dinners.*

Esmée's mention of gardens, their code word for Italy, means this note might be worth deciphering first. French 75s mean Esmée was at the Ritz talking to Frank, who is proving to be an invaluable member of the Resistance. Frank has obviously told Esmée about someone who has information for Alix on Italy. And that information—or person?—must be waiting for her at the Paroisse Française—the French Church—in Bern: the fourth in the list, as they agreed in the elevator. There's no other reason Esmée would send agnostic Alix to confession with a prayer for an identification phrase.

And Saturdays, the fourth on the list, must be the right date. There are three more Saturdays left in July—the letter's taken two weeks to arrive. She knows what her plans will be for the following weekend— and the weekend after.

She burns the letter carefully, watching the words vanish, hoping that whatever she finds in the confessional will be something that will help Matteo and Chiara. Until then, she has to try everything else at her disposal.

She starts with cabling Leone. I'M DELIVERING ON MY END OF THE DEAL, she writes, appending a full report of everything she saw in Italy and everything the partisans told her—the morale of the Nazis, the Fascists, and the Italian people; details of Pietro Koch's torture center in Milan, known as Villa Triste; information about the Battaglione Lupo, a group of Il Duce worshippers paid to hunt out partisans; the roundups, everything. Now, DAMN WELL DELIVER ON YOURS, she finishes. BISOUS.

Leone responds within an hour. Reading between the lines of his cable, she thinks he's as frustrated with the British as she is and has used her report as welcome ammunition to get things moving. For which she is hugely grateful. Proper OSS resources will stop another mass murder and boost the partisans' morale so they can at last become a force the Germans are too afraid to toy with.

* * *

One week later, Alix receives a note from Matteo, confirming he has men in the drop zones ready to receive the packages from OSS. He tells her he keeps dreaming of men with wounds he can't heal. *I also dream I won't ever see you again.*

Alix closes her eyes against the words.

The note she writes in response says that she dreams of lying in his arms—not on the floor of a shepherd's hut in the aftermath of a murder, but in a room with nobody else around. Just the two of them. It's meant to bring the future closer to him, and besides, she does dream that.

Does it mean she's unfaithful? Perhaps it does. But she hopes Bobby has someone to dream of too, some vision more extraordinary than their one disappointing night together to keep him hopeful.

\* \* \*

On Saturday early evening, Alix dresses in her most demure suit, places her fedora on her head to hide her hair, and goes to the French Church. It's an odd building, tall and thin with narrow arched windows running along each side, a strange little turret perched halfway along like a spire forbidden to grow. It's the oldest church in the city and she can feel the weight of its faith shroud her, the prayers of centuries whispering to her. A shiver prickles her skin.

She enters the church through the back door so that no one waiting for her to waltz through the main entrance will see her.

Inside, white stone arches cast shadows everywhere, as does the wooden mezzanine running over the altar. Above that, the gold pipes of the organ rise up like kings. She does not belong in this place and if it weren't for Matteo and Chiara, she would turn and run.

She makes herself breathe. Makes herself stay. Makes herself think of Matteo's face when the first American plane flies over tomorrow night with two OSS agents, two radios, guns, ammunition, money, tobacco, dynamite, fuses.

Calmer now, she locates the confessional booth, which is dark. Small. Hidden from all eyes. She'll have only a gun and her wits.

Shutting the door to the booth alerts whoever is on the other side that she's arrived and she hears surprise in his voice when he says,

"Salut ô Reine." He was obviously expecting to be warned of her arrival, which means she was right to take the back entrance.

"Mère de Miséricorde," she says, giving her response.

"*Une femme.*" There is even more surprise in his tone now.

"*Oui.*"

Something about his voice makes her glad he doesn't know who she is. It's a whiskey voice that scrapes over consonants, marking him out as a non-native speaker, no matter how hard he tries. There's a rattle of ice on his "r" sounds, rather than the required friction at the back of the throat. A ruined cocktail of equal parts champagne and schnapps, served on the rocks. Dangerous.

He's speaking French because he doesn't want her to know what his maternal tongue is. She suspects it's German—the rattle betrays him. She wonders how her Los Angeles accent alters her consonants and hopes they sound like the bubbles in the French 75 rather than the hangover. She thinks this last in an attempt to resurrect her humor. But her fists clench in front of her like a penitent's as she tries to press away the apprehension.

One of the pews creaks as the wood expands. A whistle of breeze creeps under the door. The piety in the air is suffocating.

At last he says, "You're interested in Italy."

She waits, letting her silence express her interest.

"Several German commanders are interested in bringing things to a faster end in Italy," he continues. "I was advised you can put us in contact with someone who might consider negotiations for a..."

Surrender? Is that what this is all about? Her heart quickens so much that she can hear it beat. If the Germans surrender in Italy, it will break the morale of German soldiers everywhere. The war *will* be over. She squeezes her eyes shut and almost smiles.

"A concession," the man finishes.

Conceding equals surrendering as far as Alix is concerned. "Why?" she asks.

"I don't think anyone doubts who'll lose the war now—it's just a question of how long it will take."

"You'll need to prove this isn't a setup."

"*Bien sûr.*" He tells her the name of a guard at Le Nuove prison in Turin who has release papers for five partisan prisoners. She can choose who should be released. They will speak again once the prisoners are free and his power and cooperation thus proven.

He is so smooth. This is a transaction, and his lack of emotion frightens her more than his voice. If his heart is not on the negotiating table, then *he* has the power. He has nothing to lose—but Alix does. She can never let him discover that.

"Leave any communication for me in the fifth hymnbook from the top of the pile," he says crisply. "Page one hundred and two. *Ciao.*"

It's her cue to leave.

She cables Leone immediately to confirm that Peach—the supply drop to the partisans—is still going ahead the following night. She needs to get hold of Chiara to tell her about the prisoners, and the only way to do that without it taking too long is via the new wireless operator who's being dropped into the Val di Susa tomorrow. She receives an affirmative response.

It's impossible to sleep that night and the next so she waits in the office and kisses the cable when it comes through at almost four in the morning. BISOUS, PEACH A SUCCESS. RADIO CONTACT ESTABLISHED. LEONE.

I NEED SORELLA SENT BACK TO DRUM ASAP, she cables back, wishing Bern—or Drum as it's referred to in code—had a receiver station for radio messages.

WILL PASS ON.

Chiara arrives two nights later and is thrilled to hear that Matteo can choose five prisoners to be released.

"It might be a trap," Alix warns. "Don't send Matteo to Le Nuove or he could end up inside."

"He'll go no matter what I say," Chiara replies and Alix knows it's true. This is one mission Matteo won't let anyone else execute.

Five nervous days later the message arrives from Leone: RADIO TRANSMISSION RECEIVED FROM BACIO: FIVE PRISONERS RELEASED. ALL SAFE.

Alix adds a new code name to National Gallery, Bern's master cryptogram list: La Voce.

But it's not enough for Dulles. "You never trust anyone after one successful offering," he says. And she's inclined to agree with him.

* * *

The next day, Dulles sits down in front of her and says, "It might all be over later this month. This war depends on one man and if he isn't around..."

Alix's heartbeat quickens. The only man Dulles could be talking about is Hitler and the only way for him not to be around is if he were dead. "The Allies or Germans?" she asks, wanting to know who's behind this coup or assassination.

"The Abwehr agent. Gisevius."

Alix goes to bed that night beaming. Hitler's death is imminent. It will save Italy from being ruined by more bombs. Matteo and Chiara will survive. And Matteo *will* see Alix again.

And so July progresses with Dulles in a buoyant mood, expecting news of Hitler's death every day. Alix works late every night coordinating supply drops to the partisans who are winning more and more small battles against the Germans.

She's cabling Leone near midnight toward the end of the month when Mary strolls in from Dulles's private rooms. "I was supposed to meet Allen here for dinner at eight o'clock." Her tone is easy, her eyes sad.

"I don't know where he is." Alix fixes Mary a martini and adds, wanting to cheer her up, "It's good that Gisevius has come through."

She assumes that Mary, who's been cultivating the Abwehr agent along with Dulles, knows about the assassination plot.

"Is it?" Mary asks, eyes narrowing and Alix realizes she has no idea—but that if she'd once contemplated going away for a weekend with Gisevius then she must have feelings for him that go beyond what an agent should feel for an informant.

Alix drops into a chair. A husband. A lover. An informant Mary considered sleeping with too. What a mess. All Alix can say is, "You know if Dulles hasn't told you, I can't. I'm sorry."

Mary shrugs, a small, powerless gesture and subsides into a chair too. "Don't be. Allen's reticence is a job requirement, not personal. What's personal is when—" For the first time since Alix has known her, Mary stops herself before she delivers whatever brutal truth she'd been on the point of uttering.

"You know," Alix says into the sudden silence, wondering if this time, what Mary won't say is something she needs to say—and if Alix can somehow be the one to offer the advice or wisdom or even just comfort. "You're the only person who's ever told me about the real intricacies of marriage and children and fidelity. Maybe learning how to run clandestine messages into Italy will somehow help me in my life after the war but I'm guessing the things you've told me might help me more." *Because I intend to do the exact opposite*, Alix adds, but only to herself.

"Well then, I suppose I shouldn't miss this chance to enlighten you further." Mary's voice is stretched thin to the point of breaking. "You think my husband is the better man because he's the one being cheated on."

Alix winces, having not been aware her undeserved judgment upon Mary sat so obviously in her eyes.

"Soon before I married Jean," Mary continues coolly, "he showed me a pile of letters he'd had my servant send to him while he was away, reporting on my behavior, my visitors. So I told Jean I didn't want to marry him anymore. He hit me so hard that he knocked me out. That's not an intricacy; that's life and love right there and it's why what Allen does or doesn't do can't hurt me."

"That's not love," Alix protests, wishing she'd never allowed this conversation to continue. Love is what you would defend with your life, not what you would destroy. But if it isn't love, is it life? She feels herself shudder. If it is, it's almost as bad as war.

Mary tosses down another martini, having obviously not yet concluded this evening's lesson. "Yesterday, Allen rushed into my hotel room. *Quick*, he said. *I need to clear my head.* Then he had me on the sofa and in less time than it takes me to recount this story, he was done. When he left, he told me it was just what he needed. I didn't even think—*but what about what I needed?* I stopped thinking things like that a long time ago. All of which is to say—there is no love. There are only transactions. A woman's bank is never empty for any man wanting to transact with her."

Alix stands. She's just seen a future she'd rather not see: her and Bobby in an apartment he would own, able to hit her—*he would never do that, would he?*—able to have another woman whenever he needed to clear his head. Alix would be like Dulles's wife, aware of the affair but pretending not to be, or like Mary—taking her own unsatisfactory revenge. And what of the other transactions Alix is involved in, with men who hide themselves behind confessional screens and barter in prisoners—in human lives? What will she be required to offer La Voce in exchange for those lives?

Mary ends the lesson by saying, voice no longer thin but pragmatic. "Allen told me upfront he couldn't marry me. *But*, he said, *I want you.* It was supposed to be a good enough offer. It must've been. I accepted it."

Before Alix can reply, the door flies open and Dulles enters, the strong stink of alcohol about him dangerous in a room with a fire blazing.

"Mary," he shouts. "Where's the dinner?"

Alix wishes she could throw the dinner at him on Mary's behalf.

\* \* \*

"He's still alive." It's a few days later when Dulles curses profanely then droops across his desk, a man with dashed hopes. Alix has never thought about Dulles as having hopes, just demands. But even he can't order Hitler's death. The bomb Gisevius's accomplices took into Hitler's bunker blew up but the Führer has a thousand lives. And he hardly used one, escaping with barely a scratch.

The repercussions are immediate. The conspirators in Germany are rounded up. Gisevius disappears, taking his link to the Nazis' inner circle with him. The glorious future Alix had been hoping for retreats. Mary requires a week of martinis. The pressure for a break-through in Italy intensifies.

"We need a fucking victory," Dulles says almost every day.

So Alix works harder than ever with Chiara and Matteo to extend the courier service to Milan. She equips the partisans with supplies she organizes through Leone. And those supply drops finally reap the victory Dulles wants.

*Bisous,* Matteo's note to Alix reads, *there are more than sixty thousand men in the mountains now. We've blown up seventy-five bridges and put twenty railway tracks out of action. The Nazis surrendered to us in Domodossola, Cannobio, Piaggio Valmara, Creola, Varzo, and the entire Formazza Valley. Need arms and supplies to hold ground as expect reprisals. Bacio, bacio.*

Matteo always finishes his couriered messages to her the same way: his code name with a capital letter so she knows who the message is from, and then the word repeated a second time—a kiss just for her. Every message from him is precious because it reaffirms that he too must have a thousand lives. And this message is more precious than usual because the results of Alix's work and Chiara's work and Matteo's work and the work of every *staffetta* and partisan are unarguable—a dozen towns under partisan control in Nazi occupied Italy!

Nothing can go wrong now. The partisans are winning battles. They only need to hold the towns they've taken until the Allies can break through the Gothic Line and into the north. Surely that must happen soon.

# TWENTY-TWO

In an effort to make it end even sooner, Alix leaves a note in the hymnbook for La Voce. She will test him once more and then she and Dulles will let him have his meeting with Allied Command to talk about surrenders. Paris is liberated now so why not Italy? She almost skips to the French Church on the day of their meeting, smiling at the crisp chill of approaching winter touching her cheeks, the prospect of freedom for all of them, perhaps by the end of 1944.

But her steps slow when she enters the church. She can smell him. Expensive cologne has a weightiness that either lingers or suffocates, depending on how one feels about the wearer. She has to think consciously about breathing as she slips into the confessional booth.

"Where is your favorite place in Paris?"

His words catch her completely off guard and her unthinking, "What?" alerts him to her surprise. She needs to stop thinking about freedom and recover her wits. "The Ritz," she says, remembering what Mary told her: if you share something personal with someone, they'll do the same with you—if they're truly on your side. And that's what Alix needs to know—can she trust La Voce?

He laughs.

"And yours? A place where your German accent isn't discernible, I expect," she pushes, knowing her words will irritate him and hoping to throw him similarly off guard. "It would need to be somewhere noisy. A bar? A brothel?"

"The Ritz," he replies coldly.

"Liar."

The scrape of his chair. He's going to leave.

She pushes further. "You not afraid of a woman, are you?"

She can hear how very still he is standing on the other side of the wall. "I only want one more proof," she says. "Then I'll arrange your meeting with the Allies. We both have bosses to please."

She's phrased her offer to imply she wants something from him, thus giving him a little power back. She lets him savor it before she asks, "What do the Nazis have in store for the partisans?"

His laugh is false and loud and she thinks he's used it to cover his surprise. He'd been expecting something harder to give. Damn. She's exposed herself.

"Operation Nachtigall," he says, the creak of wood telling her he's sitting down again. "The autumn of fire. Four thousand troops, as well as tanks, will soon be heading for the valleys around Turin to clean up the partisans."

She'd steeled herself before he began speaking so, despite the shock of his words, she replies with a lighthearted, "Where in Paris is your favorite place, really?"

He's quiet a moment then says, "A Paris brasserie is like no other restaurant in no other city. It's not just the food, it's the sense one has of being…indulged. I plan to return there once this is all over."

When he stands she makes no attempt to stop him. They both have what they need. But then he says, "I hope your partisans understand how well they are loved by you."

His words spark with malice, a blade drawn and then re-sheathed with the answer, "It's Brasserie Lipp." Three words spoken with the low wistfulness of truth.

\* \* \*

*No, no, no*, Alix thinks on November 13 as she listens to *Italia Com-batte* on the radio, already knowing what General Alexander, the commander of the Allied armies in Italy, is about to say. The Allies haven't progressed far enough through Italy; they're bogged down in Bologna behind the Nazis' impenetrable defense. Mud and rain equal deadly and drawn-out fighting conditions so the Allies are bedding down for winter, preparing to hold ground rather than advance. Alexander is telling the partisans that despite having survived the autumn of fire—in part thanks to La Voce's forewarning—they must stand down for winter too.

But how can a partisan army stand down? They can't return home—the Nazis will kill them. Their only option is to hide in the icy mountains throughout winter, freezing, with little food, relying on *staffette* to bring supplies. They'll lose every town and valley they've fought for—with no more Allied airdrops, they'll have no more weapons or ammunition. Worst of all is that the Nazis will hear this broadcast—it's on a public radio station, for Christ's sake. Alexander might as well have the partisans march out of their hideouts with their hands up. Matteo does not have enough lives to survive this.

Alix does the only thing she can. She catches the train to Zermatt and waits in the shed in the grounds of Nina's lodge, knowing that Chiara and perhaps a dozen furious partisans will come through the border, probably pointing their guns at Alix and telling her the general has just signed their death warrants.

The door to the shed opens after midnight. "What the hell, Alix?" It's a furious Matteo instead, which is worse. She would rather a dozen armed partisans.

There isn't a single word she can say. She's the one who got Matteo and Chiara and everyone else into this mess—she's Ariadne and her web is lethal.

She offers the only plan she has, standing in the dark of a shed lit by a single oil lamp that burnishes to gold the anger and the hurt in

Matteo's eyes. "The source who told me about Nachtigall can tell me where the Nazis are planning to attack next," she says. "I'm going to make him warn me in advance of as many roundups and attacks as possible so you can at least be prepared."

The anger dies in Matteo's eyes, replaced by something harder to witness—exhaustion. She has no idea how he keeps up the morale of the thousands of partisans who've just heard that the Allies are turning their backs on them. She has no idea how he can even stand right now.

"You need to sleep," she says. "At least sit down."

He slides his back down the wall and sits on the floor, resting his elbows on his knees, staring at nothing.

Alix presses her lips together against the painful ache in her throat. She lowers herself to the ground beside him and places a gentle hand on his.

"I don't know what kind of man I'm going to be by the time this ends," he says to her abruptly, voice hoarse. "If it ended now, I could look back and say the things I've had to do were necessary. But if it keeps going for months or years more, then…" He shakes his head and Alix's grip on his hand tightens.

"I used to fix people," he says, eyes flickering toward her face and then away. "Now I'm the one responsible for them needing a doctor. Or worse."

"Matteo," she whispers, moving closer, trying to hold on to his eyes. "You have never burned a man alive. You have never marched into a town and made women and children watch while you murder their innocent husbands. Maybe you've had to kill—but you've never murdered. I know that."

He rests his forehead against hers. "But how long before I do?"

How can anyone not cry when they listen to a man who is fighting for freedom berate himself for the things that war makes him do? She touches her palm to his face and he turns his mouth to kiss it.

She is left that night with the brand of Matteo's mouth upon her palm. She holds it against her chest, wishing she could take that scant evidence to General Alexander and have him look upon it and understand that war is also the blood and scars inside a man's heart—invisible, but harder to bear perhaps than the wounds that kill.

\* \* \*

On her way back to Bern, she reads in the newspaper what the CLN have said to the partisans in response to General Alexander. *Durare*: endure. Do not weaken.

Nor will Alix weaken. She will bargain with La Voce for what she needs.

She goes straight to the French Church, finds the hymnbook and turns to page one hundred and two. The hymn is called "When the Bridegroom Cometh." As she tucks her note inside, her eye falls on the words:

> *When the Bridegroom cometh*
> *Then we all must appear,*
> *'Round His throne eternal and our sentence hear;*
> *Will you hear His welcome*
> *To eternal light,*
> *Or, Depart, ye cursèd, into endless night?*

She shivers as she steps back out into the night.

Every day she checks the hymnbook for a reply. Every day she plans and organizes with Dulles.

One week later, a reply comes. She returns to the church that night as directed and walks in through the front doors. She tells La Voce, "A meeting in Lugano has been arranged with the people you need to speak to about a surrender of Italy. But the meeting will only go ahead if you give me advance warning of the next Nazi attack on the partisans."

This is it—the moment she has compromised herself. Dulles will certainly fire her if he knows she has told La Voce the meeting is dependent upon conditions. The meeting is set and scheduled and Dulles is a rooster crowing over the fact that he might be responsible for bringing an end to one part of the war. He'll hold the meeting regardless of what La Voce says.

Being beholden to an informant she knows nothing about is as precarious a position as you can find yourself in. But Matteo is in a precarious position too. *How long before I do?* Those words echo in Alix's sleep every night, accompanied by the image of Matteo with a knife in his hand and a body at his feet.

"I've already proven myself a reliable source," he says. "I won't give you anything more."

"Or can't?" she says, knowing she's at the edge of too-far.

But his control doesn't slip—unlike hers. "I will give you the date and location of the next raid on the partisans only when my commanders are in Lugano for the meeting. I will not give you any more for free."

She agrees. There is no other option. *Never confuse how much you like someone with the quality of their information,* Dulles has told both her and Mary. Alix might be afraid of La Voce, but that doesn't mean he won't be useful.

She returns to Herrengasse and urges Dulles to bring the meeting forward, telling him La Voce's superiors have cold feet.

On the day of the meeting, a note appears in the hymnbook with the details of the next raid on the partisans. She just has time to cable Leone to ask him to radio the partisans. They're able to move to a new location and hide both themselves and the townspeople without anyone suffering so much as a scratch.

Dulles returns from Lugano more rooster-like than ever. Of

all people, Obergruppenführer Karl Wolff was in attendance. La Voce has well and truly come through. He must work with Wolff in some capacity, given he's the man Wolff trusted with the job of getting the Allies to the negotiating table. And, Alix reflects, if Dulles and the Allies are dealing with Karl Wolff, it's unlikely she'll ever have to ask anything of La Voce again.

# TWENTY-THREE

**New York Times**

March 1, 1945

*Tension is mounting in Europe as reports that Hitler and the cream of the Nazi troops, the SS and the Gestapo plan to withdraw to an Alpine Fortress in an area bordered by Switzerland, Italy, and Austria for their final stand. Predictions of a bloody battle that will drag the war out for months or years more have the President and the Supreme Allied Command on edge. Ejecting fanatical German forces from this heavily defended area without losing thousands more lives is likely to be one of the most difficult tasks of the war so far. The elite troops Hitler has chosen to be the primary defenders of this fortress are so feared they are known as the Werewolves.*

*This mountain hideaway, known as the National Redoubt, comprises a system of air-conditioned caves stocked with enough water, military equipment, and food to keep the German army comfortable for at least twelve months. Almost all of the available troops in Italy will be able to withdraw, unhindered by the Allies, to the National Redoubt as there is a clear and open path from the north of that country into the Alps.*

"Fucking werewolves," Dulles growls as he slams the report onto Alix's desk.

Alix pours him a drink even though it's only nine in the morning. "Bacio told me he isn't sure the Redoubt actually exists."

"Fucking Bacio," Dulles growls again and Alix understands that today everyone is an expletive rather than a human being. She makes the whiskey a double, then pours one for herself.

She's managed to get the partisans through winter mostly intact thanks to La Voce's information and the partisans' ingenuity. They're readying themselves to fight properly by the Allies' side at last, believing the end is tantalizingly close. But if there's a mountain retreat where all of the Nazi troops in Italy can hide and thus extend the war over yet another winter and perhaps another...Nobody will survive that.

"What if it's just brilliant propaganda?" she says, burying thoughts she doesn't wish to contemplate deep in the pockets of her mind. "Leone's also heard rumors that maybe the Redoubt isn't real." But she can hear the doubt in her voice.

"Do your research," Dulles says as if she hasn't already been doing that. "There are no goddamned Allied troops in Northern Italy, no one except your partisans to stop every Nazi division escaping to a fortress where they might hold out for years. Ask La Voce. Use your damn informants."

\* \* \*

Alix doesn't want to ask La Voce anything. But then another cable arrives from AFHQ that makes her close her eyes.

ULTRA INTERCEPT PICKED UP REPORTS THAT ENTIRE GERMAN HIGH COMMAND ORDERED TO REDOUBT AREA. NEW AERIAL PHOTOS

SHOW ANTI-TANK DITCHES, LOG PILLBOXES, DUGOUTS, AND BUNKERS IN REDOUBT VICINITY. RUNWAYS FOR JET AIRCRAFT BEING BUILT. REQUIRE FURTHER INTELLIGENCE. URGENT.

Alix wants to throw the cable at the wall. This cannot be happening. How the hell can she tell Matteo and the partisans this? How can she keep their spirits up and keep everyone alive for another indeterminate period of time?

She goes to her apartment and, from her wardrobe, selects a Vionnet gown the house gifted her when she worked at *Harper's Bazaar*. It's so white its folds almost shimmer blue and it's made of a silk-jersey so supple that it hides very little as it skims over the curves of her body.

Thus costumed, she takes herself and her dress to the Bellevue Palace Hotel and flirts with every man in the bar, doing the research Dulles demanded of her. But only the same rumors she's already heard about the Redoubt swirl.

It's almost midnight when one of her couriers appears with a message: Matteo is waiting in Nina's shed at the ski lodge. It can only mean something terrible has happened.

Alix requisitions a car, speeds to the border and finds Matteo there with eyes skewered of all hope. "Chiara's in Villa Triste."

*No, no, no.*

Villa Triste in Milan is run by the Italian Pietro Koch, a man for whom the word *murder* is too fine. He's a butcher, and the villa is his torture chamber. Starving prisoners are made to watch through the bars as Koch and his band snort cocaine, drink champagne, and then select a number of captives whose bones they break, whose teeth they tear out. All the while a semi-naked woman dances maniacally alongside, transforming torture into something so depraved Alix can hardly turn her mind to it.

La Voce is her only hope now.

*I will not give you any more for free.*

She shudders. What will he want? And she wonders, with sudden revulsion, if La Voce had always known she would need him, eventually.

"Stay here," she says to Matteo. "It might take me a couple of days. But I'm coming back. Nina will look after you."

She drives too fast to Bern where she goes to the church and finds herself—agnostic Alix—on her knees weeping as she tries to write La Voce a note. She hears a noise—footsteps—and she whips around. No one is there. But a hymnbook near the door is open and a note is nestled in its pages.

*You want Matteo Romano's sister*, it says and her heart spasms with fear. She's being followed or Matteo's being followed or they both are—that's the only way La Voce can know what she wants. Either way, the Nazis, or at least La Voce, know who Matteo is.

*I will free two partisans from Villa Triste*, the note reads. *They will meet you at Trattoria Joia on Via Paolo Uccello in Milan at eight in the evening two days from now. They will have an offer for you from one of my subordinates. If you accept, the Romano girl will be freed.*

*You bastard*, Alix wants to shout. He could make the offer now. But he wants Alix to go to Italy to get it. He's playing with her. And she's certain that someone who works for La Voce saw her crying just now, which means they know Matteo is her vulnerability. How will they use it?

Is this whole thing a trap she's running into? Is loyalty—or guilt, perhaps—blinding her to consequence?

But how many teeth can Chiara endure having ripped out before she gives up Matteo and all the partisans?

Alix walks out of the church and in the direction of Herrengasse. Then she slips away into the square dominated by the Child Eater Fountain and through the covered arcades, weaving up one and down another, listening and watching, certain she's lost anyone who might have been following her.

Eventually, she ends up in a cheap hotel behind the church where she writes letters to her couriers, arranging to have Matteo moved to a house near a different border-crossing point, one they haven't used yet. She waits until it's dark again and borrows a different car from another person on her payroll, then drives back toward the border. She and Matteo speak only briefly, just long enough to tell him her plan.

The border crossing is exhausting—there are more steep inclines than on the previous route and the forest is thick and punishing. They cross through nearer to Lake Como and the Fascist State headquarters, closer to danger, then take several indirect trains, crisscrossing down to Milan.

It's only when they reach the central station that Alix says to him, "You can't come with me. I'll meet you here in an hour."

Matteo shakes his head vehemently.

"This might be a trap to capture you," she says.

"It might be a trap to capture you," he retorts.

"I'm worth nothing to the Nazis," she says. "La Voce knows the surrender negotiations will be called off if anything happens to me." She has no idea if this is true or if Dulles would just shake his head and sigh over the inconvenience of having to send his own cables.

She walks to Via Paolo Uccello, having memorized the route, knowing that to take out a map and appear lost is to send herself to prison. She's had to tuck all of her red hair up into a scarf, has exchanged her trekking clothes for one of the *staffetta*'s coats.

She tries so hard not to look at the posters that read:

*10,000 lira and ten kilos of salt for every partisan turned over to Pietro Koch.*

*25,000 lira for information that leads to the capture of a saboteur.*

*100,000 lira for a partisan leader.*

Each poster bears the address of Villa Triste and she is horrified to discover that it's on the same street she's walking along now, that it's four doors ahead, then two, that she is passing it and it looks like any ordinary townhouse and Chiara is on the other side of the wall.

The posters are bold and bright and intact. The rest of Milan is a ruin.

To her left, an entire side street no longer exists, buried beneath a pile of rubble. The Duomo is a carcass of broken stone and toothpicks. Walls without roofs stand like ancient archeological relics except that people pass into and out of them, people who look like ruins too.

There is no air, only dust that hangs like a smothering hand over her mouth. There is no blue sky.

A stone falls from the teetering tower of a broken building and no one except Alix jumps. This is a place where death falls from the sky so often it has become unremarkable.

A little farther along she sees, beside one of the awful posters offering cash in exchange for humans, a corpse. A placard has been hung around its neck, stating: *The Germans pay with money, the partisans pay with bullets,* and she understands that the dead man was a Fascist or Nazi and the partisans have exacted their revenge.

If she cries, the tears will leave streaks in the dust on her face.

The trattoria, when she reaches it, is a relief. How can walking into what might be a trap be a relief?

The two freed partisans are easy to spot—they have the same drained look as Matteo but their faces are colored with bruises and blood and they have no teeth. They are the augury of Chiara's future, and perhaps Matteo's too.

She gives them the code word and they respond in kind. So far, it is what La Voce promised, with no sign of an ambush, but she keeps her hand on her bag with her gun.

The partisans tell her they must return to Villa Triste by nightfall with her answer to the proposed trade or every inmate in the prison will die.

"What's the trade?" Alix asks, certain that every fiber of her being will revolt against whatever the Nazis demand.

"Pietro Koch wants safe passage to Switzerland. He knows the Allies will win eventually and he doesn't want to be left to their mercy." The partisan looks as if he will spit on the floor of the trattoria, such is his disgust at the idea of anyone allowing a man who commands a torture chamber to run away to freedom in Switzerland. "In exchange, he'll free all the prisoners at Villa Triste."

If Alix had wanted to cry before, now she wants to weep. It is not an offer. It's a travesty.

And she cannot authorize anything of the sort. How can she, who sits on her safe throne in Switzerland, authorize the salvation of the vicious murderer who runs Villa Triste? What will the families of the hundreds of people killed and maimed by Pietro Koch say to her if they find out she let him go free in exchange for the life of her friend?

La Voce is, she realizes now, the kind of man who lurks in the background behind the powerful men, ready to be called upon when the filthiest deeds need to be done. And she has thrown her lot in with him. A hundred showers and she will never feel clean, not after this.

She cannot make this decision because she does not have to live with its consequences. Only the partisan leaders can do that.

She asks the two men to wait for her. The look on their faces is one she knows no word for. It's beyond despair—they have forgotten not just hope, but the idea of hope.

At the station, Matteo moves quickly toward her and stops when he sees her face. "No..." he starts to say.

"It's not Chiara," she rushes to reassure him. She tells him what Koch wants.

Matteo punches the wall. Alix is the one who recoils with pain.

She takes his bruised fist in hers and hurries them away—Matteo's mere presence in Milan is danger enough without him drawing attention to himself.

"We have to take this to Parri," Matteo says dully.

Alix nods. As one of the leaders of the CLN, Parri is the only one who can make this kind of decision.

"Parri's wife..." Matteo stops and Alix knows that if she weren't holding on to his hand, he would punch another wall until his bones are broken. "Lisetta, Parri's wife, was taken with Chiara. She's in Villa Triste too. And she's pregnant."

When Alix saw Matteo's sister hanging from a tree with her stomach sliced open, she'd thought that was the worst thing she would ever witness in her life. But she was wrong. Deeper horror exists even than that. Parri will have to decide the fate of his wife and unborn child, will have to bow down before evil in order to save them. What man should ever have to do that?

They don't speak as they walk to the apartment where Parri is hiding.

He listens to them with empty eyes. Then he crosses to the gramophone. He selects a recording and two bursts of music erupt into the room followed by the sound of cellos weeping. Beethoven's *Eroica*, a symphony for heroes.

And Alix knows what Parri will do.

The three of them listen in silence. When the music ends, Parri says, "With hyenas, we do not deal."

There are no tears in his eyes when he speaks, his words signing the death warrant for his wife and unborn child—and for Chiara too—but Alix can hear the sound of them falling inside him, like the percussion to the heroes' symphony.

* * *

After they leave Parri, Alix looks up at Matteo and what she sees in his eyes makes her heart shiver.

"Tell me that dream again," he says. "The one you said would be my future."

"I said," she begins and her voice cracks. "You would have your own dark-haired Madonna, a band of children, and a medical practice too. That everyone in Piedmont would speak of the handsome doctor who fought bravely in the war and who devoted his life to healing. And you said that sometimes your Madonna might have…"

Her voice breaks again, split open by words that were once said so hopefully and are now a wretched plea for Matteo not to do the things that are in his eyes. "That your Madonna might have red hair," she whispers.

She draws him into the darkened corner of a bomb-shattered building and pulls off her scarf. "Red hair like this. And I didn't say, but I wanted to, that she will kiss you like this."

He reaches for her at the same time as she reaches for him and their kiss is like no kind of kiss she has ever heard of or imagined. It is not from a storybook; it's hard and sad and plaintive, mouth locked to mouth. The press of their bodies painfully tight against one another is an imploration from her to him that he not do all the things the moment with Parri has made him capable of. And it is also the plea from him to her that he will somehow find the strength not to do those things either.

"I love you, Alix."

The words are a breath against her ear, so faint and fading that they're gone before she can be sure she's heard them. She kisses him again, more urgently than before, and he responds in kind, gifting her the kind of love that breaks her heart right open—the only kind of love the world will let her have from him.

When they release one another, her cheeks are wet with his tears. She has no idea what Matteo will do now, whether he is still the man who gave her a note with his name written inside because he thought Matteo was someone worth preserving—or whether La Voce has won another victory he didn't even know was within his reach.

\* \* \*

A violent, clawing devastation propels Alix back to Bern. She doesn't creep or tiptoe or look over her shoulder—she wants La Voce to follow her. She wants this showdown.

She goes straight to the confessional booth where she knows he'll be waiting.

"That wasn't a deal," she says. "For Parri, that was agony."

"And for your friend Matteo? How did he react to the news that his sibling is soon to be murdered?" he inquires.

She wants to open the door, let in air, let in hope and light and everything she once believed robust and unbreakable. She wants to let out evil, but it is everywhere.

But—was there a slight strain on the words in La Voce's last sentence? Alix's mind scrambles through all of the voice training she's undertaken, searching for the tiny splinter through which she can tunnel into his mind, rather than always be groping for purchase.

"You know it was agony for him too," she says at last.

"All right," he concedes. "It wasn't a deal. It was a tease. You see, I want you all to search deeper inside yourselves than even the filthiest, darkest places—the ones you pretend don't exist. I want you to find the answer to the question—what are you capable of doing to a man who is merciless toward someone you love?"

A savage pause. La Voce's words are an echo of what she was thinking in that bomb-ruined building, holding Matteo in her arms.

"Parri knows the answer to that now," La Voce continues. "But I'm not especially interested in Parri. I'm interested in you, and in Matteo Romano. His sister is still alive—for now."

She wants to thrust her face right up to the screen and shout, *I'll do anything! Just tell me what to do!* Then her fingers tighten in the hard clench of her fist. Anything? Could she be merciless? And she knows the answer. No. She's not made of that stuff.

It's both a bitter blow, and a tiny flicker of light.

Until La Voce speaks again.

"My deal is this." He pauses for effect. "Next week, you will come to my room at the Bellevue Hotel. And you will wear your white dress."

She only has one white dress—the Vionnet gown she'd worn to the Bellevue the night she found out Chiara was in Villa Triste.

La Voce knows she has a white dress. It can only mean he has seen her.

And he's just told her to meet him in his hotel room. It can only mean that he wants her.

She understands now that this man has no interest in the traditional sort of power one acquires when dealing with men who rule nations; he wants the kind of power one has when playing with their souls. And her soul is the prize, or perhaps the sacrifice. She's the no-longer-sacred cow, given up for slaughter.

# PART FIVE
## PARIS, 1947

*It wasn't easy working back then...It wasn't* right *to work.* —Nancy White, niece of Carmel Snow

# TWENTY-FOUR

W e need to get out of here," Anthony said.

Alix shook her head. There was an unconscious man on the floor of her *pension*. Anthony March was side by side with Fortunée, Alix's nemesis. And Bobby had wanted to find Matteo.

"Hurry up, Alix." Anthony looked as if he were going to take her arm and propel her out the door. He said to Fortunée, "Can you clean it up?"

"Drop me in Montmartre," Fortunée said. "I'll find someone who can help."

God, they spoke as if they were working together. Anthony, and the woman who'd had Alix fired. There was no chance she was going anywhere with the two of them.

What were her options though? To walk the streets of Paris, suitcase and hatboxes in hand—while possibly being tailed by La Voce or someone working for him—until she found a *pension* or a hotel that would open its doors to her at three in the morning, or . . . *Merde*. She had no options. Suzanne would ask questions and Alix didn't want this intruding on her work. Esmée? She hadn't been at the ball, which might mean she was out of town.

She shook her head at Anthony again. "You and Fortunée can leave. I don't need your help."

"Goddammit, Alix." Somehow, even though Anthony was the one who had clearly lied, he was swearing at her. Then he started to all but shout. "You've been waiting for me to screw this up from the out-set. Searching for evidence of my shortcomings. I have plenty—you don't need a spy's training to find them, just a set of eyeballs. But you know what? You have a few shortcomings too. You don't trust *any-body*. I bet there are a million good reasons why. But I can explain Anjelica—or Fortunée or whatever the hell name you know her as—if you just come to the Ritz. I should have told you about her before, obviously. But would I be so dumb as to bring her here now if I was working against you? No. So let's go."

Of all the things she'd thought might happen since Anthony and Fortunée had appeared in her room, him castigating her for her short-comings was not one of them. She was aware only that her mouth was open, but empty of words.

Anthony swore again, and ran a hand through his hair. "Sorry. I'm pissed at myself for letting you leave the ball alone. We need to go. Please?" he added after another beat of silence from Alix.

It was so damn hard to trust. But if she walked away now and didn't let him explain, she'd be back to never trusting anybody. *What a goddamn way to live.*

So she picked up her things.

Almost immediately they were in Anthony's car. They sped along to Rue Pigalle, where they stopped to let Fortunée out. The whole time Alix held Matteo's note tight in her hand, her fingertips resting against the fabric of a gown that had promised a different kind of night.

"Come back to the Ritz when you've finished, Anjelica," Anthony said as Fortunée stepped onto the pavement.

"Anjelica," Alix repeated, the only word she'd spoken since they left.

"Some men think I'm an angel," Fortunée said before she strolled away, hips swinging exaggeratedly.

The car started again. "Stop," Alix told the driver after they'd turned the corner.

"What for?" Anthony demanded. Then, "Please don't go, Alix."

"I'm coming back," was all she said, before she climbed out and hurried over to the telephone booth they'd passed, praying someone would answer.

After that, it was a long and wordless ride to the Ritz.

\* \* \*

Once inside his suite, Anthony turned on a lamp and watched as Alix fled to the window and stared out over the Place Vendôme. In the car, he'd tried to think of a way to explain so it didn't sound so bad but he hadn't come up with anything. So he started with the facts.

"I met Anjelica, or Fortunée, in Italy. She was one of my informants. She came to see me in Paris last year to tell me that if I needed her skills—in spying, nothing more," he was quick to add, "then I should get in touch. When I heard about you coming to Paris, I asked her to try to get a job at Dior so she could keep an eye on you."

A rap at the door of his suite made him jump but it was just the coffee he'd ordered on the way up. He sent the housemaid away and poured out two cups, leaving one on the table nearest Alix. Then he told her the truth, which was what he owed her and what he'd promised her.

"When I saw her at the ball, I almost convinced myself I'd just forgotten to tell you about her. But the real reason I didn't tell you was because I thought admitting I knew a prostitute and that I'd paid her"—why did it sound so much worse aloud than it did in his head?—"would confirm every last suspicion and preconception you have about me."

"But now I've found out, can't you see it does that anyway?"

"And can't you see that you're a hard woman to confess to?"

There was more than a note of anger in his voice again and Alix whirled around to face him. He froze, waiting for her to stalk off. But whatever expression his face wore—if it reflected his feelings, it must look damn bleak—made the anger tumble from her eyes.

Instead, tears welled up and one spilled out, falling down her cheek.

Through every conversation they'd had about all the terrible things in their pasts, she had never cried. And he felt suddenly as gut-punched as she'd looked when he'd walked through the door of her *pension* with Anjelica.

The world had done its best to hurt Alix—making her an orphan at age thirteen, letting OSS pick her up and send her to war where they'd left her to manage a Nazi who most likely had the blood of tens of thousands staining his soul, then sending her back to Manhattan to work for men who would not have respected her wit or the fact that she was completely unlike any other woman on the planet. And now he'd hurt her too. *Fuck.*

"*Merde.*" She swore too, turning back to the window. "I'm sorry," she said, twisting her head to look back at him so he could see the equally bleak look on her face. "I never used to be a hard woman. Matteo once called me an angel. But it turned out I was the devil, leading him to his death. That's why I'm hard."

Anthony swore again and took one step toward her. "I didn't say you were hard. I said you were a hard woman to confess to. You know why? Because you wear your integrity like you wear that dress—as if it's your skin. Whereas I've forgotten how to even spell the word." *Shit, where was all this coming from?* Maybe from needing to be the one person who didn't make her weep.

"On the street in Montmartre a couple of weeks ago," he went on, letting it all come out now, "you were so passionate about Dior that you put your body in front of a mannequin to protect her. And all I could think was—is there anything in my life I'd put my body on the line to defend? And the answer was no. That's why you're a hard woman to confess to."

He moved back to the desk and tipped the contents of his coffee cup down his throat. "Forget it. Tonight has been, from the moment I was in the swimming pool with you—" Wanting to slide his hands over the curve of her waist. To scoop her jaw into his palms and kiss her and kiss her and never, ever stop.

*Jesus.* He rubbed a hand on his brow, replaced the coffee cup in the saucer, took a deep and steadying breath, and started again. "Tonight has been a little like being back in Italy and my head is spinning. Which means…"

She lifted her eyes up to meet his and it just about undid him because the tear was still there, as if she believed that wiping it away and letting him know she didn't want him to see her cry would be the greatest weakness of all.

"It means you don't need to apologize," he said softly. "I shouldn't have said that you not trusting people was a shortcoming. I should have said it's your scar. And my scar is…" He hesitated, not knowing if he could say it.

*I tend toward excess*, she'd once told him. No, *he* did. Women, parties, drinking. All the easy things that acted like armor, meaning nobody would ever see past the wealth and the expensive suits and the apparently handsome face and find Anthony, a man who mightn't even be worth finding.

"Cultivating a reputation like mine means I can tell myself everyone knows upfront what they're getting," he said quickly, wanting to get this over with. "I can tell myself it's not my fault if they decide they think they can change me, or if they get hurt because they knew what I was like from the outset. But that is such a cop-out."

He came back around to the front of the desk so he was closer to her and he made himself say it. "All of which means that maybe finding this man isn't worth it for either of us." *For you*, he meant. His fingers flexed as if they were going to reach out and touch her and he shoved them into his pocket.

Alix turned her back to the window now, resting her hips against the sill, skirt spilling around her, the space between the two of them like an untraversable ocean. "But won't we hate ourselves even more if we stop looking for him?"

There was something like desperation in her words, a subtext that rang out so loudly: *I'm so tired of hating myself.*

And it was the subtext he responded to when he replied, "Me too."

Silence. Not like in the car though. This was a silence between two people who felt so exactly the same about something that it was both painful and lovely to be so intimately understood.

"Anthony…" She paused, finally swiping the tear away. "You are so much more than your reputation." She offered a gentle smile along with her words and now he was the one wanting to weep. He'd never known that tenderness could make you ache more than any blow ever could.

He took one hesitant step forward. He didn't know why. Just that he had to.

So did she.

The buzz of the doorbell halted them both. Their eyes parted.

"That must be Anjelica," he said, voice thick and slow. "I don't know how much you were listening to in the car but I asked her to find some-one who could deliver your would-be attacker to the American hospital where they'll keep an eye on him until I question him in the morning."

But he opened the door to Esmée.

\* \* \*

"Why are you here?" Alix heard him ask warily and she took the chance to let out a quiet breath, to touch her fingers to the corners of her eyes and dab away any dampness still there, to lock away whatever it was that hadn't just happened between her and Anthony.

"And why doesn't the front desk call up and announce my visitors anymore?" he continued.

"Charles knows I'm not a mere visitor," Esmée said.

Alix interrupted. "I called her from the phone booth," she told Anthony. "You asked Fortunée to come back. I wanted someone here too."

Esmée dropped into the sofa. "You know I love you," she said to Anthony. "But tonight I'm on her side."

"I sometimes wish my mom hadn't stopped me from pushing you in the lake," he said with affectionate exasperation in his voice as he sat down beside Esmée. "Why weren't you at the ball? I looked for you."

Esmée shrugged. "This afternoon I saw the woman who I suspect denounced me to her German lover, resulting in me spending those nights in prison. After that, I had a low afternoon. Too low for a ball."

"I shouldn't have called," Alix said remorsefully.

"Maybe having something to do will be better for me than hiding beneath the bedsheets." Esmée smiled at Alix. "You look astonishing, by the way—even for you. I hope you enjoyed the ball?" She asked Anthony this last.

"I did," he said, glancing at Alix as if he wasn't sure she would say the same thing.

"*We* did," she amended, and she saw the hint of a smile touch Anthony's lips.

The door opened again. Fortunée didn't bother with the bell—she stalked in like an actress entering the stage and expecting applause.

But this was not Fortunée's show. It was Alix's.

She shrugged off Anthony's jacket, snapped on another light, crossed to the wall covered with paper and said, "Neither Anthony nor I are going to the Parc des Buttes-Chaumont tomorrow. It's a setup. Fortunée is going instead." Instantly she felt more like her old self—strategic, smart, and damned if she was going to let La Voce fool her.

Alix addressed her next words to Anthony. "Since you're like Washington with the money and resources and I'm like the unpromising

informant you scrape up off the street with only smarts, wit, and beautiful dresses to her name, you're the one who'll have to pay her."

It had the effect of making him laugh and Alix felt energized
again, despite the late hour—everything between her and Anthony
back to normal at last.

Fortunée interrupted. "Is anyone going to ask me if I want to go to
a park?"

Esmée snorted. "I have a feeling you two aren't friends."

"Anj—" Anthony stopped, then started again. "Before you called
me," he told Alix, "Fortunée—who's been palling up to Becky for a
while—told me that Becky thought she was meeting a maquisard
tonight who had information about you and who wanted to help her
avenge her brother's death. Becky didn't share his name with Fortunée, just that she'd had her godfather check it out and it all matched
up. Which means La Voce's posing as a goddamn Resistance hero.
That's the identity he's taken on."

"That," Alix said, "is a very smart thing to do. It means I can't just
go and tell her who La Voce is because she won't believe me. Still, I'm
going to visit her tomorrow. Esmée, can you tail her afterward to see
what she does? Anthony, you need to go to the hospital and interview
the man I knocked out, find out who paid him. I need Fortunée to
go to the park and see what happens when I don't show up. And the
other thing is—for La Voce to have planted that conversation at the
pool, he must have found out my name. I suspect that was the currency Becky used to get her meeting with him."

*You will wear your white dress.* La Voce's words from 1945, each a
sharp pin perforating her confidence, letting the fear seep in. By avoiding him at the park tomorrow she was saying to him, *I'm onto you.* It
was unlikely to make him happy.

It took every atom of will she possessed to drag her mind out of the
Paroisse Française and back into Anthony's suite.

"Couldn't you be Mary Smith instead of Alix St. Goddamn

Pierre?" he was saying to her. "Your name makes you too easy to track down."

Alix walked over to his desk and sat in his leather chair, wanting to escape his very intense gaze. "I look nothing like a Mary Smith."

Anthony crossed to the desk too, placed both palms onto it, leaned forward and it was almost like he'd forgotten everyone else was in the room. "Can you drop the one-liners for five minutes? You can't keep wandering the streets of Paris with a murderous Nazi on your tail."

"But it's fine for *you* to wander the streets," she said, trying to mask fear with irritation. *A murderous Nazi on her tail.* A man so ordinary looking and with a new identity so well constructed that he'd been able to assimilate into life, pretending to be a normal, non-monstrous human. A man whose presence on the other side of a confessional booth had been enough to make her choke. And now he knew her name.

She felt her back press deeper into the chair, saw Anthony open his mouth to say something else to her, but then he caught sight of the way her hands were wrapped around her upper arms, leaving white, bloodless marks on her skin.

Damn La Voce for still making her panic. She unpeeled her fingers and tried to relax but could still feel that she was holding her body more stiffly than a Stockman dress form.

Anthony closed his mouth, picked up a bottle of brandy and poured out at least a quadruple. He'd managed only a sip before Esmée crossed the room and said to him, "That much liquor at three in the morning will hurt come daybreak, *mon cher.*"

Anthony looked for a minute like he was about to toss the contents of the glass at Esmée but the telephone rang, making them all jump.

"Probably your friend at the hospital," Fortunée said. "He told me he'd call you for instructions."

Anthony answered the phone with a curt, "Yes."

Esmée scooped up his glass and said, "Can I leave you two alone for a few minutes? I need to get rid of this."

Fortunée looked at Alix. Alix looked at Fortunée. Esmée didn't wait for either of them to reply before she disappeared into the bathroom.

Alix supposed that if she was going to rely on Fortunée then she ought to find out a bit more about her. She left her seat at the desk and joined Fortunée on the lounge. "Why did you go to Italy during the war?"

Fortunée stretched and helped herself to one of Anthony's cigarettes. "I was in Marseilles when the Germans took over the free zone in '42 and after that it wasn't as much fun," she said lazily. "When Naples was liberated by the Allies, I went there. I wanted freedom, not occupation."

"So why come back to Paris after the war?"

Fortunée rolled her eyes. "Paris likes to pretend she's suffered. But nobody bombed her to rubble. She's in better shape than she lets on."

Fortunée was proving to be more astute than annoying. "So you follow—"

"Fortune."

Alix couldn't help laughing at the pun. "Maybe I can relate to that," she admitted. "I've been following—I don't know, fortune, adventure, something—my whole life."

Anthony hung up the phone at the same time as Fortunée replied to Alix. "Or maybe you're just following an indistinct dream you'll never reach."

Alix's eyes locked with Anthony's. Was that what they were doing?

Fortunée clocked their shared glance and added, in Anthony's direction, "I'm going to try America next. I just need a rich American to get me there."

"Then you're looking at the wrong person," Esmée interjected, reentering the room. "Now, before the telephone rang, I think we'd settled on our plan. The hospital will take care of Alix's victim until you can interview him in the morning?"

Anthony nodded.

"Good," Esmée continued. "Then if La Voce or his hired hands are expecting Alix at the park tomorrow, she'll be perfectly safe at Maison Christian Dior. We can reassess the level of danger to her tomorrow after the encounter with Fortunée takes place."

Both Anthony and Alix stared at her, Anthony with something of fury in his eyes and Alix with admiration at how beautifully Esmée had dismissed all of Anthony's overbearing concerns for her welfare.

Alix managed a grin at last. "As long as I keep a bag of flour with me, I won't be in any real danger."

Anthony almost succeeded in maintaining his intractable demeanor but then a smile tweaked at the corner of his mouth. "I cannot believe that while wearing such an incredible dress you knocked a man out with a bag of flour," he said.

Alix laughed. "I'd never make it as a gangster." Then she yawned hugely, the late hour finally catching up. "We'll all meet back here tomorrow evening?"

Esmée nodded, kissed everyone goodnight and managed to wrangle Fortunée out too. The minute Anthony had closed the door, he rested a hand against it and said, "We need to talk about Bobby."

"Why is my life such a goddamn mess?" Alix said tiredly, returning to her nest in Anthony's chair. "You know, occasionally over the last couple of weeks, I've started thinking about what I'll do with my life when this is all over. That rather than just jumping from job to job, lasting only long enough to irritate the man in charge, I'll figure out what I really want to do and do that instead. Then something like this happens and I think I'll never get to that place."

"You will," Anthony said. "Maybe you don't feel especially lucky not to have family and expectations, but at least you can imagine choosing what you might want to do. And I bet you do whatever that is."

There was a frustration in his voice that made her say, "A March son doesn't get to choose, I expect."

He shrugged. "Not when he's the only one left. I could just tell my old man I don't want to run a goddamn business; that I want to write. But only a bastard would hurt his father that much." He turned away to face the gold light cast by the lamps in the square, which softened night to eventide.

"But we were talking about Bobby, not me," he continued. "And I feel like there's a question we haven't asked."

Alix frowned. "You mean why Bobby wanted to find Matteo?"

Anthony crossed over to the papers on the wall. "Not just that. Bobby is in so many of these questions. Why did he want to lead that mission? Why not the one before or the one after? And the question we haven't asked," he faced her again, "is whether La Voce was being generally cruel in killing those men or whether he was being specifically cruel. Did he want to kill all those men, or one of those men, for a particular reason? And if he did, that means he knew who was going into the mountains that day."

Alix stood and walked over to the window, thoughts spinning as fast as thread wound onto a reel. "Are you saying either that La Voce wanted to kill Bobby, or that Bobby somehow told La Voce who was going on the mission? That is one gigantic leap to make."

"I know," he confessed, looking less certain now. "Because how would anyone communicate with La Voce anyway? But, Alix, that note—"

Alix pressed a hand to the windowpane and cut him off. "I put a wireless operator into Karl Wolff's headquarters so the Germans could communicate with Dulles about the surrender negotiations without always having to go back and forth over the border. Maybe someone transmitted the team to the operator. And maybe someone at Wolff's HQ saw the transmission—someone like La Voce."

Neither moved. They both stared at one another, her gut practically screaming at her that yes, there was something in this theory, his doing the same if the look on his face was anything to go by.

Then she lifted her chin up to the strip of darkness above the golden-black sky so Anthony could no longer see her eyes and said, "Matteo told me he loved me. I loved him too."

Anthony didn't move or speak. Nor did Alix. Her most private and sacred feelings lay strewn all around, like a mask torn off, its sequins shining like tears on the floor.

But there was more she needed to say. She tried to gather her self-possession, to speak without her voice quavering. "That can't be why Bobby wanted to find Matteo though. Bobby...He wouldn't have fought for me. I told you before that he was a nice guy. And he was. Not deep, nor shallow. Not funny, nor serious. Not smart, not dumb. He was..."

There was a definite hitch in her words as she remembered the Alix who'd accepted Bobby's proposal back in 1942—an Alix who had no idea that war could kill you, but you'd still somehow have to go on living. "He was all the in-between spaces and none of the wild and heady extremes," she finished, much too sadly.

"Alix."

She turned only her head back to Anthony, who said, very softly, "Like I said before, Bobby could be an idiot."

What subtext should she unthread from those words? She didn't know. But one thing she did know was that she would never describe Anthony to anyone as just a nice guy. Which was beside the point.

She refocused on the problem at hand. "How would Bobby have known about Matteo anyway?"

"I don't know," Anthony said. "But he did. Let me send a telegram to someone who worked my cable desk at Brindisi. Maybe they saw something. And I guess that's only one possibility. Maybe Bobby isn't the key. Maybe La Voce's motivation is. Maybe there's a reason why he wanted to screw up that particular mission. If we can find that out, then we have the power when we meet with him. I'll talk to my guy on the cable desk about that too. Maybe there was something going on in the Nazis' Italian command around that time."

Alix sank her hips onto the sill, her spectacular dress glimmering silver in the lamplight. *Bobby isn't the key.* She focused on that, because he couldn't be. It was the latter of Anthony's theories, not the former, that would give them their breakthrough. And if they had a breakthrough, they might win this. Might find La Voce and confront him with whatever dastardly reason he'd had for killing those men. It had to be something personal—there was no other reason for such slaughter. They would make him hurt the way she hurt. And then they would get him locked up forever.

And Alix would plan her future. Something to build on what she'd learned at Dior. Something of her own. Something spectacular.

She smiled at Anthony. He smiled at her. It was a smile that seared through her like fire.

It was time to leave.

She crossed to the foyer even though she had nowhere to go.

Anthony pushed himself away from the wall and gestured to her hatbox. "You don't have another bag of flour in there, do you?"

She raised an eyebrow. "No."

"Okay. My father has a suite here that he uses whenever he's in Paris. It's empty right now and it's safe. Nobody can get up to this floor unless the staff let them—or unless you're you or Esmée," he added wryly. "Nobody, including La Voce, will know you're here. Use the suite for as long as you like. I know you hate it when I try to tell you what to do so—stay for one night and move back into a tiny *pension* if you want to, despite the fact I think you're taking a big risk. Or stay for a month until we figure everything out—enjoy living somewhere with matching teacups and comfortable sofas. It's up to you."

Before tonight, she would have refused any such offer from Anthony. But she was exhausted and scared and somewhere comfortable sounded like just the ticket. Besides, she only needed somewhere to stay for two weeks. After that she'd be in America with Dior for a couple of months.

All of which meant she had just two weeks to find La Voce—or two weeks for him to find her. But together with Anthony—come what may—she would be the one to track La Voce down first.

# TWENTY-FIVE

Despite having had only two hours sleep—but quite possibly the most comfortable sleep she'd ever had in her life—Alix decided that Becky Gordon was, like a Bloody Mary, worth tackling early. "And with plenty of cayenne pepper," she muttered as she armored herself with Dior.

At *The Times'* Paris headquarters, she showed herself through to the offices while the receptionist was away from her desk, her nose searching out the heavy dose of Old English Lavender perfume that usually trailed Becky.

Thirty seconds after locating the scent, Alix swept through the doorway of a well-appointed office—if you liked chintz—where Becky sat reading the newspaper and sipping tea.

Becky's teacup wobbled. "How dare you come in here like this."

"Like what?" Alix inquired, helping herself to a chair, lifting the teapot and pouring herself a cup. "Like someone wants to strangle you?"

"Well, you have a lot of experience at ending people's lives."

It took all of Alix's self-control not to let her own hand tremble at that. Becky's brother had died. Yes, Becky had been vindictive in seeking her revenge but didn't Alix deserve it? It was so much easier to be a brazen, quipping, one-woman show when one's emotions were disengaged, but this... This was different. "I'm sorry about your brother," Alix said.

Becky's hand crept up to twist her pearls into a knot. "I was supposed to be marrying a viscount like my father at the very least but now I'm working here because my brother is dead and my parents' estate is, under of the laws of primogeniture, in the hands of a hideous uncle. I have nothing—nothing at all." Becky's tone was both disbelieving and brittle. "If my brother were still alive, so many things would be very different."

"Ruining my life won't make yours any better," Alix said quietly. "Take it from me, revenge as a way of life is…" What? A gangrenous, damaging thing.

"Exactly what you deserve," Becky finished. "Now please leave. No, first, you can read this."

Becky pushed that day's edition of *The Times* over to Alix. It was opened to Becky's weekly column about the social goings-on in Paris. It usually had a gossipy, snide edge to it so Alix rarely read it.

Today's column was headed, "The Shopgirl Goes Shopping." It was about a certain not-so-young redhead of dubious background and without a penny to her name, inveigling herself into a position at a couturier that would allow her to rub more than just her shoulders with the kind of people an orphaned girl of immigrant working-class parents would usually serve dinner to in a maid's uniform. "She *is* serving something," the article went on. "Herself. But we all know that the shopgirl ends up back in the shop in the last chapter of the story and the newspaper heir marries the princess."

Alix stood. "And where does the English Rose who's no longer marrying a viscount end up? In the arms of a—"

She cut herself off. There was nothing to gain by telling Becky she'd joined forces with a murderer. La Voce would already have spun such a convincing story about Alix's evils that Becky was certainly lost to the man responsible for her sadness.

So she kept her eyes fixed on Becky and tried not to think about how much gossip was spreading in the fitting rooms at Dior about the shopgirl who was the newspaper heir's latest and temporary diversion—and how much gossip Dior would be willing to withstand before he had to let Alix go. Instead she asked, "Who am I supposed to be meeting at the Parc des Buttes-Chaumont today?"

Becky, for all her acting ability, couldn't hide the flinch.

And Alix knew—because she'd learned a few things about La Voce during the war—that he was playing Becky too. He'd known that Alix was watching and listening last night. He'd known Alix wouldn't go to the park. He'd wanted Becky to prove herself incompetent at the task of frightening Alix away because then Becky would be ever more in his control.

No, La Voce was still planning his move. There would be a feint and then the finale—just like there had been in Switzerland. And Alix needed to stop wasting time on Becky and get ahead of La Voce so this time the finale didn't end like it had in Switzerland.

She only said to Becky, "You'll be much less hurt if you stop now than if you keep going. But I expect you're going to ignore that piece of advice too."

\* \* \*

She telephoned Anthony at his office straightaway. "What happened at the hospital?" she asked.

"He said he'd been paid by a woman. To frighten you."

"Becky. Just what I thought. Right, can you ask everyone to come maybe an hour later tonight? And tell Fortunée not to bother going to the park. Can you and she..." Alix paused. She was giving orders like a major-general. And these orders were personal, not tied to some faraway campaign, which made them harder to voice.

She tried again. "Can you and Fortunée put together a dossier on every man who went up the mountain that day? Focus on Bobby. What operations he worked on, how he might have known Matteo.

We need to see what the connection is between Bobby, Matteo, and La Voce. There's something there, I know there is. I know La Voce knew Matteo. He also knew Matteo was my..." *My fracture. The part of me that is broken still.*

She heard movement, as if Anthony had stood, cradled the receiver in the crook of his neck and moved across to the window, just like he might have done if they were talking together in the privacy of his suite. "Go on," he said quietly.

She closed her eyes. He didn't care that she wasn't being a spy right now, he cared that she was being a human.

So she kept on being a vulnerable, imperfect human. "Matteo was my Achilles' heel. And La Voce was..." Another pause. "An accurate marksman."

*Words can never hurt me*, a childhood rhyme promised. It was wrong. The words she was saying hurt her badly.

"Alix." Anthony's voice again, like a hand holding onto hers. "If I could light you a cigarette right now, I would."

So she pretended he had, inhaled for courage and let all the other painful words come out. "I compromised myself at the end. You're not supposed to value some lives over others, but I did. And La Voce knew that, just like I've always known that what La Voce did was personal—he wanted me to be as guilty and ashamed and wretched as I am but maybe I overlooked something in thinking it was just about me. Maybe..."

She took several seconds to gather herself. "Maybe he wasn't using Matteo just to get to me."

"You mean," Anthony said very carefully, perhaps trying not to press too hard on this unhealed wound, "he was using Matteo because he wanted to hurt Matteo too?"

"I think so. And we need to know why."

\* \* \*

The next part of her plan involved calling Frank at the Ritz and asking him for the largest favor so far. He told her he'd see what he could do. Now all she had to do was hope—and do some work.

She'd no sooner sat down to do just that when the phone rang.

"Where did you stay last night?" Esmée asked without preamble.

"At the Ritz," Alix said without thinking.

"Dammit, Alix."

Alix hastened to explain. "I'm not sleeping with Anthony. And I don't mean that in the sense that he doesn't do 'sleeping' as in a continuous arrangement that extends beyond one encounter. I mean that I haven't slept with him. Period."

*Forget that moment in the pool*, she told herself. Forget the tight clench in her stomach as she'd watched a drop of water slide down his chest like her hand had wanted to. And forget that movement they'd almost made toward one another in his suite last night.

"I stayed in his father's suite," she told Esmée, very firmly. "Ignore Becky's column."

"I wish I could. You don't need me to tell you this, but make sure no one finds out you're staying in the March's suite," Esmée said more gently now. "You know how Paris will treat you if they do, especially with Becky goading them on. I do not want people to forget you got the job at Dior on your own merits. I do not want anyone to call you someone's mistress. I do not want…" Esmée's voice faltered.

"I don't want that either," Alix said in a low voice. "Just like I don't want people to believe you're nothing more than another rich woman in need of a husband."

A muffled sniff, then Esmée's voice came back on the line. "If only you weren't so goddamned poor, Alix St. Pierre. If you had money and family and connections, you could just about get away with it."

"Then I wouldn't have to rely on Anthony's charity in the first place," Alix pointed out.

Esmée was silent and so was Alix, and she almost rang off because this was one too many things to deal with right now, but then Esmée said contemplatively, "There was one brief and shining moment, wasn't there, when it looked like the world would change. For four years we spied and we worked damn hard and we saved people's lives and we made a difference and nobody cared too much that we were women. And then it all ended. Went backward, even."

"Did you know," Alix said, "when I returned to New York, they asked me to make posters telling women to quit their jobs and go home and cook nice dinners for their husbands? I told them I didn't know how to spell *husband*."

"I bet you did."

"We mattered for a bit, didn't we?" Alix said, unable to prevent nostalgia making her voice heavy. "Sometimes I think I imagined it all."

Esmée's response was fierce. "Don't let the women in Dior's fitting rooms ever find a way to get their teeth into you. If they do, they will be merciless. You'll become, just like that," Alix heard Esmée's fingers click, "the American libertine who is Anthony March's latest infatuation, whose Dior is paid for by him, who depends on him. They will make you into nothing."

* * *

*To Lillie,*
*From Paris*

*I just spoke to Esmée and what she said put so many questions into my head. Questions like—did you ever believe that marrying Peter would give you the best life of all? I suppose I know the answer to that—to keep your place, even before your father lost it, you had to marry.*

*But what do I need to do to keep my place? What even is my place? It's a space that doesn't exist, between worlds—knowing people from the world of money but not coming from the world of money. Working, but not working-class enough to be of interest to a waiter, say, or an accountant. How will Esmée keep her place? Only by marrying some other wealthy aristocrat who'll be unfaithful— and so will she. A* faux mariage *that will trick society into thinking they're playing along.*

*But what game will I play?*

*All my love and* bisous,
*Alix*


Alix screwed up the letter. She needed to stay in the present for the rest of the day and concentrate on the mounting pile of paperwork: correspondence with Neiman Marcus about the award Dior was collecting in America, as well as letters to the stores *le patron* was to visit in the States. Time was ticking down to their departure date. Two weeks to trap La Voce—or be trapped by him.

She ignored her phone, which rang too shrilly. She worked so hard that at first she thought she was hallucinating the sound of a nightmarish voice. But she heard it again, altered by being out of the confines of a confessional booth. She hurried out of her office where she was met by an impenetrable wall of seamstresses bearing sheet-covered gowns.

"*Bien sûr, mon ange,* you may have as many as you like," the voice said now, clearly, distinctly, and most certainly loud enough for her to hear.

"Excuse me," she said to the throng of seamstresses, only to cause a greater commotion as one or two tried to oblige her by turning sideways, a movement that made them knock into the gowns in front and behind. Each gown's bearer wobbled, which threw the next seamstress in the line off-balance, and now Alix was facing an obstacle course of dresses thrusting forward and back like silk-bladed knives.

"It will be quicker if you just go on and I'll come behind," she said, trying to hide her impatience.

Near the door, she saw Esmée's white face. And Alix knew why her phone had been ringing. Esmée, who she'd asked to follow Becky, had been trying to warn her.

By the time Alix reached Esmée, Esmée could only shake her head.

"He's gone," she said. "I tried to delay him without making it obvious because we don't want him to find out who's helping you." She shook her head again. "He was here with Becky. I saw his face, Alix. I know what he looks like."

Alix couldn't move. La Voce had come to her workplace with Becky. He had stayed just long enough to be sure she knew he was there. This was his feint. He wanted her to know that she was the mouse—and he was the cat.

But the time had come for Alix to be a goddamn lioness.

* * *

The first knock that sounded on the door of Mr. March's suite was impertinent and Alix knew it was Fortunée. She swept in, cleavage spilling like champagne froth from her dress. She glanced around the room, frowned and said, "I thought there'd be drinks."

"You thought wrong," Alix said grimly. One glance at the menu had told her she couldn't afford to provide sustenance even for herself. Then she forced herself to smile, to remember that Fortunée had paid her debt today, that maybe they were both just adventurers who'd made best use of their assets. "Perhaps we should bury the hatchet. It might be easier."

"But not as much fun."

Fortunée could damn well help herself to water from the bathroom.

Another knock, low and private and somehow sultry—it had to be Anthony. He went straight to the phone and ordered French 75s, a kir, champagne, and vermouth on the rocks, as well as an extensive selection of food, requesting that everything be charged to his room.

Mid phone call, Esmée arrived and thus Alix's motley crew was assembled. She was glad spymaster Dulles wasn't there to see who she had to rely on.

Esmée kissed Anthony's cheeks. "I hope you got me a kir."

"Of course," he said, smiling at her.

Esmée sat on the sofa, Anthony took a seat beside her and Fortunée, who'd been watching the kisses and the smile with shrewdly narrowed eyes, said to Anthony, "She's not the kind of woman a man like you needs for a wife. She doesn't have any interest in managing a man's life. I know these things."

Esmée convulsed with laughter and turned to Anthony. "Please don't listen to her and break off our betrothal."

Anthony laughed too, head resting back on the sofa, relaxed and wearing what appeared to be no mask at all. "But you promised."

Fortunée's cleavage deflated still more.

Esmée threw her a placatory smile. "You're right. Despite my promise to him, a lifetime of entertaining Anthony's colleagues' wives is not for me. Besides, *mon cher*," she said to Anthony, "when you return to Manhattan, you'll find more than enough women who are like water, waiting to be poured into your life and take on its shape."

*Women who are like water.*

It was so achingly apt as a way to describe how Lillie was raised, how the girls Alix went to school with had been raised, how her sex in general was raised to believe their purpose was to suit a man's life. And Anthony was a man who'd equally been raised to believe in marriage to a formless girl who would be happy to exist as Mrs. March only.

Alix felt momentarily sorry for him—that an intelligent man who'd probably be a better person for marrying someone like Esmée would do the exact opposite because tradition and society had laid out his path for him and it wouldn't occur to him to step off it. And then she felt angry at herself for feeling sorry for him when she should feel sorry for the woman who would exist as Mrs. March only when she could perhaps have been so much more.

"I—" Anthony was frowning at Esmée, whose words had sounded more like an accusation than a future.

A knock sounded, interrupting them. Alix let in Michel the bellboy, greeted him with a smile and a few francs, which he returned to her, protesting that she was his favorite customer. He poured the drinks— vermouth for Anthony, champagne for Fortunée, a French 75 for Alix. Glistening in the middle of everything was a chocolate tart the likes of which Alix had never seen and she looked from it to Anthony.

"That's impressive," she said.

"Glad I've finally managed to impress you," he said wryly.

Armed with a slice of tart, Alix kicked off her shoes, and adjusted the belt that nipped in the waist of the leopard-print Jungle sheath dress that Madame Bricard had brought to her, advising that it was too damaged to be shown to *les femmes* and Alix might as well have it—except it didn't look damaged at all. By the time she discovered that, she couldn't make herself give it back.

She raised her glass. "Here's to all of you. Thank you." Then she said, "La Voce was at Dior today."

Anthony's fingers whitened on his glass. "Jesus, Alix, why wasn't that the first thing you said?"

"The tart distracted me," she said lightly. "And before you go getting all high-handed and telling me not to make any jokes, just hear me out."

He stared at her, grimly unconvinced.

"La Voce has flown under everyone's radar since the war, has had contacts important enough to get him a secure new identity as a former Resistance fighter. Which means he's made a life for himself here in Paris and he doesn't want anyone destroying that by exposing who he is. That's what's important to him—his identity. It always was, even in Italy. So he needs to get me out of Paris without making a scene or doing anything messy that could be traced back to him. That's his weakness. And him coming to Dior today was his way of telling me he's getting ready for his final move."

Anthony was at her side, vermouth finished in one long swallow. "Which means he wants you to worry over when and how it will happen. You're not making me feel any less high-handed, Alix."

Esmée interrupted. "Nor me. I sat down with a contact today from my former network. He's an old photographer and his job during the war was to find and take photos of the Nazis—to keep a library, if you like—so that if we needed pictures to pass on to agents, we had them. I looked through everything he had and I found this one."

She held up a photograph. "I'm certain he's the man I saw at Dior. Attached to it was a sheet of notes. His name was Friedrich Weber—a name that's also on your list from Frank. The notes indicated he was a killer of the kind you really oughtn't to have a showdown with if you value your life."

"You took the words right out of my mouth," Anthony said.

"I'm not waiting here in my safe tower for him to make the next move. You never win from the defensive position. You know that. And—was there a negative too?" she asked Esmée, who nodded. "That will be very useful."

Alix lit a cigarette and exhaled the smoke—along with the creeping dread of ever hearing La Voce's voice again—before continuing. "My plan is that we make the showdown happen where we can control it, using me as bait. If he wants to avoid the spotlight, La Voce or Weber or whatever name he's using now isn't going to attack me on a street or in a public place. He's going to want somewhere discreet. He's going to want to find out where I live and do it there. Which means—if Becky finds out that Alix St. Pierre is staying in Anthony

March's father's suite at the Ritz, she'll tell everyone in Paris," Alix went on stoically, retreating to the window and able now to blame the catch in her voice on the smoke. "Then La Voce will know where to find me." *And my reputation will be ruined,* she didn't add, because wasn't it already?

"Alix—" Esmée said desperately.

The Ritz, Alix remembered telling La Voce, was her favorite place in Paris. It was as if Fate had planned this all along.

Then came a knock at the door. This was the only part of her plan that might well take the roar out of her leonine spirit. If it was just one or two people, then the showdown would be almost impossible to manage. Had Frank made miracles happen—or was Alix going to have to rethink everything?

"Who's that?" Anthony demanded irritably.

The door opened and in came the miracle.

There was Charles from reception, Jean-Luc the concierge, Michel the bellboy, Agnès the housemaid, Benoît from the Little Bar. And behind them, at least a dozen more sets of eyes and ears belonging to people Alix had spoken to or laughed with or thanked each and every time she'd entered and exited the Ritz. Last of all was Frank.

"You're not at the bar," she said, bewildered.

"I figured this was more important," he said with a grin. "And there are at least half a dozen more who are on shift and can't come up but I'll brief them later. We had enough of Nazis during the war. Some of these kids," he gestured to the Ritz staff in front of him, "are still mourning the mothers and fathers the Nazis took from them. So, we're here to help."

If she blinked a thousand times, she wouldn't be able to hide the fact that her eyes were drenched with tears.

"I feel like all I've done today is ask you this question, but what's going on?" Anthony asked, looking from her to the people crowding into the room.

"The showdown will only work the way we want it to," she said, smoothing the front of her leopard-print dress—which had turned out to be very well chosen—and feeling as if there was a hell of a lot more about Alix St. Pierre that was worth saving than worth forgetting. "It will only work," she repeated, "if we know our opponent is coming. There are more than enough people here who can look at that photograph of La Voce and tell me—and you," she said quickly to Anthony, who looked like he might kill her himself if she didn't make him part of this showdown too, "—when he arrives. They can also get the authorities here the minute we need them. If we have warning and are prepared and the authorities are ready to move, then we're more likely to win. And I'm damn well winning this time. We both are," she said to Anthony who, at last, smiled.

\* \* \*

When the army of eyes and ears had left there were still more than a few logistics to hammer out, and Anthony wasn't going to let anyone else leave until those logistics were forged into a goddamn masterpiece. He knew he was pacing like a novice before their first mission but he couldn't make himself stand still.

"You're tailing Alix," he told Fortunée. "I'll pay you whatever you want. I don't care what you say about him not attacking you on a public street," he said, eyes fixed on Alix, "you need someone looking out for you. And find someone to tail Becky," he heard himself all but bark at Fortunée. "We still need to keep an eye on her."

"I'll do that," Esmée interrupted. "Let's not forget I spent the entire war tailing worse people than Becky."

Anthony nodded. "And both of you get word to me the very second you so much as smell him anywhere near Alix."

They both nodded, most likely because the tone of his voice meant nobody would dare disagree with him right now. He did not like the idea of using Alix as bait one little bit but her plan was rock-solid and she'd likely throw the chocolate tart at him, or worse, if he told her, without any logical reason, that he didn't want her to do it.

But there was one very illogical reason why he hated the idea. He halted by the window, unable to pace anymore. He was afraid for her. No, not afraid. Terrified.

Maybe the ferocity in his voice told her that. One of his hands was gripping the sill beside hers now and he watched her reach out a tentative finger, letting it touch his hand for just a moment, as if she was trying to say, *I'll be okay*. He lifted his thumb, brushing it over the back of her hand and said, voice very low so only she could hear, "Let me worry about you."

For a second their eyes caught and something fierce tore through him. Then she turned her head away and stared hard and unblinking through the window. But she left her hand where it was, resting beneath his, an ember ready to ignite.

If only it was just the two of them in the room. If only there had never been Nazis.

He made himself shift his hand from hers before he told her what he and Fortunée had found out that day.

"Bobby spent almost the entire afternoon before we left for that mission sending cables to someone," he said.

She straightened into perfect posture, walked to the coffee table and picked up her champagne *coupe*. "Do we know who he was cabling?"

He shook his head. "No. But I might have worked out how Bobby knew of Matteo. You said you were in Italy twice?"

She nodded.

So he explained that when Bobby had been in the field, it had mostly been in locations farther to the south than Piedmont. But that his last mission before April 10, 1945, had been a little farther north, not near where Matteo was located exactly but... "But what?" she asked, looking very apprehensive.

"You hear stories when you're in the field," he said. "I heard more than a few and," he nodded at Fortunée, "she heard them as well when she was in the north a couple of times. One of the stories was about a partisan leader and a red-haired American agent who'd come flying down the mountain one day and told a uniformed British agent that she'd..."

He cleared his throat but really, he'd sworn more than enough in front of her by now. "That she'd cut off his balls if he didn't take off his uniform and show the partisans some respect. And that the partisan leader had then kissed the red-haired lady very..." he faltered. "Very impressively," he finished.

Unbelievably, Alix started laughing. "Oh my God," she said. "I didn't even mention that British idiot's balls. Matteo did, I think. And there was no kissing—not then. But your story sounds much better for late nights around campfires. I don't see," she went on, still chortling, "what that has to do with Matteo and Bobby."

"I never heard that story with any names attached to it," Anthony said, feeling his hand move to his shoulder blade, which was grousing like his old man. "But..."

"I did," Fortunée said. "I heard, one time, that the partisan leader's name was Matteo."

"And if Bobby knew you worked for OSS..." Anthony began.

"And he clearly knew you had red hair," Esmée continued.

"Then he might have thought I was flying around Italy kissing partisan leaders named Matteo," Alix finished. "And now you think Bobby was sending cables that afternoon to the wireless operator I'd embedded in Nazi HQ because he wanted to make sure Matteo died on the mountain in revenge for kissing me? Bobby would never do that," she said vehemently. "He didn't care enough."

"Then Bobby—" Anthony cut himself off before he could say, *Then Bobby was a goddamned fool*. "War changes people," he said instead. "Makes them do things they wouldn't otherwise do."

"I know that," she said, sending a sharp look his way. "But all that theory does is shift some of the blame off La Voce and onto Bobby. I sat in a confessional booth with La Voce," she said, fury sparking off every word. "And I know he deserves all of the blame for what happened that night. All of it," she reiterated. "Bobby's a red herring. Some leads go nowhere, like this one. We'll probably never know who he was cabling and it probably doesn't matter anyway. Forget Bobby. Focus on La Voce instead. We still don't know what was driving him. And it damned sure wasn't a fairy tale about a red-haired woman cutting off someone's balls."

"Okay," he said, relenting and taking this last chance to control anything at all about what might happen next. "Wait a few days before you go telling everyone where you're living, Alix. Even if he sees you going to the Ritz, he's just going to think you're here for a drink or dinner. Nobody who knows anything about where you used to live," he gave her a brief smile, "is ever going to imagine you can afford to live here. The four of us are going to use every connection we have to find out everything we can about Friedrich Weber, down to how many damn freckles he has on his nose. We need to know, before he comes to find us at the Ritz, what he personally achieved that day, besides the deaths of nine men. And nobody is sleeping more than a few hours a night until we do."

# TWENTY-SIX

When Alix woke the next morning, luxuriously swaddled, she almost rolled over and went back to sleep, such was the lure of a soft pillow and a silk coverlet. If she kept her eyes closed, she could concentrate on the hope that in a few days' time there might be justice, rather than the knowledge that to achieve that hope, she first had to sit in a room with La Voce.

There were also only a few days left before the world believed she was Anthony March's mistress and all the consequences of that would fall like a scarlet letter upon her. If the gossip became too much—if the women of Paris decided they didn't want to buy their dresses from a business that sheltered a redheaded temptress—Dior would have no choice but to let her go. Or she would leave first, so he didn't have to make that decision. There was no other way. And she supposed she'd bounced around from job to job before and done all right. She could do it again.

Except this life, even despite La Voce, was one she'd come to love. She loved working with creative, inspiring, kind people like Dior and Suzanne and Madame Bricard—and even goddamned Fortunée. And she very much liked working with Anthony. He made her think, he made her laugh and he made her feel more than a few things. But after all of this, she wouldn't see him again. If you ruined your reputation over a man, you didn't keep on ruining it by continuing to go out with him to jazz clubs. Dior's clients didn't mind when the mistresses came from their own milieu and slept with someone similarly patrician. But a woman like Alix, who worked because she had to, wasn't permitted any other transgressions.

Her eyes were well and truly open now. She climbed out of bed and opened the drapes. Sunshine bathed her in gold and hope. So she decided to just dress in green silk and walk amongst crowds to work—Fortunée strolling unobtrusively behind her—and revel in the scent of Paris in summer: a combination of roses and espresso and the last waft of tenacious May lilies.

Near the end of the day, Dior came to find her. "I have had to bring our trip to America forward," he said. "We depart on Monday."

"This Monday? A week early?"

"*Oui.*"

She no longer had the luxury of waiting for a few days while everyone gathered intelligence on Friedrich Weber. She needed to force the showdown before she left for New York.

It was an effort to silence her gasp of shock.

Dior was still speaking. "There's another thing," he said. "I've agreed to something on your behalf because I wish very much for you to do it. You're to sit on the other side of the sofa for a change. A newspaper wants to interview you."

"Me! *Mais non*," she said adamantly.

"*Mais oui*," Dior said, very firmly. "You would never let me pass up such an opportunity. It is a feature story with photographs. I've designed a dress for you."

"Which newspaper?" Alix asked, wondering why the editor had gone to Dior rather than to her.

"The *New York Journal.*"

"*Mais non*," Alix repeated.

Dior stood up. "All I ask is that you think, as you always do, of what is best for the *maison*. If it is best to refuse, then so be it. I will leave it up to you."

Then he was gone and Alix wanted to shout after him, *That's very sneaky!* Because when he put it like that, how could she say no?

But how could she face an interview with Anthony? She'd watched so many feature interviews before. They were intimate affairs, taking much time, during which the journalist subtly burrowed into the hidden crevices of a soul and excavated the blue ice that lurked, spectacularly unknown, beneath the white. What if Anthony did the same to her and found nothing?

She left the *maison* then. She saw Fortunée pick her up from a block away as she began to walk down to the river. It was evening now, the best time to look across to the iron threads of la Tour Eiffel embroidered onto the skyline and think about all the good that had happened in the past nine months: finding a mentor like Dior, thrusting a couture house into the world's spotlight, watching women lift their heads high as their New Look dresses whispered promises against their calves.

And now she asked herself a different question—what if, when he interviewed her, Anthony found something worthwhile?

She remained where she was as dusk bowed down before true night. Nine months ago she could never have imagined she'd be thinking of the good things she'd done—and of the good that might yet be inside her. Which meant that, come what may, she wouldn't let the gossips make her into nothing.

Out there in the world were other women like her. Not many, but some. War had helped her to find a few—but how would the women who grew up without a war find their own kindred spirits?

She smiled, something like one of Dior's *petites gravures* drawing itself into her mind in the shape of words and pictures and encouragement and advice. A magazine, perhaps. But not a *Harper's Bazaar*. Not a *Vogue*. She didn't know exactly what it was, but it would be hers—and it would be for every woman like her, now and in the future.

Until then, she owed it to herself to finally bring to an end what had started in a nondescript room in Washington five years before.

At the Ritz, she bypassed Carmel and Christian Bérard in the Little Bar. Their eyes sparkled with alcohol or opiates and mischief, insensible to the beautiful room and the crystal glassware and the way the light touched the bottles of champagne and turned them into liquid gold, both so desperate to run away from life and into numbness, which they mistook for joy.

She walked over to Frank and said, "It's time. Can you have one of the bellboys mention to Becky that I'm staying in Mr. March Senior's suite? And can you have them do it tomorrow evening?" That would give her time to let Anthony know what was happening.

"You sure you know what you're doing?"

She smiled. In some ways it had been easier when she was with OSS as the money and resources had been almost infinite. But friends and acquaintances were proving to be the most priceless assets of all, in so many ways beyond the material.

"It's taken me a while to figure it out but, yes, I do."

* * *

Anthony thought there was a good chance she might kill him. But first, he was going to enjoy this moment. He checked his watch. Just after seven in the morning. He rapped on the door again.

It flew open. Alix, barefoot and in a very unusual but incredibly sexy pair of—*pajamas?*—stared at him. Whatever they were—russet-colored pants that somehow joined to a top that left her arms sinuously bare—it made her hair flare like fire, made something inside him flare too.

She blinked and rubbed her eyes. He grinned.

"Oh God, you're paying me back, aren't you?" she said as she followed him in and collapsed onto her back on the sofa.

"I know how fond you are of early mornings." He sat on the opposite sofa and lit a cigarette, still smiling. "And I know you're going to avoid giving me an answer about the interview so I've come to get it myself. I've ordered coffee, of course."

Alix yawned hugely. "Okay, I'm a horrible person. You can leave now you've made your point."

"But I don't have an answer yet."

"Nobody is interested in an interview about me." It was what he'd thought she'd say.

He leaned forward, elbows on his knees, hands clasped in front of him, needing her to listen. "Carmel Snow gave me the idea. I thought about the fact that one American woman is single-handedly responsible for what almost every other American woman wears. Who else—what man—has that kind of power? So I decided to do a series of interviews with different women who in some way shape the world. When I asked if I could interview her, she told me you should be one of the women too, given you're responsible for what most of Paris wears, and half of America as well. Carmel won't agree to be interviewed unless you do, so…" He shrugged nonchalantly. "You wouldn't want to cost me the interview with Carmel and ruin the chance for everyone to know more about your former boss and good friend, would you?"

Alix began to laugh. "I've been thoroughly bested, haven't I?"

"I didn't want to say that…" He tried not to smile but it was impossible. Her laughter was always so damn infectious.

"You did so," she said, still laughing. "And you know what? Yesterday I was thinking about what I might do when…" She stopped and appeared to rethink her words. "I might be crazy but I'm thinking about starting a magazine targeted at poor orphaned girls who wear trousers in bars and forget to get married and actually like working and are too stubbornly self-reliant. As you can tell, it's guaranteed to have about three readers but maybe I'll do it anyway. And maybe this interview is the perfect place to start talking about the kinds of things those three girls need to hear."

He was supposed to laugh, he knew, but it wasn't funny. It was perfect—except he knew exactly two other women who were as stubbornly independent as Alix: Esmée and Fortunée. The world had a lot of changing to do, he guessed, but maybe this was one of the ways to change it.

Before he could say anything, she added, very quietly, "I'm leaving for New York on Monday with Dior. I'll be away for a couple of months. So it has to happen before then. Becky will find out tonight that I'm staying here. Frank will have eyes all over the Ritz by this evening."

It was tempting to swear very profanely. He expelled a long breath, mind trying to grasp a foothold on the perilous and unexpected. "That still gives us a couple of days. He's not going to come after you within five minutes of finding out where you're staying. He's going to want a solid plan. And Fortunée has a lead on a guy who once knew Weber—so maybe we'll know what was driving him before then."

It sounded like so many useless pennies tossed into a well in the hopes that one would grant a wish.

"Isn't it a waste of your time doing an interview with me when you won't be able to publish it until after whatever is going to happen with La Voce has happened?" she said then, as if somehow Anthony's time was more important than a Nazi knowing where she lived.

He didn't answer right away. Not when all he felt like doing was hustling her into a car and driving her to the nearest port and taking a ship with her to somewhere far away from Nazis and the past. But the look on her face told him she was going to face La Voce, come what may, and there was nothing he could do about it.

Except be there when it happened.

He lit another cigarette and eventually she looked over at him, green eyes very serious, the pain that backdropped her heart apparent in the dark rim of obsidian circling the green.

So he told her what else was driving him, that it wasn't just about

securing an interview with Carmel. "I have to believe it will all work
out the right way," he told her. "So I have to plan for a future time
when there is no La Voce and I can print an interview with you and
the only consequence is that more people will know how much of
Dior's success is down to you."

He watched the slow blink of her eyes. "I want to believe that too,"
she said.

He wanted to promise her that it *would* happen, that he would
make it happen. For her. This wasn't even for him, this quest—not
anymore.

"I'll do the interview," she said then, and he thought there was a
good chance every atom of his being was smiling immoderately at
the news. Since when had any woman ever made him so goddamn
happy?

But she was the one woman in the whole of Paris he would never
touch, no matter how happy she made him. He had promised to treat
her like a business partner and she had finally given him her trust and
he would have no integrity at all if he broke it. So he stubbed out his
cigarette and stood up.

"Can we do the interview tomorrow? Say, two in the afternoon at
your office?"

She nodded.

On the way out he saw two of her dresses draped over the back
of a chair. He knew enough about Alix now—*I came back to Paris
last year with exactly three suits, one blouse, one pair of trousers, and no
ballgowns,* she'd said—to know that she wouldn't leave her Dior lying
around for no reason.

"Is there a problem with the wardrobe in here?" he asked. "You
can get someone up to fix it."

She winced and he was about to say—no doubt awkwardly—that
she didn't have to pay for the repairs when she said, "I'm selling them."

"Why the hell are you doing that?" One was the magnificent dress she'd worn to the ball and he couldn't believe she'd give that up for any but the most pressing reasons.

Her voice was very small when she said, "I need to pay the bell-boys and the rest of the staff who are looking out for La Voce. You're paying Fortunée so..." She shrugged. "I won't need a ballgown if I'm dead. I'm better off investing the money in staying alive."

"Alix." The urge to swear was worse than before. If he'd thought telling her she didn't need to pay for wardrobe repairs in his father's suite was ham-handed, this was ham-footed. And he'd promised he wouldn't say anything, but breaking this confidence didn't hurt anyone—and maybe it would help. "I'm not paying Fortunée. She wouldn't take any more money."

She stared at him, speechless. At last she managed, "Why not?"

"Despite what happened with that sketch, she likes to fight damn hard for the wronged."

Another long, slow blink, but he saw the shine in her eyes before she could hide it. "I can't ask everyone to do this for me," she said a little desperately. "Esmée. You. Fortunée. You all have so many other things to do."

"You're not asking us, Alix. We offered. Besides..." He grinned now, needing her to keep her dress and forget about paying the god-damn bellboys when he had a ton of useless money just waiting to be spent, "who said Fortunée's doing any of this for you? I thought she was doing it for me."

She smiled, but only a little, then glanced over at her dresses. "They're just dresses," she said.

"All right," he said, knowing he couldn't hurt her pride by doing anything other than acquiescing. But damned if he wasn't going to call Esmée the minute he left and get her to send her maid around to buy the dresses, which could be gifted back to Alix when this was all over.

She opened the door but before he could step through it, she put a hand on his arm. "Thank you," she said, studying the floor very intently. "I thought you were going to pull out your wallet and buy the dresses and if you'd done that it would have been..." Another shrug. "Mortifying."

*Fuck.* The only thing he wanted to do right then was slip his arms around her and hold her. He knew her face, had studied its contours and expressions; knew her hands, the way they moved through the air when she spoke, but he had no idea what it was like to draw her in, to use something other than words to tell her he was sorry the world was a messed-up place and he'd do whatever he could to make it feel less like a three-ring circus.

"Alix," he said, trying to keep his voice even, wishing she'd look at him, "just remember you're not on your own."

She did look up at him then and for one long second the pain fell out of her eyes. "No. We have Fortunée and Esmée in our team of misfits. And one another."

The way she said those last three words made them sound replete with everything he'd ever wanted in his life. For the rest of the day, he caught himself with unsmoked cigarettes burning down in his fingers while he stared at walls and saw only red-haired, green-eyed, dazzling Alix St. Pierre.

# TWENTY-SEVEN

The day of the interview was impossibly crazy. Three days until she left for America and Dior's tour schedule still needed to be finalized. Alix reached for the telephone on several occasions to tell Anthony she'd have to reschedule. But suddenly it was two o'clock and too late to cancel.

She only just had time to clear the grand salon of mannequins and models and *arpettes* before Anthony arrived, wearing the same navy suit, white shirt, and diamond-patterned tie she'd admired the first time they'd met in her office. He looked stomach-clenchingly good, a thought that made it hard to meet his eyes. How the hell was she going to do an interview with him if she couldn't even look at him?

She swallowed down a glass of water in an attempt to cool off.

It didn't work.

"We'll start the interview while the photographer sets up," Anthony said to her, as self-assured as always. "We'll break to get the shots, and then resume. Spreading the interview out works better for everyone. If you don't mind."

She sat on one of the little delicate Louis Seize chairs that the clients ordinarily perched on. Anthony did too but it was all wrong. He was too tall for the chair and he seemed uncomfortable and now she felt awkward too.

"Come with me." She led the way to the staircase and up to her favorite step, tucking her skirts in around her, letting him have the wall to lean his larger frame against. "I hope you don't mind the traffic. I think better up here."

"I want you to be relaxed, which is not a state I've seen you in too often—except when you have chocolate tart in hand. So if a staircase is what it takes..." He paused, then asked, "Before we start, has anything happened that I need to know about?"

"I haven't heard that Becky's started gossiping yet. So I think I'm safe for now."

"Good." He opened his notebook and tapped his pen against it. "I thought we'd start at the beginning. You told me your parents died when you were young but you never told me what they were like. Your mom, what do you remember about her?"

Alix felt her eyelids shut and an image appeared of her beautiful mother in a beaded sheath dress that she'd made for herself—and that actress Louise Brooks had asked Alix's mother to make for her too. Her parents had twirled around the living room of their tiny apartment the night Louise Brooks ordered a St. Pierre original. Alix had watched them with the same lump in her throat that she felt right now.

"She was always happy," she replied, words coming slowly as she opened her eyes and stared out at memories. "She couldn't have been, not really. Our apartment had one bedroom for all of us. She made clothes she was told to make by the studio. But she always smiled when I was there."

Anthony lifted his eyes up from the page. "That must have been nice," he said, and if she wasn't mistaken, his voice was a little wistful.

"Your mom didn't smile a lot?" Alix guessed.

Anthony demurred. "We were like most families. Washed and dressed by the nanny and lined up to parade before the parents at five every evening, whereupon my oldest brother would be scrutinized from head to toe and scolded for so much as a scuff on his shoe. My middle brother would get away with a scuff, but not for failing to give his opinion on the most important news headlines of the day. I got away with almost everything by doing something to make my mother laugh—and if I made her laugh enough, she'd keep me by her side for a few minutes longer. I used to be so damn glad I wasn't my brothers but now…" He shrugged. "I don't know. Maybe it would have been better to have been pulled up more for scuffs rather than indulged for my precocity as an entertainer."

Alix smiled. "I don't think your upbringing did you much harm. Your shoes are always shiny, you manage a newspaper so you must know what the important headlines are, and I quite like precocious entertainers."

The echo of her last words sounded incredibly flirtatious. She flushed. Anthony's eyes traveled with the blush as it spread down to her collarbones.

"If I managed to somehow charm you," he said, voice huskier than usual, "then my upbringing wasn't so bad."

And it was then that Alix realized she was completely and utterly charmed by the man on the step beside her.

A pair of seamstresses came up the stairs, laughing, interrupting the line of sight between Alix and Anthony. But Alix could still feel the tremor in the air around them.

Once the *petites mains* had passed, Anthony cleared his throat and studied his notepad once more. "So tell me how you went from a kid who lost both her parents when she was thirteen to the Directrice of the Service de la Presse for what's now the most famous couture house in France? What drove you to work so damn hard, rather than falling into the more likely path of vice and failure for an orphaned girl in 1930s LA?"

"I have plenty of vices, as you know," she said lightly, but then the timbre of her voice changed. "For a time they almost got the better of me, but…"

Anthony opened a packet of cigarettes, lit one, and passed it to her.

She drew her knees into her chest, wrapped her arms around her legs, took the cigarette and inhaled gratefully, passing the cigarette back to him before continuing.

"Being beholden to someone for everything is…Perhaps I sound ungrateful—the van der Meers really did go above and beyond any obligation when they took me in. But while owing someone everything is romantic and lovely in a film, in reality it's a thin and transparent square of ground that takes just a flick of a finger to shatter and then you're left clawing at air, waiting to be saved again. I couldn't live like that. So I had no choice but to do whatever I could to forge and fashion my own life."

Her last words came out vehemently, so much of Alix in them and everything she'd feared—that he would crack her open and see right into her—was happening. But she wasn't afraid of it anymore, not when Anthony's eyes, the darkest she'd ever seen them, were saying to her, *Tell me and it might hurt less.* And perhaps it did.

"How much of this is on the record?" she asked quietly.

"I promise I'll respect the line between public-Alix and the private woman I'm getting to know." He returned the cigarette to her, one of his fingers lingering against hers just like it had the other night in her suite at the Ritz.

The clench in her stomach this time was fierce. She should not, could not, fall for Anthony March. Except that all she wanted was to bury her head in his shoulder and feel his arms around her. To look up into the midnight blue of his eyes and be dragged down into them.

"Monsieur March! *Quel plaisir.*" Suddenly Madame Bricard was beside Anthony, chuckling throatily and sharing an anecdote about *chérie* Alix—how she'd named all the fabrics in the first collection as if she'd been born into couture.

No sooner had Madame Bricard stood up than Suzanne took her place, telling Anthony how she'd met Alix before the war when she'd worked in advertising.

Suzanne had barely finished when Madame Carré sat down, solemnly describing how she often entered the workrooms to find her seamstresses testing out a new way of stitching a sleeve or a collar on Alix. "It's why she fits the models so well," Madame Carré concluded. "The seamstresses know her measurements by heart."

"It's also a very ingenious way of adding dresses to your wardrobe," Anthony said and Alix laughed at being caught out, then realized the photographer was crouched several steps below, taking a photograph of her laughing with Anthony.

"I'd planned to get changed..." She ran her hands over her crumpled skirt and stood up.

Anthony nodded. "Okay. We'll finish the questions later."

Alix hurried away and found Dior in the *cabine* with Diablesse— a scarlet wool dress with a full pleated wool skirt, long sleeves and an emerald belt that matched her eyes. "I love it," she breathed, stretching out a hand to touch it. "The independent woman inside me wants to say you should stop giving me dresses but—"

For the first time ever, Dior interrupted her. "A true publicist would want all the most beautiful women in Paris to wear Dior gowns. I'm simply being a publicist for a few moments."

"Does that mean I can be a designer for a few moments?" she asked cheekily.

Dior laughed. "You can put on your dress. The photographer is waiting."

When she'd done so, Dior said to her, "It's a myth that redheads shouldn't wear red." He spun her around to face the mirror where she saw that the red was like a magnificent correction tape, altering all of her slightly imperfect features, or emphasizing the better ones. Her cheeks glowed, her hair shone and her eyes did too.

"Talking to Monsieur March makes you even more beautiful, and I'm being neither a designer nor a publicist when I say that." Dior smoothed the shoulders of the gown. "I'm being a friend."

And like a true friend, he didn't make her respond to that unsettling statement but slipped away so she could make her way back to the landing with the quiver in her heart unexamined by anyone except herself.

* * *

Once on the famous staircase, the photographer whistled, picked up his camera, and said to Anthony, "You didn't tell me she was so gorgeous."

"I think you mean dazzling," Anthony said quietly, and his gaze locked with hers and it was like being back in the Piscine Deligny at the ball and Anthony March was all she could see.

For the next half hour, as the photographer told her to turn this way and that, Alix's eyes didn't move away from Anthony's, couldn't move away from Anthony's—were caught there as if forever.

She felt her cheeks flush still more, her breath quicken. She was barely aware of the photographer shouting, "Beautiful! Just like that," could hardly understand that he was done in record time, that he was leaving her and Anthony to finish the interview, that she was taking Anthony down to the solitude of the grand salon.

There, sitting opposite one another, she told him so many things: about that terrible night in Manhattan when she'd gone out with Carmel and tried to drown her fears and sorrows, but there were too many so she'd almost drowned herself instead. She told him it was why she'd come back to Paris and why she tried to only ever have one drink now. She told him about Christian teaching her what proper pride was.

She told him about Matteo.

"I only kissed Matteo once," she said quietly. "It took maybe a minute but I'll remember it for my whole life." She shrugged. "Maybe it was unforgettable because Matteo and I were impossible. Maybe only the things you can't have are so beautiful they make your bones melt."

"Maybe that's true," Anthony said. His eyes dropped to her neck, landing there like an after-midnight kiss, making her bones melt. "But maybe it isn't. Maybe sometimes in a life there's a moment when you get just what you thought you wanted—and it turns out to be everything you wished for."

A moment—one that lasted so long the sun had fallen out of the sky and evening had swept elegantly in, wearing dark blue damask the color of Anthony's eyes. What had started at two in the afternoon had continued on until almost seven o'clock.

Dior's voice broke into the glittering silence. "I hope you're describing her as the star she is."

Anthony spoke to Dior but his gaze was on Alix. "There isn't any other way to describe her."

She moved to the window, resting one hand on the glass, hearing Anthony's and Dior's voices blur together. Then *le patron* left and Anthony was beside her. She felt herself move a little closer to him, a lot closer really, everything between them disarranged and sparkling, the pulse at his throat palpably beating.

"Anthony," she whispered, then stopped, words lost in a rush of nerves.

"What?" he asked, voice huskier than she'd ever heard it, so husky she knew she wasn't imagining this.

"Can I come to your suite after I finish here tonight?"

"I thought you'd never ask."

It was almost too hard to nod and draw back but she could hear someone approaching. "I have some things I need to do. I'll come as soon as I can but it might be a couple of hours."

"I can wait," he said, offering her the kind of smile that made her eyes trace over his mouth and along his jaw and down to where his shirt was buttoned, a button she wanted more than anything to undo.

"Alix." He was the one whispering her name now. "You have to stop looking at me like that or there's no way I'm going to be able to leave."

"Sorry," she said, smile deepening. "But you can be quite disarming when you try."

"I'm not trying yet," he said, smile broadening too.

\* \* \*

Why, tonight of all nights, was there so much to do? Alix was sure she would never be able to leave the office as everything for the American tour landed on her desk: a million transatlantic cables from buyers, interview requests from magazines and even radio. And Mesdames Bricard, Carré, and Raymonde, all nervous about allowing their figurehead to depart in three days' at time, constantly stopped in at Alix's office to remind her of his preferences: *He needs time for solitude; he prefers English food; make sure there are always fresh flowers in his room.*

There were clients still in the *maison* despite the late hour as last-minute appointments were crammed in before Dior left—not that he ever attended fittings. But it was as if, Suzanne said wearily, everyone thought the *maison* would come to a halt without its figurehead and with only the women remaining.

Alix took her a coffee, knowing Suzanne wouldn't have had time to eat or drink anything. But she regretted her action immediately when she heard, just before she stepped into the fitting rooms, her own name spoken by a couture client who had the distinctly English accent of Becky Gordon.

"The story is she's staying in a different room to his, but who believes that?" A chorus of titters followed.

Alix's skin turned icy cold even though she'd set this in motion. The bellboy had spoken to Becky. And La Voce was making sure Alix knew he'd discovered where she was staying.

Another client spoke. "At least we know how she managed to afford the gown she wore to the Comte's ball. The March pockets are bottomless."

Becky replied. "But Anthony March's infatuation won't be. It never is."

"I feel sorry for her." The client's tone indicated not one shred of sympathy. "She's in that dreadful class of women who are stuck in-between. Too independent for a bourgeois man; too educated for the proletariat. And too poor for the rich. Her only option is to become the kind of woman men sleep with, but never marry."

And thus Alix's sentence, which she knew anyway, was passed.

She retreated to her office with Suzanne's coffee still in hand and sat very still for a long time. But soon another cable arrived and she had to focus on her work, not showdowns or La Voce or the fact that she couldn't possibly go to Anthony's room now. It was hard not to think about the clutch in her stomach when Anthony had said, *I thought you'd never ask*. Hard not to unhear the hunger in his voice.

Then her head snapped up. Why was she letting La Voce take this from her too? He'd taken so much and she would not give him this, the one man in the world who knew who she was, who had touched his thumb to her hand and told her he wanted to worry about her, which was something so much more than simple desire.

She picked up her purse and tried not to think about the fact that it was midnight and very unlikely that Anthony would have waited up for her.

When she reached the doorstep, she hesitated. Because there was also the matter of getting back to the Ritz safely. But right out front, Dior's driver stepped out of the convertible Citroën 15 Six and beckoned her over. Dior had sent the car back to wait for her. "*Merci*, monsieur," she whispered to the night.

\* \* \*

She stopped momentarily at the Little Bar and Frank shook his head. No sightings yet. She was safe for tonight at least. She took the elevator, pausing as she stepped out. Anthony would be asleep, would think she'd changed her mind. Would it hurt him? Or would he just shrug?

She turned left toward her room.

She could tap lightly on his door. If he was asleep, she wouldn't wake him.

*He won't be waiting*, she told herself as she approached, *so don't be disappointed*. She knocked very softly, hovering for several seconds before turning away, unable to stop the downward turn of her mouth.

"Alix."

She spun around. Anthony stood in the doorway wearing dark navy pajama pants, nothing more.

"Are you going to come in?" he asked, the smallest note of vulnerability in his voice as if, far from shrugging, he'd been discountenanced by her lateness.

"I'm sorry," she said. "There was so much to do. I didn't want to wake you..."

"I wasn't sleeping. I was reading. You can come in. If you still want to." He stepped aside to let her pass and she walked across to the window.

Anthony stood on the opposite side of the room and said, "You always stand in that same spot. The farthest point in the room, as if you come here wanting to step right out again."

She turned to face him, this man who knew her habits and the dark side of her soul. She had to tell him. No matter that it might ruin what had been meant to happen. "He knows. Becky was at Dior, gossiping about it in the fitting rooms."

Anthony braced his arms on the back of a chair. "You have a gun, don't you?"

"Yes. Did Fortunée find anything yet?"

He shook his head.

Alix stared out into the black night beyond the window and saw the golden light picking out the gilding on the balustrades. The branches of the horse chestnuts unfurled like lacework against the velvet sky and the graciously curved white stone balconies opposite hung like ballgowns at rest. Paris was so goddamned beautiful sometimes. And so was life.

She turned to Anthony and smiled. It was time not to think of La Voce for an hour or two.

# TWENTY-EIGHT

At her smile, Anthony took one step forward. Lamplight shone on the curve of his hipbones emerging from his trousers, on the muscles of his arms, on the faint trace of stubble over his jaw and she wanted, with a desperation that absolutely unnerved her, her mouth on all of those parts of his body.

But…what followed would be something she wouldn't be able to fake her way through. A man like Anthony would be able to tell.

She felt the creasing of her forehead into the slightest frown, saw Anthony's brow furrow in response. She had to either explain, or leave.

"You'll laugh when I tell you this," she said.

He was by her side in an instant. "I won't laugh," he said, voice soft.

She wanted a French 75, a cigarette, and chocolate tart for courage but she was going to have to say it without a shield. "I know you don't like to talk about it, but it's a fact that you're vastly more experienced than I am. And…" She sighed. "I slept with Bobby just once and he—not that I want to share details—but…"

She inhaled for both air and resolve and the words came out in a rush. "My skirt was up but not off, and his trousers were down but not off and it all happened like that. He was my one and only before the war. Then after the war, back in Manhattan—it was the same with other men. My bosses, mostly. Not that there were many, but it was always done quickly in an office in the dark with only the bare minimum of clothing removed." *Stop.* Her hand gripped the windowsill as if that would help. "All I meant to say was that nobody has ever seen me naked before. And..."

She drew in another breath, cheeks burning with embarrassment or shame or both as she finished. "I've never seen a naked man either. And I have a feeling that whatever happens with you is going to be different and I thought I should tell you because you might prefer not to anymore..."

She closed her eyes, mortification making her hands clench into protective fists. *Why* couldn't she have just pretended? Maybe he wouldn't have noticed.

"Alix."

She opened her eyes very slowly.

Anthony was standing right in front of her, looking down at her with a dark and heavy-lidded gaze that was so exactly the same as the one he'd worn earlier at the *maison* that she heard herself inhale sharply.

Then he slid his arms around her and drew her against him so that her cheek rested on his chest, the whole of his body enfolding hers. His hands on her back drifted up and down, lightly, gently, and she squeezed her eyes shut as that one moment of tenderness filled all her senses.

Never before had she been held like that, as if she were precious.

\* \* \*

Long seconds passed in that silent embrace. Alix was barely breathing, reluctant to move and disrupt the still, quiet beauty. But it was impossible not to be aware that, under her hands, the muscles of Anthony's back were tensed, waiting.

Waiting for her.

The quick turn of her head into him was sudden and necessary and then all she could feel was the heat of her exhalation momentarily filling the unbearable space that existed between her mouth and his body. She dragged her bottom lip over his chest.

Anthony's hands on her back stopped moving, the grip of his fingertips not quite so gentle now. "Alix." His voice was very husky.

She tipped her head back to look up at him.

"Tonight, you can do whatever you want, and nothing you don't want," he said.

Her mouth curved into a smile at last. "I don't even know where to start with an invitation like that."

Anthony's eyes darkened to black.

"Perhaps I'll start here," she murmured, bringing her hands around to his chest, fingertips climbing up to his collarbones and then down to his stomach, which was firm and toned, somewhere she could spend hours, she was sure, with her mouth. She pressed one light kiss onto his chest. Then another. And another, each less gentle than before.

She began to move in a slow circle around him, mouth leading, hands following.

"Alix."

The way he said her name made her shiver. But she kept to her lingering pace, trailing kisses over his back now, standing on her tiptoes to reach the smooth and delicious curve of his shoulderblades and the scar from that night.

She touched a fingertip to it. "If you weren't so tall, I could kiss it better," she said smiling a little. "I'll have to save that for when we're lying down." She felt his muscles tense still more as if the idea of lying beside her was a pleasurable kind of torment. He reached for her and drew her around to face him.

"What next?" he whispered.

Her hands slid down to his waistband. "I don't think you need these."

His inhale was decidedly unsteady. "You're killing me, Alix," he said and she smiled again, tilting her face up toward his, knowing he wouldn't kiss her, not yet; that he was holding back because once their mouths met, it would be too much and this slow and exquisite torture would have to end.

She slipped his pajama pants off and stepped backward, driven by impossible impulse, her eyes moving the same way her mouth had just done over Anthony's body, every trace of hesitancy gone now. She met his eyes. "Well, that would make even the Rue Pigalle blush."

He laughed. "You are..." he began. "I don't even know how to finish that sentence. You are at the same time the most sophisticated and unworldly woman I know and I wouldn't change any of it. Come here. It's unfair that you have so many clothes on."

"I'll do it," she said. "There are so many hooks and it will take forever—"

"Alix," he broke in. "Do you think my attention span is so short it can't withstand a few hooks? I've been looking forward to getting you out of this for *hours*." His emphasis on the last word told her he'd been as impatient for her to arrive at his suite as she had been to get there. "Actually I've been thinking about this for days. Weeks, even."

She was back to blushing. "My hooks and buttons are all yours."

He ran the back of his hand along her jawline and down her neck until he reached the first button, which he undid slowly, his fingertips traveling up and down the V of skin uncovered. He turned his attention to the next button and then the next before unbuckling the belt at her waist, stepping back and letting his eyes roam over her body too, even though he'd revealed hardly anything: just her collarbones, her brassiere, her navel. But he still drew in a sharp breath and said, "You have no idea how hard it is not to rush straight to a bed."

"But I thought that's what we were—"

He cut her off. "No. We are going to have a lot more fun than that."

*Oh God.* "Anthony..." She said his name for the first time since she'd stepped into the room, her hand reaching for him, not sure she was going to be able to resist the temptation of not kissing him for much longer, a sensation that only intensified as he ran his thumb over her lips.

At last her dress was off but there was so much more to remove—girdles and stockings and underthings. "I want to click my fingers and have all this gone."

He smiled. "Not so fast." Which was just plain teasing.

"Anthony," she said again, hands climbing up his back and then around to his chest and then down a little lower, "you are driving me completely crazy."

"Believe me," he said, lips at her temple, hand wrapped in her hair, "the feeling is mutual. Let's make sure we're closer to a bed."

Once in the bedroom, she sat on the edge of the bed and he kneeled between her legs so he could unclip one stocking and then the other, rolling the silk away. Then he circled the thumb and forefinger of each hand around her ankles, ran his thumbs along the insides of her calves, her knees, her thighs.

If he didn't remove her bra and knickers soon, she was going to die. The pace and sound of his breath, matching hers, told her that must surely be next.

But he only lifted his hand to the strap of her bra, tracing over the silk. Now she wasn't breathing at all, and nor was he, their gazes threaded together, so much of the intensity coming from watching the play of expression over his face, the shift between light and dark in his eyes, the beat of his pulse at his temple.

She had never wanted anyone the way she wanted Anthony March.

"Come here," she said, words an urgent whisper as she wrapped her legs around him, heard him groan, his eyes a brilliant, glittering lapis. "I need to kiss you right now otherwise—"

Then she was on her back on the bed, his body on top of hers. And the kiss when it came was as soft and slow and teasing as everything that had come before, making her arch into him.

In reply, Anthony touched more barely-there kisses onto her neck and her throat but none of it was enough and there were still too many clothes between them so she reached around and unhooked her bra, tossing it onto the floor.

The want in Anthony's eyes was almost too much.

"I don't know how much more of this I can take," she gasped.

"That's a shame." He smiled languorously. "Because there's a lot more still to come."

\* \* \*

Even after they'd finished he couldn't look away, his hand running up and down her thigh, hers caressing his hipbone. Normally he'd be reaching for his clothes, eager to avoid aftermaths of any kind because people got hurt when the fallout showed them an event wasn't the same for all parties involved. But he and Alix had been chasing an aftermath for weeks, and right now he wanted the quiet epilogue to what had come before. Wanted to study her spine, the backs of her knees, the curve of her waist—all the hidden and secret places that made up Alix St. Pierre.

"Alix," he said at last, needing to be certain. "After what you said at the start...are you all right? We did a lot just then and you're unusually quiet..."

"No, I'm not all right. Not at all..."

*Merde.* Anthony tensed. "Sorry, I..."

Then she grinned and stretched her arms enticingly above her head. "I am luxuriously and gloriously replete. For maybe a half hour or so..."

He couldn't not kiss her, tongue brushing against hers, starving still. If the rest of his life involved only kissing Alix St. Pierre, he would be entirely happy.

"I don't think I said this before I left Dior earlier, but thank you," he whispered. "For telling me about your mom, and the van der Meers, and Carmel, and Dior. I know some of it probably wasn't easy to say. But I'm glad you told me."

"Me too," she said. "But…"

"What?" he asked, hand dropping to the small of her back to draw her into the inch of space remaining between them.

"It made me realize that, even though we've talked about what we did during the war, there's a lot I still don't know about you."

He supposed that was true. "What do you want to know?" And he thought that for the first time in his life, he would let someone turn him inside out, would allow her to understand the childhood tattooed onto his bones, to trail her fingertips over the scars of his adolescence, to read the history written on the underside of his skin.

"You haven't told me anything much about your dad and…Well, at the ball I got the feeling part of the reason you came to Paris was to get away from him." She shook her head, pulling away as if uncertain that being naked in a bed with him meant she had the right to ask him anything. "I'm being nosy."

He caught her and held her against him. "Don't move," he murmured. "This feels too good for you to be going anywhere."

A smile flitted across her face. He propped his head up on his hand, feeling his eyes melt as she snuggled into his chest.

He thought about how to answer her question and settled on, "I went back to Manhattan after OSS discharged me. I tried to do the right thing by my old man, but…" He reached over to the nightstand for a cigarette, his usual procrastination device.

But she kept her eyes on him, waiting for him to finish.

"Come here," he said, lying on his back and drawing her head onto his shoulder, inhaling smoke from the cigarette and passing it to her. He was silent for only a few seconds before he continued.

"I couldn't care less about advertising revenues, but you have to when you're in charge. My father and I had too many conversations along the lines of, 'Your brother wouldn't have done that,' or 'Can't you be a bit more like your brothers?' before I knew I had to leave or else I might knock his head off. The editor of our international edition took a job elsewhere mid last year and I just about ran to Europe to claim the job for myself. Now he and I speak maybe twice a year for birthdays or board meetings and . . . It's better like that."

Esmée's words about him taking up his role as Mr. March Junior at year's end, and finding someone to fill the empty position at his side as Mrs. March, darted into his head. Was he too like water, waiting to be poured into a future he'd thought was the only one that existed? A future where an important job and a place in society were the only things that mattered and a wife was a necessary acquisition—someone to host dinner parties, bear children, and turn a blind eye to infidelity. When he thought about it like that, he wondered if it wasn't just his old man he'd been running from when he'd come to Paris. In the life he was supposed to have, he doubted he'd ever have met someone like Alix, a thought that made more than just his shoulder sting.

"Is it really better for your father—who lost his entire understanding of what the future would be when two of his sons died—to have his only living son become a stranger?" Alix asked quietly and he held her tighter, thinking of the thirteen-year-old girl who'd watched her parents waltz around a tiny apartment and who'd then lost her expected future when both those parents died.

"Sometimes when people are grieving," she went on, "they don't say what they mean because it's too painful to say, *I want to talk about your brothers, but I don't know how.* Maybe what your father said wasn't about you. Maybe he just wanted you to reply, *I know my brother wouldn't have done that. He would have done this.* And then you could have talked about him together, for just a minute or two."

There was a very long pause thereafter and Anthony was only roused from it when his cigarette burned down too far. He frowned, stubbing it into the ashtray.

Alix rolled on top of him, leaning her forearms on his chest. "Did

I upset you?" she asked, touching one hand to his cheek. "That's not what I wanted to do."

"I know," he said, winding his fingers into hers. "I just never thought about it like that. While my first impulse was to tell you in very colorful language that you're wrong, my impulse now is to..." He hesitated. "What you said means that in coming over here, I deeply hurt my father. I hate myself for doing that."

Alix brought his hand to her mouth and kissed his knuckles. "Then send him a telegram, write him a letter...Make a gesture so he knows he still has you."

"Maybe I will," Anthony said, stroking her hair again. "Thank you."

"My pleasure," she said softly.

"Speaking of which." He grinned. "Are there any more of my troubles you'd like to solve?"

"Yes, there is."

He lifted a quizzical eyebrow.

"The trouble is," she said, wriggling up a little higher, "you're too far away."

The other trouble was, kissing Alix was not something that would ever end quickly so the kiss lingered, deepened, and then he turned her onto her back and braced his body above hers and the look in her eyes made him tighten his grip, knowing this time was not going to be slow and teasing and gentle, but fierce and wild and perfect.

* * *

At four in the morning with Anthony sleeping peacefully beside her, Alix unwound her limbs from his. The last few hours had been sublime and she didn't want to ruin them with mornings. If she left now, it could be just what it was—the most incredible night she'd ever had. She expected nothing from Anthony, knew she was simply an amusement on his path to becoming a responsible adult. Although, she thought with regret, it would be very hard to sleep with anyone ever again after that.

And even harder to pretend that she didn't care.

Going to work was the best distraction, even though it was Saturday. She could make sure everything was in place for Monday's departure, and might be able to stop thinking for an hour or so about when La Voce would come.

Her phone rang in the afternoon. "I can't get into the *maison* because of that stolen sketch," a voice said. "I'm in the telephone booth down the street."

"Fortunée?"

"No, Marie Antoinette."

Alix chose to ignore the sarcasm. "Just a minute."

Being Saturday, there weren't many people around so it was relatively easy to smuggle Fortunée into her office.

"He's gone," Fortunée said, studying Suzanne's brandy bottles and helping herself to a glass.

"Anthony?" Alix's voice was discernibly shocked.

Fortunée smirked. "Monsieur March is in his office. I'm talking about the man I had a lead on, the one I thought might tell me something about your La Voce."

"Dammit. Give me that." She indicated Fortunée's glass.

Fortunée handed it over with reluctance. "You probably don't want more bad news but I'm out of leads. Don't think I know any other way of helping you figure out Weber's motives." Fortunée retrieved the glass and finished the liquor.

"Wait." Alix made sure to turn her full attention on Fortunée. "Thank you. I mean it. You did more than you needed to and I won't forget it. If I can ever do anything for you, let me know."

"You'd make a fine *grande horizontale*. And I'd need a redhead if I ever opened a place of my own."

"I would never…" Alix spluttered, then she caught Fortunée's grin and laughed. Fortunée did too.

"I might even miss you, you know," she said when she'd recovered. "I never had real siblings but I'm lucky enough to have known a few people who've been almost better to me than kin."

"Well, listen up because this is the only sentimental thing I'll ever say to you in my life. Monsieur March knows I'll do anything for him. So you'd better not hurt him. Then I'd be mad and I'm not nice when I'm mad."

Alix reached up to twist one of the buttons on her dress too ferociously. "I have a feeling it's most likely to be the other way around," she said very quietly.

Fortunée sighed. "It's a hell of a lot easier not to give a man your feelings," was her parting advice, delivered almost gently.

"I know," Alix whispered to the empty room, remembering Mary's words from nearly five years earlier. *Power is the opposite to love.* And right now, Alix was powerless to do anything at all about her feelings for Anthony. They were inexorable—and that was both intoxicating and catastrophic.

But—power is the opposite to love. *"Mon Dieu."*

*I'll do anything for him,* Fortunée had said. And, *what are you capable of doing to a man who is merciless toward someone you love?* La Voce had said to Alix. At the time, she'd wondered if it was more than just a question. Now she knew it was the last piece of the puzzle.

* * *

She called Anthony's office straight away. *Please let him be there.* A woman picked up, and told her that Anthony was in a meeting. Over a hubbub of voices, she heard Anthony ask impatiently, *"Qui est-ce?"*

"Mademoiselle St. Pierre."

Anthony's voice came down the line. "Alix?"

"You sound busy. I can call back. But…" She was speaking incoherently fast.

"Wait. There are about ten people in my office—the Conference of European Economic Cooperation is on in Paris today and we're covering it, but I can spare a minute," he explained. "What's happened?"

"La Voce," she said, trying to make this make sense. "I said before that I thought he was going after Matteo. Now I know he was. I don't know exactly what Matteo did but I think it was to someone La Voce cared about—a sibling perhaps, as he wasn't the kind of man to have a lover. He said something to me once about having to learn what you might do if a person was unsparing toward someone you loved. And the way he said it, it was more than just words. I know I sound crazy and I'm babbling but—"

She heard someone call, "Monsieur!" Anthony told them to wait, then returned to her and apologized.

"You know we had agents embedded in the partisan groups," he said, speaking low and urgently, obviously not wanting anyone in the room to hear. "I've telegrammed all of them and one of them came back to me with a story about a German hostage—the brother of someone high up in Wolff's command—who was stabbed and killed by a partisan just before you came to me with Operation Lycaon. The person Fortunée was trying to talk to was a Nazi taken hostage with that man. Fortunée was going to see if she could get the Nazi to tell her anything about the man who was stabbed to death. And maybe…"

"It was Weber's brother and he planned Lycaon to avenge him," she replied, very quietly. "And Matteo…" She couldn't say it.

"Was the one who killed him," Anthony finished for her.

"Well," she said, voice cracking, knowing for certain now that she hadn't just handed La Voce Matteo's body, but his soul too. "We have the motivation we wanted. But it couldn't feel…" *Less like a victory.*

How could she make herself finish her sentence when she could still feel, tearing her to pieces again, the heartbroken love she and Matteo had shared?

"Alix." Anthony's voice was like a gentle hand stroking over her cheek. "I'm sorry."

"Me too. But that doesn't help Matteo. Nothing can."

\* \* \*

Memory. Such a crushing thing. She could smell Milan in '45 now—dust, incendiaries, the salt of a million tears. Could hear the pall of quiet broken by the sudden toppling of a wall. The rough scrape of Matteo's stubble against her cheek. His almost soundless whisper, *I love you, Alix.*

Her elbow was propped on her desk, her face hidden in her hand, a million tears untethered. "I'm sorry, Matteo," she wept.

She could say that every day and it would never be enough.

\* \* \*

Work, she thought a long time later. It was all there was to beat back memory. But look, on the floor just over there was a crumpled ball of paper that had missed the wastepaper basket. She was still writing to Lillie. Which just proved that nothing beat back memory.

But maybe something did. Good memories. Precious ones. Because she couldn't let herself be dragged back down. Had to stay strong for long enough to do the only thing she could for Matteo.

And she had new and precious memories—had just had one precious night. *Think of that now*, she exhorted herself. *Use it to focus on the present.*

Anthony, the touch of his lips on every part of her body. The press of her mouth all over his. But also, the knowledge that it probably wouldn't happen again. She was leaving for New York in two days. And the showdown with La Voce would quench any time left for ardor.

"You're so flushed. Do you need some air?" Suzanne asked, entering the room unexpectedly to change for aperitifs. Then, "How did your interview with Monsieur March go?" as if the one observation had nothing to do with the question that followed.

"Fine," Alix said, but even she could feel her cheeks flushing.

Suzanne began to unbutton her jacket. "*Chérie*," she said, "I know you think you cannot have this," she waved her hands around Alix's office, "as well as a forever after, till-the-end-of-time romance. But don't cut off the bud before it can blossom just because you think tomorrow's frost might destroy it anyway. Wait and see what happens."

"I'm not sure that botanical metaphors are your strong suit," Alix said. "Anthony March is not a till-the-end-of-time man for someone like me. Wealthy newspaper heirs require women who make their lives easy, not more complicated."

Suzanne sighed as she stepped into her cocktail dress and beckoned to Alix to help with the closures. "That is what Anthony and every other man like him needs. But it might not be what he wants." Her voice became very gentle. "I have much faith in Monsieur March. More, perhaps, than he has in himself." Then she retouched her lipstick and left the office.

Alix shook her head. Suzanne knew better than to talk about a world where what people wanted actually mattered. It certainly didn't, not if you were a woman. She needed to stop thinking about Anthony, otherwise she'd only make what she'd said to Fortunée—*I have a feeling it's most likely to be the other way around*—come true.

# TWENTY-NINE

At the Ritz, she checked in with Frank, who again shook his head. It would be tomorrow, then. Of course La Voce would have discovered—from Becky—that Alix was leaving for New York and of course he wanted to wait until the last excruciating minute. It was exactly what he'd done as the men set off into the mountains in 1945.

When the elevator arrived on the third floor, she exited and turned left toward her room. The sound of movement came from up ahead. She froze.

Her gun was in her purse. She slipped her hand inside and took a few steps forward, silent, slow.

But it was Anthony pacing outside her door, smoking a cigarette.

She stopped short and tried to remember to breathe.

"Hey," he said softly, catching her eyes in his and that was that.

They both moved at the same time, toward one another, her hand sliding along his jaw, his gripping her hip, drawing her in, kissing her in a way that was headier and fiercer and more urgent than anything she remembered from the night before.

"I can't stop thinking about you," he pulled back just enough to say.

She reached for the door and they tumbled inside, backing into the wall where she tugged him against her, expecting it would happen right there, half-clothed and fast because it felt impossible to wait for.

But Anthony shook his head and said, "I want you naked every single time." Then he added, "I didn't mean that to sound like a demand."

She laughed. "I don't mind it when you demand things like that. And you've saved me from saying the same thing."

*  *  *

"What are we doing?" Alix asked later when they were lying in her bed, the back of her body held tight against the front of his, his hand wandering up and down her hip, one of her hands threaded into his.

"Recovering," he said, and she could hear the smile in his voice.

"You know what I mean," she said very quietly.

There was a pause. "I know what you mean."

But what was the answer to her question?

"Alix," he said. "If we're going to talk about this, I need to see your face."

She rolled over and Anthony propped his head up on one hand, the other still traversing her body.

"Tell me why," he asked, voice like a soft, velvet caress, "after Bobby died and the war ended and you went back to New York, you didn't date anyone seriously? I'm guessing you didn't, based on what you said the other night. But I can't understand it. You are *beautiful*. Not just that. You make me laugh more than anyone ever has. You're smart and loyal and selfless, and if you gave even a quarter of yourself to a man the way you gave yourself to me last night, I can't see how they would ever let you out of their bed."

"I need a cigarette," Alix said, rolling onto her back and wishing she'd never started this conversation. Her reasons were to do with things no man understood.

Carmel did, perhaps. Her balm was enough alcohol to pickle her soul. Mary understood too. All Alix could see now was Mary's face when she'd told Alix that her husband beat her and that Dulles liked to rush into her room before meetings for a pick-me-up. Who was there to pick Mary up?

In the silence of her hesitation, Anthony lit two cigarettes, handing one to her. "I have a feeling you're going to want your own," he said, moving closer, breaching the small gap she'd created when she'd rolled onto her back.

She inhaled deeply and watched smoke drift upward like hopes and dreams, vanishing before it reached the highest point in the room. "You have to understand," she said haltingly, "what it's like for a woman. It's..." How to explain?

She tried again. "Did you know that no matter how much you earn, a woman has to bring along a man to cosign any credit application she makes to a bank? You have to get permission from your husband to keep working, that's if your boss doesn't fire you first. It's not usual for women to work after they're married unless you're wealthy like Suzanne and your 'job' is seen to involve nothing more than gossiping with other wealthy women. Carmel is the other major exception to the rule but..." Alix shrugged. "She never sees her husband. She hardly saw her children when they were young. All she sees is the bottom of her empty glass, and for only a second before it's filled up again."

Ash spilled from her cigarette onto the sheet and she swore, batting it away. Anthony tried to catch her eyes but she kept them moving around the room.

Another attempt at answering. "From the moment I arrived back in New York in 1945 I avoided intimacy because it would have meant facing what I could give up and what I couldn't. If I was married, I would no longer be sitting at the spectacle of Dior's very first showing, knowing I contributed a little to that. I would no longer walk down the Rue de la Paix and see that every second gown is either a Dior or influenced by Dior and know I had a hand in that. Instead, I'd pace up and down inside an apartment in a nice part of the city, desperate for the doorbell to ring so I'd have something to do."

Anthony's hold on her tightened almost uncomfortably, but it was what she wanted—to feel that he was hearing her. "Does anyone ever think," she segued, "that the men in the mountains in Italy would all have died without the *staffette* bringing them food and clothes and messages? Just like all the men today couldn't do what they do without the women at home organizing parties and managing children and households and the social networks that support the business the man does. We make the world possible—but the world makes almost everything impossible for us. During the war, every second poster on the street showed a woman at work with the headline, 'You Can Do It.' And we *did* do it. But now, you open a magazine and in every picture, the women are in their kitchens. Nobody wants us for anything but domestic duties and decoration now the fighting's stopped."

She inhaled furiously on her cigarette, letting the smoke sting her eyes, blaming the dampness on that. Saying it aloud didn't change it. But she was so goddamn angry all of a sudden that it came out anyway.

"What if I did get married and had a daughter? What am I supposed to tell her? *Yes, my darling, working and succeeding at that work is fulfilling in a way that few other things are, so dream and dare to do whatever you want.* But then I'd have to say, *Oops, sorry, I forget to mention that when you marry, you'll have to pack your dream into a box and never take it out because it will hurt too much to remember what you used to be.* So I don't even know if I want children because I don't want to tell anyone I love any of those things."

She felt the tears trickle down her face and she swiped wrathfully at them, held up a hand to halt Anthony, who was moving in to say something but, if he did, then she might cry properly. And if she let herself cry over this, then how would she ever stop?

"A woman can be ruined so easily by a man, Anthony," she said, her voice so thin it was almost transparent, the weariness setting in as she returned to the place where she'd started. "Even though my friend Lillie and her mother weren't responsible for her father losing all their money, they lost everything too. They had no money saved because a married woman isn't allowed to have a bank account in her own name."

She crushed her cigarette in the ashtray, rolling a little away from Anthony so her next words were spoken with her face averted. "Unmarried, my money and my mistakes are all mine. As a woman, the world is full of gates and locked doors and barriers, and marriage just adds so many more. So I've become the woman no one even dates, let alone marries. The redheaded, trouser-wearing, outspoken work-aholic who's trying not to let her vices overtake her like Carmel has, who's left with furtive trysts in dark corners that solve nothing and only make me cry."

Her throat choked with all the injustices she could do nothing about—and the hopelessness too.

"Alix," Anthony said. He shifted his body over hers and kissed her forehead so gently that the ache in her throat was too much, the tears in her eyes too many to contain. "Please look at me," he said. "I know you don't want to because you're hurting—but please?"

He stroked her hair, one arm braced along the side of her body, and she relented, meeting his eyes at last.

"I look at you," he whispered, "your incredible red hair spread out on the pillow, your eyes shining because you don't want to cry in front of me and I want to cry myself for what the future will do to you. There is no way you can be stuck in someone's apartment arranging dinner parties. You are *spectacular*. The world needs people like you out in it, not trapped in a Manhattan apartment with regrets hidden behind a hostess's smile. I imagine all the things that might not hap-pen if you're not out there making them happen and that future isn't one I want."

There was such compassion in his voice, so unexpected, that it eased her throat a little and gave her the courage to say the very last thing.

"I sometimes wonder," she began, haltingly, but his eyes beseeched her to keep going, "what I'll regret more when I'm seventy and alone. Will I regret the aloneness, the lack of a husband and children—will I want to reach into the past and tell myself right now just to date anyone who asks and acquiesce to the life I'm supposed to have? Or will I, when I'm seventy and have four children and fifteen grandchildren and have managed three dinner parties a week for forty years, want to stand in the doorway and scream at myself right now to never, ever acquiesce? How can I know, when I've never really had a family, whether it's worth giving up? How can I know what I'd treasure most when some of those treasures have never found their way into my hands?"

So many unanswerable questions. No, not unanswerable. Unaskable. Because it wasn't for a woman to ask or to dream—it was for her to obey. And to stay at goddamn home.

Anthony's brow furrowed as if he were trying to find the right answer and give it to her, the most precious gift of all. "Things change, Alix. You know they do. I mean, twenty-five years or so ago, women weren't allowed to vote. But now they can. So…"

He faltered, then reached over to stroke away the tears spilling onto her cheeks.

"I think…" she whispered, knowing she was coming to the end of the words she could say without outright weeping, "that one woman alone can't realign the stars to alter the future that's already written for today's women. What will be in twenty years time is already decided because the men of today—who make the decisions—have grown up in this world. They'll want to preserve it, no matter what."

"I'm sorry, Alix," Anthony said. "I wish—"

Before he could continue, she reached up to kiss him because what she needed right then was intimacy in a way she hadn't needed it or craved it or understood it, ever. The kiss was slow and deep and sad and he kept his hands cupped around her jaw, catching her tears.

Anthony March would, if he found the right woman, be a devoted husband, she thought suddenly—and the idea was bittersweet. She wanted that for him, wanted him to have that future rather than the one where he married a woman who fitted well into his life but didn't fit him—a woman he grew bored of in a year's time and became the husband who flirted with the *vendeuse* while both his wife and his mistress shopped at Dior. He wouldn't find the former if Alix took up space in his bed.

And all Alix would find if she remained there were things that would shape her into an Alix she didn't want to be. Mary's voice was calling out to her from the past, repeating the story about Dulles rushing in to clear his head: *"But,"* he said, *"I want you." And that was supposed to be a good enough offer. It must've been. I accepted it,* Mary had said.

But Alix couldn't accept being merely wanted.

"Anthony," she said, drawing back reluctantly from the kiss it was too easy to stay raveled in. "We can't keep doing this."

His jaw tightened.

"*I* can't keep doing this," she amended. "People talk—they're already talking thanks to Becky—and the unmarried woman in an arrangement like this is the one they talk about. Nothing I do anymore will be meaningful or expert because I'll be called your mistress, and we all know the one and only thing mistresses are expert at. So this—us, whatever we are—has to end now."

Her hands gripping his back spoke different words than her mouth. Her hands said what her heart wanted, which was to stay there forever. But hearts, as she'd learned in Italy, were only meant to break.

Anthony rested his forehead against hers for a long moment. His silence told her that he understood what she was saying. That she didn't—couldn't—fit into the life that he and every other man like him had been conditioned to believe was the only life. And she was grateful that he wasn't offering any false promises, wasn't pretending that he wouldn't be returning to Manhattan in a few months to take up his role as head of a newspaper empire and to marry a woman who wanted only a large house, a lavish wardrobe, and discretion in return.

"All right," he said at last. But the fierceness of his hold on her hips said that no, it wasn't all right.

But it had to be.

His only rebuttal was another kiss, bittersweet and filled with promises that, if this was the last time they were in a bed together, it would be magnificent.

It was with that same tenderness that they made love again, Anthony's fingers trailing over her skin like erotic feathers from her forehead down to her toes as he whispered, "Tell me what you like, what you want," and her whole body responding to the intensity behind that sentence with a jolt as she reached up to his ear to murmur, "Kiss me everywhere."

And he did, his lips mimicking the movements of his hands, a light and sensual brush that never stayed in any one place for too long, until it did, and then she felt not just her bones melt, but her heart melt too.

* * *

What had just happened between them? Something had, that was all Anthony was sure of, and Alix's eyes, still caught in his, said the same. He guessed he should be going back to his room—she'd said it was over. That she didn't want to do this anymore. But he could feel the marks of her fingernails against his shoulders when she'd held onto him so tightly—like she'd never let go—at the same time as she'd told him she *was* letting go.

Which meant...

*He would never do this with her again.*

The very idea almost had him bending double. He reached for the Gauloises, taking his time to light a cigarette, to inhale and exhale and then to look back over his shoulder at her, red hair spilling like his goddamn heart over the pillow.

He gave her the cigarette, climbed out of bed, and got dressed, because he couldn't stay and make her into gossip. She didn't deserve for everything she'd done to be dismissed as having been orchestrated by him and his money. He suddenly wished he had no money—but he knew only someone with wealth could ever afford to make wishes like that.

The next and quite possibly last time he saw her would be in a room with La Voce. But all he could think about now was each time he'd shared a cigarette with her and their fingers had touched for a single, pulsing second. And everything he and Alix had done together—gone to a jazz club and not shared a dance but the contours of their sorrows instead; lain in a bed side by side and touched the linings of one another's souls.

*You are spectacular*, he'd said to her. He'd known that from the first time he saw her cross the floor in the bar three stories below them. With her, it was always going to be until the end of time—or else it would burn them to ashes.

He stood up, his feet walking away across the embers.

But a photograph in a frame on the bureau arrested him. "Who's this?" he asked.

"My friend Lillie. Why?"

"This is the same photograph that Bobby carried with him."

# THIRTY

*Lillie, what did you do?* It was all Alix could think after Anthony left and she stared at the photograph, the one taken at the county fair. Bobby had carried it to Europe with him.

*Look after her*, Bobby had said to Alix.

*How's Lillie?* It was always the first thing he'd asked when Alix had dinner with him in Manhattan before the war.

Alix hadn't thought anything of it. Lillie was the golden girl—blond and rich and beautiful. Why wouldn't anyone ask after her first? Besides, Bobby and Lillie had been friends since they were young and there'd been no reason to be suspicious because Mrs. van der Meer had been so insistent in pushing Bobby and Alix together, and dismissing his wealth as not being exceptional enough for Lillie.

But hadn't Lillie been equally determined? Always whispering to Alix about Bobby, and doing the same with Bobby. Looking at Alix with tears in her eyes the night Bobby proposed, almost as if she were begging Alix to marry him. *Why?*

Because if Bobby married Alix, the triangle would still exist—their mutual friend Lillie would always be in their lives. But if Bobby's wife was someone other than Alix, that wife might want to erase the point of the triangle labeled *Lillie* because of jealousy, insecurity—any of a hundred reasons why wives didn't want their husbands to have close female friends. And thus Lillie wouldn't be able to see Bobby anymore.

Lillie had had tears in her eyes because Bobby's engagement to Alix must have seemed like the end for both Lillie and Bobby. You only carried into a war zone with you a picture of someone you loved. It could only mean that Lillie and Bobby had been in love—and quite possibly for a very long time.

*  *  *

*To Lillie,*
*From Paris*

*If I turn my head and look over my shoulder, I'll see a bed with white cotton sheets ruched into the shape of two bodies. But some time tomorrow, a maid will arrive and she'll change the sheets, unpleat all the heat and tenderness that still hovers in the air and then the bed will be flat and cold and empty.*

*I always knew that Peter wasn't your beloved, just as Bobby was never mine. Neither of us had, with our fiancés, the communion of two people—like dress with body—one fitting exquisitely over and onto and around the other. I had started to think that perhaps one only fits oneself that way. But is that how you fitted with Bobby, Lillie?*

*All I know is that you and Bobby shouldn't have let whatever was between you become an indistinct dream that neither of you ever reached. You should have told me, told your mother, told the world— you should have taken the happiness that was there while you could.*

*But you didn't and now I can't help but ask—does that somehow explain the end of everything? Or am I just looking, still, to shift the blame from myself and onto someone else?*

*  *  *

Alix laid down her pen. *Does that somehow explain the end of everything?* One end had been in Manhattan in May 1945. The other had been in April, a month earlier when a woman in a white silk dress had sat at a bar, waiting.

And suddenly Alix knew what the finale would be.

La Voce was sitting somewhere nearby, smiling a little, waiting for her to figure it out.

She pushed herself up and put on a silk dress—leopard-print this time. Then she picked up the phone and even though it was nearly midnight, she dialed Anthony's room. He answered on the first ring.

"He wants it to happen the same way it happened before," she said, strangely calm. "He must have a set of eyes at the Ritz too. And that's okay, because I have more. So I'm going down to the bar now where I'll sip water until a key appears in front of me and then I'll take the elevator to La Voce's room."

"Alix, what the hell—"

"It's all right. I still have the upper hand. Just wait for Frank to call you."

"There is no way I'm going to let you go down there and sit in the bar by yourself while I wait for Frank to call me. Alix," he said her name again, desperately, and she wanted to hold his face in her hands, to have him look right into her, deep inside her like he'd done a few hours before, and see the endless, shimmering length of red silk-satin that was everything she felt for him.

But all she could say was, "Do you trust me?"

"More than fucking anything," he growled. "You know that."

"Then trust me now. Wait for Frank to call."

She went downstairs to the bar.

* * *

Once there, she spoke to Frank, who nodded and left to put everything in motion. He was back five minutes later with another nod.

After that, it took over an hour. Of course it did. Those were the games La Voce like to play. But she knew all of his games now and, she thought, had learned to play some of them better than he did.

The clock struck half past one when the key arrived.

Second floor. Room 207, just as she'd arranged.

# PART SIX
## BERN, APRIL 1945

*For many weeks we had been receiving reports that the Nazi intention, in extremity, was to withdraw the cream of the SS, Gestapo, and other organizations fanatically devoted to Hitler, into the mountains of southern Bavaria, western Austria, and Northern Italy. There they expected to block the tortuous mountain passes and to hold out indefinitely against the Allies…*

—General Dwight D. Eisenhower

# THIRTY-ONE

*T**he next time we meet, you will come to my room at the Bellevue Palace Hotel. And you will wear your white dress,* La Voce had said. She cannot.

Alix says, eyes fixed to the screen of the confessional booth separating her from this man, "The price you're asking is exceptionally high." She hardly believes she has the gall but, right now, she has the power. He's just told her the most revealing thing of all—what he wants. And it's something only she can give.

"I'll need more than Chiara Romano released," she says flatly. "Shut Villa Triste down. And I want to know about the Redoubt. Whether it's real. Tell me that and I'll come to your room. Leave me a note when you know if you can deliver."

He laughs, but she can hear shock at her temerity. He'd thought her journey to Milan would have cowed her. It has, but it's also given her a kind of strength she knows isn't virtue, but something much darker.

\* \* \*

Alix is uncharacteristically silent when she returns to Herrengasse. Dulles eyes her but doesn't say a word. She'd had one of her couriers send a note to let him know she was in Milan and, rather than debrief him verbally, she writes everything into a report. Dulles reads it and doesn't comment. Later, when Mary arrives, she eyes Alix too but also allows her to have her silence.

The next day is similar. Alix works like an automaton.

She could leave, she thinks at around noon. The border to France is open now that France has been liberated. She could jump on a train to Paris, knock on Suzanne's door or Esmée's door and sleep for a hundred years. The hatred she feels for herself the second after she has the thought is so ferocious that she draws in an audible breath and Dulles's head shoots up from his desk.

Chiara is in Koch's torture chamber and Alix is imagining running away.

She stands up, walks to the church, opens the hymnbook, and finds a note.

*I will not tell you about the Redoubt but I will give you an unguarded route in. Your soldiers can look for themselves to see if it's real. You know what you need to do to get the information.*

She walks out of the church and drops the note onto Dulles's desk.

"From La Voce," she says before cabling Leone.

CAN OBTAIN SAFE ROUTE INTO REDOUBT IF YOU CAN ARRANGE MISSION TO VERIFY ITS EXISTENCE.

"What does your informant want in return?" Dulles is standing in front of her with La Voce's note in hand.

"Me."

"And you're happy to do that?"

Her laugh is sharp and incredulous. "Only a man who will never be asked for his body in exchange for anything would ask that." She picks up her purse and leaves to search for air.

*   *   *

She returns to Herrengasse at nightfall. On her desk is a reply from Leone.

YES. IF THERE REALLY IS A SAFE ROUTE IN.

She presses her knuckles against her closed eyes.

She's sitting in her office in Switzerland with four walls around her and no danger of ever being snatched off a street and having her bones broken. She has the power to save Chiara and Parri's wife and all the others in Villa Triste. She has the chance to find out if the Redoubt is peopled by werewolves, if the Allies need to act now to stop a blood-thirsty alpine battle from extending the war and the body count by months or possibly years.

The war needs to end. People need to be saved.

It's so simple, really.

There is so much need and almost no fulfillment.

The sound of an incoming cable intrudes. She pulls it off, sees that it's from AFHQ Caserta and, after reading it, that it must be from Lillie.

SORRY, THIS CAME IN YESTERDAY. I KNOW I WAS SUPPOSED TO SEND IT STRAIGHT ON. I WON'T DO IT AGAIN, I REALLY PROMISE THIS TIME. CAN YOU COVER FOR ME?

Enclosed is a message from the wireless operator Alix had recently inserted into Karl Wolff's headquarters. As there's no wireless receiver in Bern, the operator's messages have to be sent to Caserta, and then relayed to Alix. This one is about a meeting the Nazis want to have tomorrow. *Shit.*

Dulles is going to flay either her or Lillie alive.

She's just taken the message in to him and he's just commenced the flaying when a different voice says her name.

She jumps and turns to find Mr. Cigar, her interviewer from Washington, standing behind her.

"I came across from France," he says congenially. "I believe I owe you a drink for all of your fine work."

She almost laughs. It's no coincidence that she, a woman with wrecked nerves, is the conduit to a mission into the Alpine Redoubt and Mr. Cigar is here. Dulles must have called him in. She's about to exchange one kind of excoriation for another.

The bar at the Bellevue is busy with all the usual suspects and several of the men nod at Alix as she enters but then turn away when they see she already has a companion.

"I don't know your name," she says as she sits down.

"Colonel Dearborn." He goes through the same cigar-lighting ceremony she witnessed nearly three years ago and she watches with impatience. A man who has so much time to waste on lighting a cigar has never stood beside a Resistance leader while he chooses integrity over his wife—and who then lets the music cry for him.

"Congratulations," he says when at last he's ready. "The work you've done is one of OSS's biggest success stories. A large partisan army in the north of Italy. Surrender negotiations well in progress."

"I have trouble believing you asked me here for the purpose of celebrating."

"You find yourself in a dilemma," is all he says.

She doesn't respond. He isn't there to help her, but to persuade her. Three men—Dulles, Dearborn, and La Voce—against one woman. That's life, right there.

He savors the first true draw on his cigar and says, "I want you to think the way you would have thought in that room in Washington in 1942. I don't want you to think like a woman who has got closer to her partisans than she probably should have."

Alix reaches over for his cigar case. He frowns and she's glad because she wants to hurt him the same way he just hurt her. She has never smoked a cigar before and is fairly sure her clip isn't perfect and she skips the raw draw for the main show. It tastes like money and power and pride, all the things she doesn't have. How can she possibly think back to that Washington office and rescue from the past an Alix who doesn't exist anymore?

Dearborn presses on. "That woman had no emotions at all about Italy—no losses and no loves. If I'd told that woman that sometimes you have to decide if the need is so great that you act first and feel later, she would have done it. You did it in coming to Switzerland in the first place. You acted based on what I said without ever really trusting me. And you worried about it later—when it was too late to change anything."

Perhaps he's right. Isn't it, after all, too late to change anything?

What will be was set in motion the moment Chiara was caught. What remains is to finish it, finally and forever.

# THIRTY-TWO

In a fit of dark humor, she calls it Operation Lycaon. The newspapers believe the Germans hiding in the mountains are werewolves, so what name is more fitting for an operation to track those creatures than that of a king Zeus turned into a wolf?

She cables the name to Leone and he replies: TEAM READY FOR OPERATION LYCAON. AWAITING SAFE ROUTE FROM YOU AND A CONFIRMED DATE.

Not long after, she receives a cable from Lillie. HQ CAN'T STOP TALKING ABOUT YOUR OPERATION LYCAON, WHATEVER THAT IS. ALL I HEAR EVERYWHERE IS BISOUS, BISOUS.

The last part of Lillie's cable makes Alix laugh as she pictures a profusion of French kisses at AFHQ. THANKS, she replies to Lillie. YOU MADE ME LAUGH AND I CAN'T REMEMBER THE LAST TIME I DID THAT.

BOBBY MADE ME LAUGH YESTERDAY, Lillie returns.

On the one hand, Alix can't believe Lillie is still cabling Bobby, and using his name in cables. On the other hand, she's glad Lillie has someone to laugh with—Alix's cables are not usually the humorous kind.

Right now, she would give almost anything to hear Lillie's laugh. It was always so free of care—the laugh of a person who knew she'd be forgiven for anything.

Will Alix be able to forgive herself for what she has to do?

She puts down the cable and opens the note on her desk from Mary.

* * *

*I spoke to Allen and while he didn't tell me everything, he told me enough. And now there's something I need to tell you. Forgiveness is a word made up by a man who expected it but never gave it in return. Survival is a word made up by a woman because it's how she lives. You will survive, Alix. So will I. And that's something.*

\* \* \*

Alix arranges herself in her white dress at the bar at the Bellevue Palace Hotel and waits for her summons upstairs. By midnight, she's drunk more than she should have and her thoughts are scattered. She wants to stick her head in a bathtub.

Because it's too late. He isn't coming. It was all a game. Chiara will die and perhaps thousands of men will too in an Alpine Redoubt that the Allies have little understanding of.

Then the summons comes in the form of a key passed to her by a waiter. She rides the elevator to room 434, opens the door, and steps inside.

"Halt!" La Voce's voice calls from within the room. "Sit in the chair."

A chair has been placed by the door and she drops into it, still in the foyer of the room rather than the room proper, hand resting on the gun inside her purse.

The tinkle of ice cubes sounds, followed by a swallow. She wonders if it excites him, the idea of her out of sight, or if it really is all about him hiding his identity.

"On the chair is a map with a route marked into the Redoubt area. Your counterparts can ascend using that route and it will be unguarded all of Friday evening and into Saturday morning."

"How do I know it's not a setup?" she asks and her words are only a little slurred with alcohol and fear of what will happen next.

"There's a package waiting for you at the border. It should be proof enough."

A package. She squeezes her eyes shut, wanting to cry. She knows it's Chiara, that her friend is free and Matteo will be smiling, not weeping.

There are no more procrastinations. Alix has her map and she has Chiara, so now it is time to pay. She stands.

"Not tonight," he says before she can walk into the bedroom. "Friday night. While your men ascend the Redoubt."

Her stomach turns over and she presses a hand to the wall.

La Voce wants her to spend more days thinking about what he will do to her in her white dress. He wants to have her while she's worrying about Matteo climbing into mountains patrolled by werewolves. He knows the torture is as much in the not knowing as in the doing.

But compared to what Koch's band will have done to Chiara in Villa Triste, it is no torture at all.

"The map is on the chair," he repeats. "Take it and leave."

She does not need to be asked twice.

\* \* \*

She cables Leone: Operation Lycaon to go ahead. 10 April. Route enclosed. Then she drives straight to the border where Chiara is waiting. Her body is beyond bruised; it is almost in shreds. Her eyes are dead.

Alix wants desperately to talk to Matteo, to look into his eyes and make him believe he is strong enough not to do all the things the Nazis have made him capable of. But if he saw Chiara in this state... "They closed down Villa Triste," Chiara says dully once she's safe in Alix's apartment. "Matteo got me to the border. He says I should stay here with you until I'm better."

Chiara turns to face the wall and Alix knows she will never be better. She hides her razor, as well as her scarves.

\* \* \*

The tenth of April arrives in a blaze of sunshine. Bern looks like a fairy-tale city awaiting a storybook wedding. The gingerbread houses glisten in the sunlight, the spire of the Zytglogge is all romance against the blue sky, and the bells of the astronomical clock peal. The glint in the eye of the child-eating ogre is the single hint that fairy tales only conclude with bliss once the heel of a foot has been sliced off to fit inside a shoe, or after the head of a horse hangs from a keep.

Leone and Matteo and the rest of Leone's men will be well into the mountains now, Alix thinks as she pulls on her white dress. Her body arrives at the Bellevue Hotel but her mind is with the men approaching the route to the Redoubt, picturing them alert for ambush, their guns ready, their intellects primed to remember all details of the fortress where the world suspects Hitler wants to meet his Wagnerian end.

She drinks but doesn't taste as she is made to wait until midnight once more for her transformation into a woman who survives rather than lives.

A key appears in front of her. She takes the elevator to room 407 this time.

Inside, a lamp is lit. The drapes are drawn.

"Hello?" she calls out.

Her echo is the only reply.

There is a note on the bed. *I'm on my way. Wait for me.*

She sits on the edge of the bed and tries to think of all the many good things she's had in her life, tries to gather them to her like talismans warding off danger. But they don't come. They hide in the shadows behind the image of Chiara's face as it had looked that morning: a ruin.

And suddenly she knows. If La Voce was coming, he would be there.

Her cry is loud and long and futile.

La Voce has proven himself the master. He made her believe she was so worth having that the possession of her body would save the lives of a group of men.

She has instead sent them to their deaths.

She takes the train to the border and there, in her white evening gown, she shivers—eyes numb to tears, heart weeping ceaselessly—and waits for someone to appear.

Nobody does.

* * *

Four days later, eyes glassy, dress dirty, soul cut to ribbons, she leaves her border vigil and returns to Herrengasse. On her desk is a cable.

NINE MEN LOST, INCLUDING BACIO. ONE AGENT SURVIVED WITH GUN-SHOT WOUND TO UPPER RIGHT SHOULDER. THE GERMANS WERE WAITING.

Dulles shouts at her but she has no idea what he's saying. His shouts become screams so she walks out of the office, still in her white dress. At her apartment she wakes Chiara, who takes one look at her face and sobs.

It saves Alix from having to say it aloud: *Matteo is dead*.

Chiara kicks and thrashes. She swears and moans and, finally, she howls.

"I'll find out who's responsible," Alix vows, over and over, until she realizes that *she* is responsible.

She leaves the apartment then.

When she returns, Chiara is gone and Alix knows she will never see her again.

* * *

Alix packs her valise and catches a train to Suzanne Luling's apartment in liberated France. Suzanne is not connected to war in any way and those are the only kinds of people Alix can face.

Once her ship from Le Havre arrives in Manhattan, Alix telephones Lillie, who's also returned from Europe. She needs—she doesn't even know—absolution, a listening ear to pour her heart into. But Lillie is incoherent.

"Bobby's dead," she cries and Alix understands that Bobby was another of the men she'd sent to his death.

*No.* Not Bobby too. Golden-haired, sweet-as-apple-pie Bobby. The man who'd comforted her on prom night; the man she'd comforted the night he proposed.

"How can you bear it?" Lillie weeps.

"I can only bear it because I know I will never forgive myself." Alix's voice is hardened as if she has no emotions left when in fact she has too many. Some of them come out when she adds in a whisper, "So many dead."

"I don't care about that," Lillie wails. "I only care about Bobby."

*But I care about all of them.* Alix hangs up the telephone.

# PART SEVEN
## PARIS AND NEW YORK, 1947

*You have to put your heart and soul into it, as no doubt everybody does who wants to succeed.*

—Christian Dior

# THIRTY-THREE

"ood evening, Mademoiselle St. Pierre," La Voce—or Friedrich
G Weber—said to her when she entered room 207 at the Ritz.

*Your turn*, she told herself, trying to grapple with the physical
necessities of breathing and moving, trying to quash the memory of
everything he'd done to Matteo and Chiara.

And to Lillie.

The urge to be sick was overpowering. But she had only this one
chance and those nine dead men deserved for her to be the strongest
one in the room this time, rather than the vanquished.

"An eye for an eye and two people are blind," she said to him, each
word enunciated with lethal clarity. "Nine deaths for one and your
brother is still dead. You killed nine people to avenge your brother
when all you wanted was Matteo. The result is the two of us in a
room together. Vengeance doesn't change anything."

She saw his start of surprise. She had the advantage. He hadn't
known she'd discovered his reasons. But the advantage sat heavily
inside her. How was any of this a victory?

He recovered well, saying in equally measured tones, "You've discovered that Matteo killed my brother in cold blood, the way one
imagines a Nazi would kill. But I don't think you have all the details."

He paused and she knew that whatever he was about to say might
well vanquish her. She didn't want to listen. But this was the epilogue.
It would all soon be over.

"The night his sister was taken to Villa Triste," Weber continued, "Matteo and his partisans took five German officers hostage. They demanded we return five prisoners in exchange, including his sister. I never once considered acquiescing. After Matteo received my refusal, he chose one man, took out a knife and stabbed him without mercy. That man was my brother. No man is exempt from savagery during a war. No woman either, perhaps."

Matteo, with the luscious olive skin and a head-thrown-back kind of laugh.

Matteo, who'd wanted to sleep with her under the stars, her hair twined through his fingers.

Matteo, who was lost even before he was dead.

She moved to the phone. "I'm calling the authorities. There are people in America who'd like to bring you to trial." She understood now that yes, justice was that simple. There was no need to speak to him, just to lock him away.

He laughed. *He laughed.*

At the same moment, the door hidden in the paneling of the room opened and Anthony entered. She'd asked Frank to make sure La Voce was given a room with one of the hidden doors that she'd seen in Becky's room. After that experience, she'd spoken to Frank about them and he'd told her the hotel was full of secret passages that were used to hide people during the war.

Anthony looked like he wanted nothing more than to rush over to Alix and simultaneously throttle La Voce. He checked himself and did neither.

And Weber checked himself even more visibly than he'd done when she'd mentioned his brother.

He'd only expected her. Her fingers clasped around the power that had swung back to her.

La Voce stood up. He thought he could run away. But there was no running. Frank would have called the police. La Voce was going to jail at last.

But he said, "Monsieur March. Just in time. Please, have my seat."

"No," was Anthony's steel-voiced reply.

"Are you sure? You might wish you were sitting down when I tell you both that the Americans know exactly where I am. And they knew where I was after the war ended because I was working with them. They gave me my new identity. They even let me choose who I wanted to be. They won't arrest me."

*No.* Alix heard herself whisper the word into the shocked silence.

She *was* going to be sick. She crossed to the window, flinging two panes open but the air was hot and still and provided no relief at all. Anthony was by her side, probably giving too much away but she was glad of the hand he placed on her back.

*I was working with them.*

She'd heard of other Nazis who were granted leniency and employment with the Allies, Nazis who'd helped with postwar intelligence and mopping up the puddles of a slaughter they'd been responsible for, simply because they had valuable information about where those puddles were located and who had made them. But she'd never imagined a man like this would be gifted clemency in return for information, that nebulous thing that, for a few years in the early 1940s, was more valuable than gold.

La Voce went on, his tone smooth and untroubled—fearless, in fact. "Karl Wolff escaped jail by acting as a witness for the prosecution. I did a little of that too, but my main contribution was doing some work for your former boss, Monsieur Dulles."

*No.* Again, *no.* This was impossible. Dulles had employed a murderer. And Dulles could have told her months ago who and where La Voce was.

It was as if Weber could read her thoughts.

"He wouldn't have told you," he said faux-helpfully. "He knew you'd be upset."

There was a wildness inside her now that made her almost incapable of seeing the consequences if she were to hurl herself at him, to pound her hatred against his chest with her fists.

"Upset?" The word was a sob. "I'm not upset." *I'm about as wretched and ruined as anyone can be.* Tears ran over her cheeks, tears that showed Weber that he had won.

He had played her like a maestro.

Anthony was moving now, striding toward Weber. "You are—"

Alix stepped in front of him, cutting him off. If Anthony hit La Voce, she had no doubt La Voce would press charges and it would be Anthony locked up instead.

"Don't," she said, knowing that, once again, she was exposing herself to La Voce. The last time it had been over Matteo. This time it was over Anthony.

She was too exhausted, too empty, to make Anthony stop just by putting herself in the way so she used words instead. "If you hit him, I will too, and then I'll end up in jail. If you don't want that to happen, don't hit him."

She was glad to hear that she sounded adamant, unwavering; every other part of her was a faltering wreck.

Anthony shot her a furious look—but he stopped.

La Voce's smile was exultant. And Alix knew now that he'd never intended to do anything so kind as to kill her. He wanted her to live forever with the ferocious ache of her guilt. What he'd said meant she would never be able to look at the faces of the nine dead boys when they visited her every night in her dreams. She would never be able to say to them, *There will be justice.*

There would never be justice. Because La Voce had been allowed to go free.

"I've done what I came to do," Weber said crisply. "But while I'm

THE THREE LIVES OF ALIX ST. PIERRE 375

here, let's take things one step further. I don't think you should live in Paris anymore, Mademoiselle St. Pierre. I've made a life for myself, thanks to your American friends providing me with a new name, and I have no wish for that life to be disrupted by someone from my past spreading rumors about me. I know the information is classified and your hands are tied by the Espionage Act so there's not a lot you can do beyond the mildly irritating. Still, I'd rather you go, simply because I don't think you want to—unless of course you enjoy nocturnal visitors to your *pension* and footsteps following you on streets. I won't be so nice if I ever see you again. As for you, Monsieur March, you can't print my name in your newspaper either—you are as bound as she is."

*You goddamned coward*, she wanted to scream but what was the point? Whatever name he went by now, it would remain unsullied. Nobody would ever know he was once a Nazi called Friedrich Weber.

There weren't enough tears, even should she have saved a lifetime's worth, to cry at the knowledge. But there was pain, so much of it.

Then she heard someone speaking. Someone who knew all the things she wanted to say, the things that were being pressed down too deep inside her by the knowledge that the people she'd worked with and given her loyalty to in Switzerland had so brutally betrayed her.

"You are very lucky that Alix is here," Anthony was saying to La Voce. "She is the only reason I'm not throwing you out the window. But I will throw you out one day. Not bodily, but bit by bit and word by word. Because you're right—I can't write about you. But I can write generally about Nazis who've escaped justice. I can talk about the things you did. I can use sources who fall outside the Espionage Act to tell the world that there were deals made that would make even the hardest man weep. I will keep writing every damn day and I will win a goddamn Pulitzer for those words, and I will make everyone look just a little bit harder at what happened after the war. You've never been tried in a court but you can be. Your acts will follow you forever because you can't undo them. And from this moment, because of everything I write, you will be looking over your shoulder for justice to catch you—and it will."

Weber's smile had gone. Anthony had opened the tiny splinter Alix had been looking for since she'd sat in a confessional booth with La Voce and made the worst of all bargains with him.

"I'm not much bothered by threats about vague words that can never actually mention me, threats I know many important people in America will do their best to thwart." But La Voce's tone was less airy than before.

"I haven't finished," Anthony cut in. "You came here to destroy Alix. But you'll have to leave here knowing you will never do that. She's the strongest person in this room. She will survive all of this and even if she's not in Paris, you will watch her grow and become even more spectacular, and that will be your cross—that you could never ruin her."

But out came the wrecking ball.

"Let's see how strong she is when I remind her that she could have saved everyone. I had the wireless operator she'd embedded in our headquarters send a radio transmission to her soon before the mission to the Redoubt was to depart," Weber said coolly. "That transmission told her to abort the operation. It might have been enough time, just, to stop your men from going into the mountains. I wanted her to scramble, the way my brother was forced to. I wanted her to feel the same fear he would have felt. *She* ignored the message. So she is the guilty one."

Then he left before she could stop him, stepping past the wreckage of her soul.

*She could have saved everyone?* But she'd never seen Weber's message.

How had she missed it? How could she have been so busy thinking about what La Voce would do to her in his hotel room in Bern that she'd overlooked a warning and the result had been slaughter?

\* \* \*

Alix fled to the bathroom, where she was sick over and over. At last she sat on the tiles, head resting against the wall, fragments of words echoing: *Transmission. Enough time. She ignored the message.*

*Knock knock. Knock knock. Knock knock.* It took some time for her to understand that the knocking was real, that Anthony was saying her name. It took her even longer to reply because the words, *She ignored the message* kept repeating, but they were taking on a different meaning now.

Those words meant that Alix had betrayed someone too. Partly deliberately and partly out of ignorance.

Her omission had been necessary for self-preservation and she hadn't understood, until now, that there were far larger consequences. And the person she'd betrayed was standing on the other side of the bathroom door, having just defended her. He wouldn't defend her after she explained what must have happened, of that she was certain.

\* \* \*

She opened the door, saw Anthony stretch out a hand toward her then withdraw it, studying her face. "You need whiskey and a cigarette," was his diagnosis. "And I can hold you if you'll let me."

There was nothing she wanted more but she shook her head. "Just the whiskey, I think." In her voice she could hear the same shudder that spasmed inside her.

He passed her a glass, frowning. "Sit down," he said, making a move to crouch beside her but thinking the better of it when she wouldn't meet his eyes.

She sipped, then drank; coughed and finally winced.

"Here." Anthony held out a lit cigarette.

She shook her head. She should tell him now. Then it would be done.

But Anthony spoke first. "You never received that warning, did you?"

Alix shook her head again.

"Then it's over, Alix," he said emphatically and with a strange kind of wonder, as if even after everything he'd said to her about needing to believe it would end well, he still hadn't been able to entirely convince himself. "You can stop blaming yourself. You did everything you could have done. *We* did everything we could have done. Whoever didn't pass that message on is the one who can carry all the guilt. And I'm going to do my damnedest to find out who the hell it was."

She needed to interrupt. But how did you make yourself say something you knew would at least hurt and most likely devastate the person you wanted by your side when you faced the worst moment of your life—the person who made your bones melt?

He went on before she could interject, rubbing a quick hand over his jaw, pacing in front of the window, words a rush. "I know it sounds crazy—we just stood in a room with a man who is the worst kind of scum and I can see he's left you totally shell-shocked but, Alix, I meant every word I said to him. He didn't ruin you back in April 1945, and he can't ruin you now. You are so much stronger now than you were then, and you can't beat yourself up about a warning you never received. Leave him behind, and go and be spectacular. And you know what else?"

He shook his head and smiled wryly, as if he couldn't believe everything the showdown with La Voce had unleashed inside him. "While you were in the bathroom, all I could think was that I need to grow the hell up. I'm nearly thirty years old for God's sake and I have more privileges than most people and I'm whining about having to take over a newspaper business. If I'm in charge of the goddamn newspaper then I can do exactly what I told La Voce I'd do. During the war, I started out knowing categorically what was right and what was wrong but, by the end, even those supposedly on the side of good did more than a few dishonorable things. So I left Italy thinking if the world was so screwed up that virtue meant compromising yourself, then nothing was worth fighting for. But that makes me just as dishonorable as everyone else. If no one fights back, then we get the world we deserve. I want a better world than one where men like Weber get away with murder—and as the owner of a goddamn newspaper I can fight him, and everyone else like him, until they can no longer draw breath. If I want to write rather than worry about finances and advertisers then I'll just get someone in to do those things, probably more expertly than I would. I actually can have everything I damn well want—"

He stopped, exhaling sharply as if something had hit him and Alix tried to smile because she was happy for him. She *was*. He would write about the war criminals who still rubbed shoulders with Parisians when they should be repenting in jail. He would win a Pulitzer. *He* would be spectacular. And he would quickly forget what she was about to say because he had so many other diversions to occupy him.

"Everything I want except you," he said, looking at her with those satin-blue eyes as everything he felt unraveled from him and wound around her. And she wanted, for just a moment, to let it.

But...Instead it was time for her to unravel.

She set down her glass, stood and let her eyes meet his. "My friend Lillie," she said haltingly. "She...she died in May 1945."

Anthony frowned, struggling to veer off in the direction she'd taken the conversation.

Alix lit a cigarette, saw that her hands were shaking as she held the flame to the tip. Inhale smoke, breathe it out into the room, watch it cloud the space between her and Anthony. Speak.

"Lillie was OSS too. She worked..." Another long drag on the Gauloise. "She worked on the cable desk at AFHQ, first in Algiers and then Caserta."

"Lillie," he repeated. "As in the person in the photograph Bobby carried. I don't..." He shook his head, trying to make nonsense into sense.

Then he looked at her, very sharply. "Caserta. The cable desk?"

Alix nodded.

"You didn't have a wireless receiver in Bern," he said slowly. "And you're telling me this because..." He paused, then swore. "There was a girl on the cable desk at Caserta who was reprimanded twice for forgetting to pass messages on to us."

*Oh, Lillie, what did you do?* The question asked itself again but Alix was almost certain she knew the answer now.

She nodded again.

And now Anthony seemed to know the answer too. "You're bringing this up now because that girl at Caserta..." He paused as if he thought in not saying it, it wouldn't be true. "That girl was your friend Lillie. Jesus, Alix."

She almost nodded for the third time because, really, what further explanation was needed? Alix was a liar—that was the true and only explanation. She had deliberately not told him that Lillie worked on the cable desk but only because she couldn't bear to talk about Lillie. She hadn't concealed the information because she thought Lillie was connected to all of this in any way.

"I didn't know," she started to say, then stopped. "I mean I knew she'd forgotten to pass on messages to me before. Twice. But I didn't know there was another message she forgot..." And maybe it wasn't Lillie, she wanted to say. But all the evidence pointed straight at Lillie.

"She forgot?" Anthony said, a kind of appalled shock ringing in each word and tearing at her heart. "She forgot to pass on a message that would have saved the nine people I watched die right in front of me? Just like you forgot to mention that she worked for OSS and that she was dead?"

"She wouldn't have known what it meant..." That was the weakest excuse of all. Every message handled by OSS potentially had lives attached to it. She stabbed her cigarette into the ashtray.

When Anthony next spoke, his voice was very quiet. "I'm guessing the person Bobby spent an entire afternoon cabling the day of the mission was Lillie. Were they in love? Did you know that too?"

"No—"

He didn't wait for her to finish. "What a waste of goddamn time it was chasing that lead down. Your friend Lillie was sending love messages via cable to Bobby, and I'm hunting down sources wondering if Bobby was up to something sinister. What if you'd just written Lillie's name down on the lists in my suite and perhaps mentioned how goddamn careless she was? Maybe we would have followed up the wireless operator, tracked that message, and known weeks ago that she was to blame, not us. Not blaming myself meant everything to me—you knew that."

Anthony jabbed his fingers into his shoulder as if he was incensed with himself when she knew he was rightly outraged with her. She'd had at least a half hour in the bathroom by herself to process all of this whereas he was just coming to grips with it now.

"I remember standing in front of you in my suite and asking if you'd written down the names of everyone you'd worked with," he said, still in that same low and disbelieving voice. "You said yes. You lied to me. Trust was your scar but ... You *lied* to me," he repeated, the tiniest splinter in those last words.

*Do you trust me?* she'd asked him only a few hours ago.

*More than fucking anything. You know that,* he'd replied.

She'd broken her word—and now she'd broken herself.

"I might have started out as a liar," he said now, eyes drilling into her, "but from the moment you called me out on my duplicitous bullshit, I have not told a single lie. I have only told truths."

"But ..." she started to say.

He was forgetting Fortunée. Just as he hadn't been honest with

Alix about that, she hadn't been honest about Lillie. And for the same reasons. Shame. How could she tell him there was one more death she thought she was answerable for? That Lillie's death was the thing that had made her hate herself most of all. Lillie had died because Alix had not been there for her, and that was the truth she could not bring herself to say.

If only she could stay focused on logic, on her rebuttal. But what she felt for Anthony had never been logical. She'd once told Anthony that Bobby was all the in-between spaces and none of the wild and heady extremes. Anthony was the wildest and headiest of those extremes. He would never take the news that she'd lied to him with a shrug and a subdued, *Oh well, that's a shame*. He was furious because he cared.

And right now, he was waiting for her to speak. When it became clear that she couldn't or wouldn't finish her sentence, he shifted, as if he didn't know whether to pace or shout or turn his back on her. Instead a furious rush of words broke from him.

"Alix, I have given you more than—" He cut himself off, and then he did turn away, standing with both arms braced against the table.

*More than any other woman*. She knew that was what he'd stopped himself from saying.

She heard someone sob and realized it was her. She pressed her knuckles to her mouth, could see that Anthony's jaw was working hard to keep something in check too. "I'm sorry, Anthony," she said bleakly. "I'm so very sorry."

He looked back over his shoulder at her, swore again, took a handkerchief out of his pocket and laid it on the table. "Here," he said, voice gruff. "I know you never have one when you need it."

Then he rubbed a hand over his jaw and pushed himself away from the table. "We're both exhausted. We shouldn't do this now. Let's . . . I don't know. Let's talk tomorrow." He crossed over to the door.

But once there, he shoved a hand into his hair, let his eyes meet hers and said in stunned kind of disbelief, "I loved you, Alix."

This was the moment where she could make everything right. If she just fell to her knees and asked him to forgive her and told him again how sorry she was, then he probably *would* forgive her. And then what? Nothing.

They'd be back to where they were before—not being honest. Because he had never told her he loved her until now.

So the words that came out of her stubborn goddamn mouth, trembling more than a little, were, "Which makes you a liar too."

His head jerked back. "What the hell, Alix? I just told you I *loved* you."

It was so easy for Anthony to say that now, when they were just about over. If he'd told her he loved her when she was pouring out her heart to him in their bed, then he would have had to do something about it—would have had to acknowledge that simply saying he loved her didn't change anything. Loving your mistress didn't alter the fact that she was a mistress.

"You want a medal for that?" she asked, voice still wobbling more than she wanted it too. "When did you decide that you loved me, Anthony? Just now? Yesterday? This morning?"

"It's not like you just decide to love someone and make a note of the time, Alix," he shot back.

"You think I don't know that?" She felt herself advancing toward the door, driven by the need to make him understand that telling her now that he loved her meant he'd omitted some pretty important things too. "I've been in love before, remember? I know what love is like. But I want to know why you couldn't tell me you loved me the last time we were in a bed together."

"Because the last time we were in a bed together, you told me you didn't want to see me anymore."

"I told you I didn't want to be your mistress. That's a different thing."

"No. You told me that being by yourself was what you wanted.

That marriage was a locked door you didn't want to be given a key to. That you didn't even think you wanted kids, for Christ's sake. That you didn't want my life and didn't want to share yours." He was shouting now, just like she was. "But that's not what this is about. We were talking about your friend Lillie, not us."

"This isn't about Lillie, not anymore. This is about truth and lying. We've both done the latter."

"But you—"

"What? I lied worse than you? Is that what you were about to say?"

She was standing right in front of him now, could feel the fury blazing from both of them and knew suddenly that this was always how it was going to end. When two people came together in the kind of tempest that made even the air around them blaze, then the grand finale could only be everything—which he had never offered her—or nothing.

"You think not telling me you loved me was a minor thing? Love is such an inconsequential emotion that it's not worth mentioning?" She gave one mirthless, incredulous laugh. "And you think you gave me more than you've given any other woman? I think you're confusing having given me more with having given me enough. You gave me only what every other man I've ever had sex with has given me. If that's more than you've ever given anyone, then I feel sorry for all the other women."

She'd gone too far. Anthony's face was very still, muscles hard with anger. And that made all of her indignation fall suddenly away, and she heard herself say in a desolate voice, "I want to be the length and breadth of someone's life, Anthony. I want to be the person with whom you travel to all the wildest and headiest of extremes, not the one you sit comfortably in the middle with. I want to be the scope you can't even imagine. Not just an afterthought appended to an already wretched conversation. And you know what else," she went on, hearing the ache of two years of keeping it inside fracture every word, "Lillie was like my sister. And you haven't bothered to ask me how losing her..." God, how was it possible to cry more than she was crying right now?

She swiped both hands over her cheeks and said the very last thing she was going to say to him. "You haven't bothered to ask how losing her made me feel. She was the only family I had left, Anthony."

And that was the cold, wretched core of her grief. To have no family at all was an irreparable tear right through the center of an already broken heart.

Silence. Anthony stared up at the ceiling, Alix down at the floor.

She didn't know how much time passed before he spoke.

"I'm sorry about Lillie. I really am." His voice was wrung out too. "But I guess, like you said, this isn't about her. It's about a whole lot of other stuff. And what it comes down to is we're two people who've been spun into different orbits." His hand closed around the doorknob.

Her eyes flickered upward and she saw that his were damp now too.

And he didn't leave, not yet. He said one more thing, words slow and quiet and sad.

"I gave you my trust, Alix. Not straight away. But from the night of the ball, I did. I gave it to you because it was the one thing you wanted above all else. I've never given that to anyone before. So yes, I did give you more."

He exhaled sharply. "I'm sorry if it wasn't enough."

And then he was gone, and all she knew was that they were both right and they were both wrong. And also that they wouldn't be talking tomorrow. Or the next day. Or ever again.

# THIRTY-FOUR

At dawn on the fifth day after leaving Cherbourg on the *Queen Elizabeth*, Alix, Monsieur Dior, and a thousand suitcases greeted the city bursting out of the water, the lower stories of Manhattan's skyscrapers still shadowed by the last remnants of night, the peaks crowned with gold from the early rays of sun. *Le patron* smiled and indulged his Norman temperament by effusing about how he would love to conquer the city. Alix stared at bad memories in the guise of office buildings where she'd once worked and tried desperately not to think about Anthony.

She'd spent most of the voyage in her room, telling Dior she suffered from terrible seasickness, which was true, in a way. Her entire world, her entire notion of herself, had lurched nauseatingly back and forth in front of her as she lay in her bed in her cabin, seeing Alix in the white dress awaiting one fate when another worse fate was awaiting her, hearing Alix telling Chiara that Matteo was dead, remembering Alix and Anthony hurting one another, and themselves too.

And most especially, recalling the glimmer of tears in his eyes as he'd said, *I gave you my trust. I'm sorry if it wasn't enough.*

*It was*, she wanted to explain. It was more than she'd ever had, that trust, and she hadn't known what to do with it. Just as he hadn't known how to cast off almost thirty years of understanding how the world worked so he could take in the scope of her. So they'd blown it up, like everything else.

There was only one possible thing she could do now to save herself.

Hours before they drew into New York, Alix forced her mind to focus on that—the transmission La Voce told her he'd sent. Shifting the blame onto Lillie, as Anthony had done, didn't make Alix feel any better. She needed to see all the transmissions that had happened around April 10, needed to understand how Lillie could have been so careless.

If Alix was ever to truly reclaim her life, then she needed to somehow let go of the other suffocating guilt she'd carried with her since 1945 and was carrying still—the guilt over Lillie's death. That had driven her as much as anything to search for solace in all the wrong things: French 75s; occasional rushed sex; telling lies to protect her hurts; not trusting because she didn't trust herself.

As soon as her official business with Dior was done, she would go to see Colonel Dearborn and ask him if she could see the wireless transmission and cable records. Maybe there was something in there that would help her unloose the blame from herself and from Lillie too. Or perhaps it was just another thread of hope waiting to wind itself around her neck.

\* \* \*

Alix and Dior left Manhattan immediately for Dallas where the fashion Oscar presentation was to be held at Neiman Marcus. The following morning, she disguised her red eyes with mascara, her sadness with red lipstick, and her shattered heart with a Dior gown. She was there to do a job, and she would put everything else aside and do that job brilliantly, for Dior. It was the last job she would ever do for him given La Voce's ultimatum. When *le patron* returned to Paris, Alix would not go with him. But she would wait until the end of the tour to tell him that. And she would let everything else wait until she was back in New York too.

The ceremony began with a parade of American mannequins in Dior gowns who strode through the central hall of the store. Gold lamé had been strung in eye-blinding brilliance from every available surface, as if this were elegant. Alix mimed putting on sunglasses in an attempt to make *le patron* stop frowning and to make herself feel a little lighter. It almost worked but, after an hour, an interval was announced.

"Can no one sit still for two hours?" Dior complained, not brightening at all when told it was time for questions from the press.

"Monsieur," asked one interrogator, "there is certain amount of flesh exposed, isn't there?"

"There is," Monsieur agreed placidly.

Alix moved in to save him, knowing he didn't have any idea about the puritanical bent of some of her countrymen. "The line depends on two things—superb craftsmanship, and the shape of a woman," she said. "The dresses simply follow the natural contours of a woman's body."

She gestured to the line of mannequins, one wearing—fortuitously or unfortuitously, depending on one's own preference for natural contours—the Maxim's dinner dress with its generous serving of cleavage. Alix swallowed the first laugh she'd felt press into her throat since she'd left Paris and Dior's mouth twitched.

"But the protesters," the questioner spluttered, for there had been a delegation from the Just Below the Knee Club at the dock to greet them in New York. "They want a return to shorter skirts and a less... liberated bosom."

Alix did not dare look at Monsieur Dior. "Then I think they will enjoy the next part of the show."

Along the catwalk strode a mannequin in the signature long Dior skirt. Behind her, a mannequin raised a placard, protesting the shocking length, the covered calves. The first mannequin tugged on a pulley Alix had had added to the dress, and the skirt raised itself to the

supposedly more acceptable just-below-the-knee length. The protester
smiled as if satisfied and left the stage, at which point the first mannequin released the pulley and down dropped the skirt.

The audience roared with laughter and Alix knew that was the
shot that would run in the papers the next day. And she thought that
maybe it would all be okay. She would stay in Manhattan and find
another job that she loved, a job where her boss made her proud of
herself and never appeared in her office at midnight with a bottle of
brandy. And she would find something in those cable transmissions
that helped her to trust herself again.

But out of the corner of her eye, she saw an advertising billboard on
the street outside proclaiming: *Cigarettes are like women. The best ones
are thin and rich.*

And she remembered saying to Anthony, *What will be in twenty
years time is already decided because the men of today, who make the
decisions, have grown up in this world. They'll want to preserve it, no
matter what.*

Perhaps she was wrong. She should have said, *What will be in
fifty years time is already decided.* Change was as fanciful a thing as
her hopes.

* * *

From there they went to Los Angeles, Chicago…City after city
until at last they arrived back in New York and it was time to visit
Dearborn—and also to tell *le patron* about her resignation from the
House of Christian Dior. She decided to tackle Dearborn first and
was sitting down to breakfast at the hotel on the day she was to meet
him, flicking through newspapers, when a picture made her stop.

It was Alix wearing Diablesse on the staircase at the *maison*, an
intimate smile playing over her lips, eyes sparkling at a man beyond
the frame, everything about her so utterly alive in a way she'd never

thought she'd be again after she left Switzerland. In the photograph, she was so obviously a woman living, rather than a woman surviving. It was a version of Alix she wasn't accustomed to. One she wanted to grasp with both hands and never let go of, no matter what happened.

*Would Mary see the picture?* she wondered. And if she did, would she believe in it?

The answer was too sad to contemplate.

She turned her attention to the words Anthony had written.

*With a name like Alix St. Pierre, she's destined to rule the world. And rule she will. She begins her conquests by disarming her subjects with her outrageous one-liners. While they're laughing helplessly, she moves in for the kill with a spool of brilliant ideas that knock out all the competition. Lastly, from atop her throne of silk, she'll smile. And the whole world will be silenced—and then fall in love with her.*

Alix's coffee cup made its unsteady way onto the table. She reread the opening paragraph but she'd made no mistake about the words.

"We seem to have conquered the press," Monsieur Dior said as he sat down beside her. "You and I both. Between us, there's hardly a square inch of column space that doesn't mention Dior. I owe you a pay rise."

She looked up at him blankly.

Dior smiled. "*Merci* is the word you require."

"Yes," she said, attempting to focus. "Thank you. Thank you," she repeated.

"You are as disarmed by Monsieur March's article as he is disarmed by you."

Alix shook her head. "He's not... Anthony is not disarmed by me. Not anymore."

"Ah," Monsieur Dior said.

He hadn't said a word about her red eyes, her unusually sober and silent demeanor, or the fact that she rarely smiled anymore. He'd just watched her silently and seriously and allowed her to hold on to her grief—until now. He pulled a small box from his pocket and passed it to her.

She opened it wordlessly. Nestled inside was a little gold star on a chain. She looked up at Dior. "It's beautiful. But..."

"I cannot wear it," he said. "So you can't return it to me. Besides, you won't have it for long, is my hope. You have always set your sights at the stars for me. I want you to do the same for yourself. So, this is a star I want you to put it back in the sky whenever you have reached up and touched the constellations for yourself."

Of course she was weeping. How could she not? "Thank you," she sobbed as he held her in his arms.

"It is also a good luck charm, *ma chérie*," he whispered in her ear. "I feel you need a little luck right now."

"You really..." She swiped at her eyes and gratefully accepted the handkerchief Dior was holding out for her. She touched a finger to the star. "You really believe in what Madame Delahaye says, don't you?" she asked, referring to Dior's fortune-teller. "And in the power of a token to... what? Change the future? But if you can change the future, then why ask a fortune-teller to prophesy it?" She frowned, not even sure what she was asking, the image of Friedrich Weber's mocking smile in her thoughts.

"Perhaps it reassures me to know there is a future. If there was only the past and the present, then..." He withdrew a little so she could see his face as he spoke. "Then we would be very different people. I think it's Ophelia who says, 'We know what we are, but know not what we may be.' A fortune-teller can perhaps foresee the events that might happen to me but not what kind of man I'll be when they happen. I try to be the right man for those events, I suppose."

Confronted with the tears shining in her eyes, another person might say in a chin-up, cheer-up kind of way, *And you'll be the right woman for the events in your life too.* But Dior didn't and she loved him all the more for that. She loved him for saying he *tried* to be the right man. Because she supposed that was all there was in the end. The effort you made to let events shape you and coerce you down a path, or the effort you made to shape yourself and steer yourself in spite of what happened.

For a brief moment in Paris, she had started to believe there was still good inside her. She had begun to plan for a future. Then she had let Weber persuade her otherwise. Which meant she had a lot to think about.

"You're a very wise man," she said to Dior.

"I'm just happy I was the right man for this moment."

* * *

"You want to look at Top Secret records," Dearborn said to her after he'd performed his usual cigar-lighting ceremony in the comfort of his leather chair behind his antique desk in a lawyer's office with all the usual adornments: framed certificates from Yale, a whiskey decanter, a photograph of a wife and four children.

"Yes," Alix replied.

"You know I can't let you."

"You can if you want to. Or if I'm persuasive enough."

"Don't," he said sharply. "Don't imagine I'm someone who can be persuaded by any of the usual means."

She laughed. "Believe me, I have no money to offer you and I'm planning for both of us to stay fully clothed."

It was his turn to laugh. "Of course. Alix St. Pierre is not one to bargain for what she wants; she's one to bludgeon for it instead."

That laugh made her voice became very, very hard. "Then let the bludgeoning begin. You owe me. You owe me for letting Weber work with OSS after the war. For not punishing him for everything he presided over. For pretending to yourselves that what he did in bringing

Operation Sunrise and the Italian surrender to the table could atone for the deaths of men and women who should be alive now, enjoying the freedom they fought for."

She thought of Matteo, who ought to be helping a patient at a hospital. She thought of Chiara, who ought to sleep peacefully without nightmares of torture.

"You owe so many people so much," she finished more quietly.

"And you think your crusade will settle the ledger?" he asked, resting his cigar in the ashtray and studying her, looking for the right answer to his question.

There was only one possible answer. Her conversation with Dior, even her conversation with Anthony, had made her understand it all at last.

"The ledger will never be settled," she said. "But I need to finish this, for me. So that the ledger is something I can endure instead of something that defines me. *We know what we are, but know not what we may be.*'" She quoted Dior, and Shakespeare, to Dearborn. "I want to be the best possible person I can be, rather than the worst."

A contemplative silence. Dearborn picked up his cigar. "You did a great many good things, Alix. One disaster should not define you."

"Maybe it shouldn't. But right now, despite all my attempts to believe otherwise, it does."

He smiled at her before blowing out a puff of smoke, hazing the air between them. "You turned out to be more than I could have imagined. And you coming here is proof of that. Few people pay the debts that only their souls demand."

He stood up. "The files are stored off-site. It will take several days to get them here. Come back next Monday. If you return about seven in the evening, I'll see that you're let in. You'll need to be gone by morning, with everything put away. And you know that, no matter what you find…" He paused.

Alix fixed her eyes on him, very serious now, not expecting it would change anything but needing to say it aloud for Matteo and for Bobby. "No matter what I find, Weber will still dine at Brasserie Lipp for the rest of his life?"

"Something like that."

"Precisely like that, and you know it."

She walked toward the door, knowing that she could at least keep her head high, having not let Dearborn get away with any obfuscations.

He turned his back and began to tidy the already tidy shelf of photographs. Before she reached the door, he said very quietly, "Perhaps I can find a way to have the authorities in Paris revoke Weber's passport and make sure he returns to Germany. And perhaps I can turn a blinder eye than I ought to toward any articles Anthony March publishes—so long as he doesn't directly contravene the Act. It might mean that a stink starts to follow Weber around. If Weber's not in Paris, you can return there knowing he's lost Brasserie Lipp at least, and that he might be looking over his shoulder, waiting for his past to snare him—which I hope it will, one day."

Alix nodded. "I think that would be a good start."

\* \* \*

Five days later—box after box, page after page of cable traffic and reports she'd written about V2 rockets and strange camps being built in Auschwitz and the number and size of the partisan brigades in the Italian mountains.

By three in the morning her eyes slipped over the words, one message blurring into another and she couldn't be sure she was reading any of them properly. She'd made her way through almost everything when she came upon a series of odd messages sent over weeks stretching from 1944 and into 1945 from the Swiss desk of AFHQ in Caserta where Lillie was, to OSS Brindisi where Bobby was.

I FOUND YOU.

I MISS YOU.

WE NEED TO TELL ALIX.

I KNOW.

SINCE I WAS TEN YEARS OLD.

ME TOO.

LOVE.

SO MUCH.

AFTER THE WAR?

YES.

Then another series of messages transmitted on the morning of April 10 between the same two people.

I'M LEADING LYCAON. LEAVING FOR RENDEZVOUS POINT IN TEN MINUTES. STILL HOPING TO FIND MAN WHO KNOWS ALIX. HAVE NOTE FOR HIM TO GIVE HER. NEED TO EXPLAIN ALL OF THIS. CAN'T KEEP IT FROM HER ANYMORE.

YOU'LL MAKE A SUCCESS OF IT. ALIX WILL UNDERSTAND. SHE'S THE BEST OF US.

SHE IS.

GOOD LUCK.

I WISH YOU'D BE THERE WHEN I GET BACK.

WOULD YOU KISS ME?

WILL YOU MARRY ME?

YES.

Filed between WILL YOU MARRY ME? and YES was the record of a radio transmission sent to the cable desk where Lillie had been working. It had been transmitted via the wireless operator Alix had embedded into Karl Wolff's headquarters. The transmission was marked *Urgent* and directed the receiver to forward it immediately to Bern.

MESSAGE FROM PAROISSE FRANCAISE CONTACT, it read. ANULLARE. Cancel.

Alix closed her eyes.

There might have been enough time to change the future. Except the transmission was stamped only as *Received* by Caserta and not as *Forwarded*.

Alix took the transmission over to the fireplace and set a match to it. She didn't stay to watch it burn.

\* \* \*

Alix caught the subway up to the 157th Street Station, exited, and walked across to Riverside Drive. In the distance, the George Washington Bridge curved over the river, crossing from one realm to the next. Just as Lillie had done.

The sadness started as soon as Alix drew within sight of the gates—that this was how it had ended, in a lonely place with green grass and blue sky for company on a good day, the spatter of mud and rain on a bad. She found the grave and touched her hand to the tombstone, eyes reading the words: *Lillie Marie van der Meer. Born July 18, 1919. Died May 10, 1945.*

Twenty-six years of life. That was all Lillie had had.

Alix dropped onto the grass and placed a bouquet of May lilies on the tomb. Then she leaned against a tree and closed her eyes. Her last conversation with Lillie appeared behind her lids, like a movie in full color, volume too high.

On May 10, 1945, she'd telephoned Lillie, who'd wept, *Bobby's dead. How can you bear it?*

And Alix had replied, *I can only bear it because I know I will never forgive myself. You wouldn't be able to forgive yourself either if you were the one responsible.*

Lillie had cried anew.

What Alix knew now was that Lillie hadn't been weeping over Bobby her friend, but over Bobby her lover, the boy her mother hadn't wanted her to marry because he wasn't rich enough. And she'd also been weeping because she'd been flirting with Bobby via cable, one of those intense and all-consuming conversations lovers have. He'd asked her to marry him and Lillie had said yes, the word she'd perhaps wanted to say to him for so long.

In the midst of her joy, Lillie had received a radio transmission she was supposed to pass on to Alix, a message from La Voce calling off the mission. But Lillie had been distracted, careless, ignorant certainly of what the message meant and she'd not understood until afterward that by failing to pass on that message, nine men had died, including the one she loved.

Alix had blamed herself for those deaths for more than two years. But there was nothing Alix could have done to stop them.

It was time to truly let that guilt go, as well as her guilt over Lillie's death, a pain she'd almost let drag her all the way to the bottom. Because she knew now, truly knew, that Lillie's death hadn't been her fault either.

Lillie had been distraught on their telephone call in May. And rather than sympathize, Alix had spoken in a pitiless voice about responsibility and forgiveness—words directed at herself, not at Lillie. Lillie had called Alix back later and Alix had ignored the ringing telephone because she'd been almost insensible with whiskey. And so that night, unable to sleep, those words she'd said unknowingly to her friend—*You wouldn't be able to forgive yourself either if you were the one responsible*—had landed in the most hidden and wretched part of Lillie's heart. Lillie had helped herself to her mother's vial of sleeping tablets. She'd swallowed one or two, Mrs. van der Meer had told Alix. But after Mrs. van der Meer herself was asleep, Lillie had returned for the bottle. She'd taken some more. And some more. Until she'd finally taken too many and she lay now, asleep forever.

Since then, Alix had believed that if she'd answered the second phone call from Lillie, then Lillie would have had someone to talk to and she would have been able to sleep without pills. But nothing would have helped Lillie sleep—because Lillie had known she was responsible for Bobby's death. She could not forgive herself.

And after the night of May 10, she no longer had to.

Alix's quest had uncovered only carelessness. A young woman and a young man so caught up in their love that one had forgotten to pass on a message and the result had been slaughter. A result no one could possibly have foreseen, but a result nonetheless.

She also understood now that Bobby had been looking for Matteo so he could tell Alix she was free. But Alix and Matteo had been as ill-fated as Lillie and Bobby.

She bent over now and placed both hands on the grave.

"To Lillie," she said with a half smile, half sob. "From Manhattan." She drew in a long breath. "I love you. I hope you and Bobby are together somewhere. I wish you could have been together here on earth. I wish for so many things to have been different. But all I can do is live a better life, one I might not otherwise have lived had it not been for all the terrible things that happened. I will, I promise. All my love and *bisous*, Alix."

# THIRTY-FIVE

The following month, Alix returned with Dior to Paris, to the little office she shared with Suzanne and her job as Directrice de la Service de la Presse. Over the next two months she wore her star around her neck as she whipped up a frenzy of anticipation more fervent than that in February for *le patron*'s second collection.

She met with editors in her office and never at the Ritz. If she went out in the evenings it was to Café de la Paix or Sheherazade, which was loud and large and opposite in every way to Tabou. She had dinner at Suzanne's at least once a week—Suzanne's dinner parties were legendary. After Suzanne had responded to one guest's snide comment about Alix having to find herself another fancy man now that Monsieur March had tired of her by saying, "Mademoiselle St. Pierre is the last person I will ever throw out of my house. But you, madame, may well be the first," few people made snide comments about Alix and Anthony's brief liaison. Still, Alix knew the best thing to do was to live a monkish existence for a time, which suited her fine as she had no interest in affairs of any kind.

Her social circles were diametrically opposed to Anthony's so she never saw him. She had her assistant communicate with Fortunée, who Anthony had employed as the fashion editor of his newspaper. That was the one thing that actually made Alix laugh out loud, with both bemusement and recognition that it was a very shrewd move. Fortunée would no doubt be excellent in the role.

Some evenings, she simply returned to the new and tiny room she'd rented at a different *pension*, and she painstakingly and page by page started to make a dummy of a magazine that wouldn't be a *Harper's Bazaar* or a *Vogue* but something more sincere. She wrote the word *Elan* on the front cover because it would be for women who were smart and spirited and, yes—more than a little obdurate. She didn't know where she'd get the money to do such a thing or if there really were only about three other women in the world as obdurate as she was but she would keep imagining she could do it—would keep turning her face up toward the constellations.

Perhaps Dearborn had told Becky's godfather—and perhaps Becky too—to sheathe their claws. Becky was still at *The Times* and she occasionally made comments about the redheaded coquette who was still trying to take a too-big leap out of the wrong side of town, and Alix still heard the rustles of whispers in the fitting rooms when she walked past, but she knew she would hear rustles and would encounter Beckys all her life given the path she'd chosen. It was best to do so while wearing a Dior leopard-print blouse and without apology.

Dearborn had cabled Alix to tell her that La Voce had been sent back to Germany. And he'd made sure rumors about his past had been scattered like bullets through his chosen town of residence— some sort of justice would be coming for him soon enough.

So Alix was happy, not in a wild and heady way, but in a contented way. There was a lot to be said for simple contentment, she thought to herself as she made up the cards for the press at Dior's second show, imagining the gasps when Diorama in black wool, with its extravaganza of a skirt that had a forty-meter circumference, twirled through the room. The only time her contentment frayed was when she wrote Fortunée's name down on the card for the *New York Journal*, not Anthony's.

He would be gone from Paris soon, back to New York, and she would never see him again.

After that, she left work, hurried back to her *pension* and changed into her Chérie dress. It was Esmée's birthday and she was holding a ball—a ball Anthony would not attend, Esmée had sworn. Alix had no dress that was appropriate as she'd sold the heavenly Compiègne to pay everyone at the Ritz for spying for her. Still, Chérie was a beautiful dress, one of the most beautiful she'd ever owned, so she would make it be fine enough.

She walked to Esmée's despite the chill and was ushered inside by the maid. She saw Esmée immediately, wearing Dior too, and wearing it better than any mannequin. Esmée was smiling at the man beside her in a way that said she was utterly bored so Alix hurried over to rescue her.

She arranged her face in an expression of horror, tapped Esmée on the shoulder and exclaimed, "*Mon Dieu!* A toad just hopped into my skirt, I swear it did. But there is so much silk I cannot find it!"

And Esmée, about to pop like a champagne cork with mirth, said to the man at her side, "A true emergency. I must assist my friend," and the two of them scurried away, collapsing into laughter on the other side of the door. Until Esmée said, "You don't really have a toad in there, do you?" which only made Alix laugh all the more.

"Come with me," Esmée said, leading Alix up the stairs to her bedroom. "I have something for you."

"But it's your birthday, not mine," she protested.

Esmée smiled and ushered her into an entire room of dresses. There, shining like a constellation, was Compiègne.

"How...?" Alix spluttered.

"Anthony told me you were selling it. The girl who purchased it from you was one of my maids. I have a tradition of giving people presents on my birthday, so it's yours. It doesn't fit me anyway. You're shorter than I am. And if you say no, I will send a plague of toads to your rotten *pension*."

Nobody argued with Esmée. And Alix didn't want to. "Can I put it on?" she asked.

"You'd better," Esmée said.

Esmée helped her to do up the fastenings and spun her around to the mirror where Alix saw a woman similar to the one in the picture that had accompanied Anthony's interview. But this Alix had a penumbra of sadness that sat between her heart and happiness. She turned away from her reflection and touched a hand to the *velours au sabre*, remembering how she'd once thought she'd found the shadow Anthony concealed, his tenderness hidden like the roses in her dress until the outer surface was slowly cut away with touch and laughter and trust.

She blinked.

Then she looked back over her shoulder at the Alix St. Pierre who'd emerged from motherlessness and war and Dior—and love.

"Will you work for me?" she said suddenly to Esmée. "On the magazine I'm conjuring up, the magazine that has no money and probably no readers but a hell of a lot of ambition?"

Esmée laughed. "Only if you promise never to mention the word *toad* to me again. And I have money, remember? When you're ready to do this, I'll make you a loan—I know you won't accept a gift. And I'll be your Paris correspondent." She lifted her head up and flourished her hand. "Esmée Archambault, Paris correspondent. Yes," she said. "That's a dress I want to slip into, much more so than Esmée Archambault, bored socialite."

Alix slung an arm around her friend's shoulders. "You know it might take me the rest of my life to pay you back?"

"Then you'd better make sure you have a long life, Alix St. Pierre," Esmée said. "We'll poach Fortunée from Anthony. She'll be bored there once he goes back to Manhattan anyway."

Alix laughed. "I don't know whether that's a brilliant idea or a terrible idea."

"My ideas are always brilliant," Esmée said airily. "And I have another idea that is nothing short of genius."

Alix raised an eyebrow and grinned. "This I have to hear."

"You should talk to Anthony."

Alix took three steps backward. "That is as far from genius as concrete underwear."

Esmée laughed. "Well, that would certainly keep us in our place, wouldn't it? Let me show you something."

She disappeared into her bedroom and came back with a newspaper, which she presented to Alix. It was open to an article with Anthony March's byline and it told the story of the women in Italy who'd worked as *staffette*, keeping the partisans alive for four long years. One *staffetta* he'd interviewed was Chiara Romano, who said, "There was someone in Switzerland who helped keep us alive too. You can never be one hundred percent successful at that in wartime, but she did everything she could, and a hell of a lot more than most."

"And this," Esmée said, as if determined to make sure that Alix ruined her dress with weeping.

It was a note, written in Italian.

*Bella, come to Italy for a holiday. I'm a poor medical student but we'll still have fun. Ti amo, Chiara.*

Alix looked up wordlessly.

"Anthony asked me to give it to you," was all Esmée said. "And now that you're weeping and vulnerable, I'm going to move in for the kill. You did something and Anthony was hurt by it, that much I've gleaned. But did Anthony ever propose a way to overcome all the many obstacles someone living your life faces? Of course he didn't. It was easy for him to leave and so much harder for him to stay. Easy for him to blame you for doing something that he chose to believe was unforgivable, harder for him to forgive."

Alix felt herself spill into a chair. "I don't think—"

"I haven't finished," Queen Esmée said as imperiously as she'd been as a seventeen-year-old schoolgirl. "One of you needs to be brave enough to give your love"—she waved her hands, dismissing Alix's protests—"one more try. A proper try, a genuine effort of the soul. Make it the most spectacular try you can think of. Because if it succeeds, it will be more than worth it."

Alix squeezed her eyes shut. What would it be like to lie beside Anthony every night, telling him about her day—her troubles, her victories, her laughs, and her losses? What would it be like to hear the same from him each evening? *Bliss.*

"I already gave it a try and it turned out spectacularly badly," she said flatly.

Esmée shook her head adamantly. "No, you and Anthony were angry. That's not the same as trying. And I'm saying this to you rather than him because you're the bravest person I know. And if he's too damn stubborn to listen to you and it doesn't succeed, then come straight back here and cry out every tear you have left and then we'll get Dior to make you a gown from your sadness and we'll burn it in the fire. Also," she said, more gently now, "if it doesn't succeed, he was never worthy of you."

Alix pushed herself out of the chair, her dress swirling around her as wildly and extravagantly and tempestuously as her history with Anthony. She reached out a hand to touch it, remembering Anthony leaning down to whisper in her ear, his breath warm against her skin, *I can't compliment you on how you look because there isn't a word I can think of that would suffice.*

And Anthony saying, *I loved you.*

And Esmée saying, *It was easy for him to leave.*

Her head snapped up. Esmée clapped her hands together and grinned.

She *would* give it a spectacular try. In bed at the Ritz, Alix had poured out every conceivable difficulty about her way of life to Anthony. He had listened to her. But that was all. Certainly, she had done the wrong thing in lying to him. But hadn't he too done the wrong thing in not letting her know that she *could* love him—that with him, it would be different?

Perhaps it wouldn't be different. Perhaps he couldn't imagine a life where he didn't sign off on bank accounts and dole out money and come home to a woman who'd arranged that evening's dinner party for him. Perhaps when he said he could cry at what the future would do to her, he meant he could cry because he knew he couldn't be a part of the future she wanted.

If that was the case, she would not let Esmée and Dior make a gown from her sadness. She would have them make it from her courage instead, and she would take that gown with her into the future— a future she would make for herself. A future she would treasure, regardless of what happened now with Anthony.

# THIRTY-SIX

Alix marched in her beautiful blue gown to the Ritz. She didn't bother to ask where Monsieur March was. He would be in the bar, of that she was certain.

She swept through Temptation Walk to the Little Bar. He was sitting by one of the windows, legs stretched out, one hand in his pocket, the other preoccupied with a cigarette, an almost empty glass on the table before him, two women at the next table batting their lashes in his direction.

She stalked over, saying, just as she'd done the first time they'd met, "Alix St. Pierre. Can I get you a drink?"

Anthony's head spun around. He squashed his cigarette in the ashtray and said very wryly, "Alix St. Pierre. You sound like you should *be* a drink."

She almost smiled at all the memories his words stirred.

Instead she gathered up her skirts and sat in the chair opposite, thinking only now that she should have come up with a strategy rather than rushed impulsively in. But love had no strategies, just risk and illogic, euphoria and grief. It was never a certainty which way the dice would fall. She would throw everything into the air, spectacularly well or spectacularly badly, come what may.

"Except I'm not anything quite so simple," she began haltingly. "I'm the woman who loves you..."

His eyes flickered over to hers, then darted away.

"I'm the woman who loves you," she repeated. "But I'm also the woman who wants to work long hours, the woman who would often not be home in time for dinner, let alone in time to organize a dinner party for you. A woman who would be utterly unlike any other partner of any other man you know and who would not accept that, in a year's time, you would get yourself a mistress and dole out jewelry to me to cover your guilt. A woman who never wants to be less than the man she's with. That doesn't mean I want to be by myself and never share my life with anyone. It means I want to know if I can shift a couple of stars off course so my future is something I never really thought possible—a glorious span of time where I can marry someone and keep my independence *and* my career."

She drew in a breath and tried to slow down so he could understand what she was saying rather than frown at her as if none of it made sense.

"I wasn't fair to you," she said more quietly, "but you weren't fair to me either. You walked away without ever letting me know that you were *possible*. And I still don't know if I should regret you because I still don't know if you were ever a chance—or if you were just a dream meant only for nights swathed in sheets . . . a dream that wouldn't have survived a single day."

She picked up his glass and swallowed the last mouthful.

Anthony stared at her for a long, long time. She tried her hardest not to look away. The blue-black of his eyes told her that he was brooding over everything she'd said, was deciding whether he was prepared to make that genuine effort of the soul, as Esmée had so eloquently put it.

Then he shook his head as if to say, *No*.

A group of fashion people bustled through the door. They called her name but she didn't acknowledge them because she was telling herself not to cry over this, but to keep to her vow of courage. It was so much harder to be valiant in the moment when something precious was finally lost.

She placed her hands on the table, ready to stand.

Then Anthony smiled, suddenly and brilliantly and said, "God-damn you, Alix St. Pierre, for always being right. I was very—not happy, but righteous, wallowing in my self-pity and my vermouth. But of course you're right again. I never gave you any good reason to trust that I wanted you just the way you are. It was easier to believe that what happened with Lillie meant you were the one in the wrong. And it was easier to convince myself that when you were telling me about your life and what you wanted, you were saying it was impossible for us to be together."

A raucous burst of laughter almost drowned out Anthony's last words and he stood up. "I don't want to have this conversation here. Can we…"

He hesitated and she steeled herself for him to suggest they go upstairs to his suite. If he did that, it was truly over, because it would mean he didn't understand any of it—that being in his magnificent room where they'd once made love tipped the power into his hands and took it all away from her. It would mean he couldn't comprehend how easily he could make her less than him.

He looked down at the table and tapped a hesitant finger against it. "Maybe we could walk down to that crazy cellar club you once took me to."

She inhaled sharply. This was it. That moment she'd written about in a letter to Lillie—the communion of two people, like dress with body, one fitting exquisitely over and onto and around the other. The crazy cellar club was the place where they first became partners of a sort; the place where they first gave one another their trust.

And Anthony had known it was the single most perfect place to bring everything to its unraveling.

"You know," he said, his voice too husky not to make her shiver, "even though we've been to a nightclub and a ball together, I've never once danced with you. I dream about dancing with you."

Her own voice was undeniably husky too when she said, "That might just be the most beautiful and unexpected thing you've ever said to me." Then she smiled. "You dream only about dancing with me?"

"Alix."

How far into love could you fall?

But... The look in his eyes told her only that he wanted her. And that was still not enough.

So she tore her gaze from his and they didn't speak as they walked down to the river and across the Pont Neuf, a different bridge to the one she'd crossed when she first came to Paris in 1937. For just a minute, Alix could see the girl from ten years before with red-gold hair and an exuberant smile. Could also see a woman with damp green eyes and an aching heart. But the Alix crossing the bridge now felt like a different one, a third Alix perhaps, made up of the other two but also of so much more.

Inside the club, the singer's voice slipped into the tiny spaces between the dancers and the smoke, and closed the gap that existed between Alix and Anthony. The table they'd shared the last time was free and he gestured to it but she shook her head.

"You said you wanted to dance with me," she said and the next instant she was in his arms, as close to him as she'd ever been because distance didn't exist inside Tabou. But rather than taking one of her hands in his and placing one hand on her back, both of his hands gripped the small of her back and her arms wound around his neck.

"That dress," he whispered, breath hot against her skin. "I've always wanted to remove that dress from your body."

"You're procrastinating," she whispered back, unable to keep from smiling.

He shook his head vehemently. "I'm telling the truth. And I'm going to tell you some more truth."

He drew them into the deepest recesses of the club, one of his hands sliding up to trace circles over the bare skin of her shoulder-blades, circles that made her ache.

"I might have said I could cry for what the future would do to you," he began, frowning a little. "That was true. But I was a goddamned coward. Because I realized the night I said it that what I'd always seen as my future—a wife who smoothed and arranged every single aspect of my life so I could do whatever the hell I liked—would never happen with you. And I told myself that was fine. But it made me question whether I could be happy coming home to a woman who'd been lunching with friends all day, a woman who'd never heard of the Marshall Plan. A wife who looked good on my arm, but who— you're probably right," he sighed, "I might have cheated on. A wife who was the future I was supposed to have. But why had I never considered whether that future was worth having? You made me think, Alix, too damn much."

He drew back a little, as if he realized he was towering over her, was speaking fast and fiercely. "I'm sorry," he said, and she tugged him back against her, not wanting that thin sliver of space he'd just created between them to exist.

His next words were intent and very serious. "I was such an asshole, Alix. I can't be sorry enough for that. You told me you didn't want to just sleep with me. And you also told me marriage was a cage waiting to trap you. So that was it, I thought. The end. And then I told you I loved you and I left you to work everything out on your own. But I don't want to do that anymore. I want to work it out with you. Don't ever lie to me again and I will do my damnedest to show you I'm worth trusting. I have no real strategy for any of this, which means I'll probably do the wrong thing a hundred times. You'll need to forgive me a lot. I'll be old-fashioned and traditional and dumb and maybe you'll want to give up on me like I almost gave up on you. But will you let me try?"

"Anthony," she said, eyes spilling over with tears at having somehow found the one man who wanted her to be the Alix St. Pierre she was right now, not one that suited him or the world. "Of course I will."

He wiped her tears away with gentle fingers then slid a hand along her jawline, thumb brushing over her cheekbone, fingers threading into her hair. They'd stopped even pretending to dance, were pressed against the wall of the club, the heat of a thousand fires blazing between them.

"I missed you so much," he said very softly. "I love you so much. I want you so much."

Then he stepped away from her.

And, somehow, despite there being no room at all in the club to do such a thing, he dropped to his knee.

The saxophone crowed with delight and the dancers gave them more space, most of them watching while Alix laughed and a very mischievous smile crossed Anthony's face.

"Alix St. Pierre, will you marry me?" he shouted above the music. "I promise to do whatever I can to make this be a marriage of equals. I promise to always love you. And I promise," he added, smile widening, sparks of lapis flickering in his eyes, "to never let you wear this dress for more than five seconds before I take it off you."

"Come here," she said, laughing still more and tugging him to his feet while the drums clattered out their applause and the dancers swung into celebratory hijinks. "There is nothing I want more than to marry you," she said, grinning and swiping tears as she added, "And to have you finally remove this dress."

He drew his arms around her again, brushed his lips over hers too quickly and murmured in her ear, "Then why are we in a goddamn club and not in a bed? And does that mean you'll be Alix St. Pierre March? Then you really will sound like a PR princess."

More laughter—there would be so much laugher in her life now, she knew. "I'll let you call me Princess Alix for short," she murmured. "And remember how I was talking about starting my own magazine?

I've already employed Esmée and I'm planning to steal Fortunée out from under you. But you can be editor-at-large and go off and find whatever stories you like, and I'll be editor-in-chief—your boss in other words—and we'll get along just fine."

It was his turn to laugh quite helplessly and then to trail his lips down her throat and along the top of her shoulder. "What have I got myself into?"

"Hopefully we'll have years to find out," she said, dragging his mouth up to meet hers.

# AUTHOR'S NOTE

Christian Dior, creator of the New Look, the man who, in 1947, turned the world of fashion on its head, employed an American to run his Service de la Presse in the first couple of years of business—a man, not a woman. This always intrigued me because, besides his business manager, Jacques Rouët, Dior surrounded himself with women, including Suzanne Luling and the three mothers: Mesdames Bricard, Carré, and Raymonde. So I decided to change history and make Dior's first manager of his Service de la Presse into a woman named Alix St. Pierre. She is a figment of my definitely overactive imagination, as is Anthony March (unfortunately!), but everyone else at Dior, even Ferdinand the doorman, is based on a real person.

There were so many fun facts I could have included in this book about life at Maison Christian Dior in those early years but I had to contain myself otherwise this book would have been twice as long! Dior was called *le patron* by his staff and he did like to work on the staircase. Fortune-tellers and good luck charms were essential to him. The speech Christian Bérard gives to Dior on the night of the first showing is recounted in *Dior by Dior*, Christian's autobiography, as is the strategy of allowing his many friends in the fashion and editorial worlds to do the talking, and thus the publicity, for him.

Dior himself tells the story of several ladies of the night arriving at the *maison* in response to his advertisement for mannequins, and he did interview all of them. He was also one of the first couturiers to forge a connection with Hollywood actresses and Rita Hayworth did wear Soirée to the premiere of *Gilda*, although at a slightly later time to that in the book. I have also moved the date of Dior's visit to America in 1947 to collect the Neiman Marcus Award for Distinguished Service in the Field of Fashion—the award Dior describes as the fashion Oscar in his autobiography, a term I have kept; it was later in 1947 than it happens in the book. The shoot on Rue Lepic, where a Dior mannequin was attacked by Parisians, actually happened too, as did all the debates in the media about the shockingness of letting a skirt fall to mid calf rather than just below the knee. It's funny to think that protesters followed Dior around America on his tour because they were outraged that his skirts were too long!

*Christian Dior: The Biography* by Marie-France Pochna was a useful source for many anecdotes, including the Comte de Beaumont's Venetian Ball at the Piscine Deligny. Other sources I used to re-create life at the House of Christian Dior include Suzanne Luling's memoir, *Mes Années Dior: L'Esprit D'Une Époque*, which I made my way through in French, one chapter at a time (and, yes, Suzanne did like to go to the Tabou nightclub!). *Christian Dior: The Early Years* by Esmeralda de Réthy and Jean-Louis Perreau; *Working for Christian Dior: The Insights of a 1950s Fashion Model* by ex-Dior mannequin Jean Dawnay; *Dior: The Legendary Images*, edited by Florence Müller; *Talking about Fashion to Elie Rabourdin and Alice Chavane* by Dior himself; *Dior and His Decorators: Victor Grandpierre, Georges Geffroy, and the New Look* by Maureen Footer; and the magnificent Assouline volume *Christian Dior 1947–1957* were all hugely helpful.

Needless to say, all of the Dior gowns in the book are actual dresses, including the heavenly Compiègne, although I have allowed this to travel backward in time as it wasn't actually created until 1954; have fun searching for pictures of the gowns on the internet! As always, I'll post lots of images of them on my social media accounts.

All of the fashion editors you meet or who are mentioned in the book are real people. Carmel Snow's incredibly successful life as editor of *Harper's Bazaar*, in such stark contrast to her terribly sad personal life, is detailed in *A Dash of Daring: Carmel Snow and Her Life in Fashion, Art, and Letters* by Penelope Rowlands and this was the main source I used to shape Carmel as a character in my book, as well as *The World of Carmel Snow* by Carmel Snow, which offers a more ebullient perspective.

To help me re-create postwar life in Paris, I used Antony Beevor and Artemis Cooper's *Paris: After the Liberation: 1944–1949*, and *To Marietta from Paris: 1945–1960* by Susan Mary Alsop, an American whose husband was an attaché at the Paris Embassy. She provides much detail about the affairs of the various men and women around her (but not her own) and the way in which marriage generally worked at the time; and the role of both women and wives. Like Alix, I also have a breathless copy of *So You're Going to Paris!* by Clara E. Laughlin, the trusted guidebook for all young women throughout the 1930s. This was essential for double-checking street names, geography, and places from the era.

Rowlands's biography of Carmel Snow also paints a fairly accurate (if depressing) picture of what life was like for women at that time, and what it would have been like for Alix. She says of Carmel's husband, Palen: "He, like many men from established eastern families, scarcely worked, at least not by our standards today. In the case of the Snows, as with so many other members of the WASP establishment—they ruled then, remember?—the fortunes had long been made, the clubs founded and joined, the great houses built. Most men married wives for whom this could be a raison d'être...As late as the 1950s, even later, American women seeking to work for fulfillment, rather than out of necessity, often had to ask their husbands' permission to do so. And many men refused it." Ouch. The discussion Alix has with Anthony about women's bank accounts and that a man's permission was required is all based on fact. It wasn't until the 1960s that women in America gained the right to open a bank account but, as *The Guardian* reports, it wasn't until 1974 that the Equal Credit Opportunity Act passed in the U.S. "Until then, banks required single, widowed or divorced women to bring a man along to co-sign any credit application, regardless of their income. They would also discount the value of those wages when considering how much credit to grant, by as much as 50%." Double ouch. And that cigarette advertisement about rich and thin women that Alix sees near the end of the book is real; but it was created at an even later time: 1967, which just goes to show how long women endured such things—and still do, to some extent.

On a minor note, you might be wondering why Alix's telegrams to Mary use the word "stop" in place of a full-stop, whereas Mary's cables to Alix don't. Punctuation was more expensive than words back then, which is why people used "stop" instead. Of course Mary had enough money not to care about such things, but Alix didn't. This is just one example of the research rabbit-holes writers disappear into when trying to be historically accurate!

Regarding the Swiss storyline in the book: Allen Dulles was dispatched to Bern in late 1942. He worked with, and slept with, Mary Bancroft, who became great friends with Dulles's wife when Clover Dulles came to Bern after the war. Mary's backstory is similar to how I have described it in the book: she was in Switzerland with her second husband, who did have his butler spy on her activities prior to marrying her and who did hit her into unconsciousness. Mary's words about power being the opposite to love come from her autobiography, as do many of the anecdotes relating to her, including the one about Dulles rushing into her room one morning, taking what he wanted, and then departing swiftly after thanking her for the pick-me-up.

Dulles is a complicated character: some people who have written about him clearly despise him and others think him something of a hero. I suspect the truth lies somewhere in between and that he could be both despicable and possibly heroic, depending on circumstance and one's relation to him.

To help create his character and Mary's character in the book, I used *Agent 110: An American Spymaster and the German Resistance in WWII* by Scott Miller; *Autobiography of a Spy* by Mary Bancroft; *Max Corvo: OSS Italy 1942–1945* by Max Corvo; and I also read through hundreds of Dulles's cables from Bern to Washington, Caserta, London, and points in between, as reproduced in *From Hitler's Doorstep: The Wartime Intelligence Reports of Allen Dulles, 1942–1945*. I have occasionally used phrases from his cables, especially in relation to the Alpine Redoubt, which was, in the end, a falsehood. But, as detailed in *Ultra and the Myth of the National Redoubt* by Marvin Meek and many other sources, the Allies were fearful about the Nazis taking their elite troops into this mountain hideaway and thus causing the war to drag on for months or years more in a bitter and protracted alpine battle. The newspapers in America were reporting on the Redoubt from around January 1945, and were calling the troops believed to be sequestering there "the werewolves." I have used some of the words from Harry Vosser's *New York Times* report titled "Hitler's Hideaway" in the newspaper article in my book.

The idea that there might have been an exploratory party of OSS agents and Italian partisans sent into the Alps in April 1945 to reconnoiter the Redoubt is entirely made up. With things like this, I always ask myself the question: is it possible? And I think that yes, it was possible that such a mission would have been at least considered by the Allies at the time, given how fearful they were of this Alpine Fortress. Given that the cables detailing both the Ultra intercepts and the reconnaissance photos of the Redoubt area are based on actual reports, you can see how the Allies grew to be concerned about the threat it posed.

The situation with the Italian partisans is mostly based on fact, although I have had to change names and dates occasionally as historical events don't always comply to the needs of a narrative. I have also simplified and compressed details of the establishment and workings of the CLN and OSS in Italy. For example, I have AFHQ move to Caserta in June 1944 whereas this move actually took place in July 1944. Other places where I have massaged fact include the battles between the Italian partisans and the Nazis in 1944, which were called the summer of fire, not the autumn of fire, and they took place, as the name suggests, over summer rather than autumn. In some instances Nazi personnel changed and officers such as Kesselring and Veitinghoff were in positions of power in Italy at various times but, to avoid confusion and details that would only weigh down the narrative, I have concentrated Nazi decision-making through Karl Wolff.

The terrible story of the Nazis' brutality in Italy—burning priests, hanging and stabbing pregnant women, setting fire to villages, and the roundups—are all detailed in Caroline Moorehead's *A House in the Mountains: The Women Who Liberated Italy from Fascism* and Ada Gobetti's *Partisan Diary: A Woman's Life in the Italian Resistance.* Also detailed are the atrocities at Villa Triste and the imprisonment of the wife of CLN leader Vittorio Foa's wife, Lisetta, and the subsequent bargaining by Pietro Koch to release Foa's wife in return for Koch's safe passage to Switzerland, a bargain Foa heroically refused, using the words I have reproduced in my book, "With hyenas, we do not deal." Foa then went to the apartment of a friend and listened to Beethoven's *Eroica* on the gramophone. Reading about that broke my heart. But you will notice that, in my book, I have replaced Foa with Parri as the reader had already been introduced to Parri and it was difficult to bring another character into the narrative. My apologies to Foa for this. Like Chiara, Lisetta escaped from Villa Triste and survived the war.

Chiara and Matteo are both composites of many of the incredible *staffette* and partisans I read about in Gobetti and Moorehead's books.

OSS Bern and the Italian partisans did set up a courier line from Northern Italy into Switzerland to run messages and intelligence back and forth between OSS Bern and the Piedmont region and CLN headquarters. Some of the liaison between the partisans and Switzerland was done via OSS agent Donald Jones out of Lugano but, again, for the sake of simplicity, I have removed Jones from the narrative and kept these activities out of Bern. Occasionally in this part of the narrative, I have also had to alter dates, timeframes, and code names for simplicity.

It's impossible to write a book like this and not feel desperately sorry for the Italian partisans. Certainly the Allies were less supportive than they could have been and General Alexander did, on the eve of winter 1944, tell the partisans via public radio to stand down for winter. One can only imagine how difficult it was for those in the mountains to hear those words.

There was much politicking between OSS and SOE, the British service responsible for partisan support, sabotage, and intelligence gathering. John McCaffery, the SOE liaison in Switzerland, did tell Parri that the Italians had only themselves to blame for their current situation and that the partisans should limit themselves to sabotage. Dulles's role in support of the Italian partisans is less easy to pin down; some sources imply that he was more interested in taking control of whatever he could and in ingratiating himself with the powers-that-be in Washington (Corvo's book is especially critical of Dulles) and other sources say that he was an important force in convincing those in charge that the Americans should play a greater role in Italy. Certainly his cables show that he was often fighting for supply drops for the partisans.

Dulles did enter into secret negotiations with the Italian high command to bring about the surrender of the Italian troops in Operation Sunrise, which was finally effected on May 2, 1945. And the Bern station of OSS did embed a wireless operator into Karl Wolff's headquarters to help facilitate the negotiations. In other places, I have vastly simplified the way OSS communications and cables worked so as not to overburden the narrative but certainly there was much traffic exchanged between OSS Bern and Brindisi, and AFHQ in Caserta.

It is also true that Karl Wolff, Obergruppenführer und general der waffen SS, or Supreme SS and Police Leader, escaped prosecution for his crimes at the end of the war due to his participation in Operation Sunrise, although he was finally arrested in 1962, but released after just six years. Many commentators state that Dulles's persuasive powers were instrumental in allowing Wolff, who was certainly responsible for thousands of deaths, if not more, to avoid likely execution at Nuremberg. A number of the sources listed above detail the fact that former Nazis with at-best shady pasts were recruited by the OSS in the months after the war for their value as informants. Later, in his role as head of the CIA, Dulles was also accused of aggressively recruiting former Nazis to the spy organization. It is from this history that I have invented the character of Friedrich Weber, or La Voce, and his deal with OSS for his freedom after the war.

Finally, I know how much my readers enjoy these notes at the end of my books—I always receive hundreds of messages about them, which I love. I hope this gives you lots of new areas of history to explore further.

# ACKNOWLEDGMENTS

Another book published! If anyone had told me, back when my very first book came out in 2010, that I'd still be writing books and having them published and read by readers more than ten years later, I'm not sure I would have believed them. Writing books is what I love; I'm so lucky to have my dream job, to wake up every day eager to get to work and make up more stories. But it's largely because of many wonderful people that I'm able to do this.

My agent Kevan Lyon is one of the most wonderful of those people. I sent her five chapters of this book and a possibly rambling synopsis and she fell in love with it (or at least she told me she did!). When someone has that kind of faith and confidence in your writing, it's a fabulous gift. Thank you for being the best agent on the planet.

Rebecca Saunders, my incredible publisher at Hachette Australia, had a very similar reaction. I remember receiving an email from her where she actually used exclamation marks (a very rare thing for her!) and said it was the best thing I'd ever written. Her belief in me has been unending since she encountered the manuscript for my first historical novel and I'm so grateful for that.

There are so many other people at Hachette Australia that I could thank—everyone, in fact!—but let me single out Kate Taperell, who is my dream publicist, and Sophie Mayfield and Emma Rafferty for their management of the editorial process. Louise Stark,

Fiona Hazard, and Eve Le Gall all deserve a special mention too, as do the sales team whose ceaseless championing of my books is a wonderful gift.

It's always nerve-racking working with a different copyeditor for the very first time but Dianne Blacklock proved to be a copyeditor extraordinaire—thank you!

Leah Hultenschmidt from Grand Central Publishing in America also greeted this manuscript with love and enthusiasm and I thank her for putting her trust in me to deliver on what the early chapters promised.

My foreign rights team of Sarah Brooks, Emma Dorph, Andy Hine, and Kate Hibbert are truly amazing and I honestly can't thank you enough for everything you do. A big shout-out to all of my translation publishers—it's such a buzz knowing there are readers all around the world who are reading my books.

There are many writing friends to thank but most especially those with whom I drink tea, chat, and write every Wednesday fortnight: Louise Allen, Holly Craig, and Polly Phillips. You guys are the best and long may our meetings continue to produce much laughter and a few words too. Sara Foster is always my first reader besides my publisher and she once again proved herself to be an invaluable part of my writing process.

My fellow Lyonesses who are the most supportive group of writerly friends anyone could ever wish for: thank you for the Friday chat time, the love and sharing of all bookish news, and the commiserations and celebrations as the occasion requires.

Booksellers and readers are vital for authors and I thank you a thousand times for all of your support. The messages that flow through from readers are bright lights amidst long days of writing, as is the thrill of seeing my books displayed and sold and recommended in bookshops.

The last word goes to the best people of all: Russell, Ruby, Audrey, and Darcy. Thank you especially for letting me run away to the beach a few times when I needed to lose myself in the world of this book. I would always rather lose myself in your world but duty occasionally calls!

# ABOUT THE AUTHOR

NATASHA LESTER is the *New York Times* bestselling author of *The Paris Seamstress*, *The Paris Orphan*, *The Paris Secret*, and *The Riviera House*, and a former marketing executive for L'Oréal.

When she's not writing, she loves collecting vintage fashion (Dior is a favorite), practicing the art of fashion illustration, learning about fashion history, and traveling to Paris. Natasha lives with her husband and three children in Perth, Western Australia.

You can learn more at:
NatashaLester.com.au
Facebook.com/NatashaLesterAuthor
Instagram @NatashaLesterAuthor